The Gift of Hope

A NOVEL

J. Willis Sanders

ISBN: 978-1-954763-37-1 (paperback)
ISBN: 978-1-954763-38-8 (hardcover)

Printed in the United States of America
Cover by MiblArt

The version of the lyrics for Poor Wayfaring Stranger used in this book is in the Public Domain, from William T. Dale, 1893.

Novels by J. Willis Sanders

The Eliza Gray Series
The Colors of Eliza Gray
The Colors of Denver Andrews
The Colors of Tess Gray

The Outer Banks of North Carolina Series
The Diary of Carlo Cipriani
If the Sunrise Forgets Tomorrow
Love, Jake

The Hope Series
The Coincidence of Hope
The Yearning of Hope
The Gift of Hope

Writing as J. D. James
Reid Stone: Hard as Stone

Readers: please enjoy the first chapter of *The Colors of Eliza Gray* in the back of this book, after the book club questions.

Amazon reviews for *The Colors of Eliza Gray*

"Captivating! ... J. Willis Sanders has captured love in this story. Love of a father to his daughter, love between brothers and sisters, and true love struggling to find a way to a future together. I look forward to Sanders' next book."

"I can honestly say that "The Colors of Eliza Gray" had me hooked from chapter one! It had me wishing for a "happily ever after" for Eliza from the beginning. Every emotion is found in this book and J. Willis Sanders definitely knows how to draw his readers in! I had read half of it before I realized it and finished it up the next morning!"

"Enjoyed this book so much! Stayed up way past my bedtime to finish it. Romantic and inspiring story. Great descriptions enabling the reader to visualize the scenes. Highly recommended."

"You won't be able to put this awesome book down! Love, love of a father and their love!!!! Please write another about how their lives are going!!!"

"The Colors of Eliza Gray is one of the most compelling books I've ever read. Beginning with a hearing-impaired abused Eliza. Taking you through her education and life altering experiences once she has her world opened to her. I truly hated it to end. Can't wait for the next book."

Amazon Reviews of *The Diary of Carlo Cipriani*

"This is the story of a shipwreck. No, a survival story. Actually, it's a history lesson worked in to the tale of Carlo's life after a shipwreck told as entries in a diary to Carlo's daughter. Wait, it's also a love story from earlier in his life, and again now. An impressive work of fiction."

"Many twists and turns, lots of tragedy but always hope. At several points you are not sure what is real and what is the narrator's madness due to his loneliness. A very satisfying resolution answers all our questions."

"This is a fascinating tale of survival, both of shipwrecked sailors and of how wild horses came to live on the Outer Banks. I enjoyed the characters and the character development, as well."

Amazon reviews of *If the Sunrise Forgets Tomorrow*

"What a captivating book. I read it in 2 sittings because we just couldn't put it down. Brought tears to my eyes!"

"To be honest, I wasn't certain I would enjoy this book. I've read other books at in the Outer Banks and a lot of them seem to be sloppily written and just capitalizing on the setting to prey on die-hard OBX readers. I was pleasantly surprised to find it very well written and descriptive. It was easy to visualize the island, the characters, and the story as it all unfolded."

Author's Note

My first novel started this three-novel series. Although each is complete in itself, they read much better if they are read in order.

For those who care to know the list and the order, it starts with the first novel, *The Coincidence of Hope*, followed by *The Yearning of Hope* and this novel, *The Gift of Hope*. Naturally, I call them my Hope Series.

The Gift of Hope picks up about ten years after *The Coincidence of Hope*. Of course, you'd rather read it than have me tell you about it.

As most authors might say, to write well, we must share the perspective of our characters, shirking our own perspective while we write. As a fan of perspective in all its forms, I hope these novels are a reflection of perspective, for what finer way to understand a person than to place ourselves within their situation?

Please enjoy,

J.W.S.

The Gift of Hope

Chapter 1

Joe swung his leg over the Harley's black leather seat, heeled the kickstand up, and balanced the heavy motorcycle. Elaine climbed on ahead of him and turned the key. The starter whined. The engine rumbled. The seat vibrated in rhythm with the *chu-chugging chu-chugging* idle. She checked for traffic and twisted the throttle. Engine roaring, the acceleration forced him against the backrest.

On a perfect day they alternated between the sun's warm light and the cool shadows of oaks and maples crossing the narrow country road in jigsaw patterns.

Below Elaine's helmet, wind swirled her long hair, sweet with the faint aroma of floral scented shampoo. Joe slid close and slipped his hands around her waist. The Harley must've reached fifty by now, and if she took the curve near the path to the river too fast, they'd end up scattered across a wheat field—or worse. Peeking over her shoulder, he couldn't help widening his eyes. The speedometer needle quivered on fifty-five, and they'd arrive at that curve in less than a minute. He squeezed her middle and set his chin on her shoulder. "Are you trying to get us killed?" he yelled.

"I'm trying to get you to hold me tighter!"

"All you had to do was ask!" Joe grinned at her reflection in the rear-view mirror, nothing but the tinted face shield with her chin below it.

She twisted the throttle. "That's what I'm doing!" The speedometer needle shot past sixty.

Joe already held her to the point of feeling her ribs beneath his fingers. He squeezed harder. "How's that!"

"Much better!" She twisted the throttle again. The needle zoomed to seventy.

The curve loomed about a half-mile away. Beyond it, the top of the huge oak that had received its fair share of car impacts over the years appeared. Just beyond that, like a green carpet shimmering in the sun, his father's hundred-acre field of half-grown wheat waved in the breeze.

"Look!" Joe yelled. "You're gonna splatter us all over that oak or run a path through my dad's wheat! With all the college tuition we owe, our parents won't appreciate our hospital or funeral bills one bit!"

The speedometer needle shot to eighty.

"Ela-a-a-a-a-i-n-n-n-n-n-e!"

Laughing like a maniac, she braked hard enough to slide them forward on the seat, the engine's rumble changing from a high-pitched growl to a low-pitched murmur each time she geared down. She steered into the path to the river and killed the engine.

Kickstand down and helmets on the seat, she combed her hair out with her fingers. "That's what I was really trying to do, you big wuss, get you to scream like a big wuss. Did you wet your panties too?"

Joe's jaw dropped—not because of her joking, which he loved, but because she attracted him like no other woman he'd ever met. Although she wasn't a beauty in the traditional sense, her sun-streaked brown hair framed her heart-shaped face to distraction. Add that to her dark brown eyes and her amazing smile, she was the most beautiful woman in the world.

He slipped his arms around her for a kiss. The motorcycle engine ticked as it cooled. In the field across the road, the wheat swished with the breeze. Pulling away, he tugged the elastic waistband of his briefs from his jeans. "No wet panties here, babe. All man, every inch of him."

Elaine burst out laughing. "*Inch* is probably right."

Joe made a growling sound in his throat. "You'll find out *one* day, I promise you that."

"Promises, promises," she said, wrapping her arms around his neck to pull him down, eye to eye. "And I'll be an old maid before that happens."

He dug his fingers into her sides, tickling her. As she jerked away, he grabbed her hand and spun her around to wrap his arms around her waist again. "Uh-huh, but you'll be a *satisfied* old maid."

"Whatever." She pointed toward the wheat field across the road, where the sun was lowering into the tops of the trees in the distance. "We better get to the river. It'll be a lot easier to build a fire while it's light."

Joe took their helmets from the seat and gave her the one with the face shield. "Can I ease your new toy down the path?"

"Don't wreck it. I worked hard to pay for it, even if it *is* used." She climbed on and slid to the backrest, and he sat in front of her

"Don't worry, I can handle it."

Elaine gave his middle a squeeze. "Maybe you can, maybe you can't. You won't find out until we get married, whenever that is."

Joe kicked the stand up, pulled the clutch lever, and turned the key. The double meaning of Elaine's comment wasn't lost on him.

The starter whined until the Harley's engine rumbled to life. He twisted his head around. "You realize I know that 'handle it' remark has nothing to do with me driving this thing to the river and everything to do with our honeymoon."

"Uh-huh, the honeymoon I keep saying will never happen. You've probably got some other farm-girl floozy wishing you'd marry her instead of me."

"Yeah, right. Where would I find another girl in Nebraska who wants my hot body as much as you do? Hold on."

Done with the somewhat bumpy, nearly mile-long ride to the river, Joe parked under the huge oak, its limbs spreading majestically over the bank of the Republican River. When he and his family had moved here in 2012, he had no idea he would grow so attached to this section of river that ran through Harlan County in southern Nebraska. Off the Harley again, he opened one of the saddle bags for a folded quilt. Now it was Elaine's turn to open her eyes wide.

"Did you sneak that in there while I was talking to your mom and dad in the kitchen? Why didn't you grab a couple of bottles of water and a sandwich or two?"

In the shade of the oak, Joe set the quilt on the picnic table. Its surface, pitted and scarred from limbs falling on it, had seen better days, but the annual coat of wood preservative he applied ever since his and Elaine's first visit here, when she'd taken to this place like he had, had slowed its eventual decay. Elaine sat while he stepped around to the other side of the tree that was large enough to hide several of him, to return with a cooler big enough to hold six bottles of water, four sandwiches, and half a pecan pie he'd snuck from the counter in the kitchen at home. He opened the cooler and leaned it toward Elaine. "No bad, huh?"

"When did you bring this down here?" she asked, leaning closer to the cooler.

"This morning. I thought we'd take a ride here when you called about buying your new toy." He took out the pie, and Elaine licked her lips.

"Wow, I haven't tasted your mom's pecan pie since Christmas break."

He took out the sandwiches and water. "Oven roasted turkey breast that Dad brined and Mom cooked this past Sunday. Hard to beat a sandwich made with that." He returned everything to the cooler. "I need to get the fire going. Let's get some wood."

They had cut their arrival time close with the setting sun, but Joe soon had a small fire burning brightly. It lit the surrounding area, including the base of the oak, the yellow blooms of the daffodil patch on the other side, and the grass by the river. Every few seconds the light glimmered on the water, sparkling on a slight wave or eddy swirling near the bank.

Elaine had spread the quilt and was lying on her side, propped up on one elbow. She patted the quilt. "Come on over here, handsome. There's a chill in the air and I need warming up."

"I thought you were ready for dinner?" Joe joined her, lying by her side.

She ran her fingers through his hair, gripped his curls, and pulled him close for a kiss. Ever since their first serious kiss here when they were sixteen, each one had been the same— absolutely perfect.

With lips soft and luscious, she continued kissing him until he pulled away, breathing hard. They had never made love, and he knew she wanted to as much as he did, if not worse.

"Okay, okay," he said, sitting up cross-legged. "If we keep that up ..."

Elaine sat up too and fingered her hair out of her eyes. "I guess I kissed you like that because I haven't seen you in a couple of weeks. Is your last semester under better control than we are?"

"Let me grab us a water and I'll tell you." He returned from the picnic table with the cooler, gave her a water and sat. "Ready for a sandwich?"

"Maybe later." She twisted the top off and took several swallows. "Oh wow, that's good."

Joe swallowed water also. "Imagine what it was like around here back when all the roads were dirt. It'd be dry and dusty at the same time."

Elaine tipped the bottle toward the oak. "You mean like back in their day, right?"

Joe glanced over his shoulder, to where the fire flickered on two polished granite headstones standing amongst the daffodils. He faced Elaine. "I imagine so with Kurt, since he lived here from about 1944 on. I'm not sure about Ruth. I don't know if she lived around here then or not."

Elaine capped the water and dropped to her side again. "It's strange how Kurt was married to your great-grandma. Then, after she died, he married Ruth, who was her best friend."

"Not as strange as how I'm named after my great-grandpa Joe, and how you're named after your great-aunt, Elaine. If we add how they got married, then how she got pregnant from their one night together—probably right where we are now—you've *definitely* got strange."

Elaine rolled over onto her back. "You'd think we'd get tired of bringing it up. Maybe we don't because it's so romantic."

"Yeah, right," Joe said. "Except for the part where he died in World War II."

"True," Elaine said, turning toward him. "As tragic as that is, it would make a heck of a book."

"Right," Joe said, shoving her. "If you like crying."

She stuck her tongue out at him. "How old were you when your grandpa told you about them?"

"About ten. He said their memories—and their story—deserved to stay alive."

Joe lay down beside her. She turned over to face away from him and slid close to pull his arm around her. He used his other arm for a pillow while they enjoyed the fire and the quiet moment.

In the branches above them, the breeze rustled the leaves. Joe loved that sound. No matter how much he listened, he never grew tired of it. It called to him, pulled him as if he were a kite riding a March wind, the line almost breaking.

Ever since meeting Elaine, he'd lived this moment over and over in two dreams, both a whisper of an unseen past. He loved her without question. Always did and always would. After all, not only was he Joseph Samuel Matthan, great-grandson of his ancestor who bore the same name, he believed himself to be Joseph Samuel Matthan, the man who died in World War II, and the man who loved Elaine's great aunt.

He swallowed as he reaffirmed this belief, but fear remained in his throat. He wanted to tell her, especially tonight. More than that he wanted to see if she suspected the same thing about herself—that she was some kind of reincarnation, which was the best term he could come up with, of her great-aunt.

He swallowed once more, easing the fear down. He should let it go. After all, he'd made it back from death, and that's what mattered. Besides, if he told her all that, and she didn't feel the same way about herself, she'd insist he pack his bags and pay a visit to the nearest mental health facility.

Elaine raised his hand from her stomach and kissed his palm. "You're mighty quiet back there, Mr. Matthan."

Joe's stomach growled. "Is that better?"

"Better than something else. If we ever manage to get married, you better not be one of *those* guys."

Joe nuzzled her neck. "Only when I have beans."

She turned over to face him. "Here I am, thinking you chose crop sciences as a major so you could take the gas out of beans. You'd be doing womankind the world over a favor—probably win the Nobel prize too—if you did." She tapped his nose. "How's school? I sidetracked us by bringing up Kurt and Ruth."

"Their history is enough to sidetrack anyone. School's fine. I can't wait to graduate and combine our incomes. How's it going with the kids at our alma mater of Alma Elementary? Do you still like teaching?"

Elaine snuggled close and lay her head on his shoulder. "More than I thought I would. When I see a kid's eyes light up when they learn something, it makes my day."

"It sounds like you're good at teaching."

"It sounds like I'm old fashioned, huh?"

"If being proud of a job well done is old fashioned, so be it."

"Do you ever think about how we haven't made love yet is old fashioned? It's almost like we were born back when your great-grandpa was. I mean, here we are, enjoying the simplicity of lying by a fire by the river, and neither of us has a smart phone out."

Joe agreed. It was almost as if she'd been reading his mind concerning what he believed to be his—or their—past. "Have you ever heard of the phrase 'old souls?'" he asked. "Maybe that's us."

"I've heard of it and ..."

"Don't stop now, babe, let's hear it."

"I've wondered that about you, but not me."

"Why's that?"

"I think the biggest thing was when we met, when you were just a scared twelve-year-old trying not to stutter while introducing yourself in Mrs. Hansen's English class. Talk about shy, I didn't think I'd ever seen a face so red. When we talked after class, you were like a completely different person, calm and funny. No, now that I think about it, that started right after I asked you about your last name. Remember when the kids laughed because you said it had something to do with hope? You laughed too, when I thought you might've tucked your face into your book instead."

Joe popped her behind. "You're just now getting around to telling me all these deep, dark thoughts you've been having about me since then?"

Elaine pulled his hand to her bottom. "Do that again, I think I liked it."

A sudden flush engulfed Joe. What he wanted to do was—No, thinking about it only made it worse, and it was bad enough already.

"I shouldn't have said that," Elaine said, tucking her chin. "Every time we come here, we practically rip each other's clothes off, and teasing makes it worse."

"You won't get any argument from me." Joe sat up." Are you ready for that turkey sandwich?"

Elaine sat up also. "How many times have you've asked me about a sandwich? Did you get some life insurance on me and put arsenic in one?"

Joe slid the cooler over, took out a sandwich for himself, and leaned the cooler toward her. "Three more, take your pick." Firelight glittered in her gorgeous eyes. To heck with eating.

She smacked his hand. "Don't look at me like that, you know what it does to me." She took all three sandwiches out. "It's just like you to put a worm in one."

He offered his sandwich. "Have at it, babe."

"She unzipped the plastic bag. "If I wanted to 'have at it," what we'd be doing on this quilt would make Kurt and Ruth roll over in their graves."

Joe rubbed her knee. "You mean because the earth would move beneath us?"

"Shut up and eat." Elaine took a bite of the sandwich. "Wow, make sure your dad shows you how to brine and cook a turkey for when we get married."

"Mom cooked it. They're a team effort, like I expect us to be." Joe took a bite of his sandwich.

Elaine tipped the crinkly plastic bottle up and swallowed water. "I'll believe we're getting married when I see—"

"Ow!" Joe spit chewed sandwich into his palm and poked around in it. "What the?" He took something out, wiped it off, and held a diamond ring up to the fire. "I asked Mom to make these sandwiches and she lost her ring in one. Imagine that."

In spite of the mayonnaise clinging to the stone, Elaine started to smile but stopped. "You had my hopes up for a second. At least it isn't a worm."

Joe took a napkin from a plastic bag in the cooler, cleaned the ring, and offered it to Elaine. "Does it fit? Yours and mom's fingers look about the same size."

"Let's see," Elaine said, taking the ring. "Who knows when I'll get my own."

She slipped the ring on, held it out toward the fire, and Joe poked her knee. "I would never have believed it."

"You'd never believe *what*, Mr. Matthan?"

"That you'd be so gullible."

She took the ring off and gave it back. "What are you talking about?"

He took the ring, took her hand, and slid the ring back on. "You tell me."

Elaine's eyes opened wide enough to reflect the fire. "You mean …?"

Joe loved surprising her, and this surprise topped them all. How long had he been looking forward to this moment? Ever since they met in 1943?

He tapped her nose with a fingertip. "You finally figured it out, huh?"

Chapter 2

Elaine threw her arms around Joe's neck and pulled him down. Sandwiches and water went flying. She rolled him over to straddle him and kissed one cheek. "You have got to be the sweetest" —she kissed the other cheek— "man ever." Then she kissed him like she had earlier, but this time she held him down, kissing him deeply, exploring his lips and tongue like never before. This time Joe responded fully, returning her deep, probing touch. Unbuttoning his shirt, she worked her way down his neck and chest, dotting him with more kisses. He moaned, hands clenching the quilt at his sides.

At this very moment she loved him more than she'd ever thought possible, and she wanted him more than she'd ever thought possible too. With each kiss and each taste of his skin, slightly salty from the unusually warm May afternoon, tingles skittered along her spine like water in the shower before it turned warm. She would want more than kisses if they kept this up.

She sat up. "Whew, we better stop. We waited this long, we can wait longer."

"How long will that be?" Joe asked, buttoning his shirt.

"At least until you— Hey, you didn't stop me. How long were you gonna let me kiss you like that?"

"Until I didn't need a shower when I got home. That was some mighty fine tongue action, babe."

Elaine smacked his leg. "You're terrible."

"How do you know? I might be good at it."

"You know what I mean. You're terrible for messing with me about my so-called tongue action."

Joe finished the last button and sat up. "Well, it's not like I've had a chance to try the same thing on you yet."

She held up the ring. "It won't be long now, but we need our own place. Have you thought about a job?"

"Not a lot, but I will." Joe touched the ring. "I'm glad we're finally—and officially—engaged, especially since you've been reminding me about it for who knows how long."

"I know how long, ever since our first kiss when you shoved me up against the oak."

"You shoved *me* against the oak," Joe said, waggling a finger in her face. "I even thought about breaking up with you."

"Phooey. I'm an angel and you know it."

"Right, an angel who likes her bottom spanked."

"All right," Elaine said, "time for a serious subject. How about that job? I understand there's an opening for a sanitary worker in Alma, also known as a trash man."

"Stop teasing," Joe said. "I need a better job than that to afford a house."

"Are any recruiters looking for people at college yet?"

"I think some are coming next week. Maybe Wednesday."

"Make sure you impress them."

"Will do." Joe picked up the ruined sandwiches and water and dropped them in the cooler. "Let's have the other two sandwiches and the pie and head home. Don't you want to tell your mom and dad about their soon-to-be son-in-law?"

Elaine took the offered sandwich "Have you told your parents?"

"I have an idea how. Minister Mattaniah called this afternoon. He said Dad mentioned I'd be home this weekend and asked if I'd play guitar and sing during the service tomorrow."

"What has that got to do with telling— No way, you're gonna announce our engagement at church?"

"Why not? It'll surprise everyone."

"Aren't you smart?" Elaine kissed his cheek. "Now we can stay longer and cuddle after we eat."

Sandwiches, pie, and water gone, Joe added a few more pieces of wood to the dimming fire. He stirred the glowing embers and returned to Elaine, to sit behind her with his arms around her waist as she faced the fire. Between the fire's warmth in front of her and Joe's warmth behind her, she was as snug as the proverbial bug in a rug.

She patted his hands. "A great meal and a fire and this place, not to mention my fiancé holding me in his arms. It doesn't get any better than this."

"We better not get too comfortable and fall asleep." Joe nuzzled her neck. "We can't be late for church in the morning."

"How did you learn to play the guitar so well? Didn't you start last May?"

"It was more like six months ago."

"Time flies, huh? Seriously, how'd you pick it up so fast? When you played that old song you first learned ... what's its name?"

"Poor Wayfaring Stranger."

"That's right. When you played and sung it over the phone a couple of months ago, it sounded great."

Joe kissed her cheek. "Thank you, darlin', I appreciate that."

Elaine turned to look over her shoulder at him. "Where'd you get 'darlin' from? That sounds old-timey."

"You know how us old souls are. Like it?"

"I don't know yet. I need to come up with a pet name for you. How about … I know, how about hot ass?"

"It's not old-timey enough. Besides, if you call me that in church tomorrow, we might get thrown out."

"Good point, not that I wasn't kidding anyway. I'll think about it and let you know."

"You do that." Joe raised his wristwatch. "It's about time we skedaddled, darlin'."

"Right, hot ass."

* * *

Taking Joe home, Elaine slowed for several deer eating the thick grass from the roadside ditches. Whether one or three or more, they raised their heads, eyes reflecting the Harley's headlight like a group of huge lightning bugs.

Within forty minutes she had dropped Joe off, given him a goodnight kiss, and was downshifting the rumbling motorcycle while pulling into her parents' driveway. She parked under a shed in back and went to the kitchen to glance at the digital clock on the microwave over the stove. A little after twelve, enough time for a quick shower. Bugs had likely flown into her hair since she'd driven home without the tinted face shield for the ride at night. She'd have to get a clear one soon.

The stairs barely creaked as she crept to her room, but Mom came from the bedroom door down the hall and closed it behind her. "You're running late. Did you and Joe have a nice time?"

Elaine was glad she'd returned the ring to Joe so he could give it to her at church. She had no idea Mom would wait up, if that was the case, and didn't want her to see it.

"Joe and I always enjoy the river. I'm bushed and need a shower. Talk to you in the morning, okay?"

"Sure, honey." Mom started to open the door.

"Mom?"

"Yes?"

"Joe's singing at church tomorrow. Will you and dad be there?"

"Just like every Sunday."

"Will the nursing home let you bring Uncle Thomas?"

"We'll make sure he comes."

In her room, Elaine kicked off the boots she'd bought after the guy at the Harley place recommended she get a pair for protecting her ankles. He also recommended a vented jacket with pads inserted into the fabric, as well as leather gloves. She bought the gloves but needed to research the jacket on the internet.

Her hair was a hot mess, flat to her head with the ends tangled. She grimaced while forcing a brush through the various knots but eventually worked them out. Jeans, shirt, socks, and panties in the hamper, she stood in front of the full-length mirror that hung on the back of her bathroom door. Thank goodness her parents had added on to the house after buying the place from her great-uncle Thomas. She admired how they wanted to keep the old home place in the family, but it was also great because Thomas, at age ninety-five, was showing the early stages of Alzheimer's, and the money helped fund his residency in the nursing home.

Still in front of the mirror, she eyed her average sized breasts, narrow waist, and full hips. Not bad. Whenever Joe finally got to see her naked, he'd likely call her "hot ass" too. She patted her tummy. What would he say when she waddled around from being pregnant? She closed her eyes and ran her hands over her skin. She wanted him more than ever tonight. Eyes open again, she glared at her reflection. He'd better get his hot ass in gear and find a job—like now.

Fresh from the shower, she fell into bed, pulled the cool sheets over her clean, naked body, and snuggled the equally cool pillow to her cheek. "Goodnight, Joe, I love you."

Chapter 3

The aroma of coffee and bacon drew Joe from his room to the kitchen table. Mom brought a filled plate to him, one to Dad, and joined them with one of her own. "Got in a bit late last night, didn't you?"

"Since you're keeping tabs on me" —he poked her arm— "like a good mom should, you tell me."

"You got here after eleven, smarty. Did you and Elaine have a nice time at the river?"

Joe didn't mind Mom asking about his love life, or rather, the love of his life, who had always been Elaine. Her questions meant she cared. "Elaine loved the pie. What's that tell you?"

Coffee cup at his lips, Dad lowered it. "I wondered where that pie went. When I opened the fridge before bed, what do you know, no pie."

"You two ate half a pecan pie?" Mom asked, facing Joe.

"She loved the sandwiches too. She wants me to learn how to brine a turkey like Dad did that one."

"Be glad to show you," Dad said, "but your mom's the expert on cooking it. She found that recipe on the internet." He spread blackberry jam on a biscuit. "Want some jam?" He slid the jar to Joe. "How about the song you're playing and singing this morning, ready to go?"

Joe took jam from the jar with his knife. "I printed a copy of the words in case I forget them."

"I thought you knew it by heart."

Mom took the jar from Joe. "I don't understand how you learned the guitar so fast. I guess we're lucky we found it in the attic."

"Me neither," Dad said. "I can't figure out how the hot and cold didn't ruin it up there either. It's like it was protected or something."

"Just one of those things that's meant to be, huh?" Joe loved Dad's way of looking at the world, probably an influence from Grandpa's story. "C'mon, Dad, with all the history surrounding our family, it wouldn't surprise me if this place is haunted."

About to take a bite of bacon, Mom lowered it. "Exactly what history are you talking about?"

"The history of my great-grandpa. It was his guitar before he was killed in World War II. Didn't Dad tell you about it?"

"I told her bits and pieces. Your grandpa tells that story to his descendants when they're old enough to understand. He told me when I was about ten, like when he told you. What makes you bring it up now?"

"Just the thing with the guitar. You didn't tell me it was his until we found it, after Grandpa told me the story he passes down."

"That's because none of us were ever interested in playing it, and Kurt was. Far as I know he never got around to it. Never mentioned it if he did. Ruth probably put it in the attic when he passed away. Are you curious about anything else?"

"I'm curious about all of it. Mom might be too, since you only told her part of it."

Mom finished crunching bacon and swallowed. "It does sound interesting. What parts interest you? I'll stop you if it's something I already know."

"Mostly the parts that make me think this place is haunted, like—"

"We've never seen a ghost," Dad said, "if you're talking about how Kurt, Elaine, and Ruth all died in mine and your mom's room."

"That's part of it," Joe said, glad Dad had mentioned that intriguing fact. "The other part is how Ruth and Grandpa took Great-grandma Elaine's ashes to the same cemetery where Great-grandpa Matthan is buried in Belgium. You have to admit, having her ashes placed in his grave, along with everything else, is a lot of weirdness to not have ghosts rambling around this place. Then, when you add how Kurt and Ruth are buried at the river, it's a wonder we haven't had to hire a psychic to perform an exorcism or two." Joe grinned so Mom and Dad would think he was joking. Still, he couldn't have been more serious, especially when he considered how he believed he was the reincarnation of his own great-grandpa, according to his dreams since he'd met Elaine.

Mom pointed her fork at him. "Smile if you want, I don't care for talk like that."

"Come on, Anne," Dad said, "he's pulling your leg."

"Oh, really? Young man, you kept to yourself a bit too much before we moved here, but since then you've turned into a real joker. How do you suppose that happened?"

"Don't you know?" Dad asked. "Elaine happened."

"I guess that's true. It might sound like I'm complaining but I'm not." Mom faced Joe. "She's definitely good for you."

"I'm glad you agree. Let me finish this fine breakfast and get ready for church. I want to get there early so I can tune the guitar and set up the stand." Joe sipped coffee and took a bite of a warm biscuit with blackberry jam.

Not only had those dreams started when he'd met Elaine, they'd grown in intensity when he found and started playing the guitar. Also, like Mom had just said, playing the guitar came to him naturally. Within a month, the chords seemed to form under his fingertips, including the more complicated bar chords and the minor and diminished chords. He'd been too shy to sing, but when he'd found the words to *Poor Wayfaring Stranger* scribbled on a yellowed sheet of paper in the guitar case, words that strangely resembled his own handwriting, he'd taken to that almost as easily as playing the guitar. With those occurrences, as well as the dreams, he'd grown increasingly sure that he was some sort of reincarnation of his own great-grandpa, who he'd heard so much about from his own grandpa.

He might share his theory with Elaine one day, but not until he was sure she wouldn't look at him like he'd grown a second head on his shoulders. He didn't want to do anything that might upset their engagement either. Besides, one dream was benign, mostly of Elaine in 1940's clothing with a yellow ribbon in her hair and kissing him. But the one that made his belief all too real was when he'd danced with her under the oak at the river beside a fire, singing *Poor Wayfaring Stranger* when she'd requested it as a wedding song. As benign as that had also been, since he'd sung it to her over the phone, which might explain it, the part of the dream when they'd made love after his singing to her was anything but benign. In fact, it was the best dream he'd ever had in his entire twenty-two years. Then again, as strange as it might sound if his theory were true, he was ninety-six.

* * *

At the church, Joe parked his pickup beside Elaine's car. He loved her windblown look when she climbed off the Harley yesterday, but it might not go over too well in church if she rode the motorcycle here, especially with a bug or two splattered on whatever dress she might have worn.

Inside, he took a bulletin from a table near the doors and noted his name under "Special Music." A few early members already sat on the wooden pews, but not Elaine.

Minister Mattaniah glanced up from the pulpit. "Hey, Joe, glad you could make it."

At the front, Joe placed the guitar case and stand on the pew to the right and offered the minister his hand. "Good to be here, Minister." He winked. "Good to be anywhere, if you know what I mean."

"If you mean anywhere *breathing,* I agree. Got anything special planned for your song?"

"It's a repeat of what I did last time. Elaine bugged me until I sang it over the phone from college because she couldn't make it to church that day."

"*Poor Wayfaring Stranger,* right? That's a great tune. I love the mystery of how the author isn't known. The message is great too, kind of about second chances, so to speak. Your song will compliment my sermon."

Joe returned to the pew and opened the guitar case. "I love it when things work out like that." He set up the stand and placed the guitar on it. "Have you seen Elaine? I saw her car out front."

"I think she's in the nursery. We have a couple in Sunday school who have a newborn."

"A baby?" Joe asked, trying and failing to stop his voice from getting too shrill.

The minister chuckled. "Something you need to tell me, young Mr. Matthan?"

"I'd rather you wait and see. You like surprises, right?"

"As long as they're good ones." The minister patted the Bible on the podium. "Know what I mean?"

"No worries. This is definitely a good one."

The minister returned to his notes, and Joe tuned the guitar, tweaking the strings with the help of an electronic tuner clamped to the peg head. Satisfied with both his ear and the tuner, he returned the guitar to the stand and took the copy of the words from the case. After taking the case to a room to the right of the choir loft, he waited on the pew.

According to Grandpa, Minister Mattaniah took the opening at this church shortly before Kurt and Ruth were married. He performed the ceremony at the river and performed both funerals there also. Kurt passed from cancer first, Ruth from heart problems about a year later.

Both were well liked in town, often seen at the Farmer's Market where Kurt sold produce and Ruth sold homemade bread. Kurt's small greenhouse still stood at home, and Mom and Dad grew a few tomato plants there as well as cucumbers. A fresh salad with those ingredients couldn't be beat.

Joe went down the hall behind the pulpit and peeked in the nursery. Elaine rested her elbows on the railing of a crib, eyeing the baby. Joe tapped the door frame. "The minister already asked me if he needed to worry about you being back here."

Elaine came to the doorway, glanced both ways down the hall, and kissed him on the cheek. "Maybe next year this time."

Joe twisted his lips to one side. Elaine was familiar with that look, and it should be enough to get his point across. "That's pretty soon. We need to have some alone time before we start a family. Like one year … three … ten."

Elaine kissed the opposite cheek. "Twist your lips all you want. If we can afford a baby, I don't want to wait forever."

"How about five years? I'd like to have you to myself for at least five years. Don't you think five years—"

"Yes, Joe, five years is fine." Elaine glanced at her watch. "Sunday school will be over in a few minutes. When the mom of that cutie in the crib comes, I'll meet you out front."

"Gotcha, babe." Joe started down the hall but stopped. "In case you were wondering" —he patted his shirt pocket— "I've got the ring right— Uh-oh."

"Don't even try it. You couldn't fool me in a million years."

Joe patted his pocket again, gave her an "okay" sign, and returned to the sanctuary. The pews were filling. In back, more people entered the double doors, including Mom and Dad. He waved and Dad waved back. Elaine's parents, with her dad pushing her great-uncle Thomas in a wheelchair, entered next, to follow Mom and Dad down the aisle.

Joe waited until they all rounded his pew. "Wow, quite the crowd. Not only you all, but everyone else."

Dad nodded toward Mom. "That's because hot line here has been on the phone telling friends and neighbors about you singing today. Can't see it myself. You're good, but not that good."

"Hush and sit down," Mom said, elbowing Dad toward the pew. "You're getting as bad as he is with your joking."

Joe joined Elaine's parents, who, not long after he'd met Elaine, had told him to call them by their first names, Jimmy and Nora. Jimmy, bald and broad, who owned a plumbing business, offered his hand and a gap-toothed grin.

"Hey there, Joe. Whatcha got lined up for us today? How about a little bluegrass?"

Joe released Jimmy's hand. "It might qualify. I've heard more than one rendition performed by a bluegrass band."

Nora, with graying hair and a twinkle in her eyes that had to be where Elaine got hers, Patted Joe's arm. "Don't pay any attention to him, Joe. When are you going to sing me one of Elvis's tunes?"

Joe laughed. "I'll make a deal with you, Nora. I'll sing one if you'll wiggle your hips like Elvis did his."

Jimmy chuckled. "That I'd like to see."

Joe knelt beside Thomas's wheelchair. With sunspots on his craggy cheeks, no hair, and deep wrinkles lining his forehead, the wizened man, born in 1927, was ninety-five years old. Despite the warm morning, he wore a baggy, brown sweater, and it almost pained Joe with how he sat slumped over in the wheelchair.

"Good morning, Uncle Thomas. I'm glad you could make it."

The old man raised his head, hazy eyes barely open. "Well, if it ain't my sister's beau, Joe. I ever tell you how she went on and on 'bout that big catfish she said you made her loose at the river?"

That story, as well as the rest, had been passed down by Joe's grandpa, Joseph Matthan, who was the original Elaine and Joe's son. The Alzheimer's must be getting to Thomas this morning, since he mistook Joe for the Joe who died in the war. Joe didn't mind. He'd almost talked himself into believing he was the original Joe too.

"I know that story, Uncle Thomas. She wouldn't believe a catfish had whiskers until she saw them herself."

Thomas laughed, a mix between a cough and a wheeze. "You showed her, didn't you?"

"I did my best." Joe stood, and a warm hand slipped into his.

"Are you harassing my uncle?" Elaine knelt before Thomas, who barely opened his eyes again.

"Hey there, Lainey. You get this beau of yours to take you fishing yet? He better. I won't have my sister be with some boy who don't know how to fish."

"Don't worry, Uncle Thomas, I can handle him. I can out fish him too."

Thomas lowered his head to its previous drooping position and closed his eyes.

Elaine led Joe a few steps away, her usual twinkling eyes downturned. "I hate how he was diagnosed with that terrible disease. When I visited him last weekend, he called me Lainey."

Joe glanced at Thomas. "I just remembered how Kurt called Elaine Lainey. At least that's what Grandpa Matthan told me. How much of that story do you know?"

"The basics. You can fill me in sometime."

Joe took a step back and looked her over from head to toe. She wore a yellow blouse and a blue, knee-length skirt, including a ponytail tied with a yellow ribbon. Joe tugged the ribbon. "Special occasion? You stopped wearing yellow ribbons in your hair when we went to junior high school."

Elaine slapped his hand away. "Hush. Someone might hear that 'special occasion' remark, and I want our announcement to be a surprise. No, I just thought I'd look springy with the ribbon in my hair."

"What you look is really nice. I should have said so in the nursery."

"You get a pass, but not next time."

Joe snapped his heels together and saluted. "Yes, ma'am. Whatever you say ma'am."

Elaine rolled her eyes. "What I say is it's time to sit, you big kid."

At the end of the pew near his guitar, Joe and Elaine sat while the pianist played. The remaining crowd took their seats, including those who were filing in from Sunday school. Minister Mattaniah stepped to the pulpit, and the murmur of small talk from the congregation ended.

"Good morning. It's great to see such a large crowd. For our opening hymn, please turn to page forty-four."

Joe opened his hymnal and gawked. Exactly like when he'd opened his school book after meeting Elaine for the first time at Alma Elementary, page forty-four appeared. A bit dizzy, he shook his head. Déjà vu? The same thing had happened a time or two lately, but not to this extent. Maybe it was a sign his plan for Elaine today would work out. Better not think about it now. A lot was about to happen, and he wanted to have his mind clear for what he wanted to say.

Done with the hymn and offering, Minister Mattaniah held up the bulletin. "As you see in the bulletin, Joe Matthan is our guest for the special music this morning. He nodded toward Joe. "Joe, come sing for us."

Joe took the guitar from the stand, looped the strap around his shoulders, and climbed the three steps to the pulpit. Another bout of déjà vu hit, and he could have sworn the congregation were his classmates staring at him right before Elaine had opened Mrs. Hansen's sixth-grade class door.

He cleared his throat. "I was surprised when Minister Mattaniah asked if I could play today. I mean, after my last time here, I thought he might not want me back." Men and women of all ages glanced at each other, but no one smiled. Joe raised an eyebrow. "Wow. Tough audience."

"Maybe you need to take 'em fishing like you did my sister," Uncle Thomas said.

That broke the ice, and a general chuckle ran throughout the room.

"All right, Uncle Thomas, I think we're an act." Joe slid the guitar pick from where he kept it within the strings near the peg head. "Seriously, I'm happy to be here to sing for you." He smiled at Elaine. "There's another reason too. Come on up here, darlin'." With as huge a grin as he'd ever seen on Elaine, she hopped from the pew and joined him. He gave her the words to the song and faced the congregation again. "I have someone to help me sing the chorus. You all know Elaine Johnson, I'm sure." Several heads nodded. Joe had expected Uncle Thomas to say something about his sister, but he'd drifted off again.

Elaine leaned near his ear. "Are you crazy," she whispered, "I can't sing."

He pointed at the paper. "It's just these two lines. Trust me, you'll be great."

"I—"

Uncle Thomas, head up from his short nap, cleared his throat. "Go on and do like Joe says, Lainey, sing us one. I heard you singing in the barn one time while you were digging worms. Sounded good to my ears."

Elaine's mouth fell open. She leaned near Joe's ear again. "You're gonna die. You know that, don't you?"

Joe winked, strummed the last line of the song, and sang:

> *I am a poor, wayfaring stranger*
> *While traveling through, this world of woe*
> *Yet there's no sickness, toil nor danger*
> *In that bright world, to which I go*

He nudged Elaine with his hip, and she joined him for the chorus:

> *I'm going there, to see my father*
> *I'm going there, no more to roam.*

Chorus done, he continued the song, with her joining in at those same two lines.

When the last notes of the song echoed about the room, everyone clapped. Jimmy clapped the hardest. "Doggone, Nora, where'd our girl get that from?"

Elaine faced Joe. "Does all that mean I did okay?"

"Hey, they didn't clap that hard for me when I sang by myself."

As the applause faded, the minister rose from the chair behind the pulpit.

"Do you mind if I make a quick announcement?" Joe asked. "Won't take a minute."

The minister stepped aside, and Joe faced the congregation again. A few people were whispering and nodding, possibly discussing the surprise of Elaine's singing, but it didn't surprise him. He'd seen and heard Elaine singing the same song in the same dream, when she'd asked him to sing for their wedding dance on their honeymoon night at the river back in 1944.

He took the ring from his shirt pocket, faced his parents and winked. Mom raised her hand to her mouth while Dad returned the wink. Joe held the ring up so everyone could see it.

"Most everyone here knows how Elaine and I have been a couple almost from the day we were old enough to date. I think it's about time, don't you?"

The entire congregation clapped, and several "Amens" scattered about the room.

Joe slipped the ring on Elaine's finger. "Yes, right?"

"What am I gonna do with you?" she asked, shaking her

head.

The minister stepped over. "You'll figure it out, I'm sure."

Joe's cheeks warmed. Elaine's cheeks turned red. She pulled him down the steps past Uncle Thomas, who grinned up at them. "It's 'bout doggone time, you two."

Chapter 4

The service over, Joe cased his guitar while his and Elaine's parents congratulated them, and while Uncle Thomas dozed again. They asked about a wedding date. Elaine said Joe had just proposed last night, so they hadn't discussed it. Also, Joe needed to graduate and find a job, and they needed to find a home, which would be small at first and within their budget.

Minister Mattaniah returned from the front doors, where he'd been shaking hands and saying goodbye to the people filing out. "If I heard correctly, you two need a home. I might know of a place like that. The owner lost his renters and needs the income to pay the taxes and make a decent contribution to his retirement account every month."

"You know a lot about this person," Dad said. "It's Ruth's old house, right?"

"I can't get anything by you, can I, Al? Did you hear the guys at the hardware store talking about it?"

"Sure did. That old store is the best place to hear the latest news in Alma."

Holding his guitar case, Joe faced the minister. "I didn't know you bought Ruth's house."

"I didn't either, "Elaine said.

"After she died, her kids put it on the market at a good price.

Interested? Probably needs a little paint, maybe a plumbing upgrade."

"You're talking my language," Jimmy said. "Me and Elaine can check it out after work tomorrow."

Joe put the guitar case down. "Don't I get a say in this?"

Jimmy patted Joe's shoulder. "If it needs a new toilet, *you* can install it. How's that for having a say?"

"As long as your daughter squirms around in the dirt in the crawlspace to check the heating and air system. She might even find a snake or a nest of spiders under there. That house is old."

"No worries," the minister said. "I put down plastic last fall when I had a new system installed." He took a ring of keys from his pocket and removed one. "Here you go. You and Elaine can take a look when you leave."

"It'll have to be a quick look," Joe said, taking the key. "I've got to head back to school. I'm not trying to get it for nothing, Minister, but I can't afford rent right now."

"Poor broke little baby," Elaine said. "It doesn't sound like the good minister is out to make enough for a cruise to the Bahamas. If it's not too high, I can afford it."

"Go ahead and make all the decisions. I guess cooking and cleaning is next."

"And anything else I can think of." Elaine picked up the guitar case. "Let's go."

Joe followed Elaine out to her car, where she placed the guitar case in the back seat. "I'll drive us over and run you back for your pickup later."

Joe opened the passenger door. "Whatever you say, Sarge."

Elaine fastened her seat belt. "Did Dad and I deciding about renting the house bother you?"

"Like it wouldn't bother you if no one asked for your input."

Her mouth opened but nothing came out. She faced the

window beside her and then him again. "I doubt I would have handled it as well as you did. Maybe it was the excitement of being able to have a place of my own."

Joe shoved her arm. "*Our* own."

"Do you forgive me?"

"As long as I get to leave the seats up on the toilets. It's been my dream to hear you splash in the middle of the night."

Elaine started the car. "Then I'll jump in bed and sit on top of you with my wet behind."

"I could handle that, minus the wet behind."

As Elaine drove through town, Joe said nothing. Passing the hardware store, he pointed. "Every time I come home, I half-expect that ancient store to be torn down for a new one, or at least remodeled. It's been a while since I've been inside it. Is the old wood stove still in the main aisle? The benches too?"

Elaine flipped the turn signal and turned right. "I guess. Dad gets a lot of his plumbing supplies from there. If Mr. Hansen took it out, he would've mentioned it. I remember going in there with him when I was a kid. The old men sat on those benches and circled around that stove like it was a shrine of some sort. It doesn't even work."

"Like you ladies don't gather at the mall and spend money."

"I hear you, Joe Matthan. All you need to worry about is checking with those job recruiters on Wednesday."

Elaine took another right and entered a quiet street lined with red maple trees budding with new leaves.

"I knew Ruth had a house in town," Joe said, "but I didn't know where. How'd you know where it is?"

Elaine parked in the driveway, shut the engine off, and plucked her lower lip. "I ... uh, I can't remember. Maybe ... huh. Honestly, I don't know. That's strange, isn't it?"

Joe wasn't about to answer. He'd been having his share of

"strange" lately too. Teasing her about it when he might eventually tell her about his "strange" dreams would cause problems until she had her own dreams—*if* she had them. Still, it was a good way to break the ice concerning his own recent déjà vu episodes. "Is it like déjà vu?" he asked.

"Well, I kind of feel like I've seen it before."

He opened the car door. "Let's check it out."

She joined him at the front of the car, and they strolled up the sidewalk. The cracks in the concrete needed patching, and the shrubbery at the sides needed a trim. The wooden steps to the porch creaked when he and Elaine climbed them, and a bird flew out from under the overhang to the left. A white smattering of droppings on the porch floor, with its peeling gray paint, marked its roosting place.

Joe pointed to a collection of twigs on the overhang. "That bird's building a nest. I better bring my pellet gun and take care of him—or her—before we—"

Elaine smacked his arm. "You will not. We can move the nest—or the start of it—to one of the shrubs. Maybe there's a chair or something you can stand on and do it now."

Joe rubbed his arm. "Sheesh. I'll have to check for a bruise when I get back to my apartment at school."

Elaine inserted the key into the lock. "Is that where you have the pellet gun? If someone finds out—"

"That's where I left the receipt for the ring. If you're gonna beat me every time we have a difference of opinion, I might have to get my money back."

"I didn't hit you that hard." She opened the door. "Want me to kiss it and make it better?"

Joe followed her inside. He turned around and patted his behind. "Too bad you didn't hit me here."

Looking around, Elaine placed her hands on her hips. "A

purple living room? The minister was right about this place needing a coat of paint."

Joe plopped into a recliner. "He must have supplied the furniture. This looks sort of new."

"That'll save us some money. The sofa and love seat match the recliner too. There's a table and wiring for a flat screen TV. I guess the renters supplied theirs."

Well durn, now I have to TV shop. At least a fifty-inch model would be perfect." Joe hopped out of the recliner. "Let's see what the most important room in the house looks like."

Elaine followed him down a hall. "Kitchen? Bathroom? I'm dying to know which one you think that is."

Joe stopped at a door that opened to a large room with a king-sized bed and pumped his fist. "All right! Lots of room for—"

She shoved him into the room. "I don't think I want to sleep where other people slept. Did I ever tell you I like to sleep naked?"

"Me too. Convenient, don'tcha think?"

"Not until we get a new bed it won't be." Elaine sat on the bed and bounced. "This one's worn out. Look at that sunken spot in the middle."

"For sure. I'd rather have the fun of wearing it out ourselves."

Elaine got up and went to two closed doors. "I guess this is the closet." She opened the doors, blinked, and plucked her lower lip like she had in the car.

Behind her, Joe slipped his arms around her waist. "I know that look. Not enough racks?"

"It's ..." She slid a couple of racks aside. "It's that déjà vu feeling again. I could swear I've been here before."

He turned her around. Bring up his own déjà vu or not?

Maybe a little, to see what she might say. "I've had dreams once or twice about places. Then, when I see a similar place, it's like I've been there before. Is that what you mean?"

Elaine's brows were knit into a V. "I'm … I don't know. That must be what it is." The V disappeared. She opened another door and went inside. "The bathroom looks nice. A shower stall instead of a tub, I like that."

Joe followed her. "A two-seater shower? Cool, we can save on hot water." He expected a comeback of some kind, but Elaine simply glanced around. He went to the toilet. "This looks new, so no changing it out. The minister did a great job keeping this place up to date."

"We need to check out that other important room," Elaine said, leaving the bathroom. "The kitchen."

Their footsteps echoed in the hall with its hardwood floors, until Elaine stopped to look around. "There's that feeling again. It's as if I were a ghost rambling this old house."

"I feel like that sometimes when I'm at home or at the river," Joe said. "Is this the first time you've felt like this?"

"Like this it is." She continued down the hall, shaking her head. "I'll get over it."

"At least the living room's the only one with the weird paint scheme. I'm okay with beige in the other rooms."

In the kitchen, a countertop—maybe granite—shined in the sun beaming through the window over the sink. The countertop's dark color complimented the matching floor tiles. Joe went to the window in the back door. "The minister didn't say anything about the deck and the screened porch, or the big backyard and the storage building. I think we lucked out."

Elaine opened the refrigerator. "It'll be a decent starter home. I still want to live in the country eventually."

Joe sat at the yellow kitchen table and patted its mottled

surface. "Sort of retro, huh?"

"I like it." Elaine sat across from him. "It has that warm, cozy feel."

Joe took her hand in his. "What did you think of the minister's sermon? Second chances and how hope is a gift."

"It fits us to a T. It feels like we've been hoping to be together for ages and ages."

Joe didn't reply. It sounded more and more like Elaine was having the same feelings as he'd been having, like returning from a dream that had lasted a lifetime. Still, his dreams were as real to him as if they had actually happened. Still again, if he told her about them, she might question his sanity and make him take the engagement ring back. After all, how could he tell her he'd already married her and made love to her in what had to be another lifetime? Maybe his dreams would fade. Maybe that's all they were, just dreams. As bad as he wanted to make love to her, he wouldn't be surprised if they were just dreams. He glanced at his watch. "As much as I hate to, I need to start back to school."

Elaine stood. "Before I make any more decisions without your feedback, do you want me to tell Minister Mattaniah we'll take it?"

Joe hopped up, took her in his arms, and gave her a quick kiss. "Sure, as long as *you* can afford it."

Chapter 5

At Joe's pickup, Elaine reminded him about the job recruiters coming to school, kissed him goodbye, and drove back through town. Nearing the hardware store, she pulled to the curb.

On more than one occasion since meeting Joe, this place tugged at her, almost like when Joe had tugged the yellow ribbon in her hair at church. The last time she was here with her dad, she waited on one of the wooden benches while he bought something from Mr. Hansen. The Hansen's owned the store back to around 1940, when the dinosaur of a wood stove she and Joe had discussed heated it. On the visit with her dad, she noted the lack of pipes for the smoke. On the way home, when she asked Dad about it, he said the Hansens installed a heat pump back in the early nineties, so it didn't need pipes for the smoke. Although his answer puzzled her because the stove and the benches remained, she credited it to some strange male ritual she'd likely never understand.

A couple passing on the sidewalk waved at Elaine, jarring her from her memory. She recognized the couple from church, just being neighborly.

At Ruth's house, she hadn't been completely honest with Joe about her déjà vu episode in the hall, but it was the first time it had been that intense. The first episode happened that day at the store with Dad. Sitting on the bench with her hands gripping the rounded and worn wooden edges, she could've sworn someone was playing a musical instrument nearby. The notes were mere suggestions—soft as a warm summer breeze at the river—but she heard singing too.

She closed her eyes to reel in that moment from her memories, similar to reeling in a catfish at the river. As quickly as the music and singing tempted her, the line connecting her to them broke, leaving her feeling as if she'd lost herself within the haze of a daydream. But unlike any daydream she'd ever experienced, this one left her disoriented and dizzy.

She opened her eyes to reveal her last memory of the hardware store: the rounded and worn wood of the bench within her fingers, the blackened wood stove, and the slightly charred floor beneath its door.

Climbing from the car, she checked for traffic. No cars or pickups threatened, so she ran across the street to the hardware store to look inside the glass door.

Since it was Sunday, the store closed and no lights on, shadows crossed the long walkway to the counter from light shining through the two front windows. About two-thirds of the way to the counter sat the wood stove. If the store had been open, she would've sat on the same bench to see if the music would play again, faint and like the whisper of some long, lost past, similar to what she'd experienced while standing at the closet at Ruth's house.

Or would she?

She returned to the car.

No, she wouldn't.

Why tempt such things? Her reflection in the rear-view mirror stared back. What did she tell Joe about ghosts rambling in Ruth's house? No, not *ghosts* rambling—it was as if *she* were the ghost rambling, or actually, a ghost sliding racks aside in the closet with a clatter while looking for something to wear.

She shook her head and started the car. Was she going insane? She glanced in the mirror once more and stuck her tongue out at her reflection. Of course not. It was likely nerves from being forced to sing in public and announce the engagement right after.

She drove away from the curb. Why did Joe make her sing when he'd never tried before? She didn't even sing in the shower or the car. The few times she tried, at least to her, her voice sounded like two cats meowing at each other right before they fought. Whatever made him ask, he seemed sure she'd sing well.

As she left Alma with the day's events—welcome and not so welcome—swirling within her mind, another question remained: when Joe had asked her to sing, he'd said, "Trust me, it'll be great," so how did he know she'd sing as well as everyone thought she did?

At home, Elaine found Mom at the kitchen table with a sandwich and Dad slicing a tomato on the counter by the sink. Mom looked over her shoulder at Elaine. "It's not often a young woman has her singing debut and announces her engagement and locates her new home within an hour."

"Want a sandwich?" Dad asked. "Your future father-in-law gave us a bag of tomatoes before we went in the church. Must be nice having a greenhouse." He slathered mayo on a slice of bread. "Maybe mayo is good for the vocal cords. You do like a lot on your tomato sandwiches."

"A sandwich would be great," Elaine said, sitting beside Mom. "As far as how I managed to get through that song, I have no idea. You and Dad know I don't sing."

Mom licked mayo from her lips and swallowed. "You do now. I'm sure you and Joe will be asked to sing again soon."

"I'm glad he's on his way back to school. I'm not sure about singing again."

Dad brought the sandwich over. "Seriously, honey, you were great. I don't know if I've ever heard two voices harmonize like yours and Joe's did. Since you never tried before, it coming out like it did—perfectly, if you ask me—made it even more special." He went to the refrigerator. "Milk? Water?"

"Milk's fine."

Mom slid the salt and pepper shakers toward Elaine. "Did you and Joe like Ruth's old place?"

"It was a lot nicer than Minister Matthan let on. It's furnished too, but I told Joe I wasn't about to sleep in someone else's bed. I'll have to get a new mattress and box spring, king sized at that."

Dad joined them with his own sandwich and a glass of milk, including one for Elaine. "If that's all you need, are you moving in soon?"

"I haven't had time to think about it." Elaine sipped milk. "I've got to call Minister Matthan about the rent too."

Mom took her empty plate to the counter. "He said something about changing out the plumbing."

"The kitchen sink looked rough. It's an old white enameled thing with plenty of chips and stains. I didn't say anything to Joe about it. He won't have time to replace it, being at school."

"Let me take a look," Dad said. "I might have a new stainless-steel sink and a single lever faucet. Any idea what size it— What am I saying, it's not like you had a tape measure with you."

"You mentioned meeting me there after work tomorrow. Is around five okay? I'll be there as soon as I finish grading tests, or a little earlier."

"Five it is."

Mom sat again and held out her hand. "Can I see your ring?" Elaine placed her hand in Mom's, and her lips formed an O. "Very nice. I always liked an oval cut diamond. You didn't seem terribly surprised."

"You should have seen me last night at the river. That's when he asked."

"How romantic. Not *too* romantic, I hope."

"We'll find out in nine months."

"You better be joking," Mom said, her cheeks reddening. "We talked about all that back when you and Joe started seeing each—"

"Yes, Mom, I'm joking. I'm still as pure as the proverbial driven snow."

Cheeks reddening too, Dad stood. "I'll finish my sandwich on the deck."

Mom waited until he closed the door behind him. "He still thinks of you as his baby."

"You don't?"

"I do but I try to be realistic—sexual urges can override reason. Didn't you know you were illegitimate?"

"I'm *what?*"

Mom stood with Elaine's plate and empty glass. "You're not the only one around here who can joke."

* * *

Elaine finished grading the tests early enough to swing by Minister Mattaniah's home. He stepped out on the porch as she closed the car door. "I saw you drive up, Elaine. No Harley?"

She joined him on the porch. "The forecast called for showers and that's not fun."

"I was somewhat surprised when I heard you'd bought it. Was it just for fun?"

"Part of it, I guess. Since the drive from my parents' house to school is about twenty minutes, I can save on gas too."

"I had a bike when I was young," the minister said, sitting in one of two wicker chairs on the porch. "A few close calls made me sell it. You never know when someone might pull out in front of you."

Elaine sat too. "When I drove home Saturday night, I didn't like the deer on the side of the road. If I have to go out at night from now on, I'll probably take my car."

"I'm sure you'd like to discuss the house. Did you and Joe take a look at it?"

"We like it." Elaine crossed her legs; the old whicker squeaked in protest. "I had no idea it'd be furnished, but I'd like a new mattress. Other than the rent, I wanted to ask about the kitchen sink."

"I noticed it was in bad shape when the renters left," the minister said. "How'd you like the purple living room?"

"Beige is much better."

"No doubt. I can have the sink replaced. Anything in mind?"

Elaine paused. Dad was one of two plumbers in town. She wanted him to do the work but wasn't sure what the minister would say. "Dad said he might have a stainless-steel sink and a new faucet. Is that okay?"

"Sure. If he installs it instead of me, I'll deduct the cost from the first month's rent. You'd like to know what that is, I'm sure. I was sort of vague about it at church."

"Maybe a little."

The minister took a slip of paper from his pocket and gave it to Elaine. "I figured you'd drop by and had this in case."

Elaine could hardly believe the price. "I wasn't expecting this. Are you sure it's enough?"

"I'm just returning God's blessings."

"I—Joe and I, that is—really appreciate this." Elaine folded the paper and dropped it into her purse.

"Glad to do it." The minister stood. "Are you moving in soon?"

Elaine stood also. "Maybe within a month, after Dad changes the sink and I get a new mattress for the bed."

"That one sure was worn out. As far as the rent, you can mail it or drop it off."

"I'll probably mail it. I don't want to take up any more of your time than I have to." Elaine took her car keys from her purse.

The minister followed her to the porch steps. "Don't forget, I do pre-marriage counseling. I hope I'm not presuming, but did you and Joe have me in mind for performing the ceremony?"

"We haven't had time to think about it, but probably." She glanced at her watch. "Thanks for everything."

The minister waved when Elaine backed out of the driveway. What a nice man, as well as a minister. She'd have to keep the idea of pre-marriage counseling in mind. He might have some insight into—

She plucked her lower lip. What he might have some insight into was her recent déjà vu experiences. Maybe they'd go away so she could concentrate on the house.

Passing the hardware store, she eased off the accelerator. She needed to check the prices on paint and related supplies to get rid of that horrid purple in the living room. More than that, she was tempted to take a seat on one of the wooden benches in front of the old wood stove to see if that faint music played again.

She pressed the accelerator. What she needed to do was meet Dad.

His white work van, with Johnson's Plumbing, Heating, and Air emblazoned on the side in red letters, already sat in front of the house. He strode from the backyard and waved as she climbed out of the car. "I thought that might be you pulling up. Running late?"

Elaine joined him by the porch. "I stopped by Minister Mattaniah's to find out about the rent and the sink. He's okay with you installing it, and the rent is better than I thought."

Dad grinned his gap-toothed grin. "What'd you expect from a minister? Let's take a look at your sink."

He waited while she unlocked the door. In the kitchen, she pointed at the sink. "It's a yucky old thing."

He took a tape measure from his belt, stretched it out along one side of the sink's edge, and did the same with the other. "Twenty-two by thirty-three, exactly like what I have in the van. Since the minister gave you a great price on the rent, I assume you're taking it. I can install the new sink in about an hour."

"That'd be great, unless you'd rather go home and do it after supper. Mom will be expecting you."

"Good point," Dad said, clipping the tape measure to his belt. "What color are you painting the living room?"

"I'll run by the hardware store before they close and check. I'll get copies of the key made and give you one when I get home."

"Good idea, it looks like a grape exploded in there." He followed her to the porch and waited while she locked the door. "Got a second, honey? I wanted to talk to you about something."

"I won't need long at the hardware." Though his tone puzzled Elaine, she had no idea what he wanted to discuss.

"It's about your motorcycle. When you said you were thinking about getting one, it worried your mom and me. It only takes a split second for an accident to happen."

Their concern was nice, but Elaine hadn't expected him to mention it. "You never said anything when I asked for a dirt bike to ride with Joe."

"That's because I'd take your bike to Joe's so you could ride with him in the woods and trails and down to the river. That's not the same as on the highway. Trees aren't driven by people not paying attention. Promise me you'll be careful, okay?"

"I wear all my protective gear. I ordered a padded jacket too. Until it gets here, I wear one of my old leather jackets."

"All that's great, but you never know what might happen. Your mom and me can't bear the thought of you getting hurt. Joe too, I'm sure."

Elaine kissed his stubbled cheek. "Aw, how sweet."

Half-grinning, Dad shook his head. "I'll 'how sweet' you, young lady. All right, get on down to the hardware before they close. See you later."

At the hardware store, Elaine pushed the heavy wooden door open and looked up as the brass bell that announced an entering customer dinged. Supposedly it was the original, installed when the store opened before World War II. She strolled down the aisle that led to the counter in back, currently un-attended. The majority of the store's fixtures, including the shelves lining the walls and the rolling wooden ladders that were climbed by whoever was waiting on a customer to reach the taller levels, stood as a reminder of the past. Modern stores had little genuine wood or genuine wood aromas, or floors layered with ancient paste wax in the corners that received little to no foot traffic. The aisle she now walked was a different story: dark with who knows what kind of stains brought in by boot soles over the years, with the wear showing in the form of a slight depression running the length of the aisle.

At the blackened cast-iron wood stove, Elaine sat on one of the wooden benches, equally as worn as the floors. Scattered near the stove's door, burns and what could have been chewing tobacco stains marked the floor. She glanced around. The floor of this old place had as much character as the rest of it.

Would the music return? Dumb question. A better one was did she *want* it to return? Life would be a lot simpler without those insane memories, if that's what they were, flaring up when she least expected them. Regardless of her desire to stay in the present, she closed her eyes and attempted to stray into the past.

And there it was, a guitar's soft strumming, plus a voice, masculine and young. She swallowed. What in the world was going on? Was she really hearing music from her past, or was she going insane?

"Why good afternoon, Elaine. I must not have heard the bell. Can I help you with something?"

Elaine opened her eyes to find Mr. Hansen peering at her from the counter. Great. Now the men who frequented this place would get an earful about the crazy Johnson girl daydreaming by the stove.

"I was … I was just resting my eyes. It's been a long day at school." She stood. "I need some paint and supplies."

She went to the counter, where Hansen pulled out a pad and a pencil. "Got whatever you need. Interior or exterior, and what color?"

Elaine looked past Hansen. Barely a whisper, the guitar and singing seemed to be coming from somewhere behind him. "Mr. Hansen, do you hear music?"

"You a bluegrass fan too? I have a radio on in the back. Keep it playing while the store's open. Have been for the last twenty years too."

"A radio?" Elaine asked, tilting her head to one side.

"Yep." Hansen placed the pencil to the pad. "How about that paint?"

"I need a medium beige interior paint. I'll get a gallon to start and get more if I need it. A couple of brushes, probably some primer, and plastic to cover the floor."

While Hansen wrote the items down, Elaine wanted to laugh at herself. The "mystery music" had been explained. Why hadn't she thought of something as simple as a radio? If she looked at the incidents at Ruth's—at the closet and while walking down the hall, when she'd had that intense bout of déjà vu similar to what she'd had at this store years ago—they could probably be explained away too. Since that was the case, she'd shove it from her mind completely.

"All right then." Hansen stuck the pencil behind his ear, got a cart from beside the counter, and headed toward a paint display. "I wasn't at church Sunday. A customer mentioned you and Joe getting engaged." He stopped at the display. "Find a place already?"

"I lucked up with that. Minister Mattaniah has a place ready to rent, except for the room I need to paint. Do you think I'll need a special primer to cover purple?"

"Just one room? You lucked out with that too." Hansen took a gallon pail from the counter and placed it in the cart. "This should take care of it."

At Ruth's place, Elaine took everything to the living room and frowned. Why call it *Ruth's* place when it was *her* place? She plucked her lower lip. If she checked the bedroom closet again, would that eerie déjà vu feeling return? What if she walked the hall to the kitchen? Might as well give them both a try. She returned to the closet and waited. Nothing. She strode the hall between the bedroom and the kitchen. Nothing.

Smiling, she locked the door, climbed in the car, and headed home. Yes, this old house was *Elaine's* place now instead of Ruth's place.

Chapter 6

Elaine closed the front door and followed the aroma of what could only be Mom's fried chicken to the kitchen. At the table, she and Dad were crunching away. Dad set the chicken down to spoon a bite of mashed potatoes into his mouth. Mom's cooking was an art form, but it did nothing for someone trying to stay trim.

"Sit and have a bite," Mom said.

Elaine fingered mashed potatoes into her mouth and swallowed. Butter, salt, and pepper—some things just tasted better with the basics. "I might grab a chicken leg and a couple of slices of bread. I want to start painting tonight."

Dad followed the potatoes with sweet tea, a slice of lemon in the glass. Mom could make a mean pitcher of that too. He set the glass down. "I thought you'd be tired from the kids at school."

"I doubt I'll do much."

Mom pointed a fork at Dad. "If you wait until your dad eats all my mashed potatoes, he can come along."

"He had a long day too," Elaine said. "I need to change clothes."

Elaine changed, packed the chicken leg and bread in a bag, and hurried to the car, only to frown when she turned the ignition. The gas gauge rested almost on E. Taking the car meant hunting in the shed for the lawn mower gas. Chicken in hand, she ran back to the house. Or she could ride the Harley.

She donned the leather jacket, gloves, grabbed the helmet—and snapped her fingers. Boots. She needed to trade out her tennis shoes for the boots. Fully clothed in the safety gear, she stopped at the kitchen door. "I'm taking the bike." She started toward the back door but stopped. "Got all my gear on too. See ya later."

"Don't stay too long after dark," Dad said. "You know how the deer are."

Dinner in a saddlebag, helmet strapped tight to her head, Elaine set off down the road.

To the west, across a field of wheat at least a half mile wide, the sun glimmered orange as it lowered into the treetops. In a curve ahead, a four-wheel-drive tractor, huge and green, capable of plowing a swath of land almost fifty-feet wide, headed her way. Diesel exhaust billowed above it. To avoid the huge tires, two to a rim, she eased the Harley to the side of the two-lane road. Those same tires had slung dark brown soil onto the asphalt, and the earthy aroma rose to greet her until she passed the dirt road where the tractor had come from, evidenced by the same soil lying in clumps at the turn. At another field, this one covered with lush grass, the aroma of fresh cow manure rode the wind and found its way under her face shield. She wrinkled her nose at the pungent smell, but she loved it as much as any other farm aroma.

Except pigs.

During the summer heat, when the wind blew just right, the scent of pigs came from a farm a few miles west of Dad's farm, and a strong whiff could almost take a person's breath away.

Pigs she could do without. Bacon, on the other hand, she could handle.

Elaine adored country living. If she and Joe had their way, they'd build a home overlooking the river. They both loved the place where they'd spent so much time over the years, picnicking, fishing, lying there on many a moonlit night while making plans for the future. Their place at the river—it had been her great-aunt's and Joe's great-grandpa's special place too, from family accounts—was her and Joe's special place as well. No matter where they were or what they were doing, the entire time they were dating it drew them like moths to the lantern they used to hang in the oak, not to mention mosquitos to their bare arms and legs if they forgot mosquito spray.

Inside the helmet, Elaine raised an eyebrow. Since the river was such a special place for her, as well as those relatives of long ago, and for Ruth and Kurt who were buried there, if she had one of those weird déjà vu experiences anywhere, she should have one there. She never had, another bit of evidence that put her curiosity about the déjà vu experiences to rest. Fine with her. Time to concentrate on her new home.

At the house, she sat on the porch steps to eat the chicken leg and bread, washing it down with a bottle of water she'd thrown in the bag at the last minute. With the brown crust still crunchy and warm, the only thing that would have made the meal any better was a helping of mashed potatoes.

Meal done, hands wiped on paper towels from the kitchen, Elaine went to the living room, placed her hands on her hips, and glanced around at the hideous purple walls. She'd never painted a room. Shouldn't be that hard. She wrestled the furniture to the center and spread the plastic along one wall, lugged over the gallon pail of primer, a paint tray, and a roller that Mr. Hansen had already attached to a handle. Using a metal tool made especially for paint cans, she pried the lid from the primer and stirred it with another tool Mr. Hansen had recommended, which resembled a giant wooden popsicle stick. Stirring done, she poured enough to cover a tray, wet the roller with a thin layer, and gave the wall several up-and-down strokes. The primer almost covered the purple. At this rate, she'd soon be ready for the next wall. She slid the tray over, wet the roller, and continued the process.

At the end of the wall, she flipped the light switch and glanced at her watch. Almost nine. Time to clean up and get home.

Lid on the primer, roller and tray rinsed in a five-gallon bucket of water—thank goodness the stuff was water-based—the smart phone in her jacket rang with Mom's tone, *I Did It My Way*, by Elvis Presley. Mom loved her some Elvis.

"Hi, Mom, what's up?"

"Me and your dad were wondering how it's going."

Elaine paused. This was parent-speak for *when are you coming home, we're worried.* "I just finished priming one wall and I'm cleaning up. I'll leave in a minute."

"I won't hold you up."

Elaine slid the phone back in the jacket and donned it and the rest of her riding gear, turned off the lights and locked the door. The Harley soon roared along the country road on the way home.

A sliver of a moon had risen above the trees across the fields, and stars scattered above her. Occasionally she'd run through a pocket of warm air, and once she caught the sweet aroma of honeysuckles, their yellow and white blooms tangled with a barbed wire fence that shone in the Harley's high-beam headlight. About a quarter mile from home, she twisted the throttle as she rounded a curve. The engine's rumble echoed back from another fence row while she leaned the bike into the curve's second half. The centrifugal force and feeling of being glued to the seat sent a tingle up her spine. Absolutely nothing compared to cruising on a motorcycle on a country road on a beautiful spring night.

Leaving the curve, she straightened the Harley. In the distant throw of its headlight, several pinpricks of light rose from the right side of the road: deer raising their heads at the Harley's rumble, no doubt. She let off the throttle. More pairs of reflective eyes, this time on the left side of the road. She braked. Not deer, a deer herd. She downshifted, slowing in case the four-legged-car-crashers decided to streak in front of her. The multiple pairs of eyes lowered as the deer went back to dinner. She eased along until she passed, twisted the throttle, and—

A huge brown blur entered the extreme left edge of her peripheral vision, followed by a jarring thud that sent her and the Harley toward the ditch. The front wheel twisted in the thick grass and the heavy bike fell on top of her, pinning her to the ground.

She managed to twist the key off, and the engine died with a sputter. Teeth clenched, she clutched her right hand to her chest. Pain throbbed in her wrist, either badly sprained or broken.

She pulled her left foot up and shoved against the seat. No movement at all. At least her right foot wasn't beneath the hot engine. She tried again, wiggling her foot, but it remained stuck.

Helmet off and in the grass beside her, she winced at the pain still throbbing in her wrist. Of all the luck. Not true. How often did someone in a motorcycle crash manage to fall in thick grass and not get hurt any worse than an aching wrist? Still, she needed help. Maybe someone would come along and—

Her phone. She'd slipped it in the jacket pocket before leaving Ruth's house. No, *Elaine's* house. She'd already settled that.

She checked the phone, which refused to come on.

A noise rustled nearby. Mr. Deer coming to finish her off?

Moo-o-o-o-o-o!

In spite of her pain, Elaine laughed. "Hi, Ms. Holstein. Can you run to my house for some help?"

Plop-plop-plop.

Elaine Wrinkled her nose at the unmistakable sound of manure plopping a wet pile to the pasture.

Moo-o-o-o-o-o! Snort.

"I can't believe it. I've been run over by a freaking deer, I can't get out from under this bike, and a cow is laughing at me."

Moo-o-o-o-o-o! The cow ambled away, hooves swishing in the grass.

The luminous hands on Elaine's watch said it was almost 9:45. If she weren't home soon, and if she didn't answer the phone when Mom called again, which she surely would, Dad would be along soon.

She lay back in the grass and kicked the seat once more. No movement whatsoever. At least she had a nice view, with the stars lighting the night sky as if they were lightning bugs winking on and off, on and off. A breeze blew from across the field, in the direction the cow had strolled, and Elaine cursed under her breath.

Pigs.

She held her hand to her chest. Thank goodness the pain had eased off. A meteor streaked across the sky, burning out directly overhead. She squirmed in the grass. Cold dew was soaking through her jeans.

Elaine closed her eyes.

* * *

Jimmy stepped out onto the porch, where Nora, who sat in the swing, eyed him. "I'm worried, and I know you are too. She should have been here an hour ago."

He took his phone from his pocket and dialed Elaine's number. "She's still not answering, I better head to town. She probably decided to keep painting."

"She still should leave her phone on so we can call."

"That's probably *why* she turned it off. Well, *if* she turned it off." He left the porch. "I'll call when I find her."

In his Van, Jimmy set off toward town. He hadn't mentioned it to Nora, but most days on his way home, he'd seen plenty of deer in the fields lining the road going in to Alma. Less than a quarter mile from his drive, yellow reflectors shined to the left. Something—or someone—had run into the—

His heart leapt to his throat. A motorcycle had crashed into the ditch. He hit the brakes, sliding to a stop, and jumped from the van, flashlight in hand.

"Elaine!" He rounded the bike, shined the light on her still form, and knelt beside her. "Elaine! Are you—"

Her eyes fluttered open. "About time you got here. I was just having a nap."

Tears filled Jimmy's eyes. He laughed while wiping them away. "I guess that means you aren't hurt bad." He shined the light toward where her leg went under the bike. "Are you hurt at all? That doesn't look good."

"If you'll get the bike off me, I'll tell you."

"Sorry about that, honey. Seeing you lying there about gave me a heart attack." He wrestled the bike up and set it on the kickstand. "Let's see if you can stand."

He slipped his arm around her and helped her to her feet. She shifted her weight from foot to foot. "My ankle's a little sore. The ribs on my right side too. I'll ache for a week."

Jimmy shined the light on her wrist that she held to her chest. "I'm taking you to the ER. Your bike will be fine until I get you home. I'll walk back and drive it in. It's no use arguing, you know."

In the passenger seat, Elaine clicked her seatbelt. "About the only thing that got totaled was my phone. Can you call Mom and let her know I'm okay, at least for the most part?"

Jimmy pressed the accelerator. "So that's why we couldn't get hold of you." He gave her his phone. "You call her. Payback for buying that Harley and almost getting killed."

* * *

At the ER, the attending physician examined Elaine, had her wrist X-rayed, and a nurse rolled her back to her curtained cubicle where Dad waited. He helped her from the wheelchair to the examining table covered with crinkly white paper. "Is the pain easing off or getting worse?"

"It's a dull ache now. I hope it's not broken. It'd be hard to work with my wrist in a cast."

"At least you won't be riding that bike anytime soon."

"Mom said if I had gotten killed, she would've killed me."

"I'd have loaded the gun for her. Buckshot, naturally."

Elaine shared a weak smile. "Maybe I should take up deer hunting."

"What you *should* take up," Dad said, his tone stern, "is not riding that motorcycle at night anymore."

Elaine covered her eyes with her good hand. Good point. If she'd been going as fast as she had when she came out of that curve and hit a deer, she, the deer, and the Harley might be scattered across a field, getting pooped on by Ms. Holstein.

57

"I hear you."

"I'm sure you do," Dad said. "But not as loud as you heard your mom when you called her, I bet."

The curtain opened and the doctor stepped in, laptop in hand. "Elaine, according to the X-ray, you have a bad sprain. That's minimal damage for someone who's crashed a motorcycle. How's the bike?"

"We haven't taken a look yet," Dad said. "Elaine was my priority."

"No doubt," the doctor said, opening the laptop. He brought up the X-ray and pointed. "As you see, nothing is broken." He slid his finger along the screen. "I wanted to ask you about this place on your wrist, called a 'callus.' It's a calcified place in a bone after it's healed. Your records don't indicate you being treated for a broken lower arm at this hospital. When did that happen?"

"I've never had a broken bone."

"I can vouch for that," Dad said. "This accident is the closest she's ever come to having anything broken. It's a wonder, with all her tomboy ways growing up. Dirt bikes, driving tractors, chasing down goats we used to have and riding them."

"Sounds like fun." The doctor closed the laptop. "It definitely resembles a healed break. Regardless, what matters is you're not hurt any worse than you are."

"What about work?" Elaine asked. "I'd hate to miss time from school."

"Don't overdo. Take ibuprofen if you need it."

"What about a brace?"

"If you can move it without too much pain, I'd prefer not. If it doesn't improve within a few days, follow up with your family doctor, but I expect it to improve." He gave her a form. "Give that to the attendant when you leave."

"Before you go," Dad said, "can you give Evil Knievel here another order?" He held his hands out as if gripping the handlebars of a motorcycle. "Vroom, vroom."

"Good idea. Elaine, no motorcycle for at least two weeks. I don't want any extra strain on that wrist. Doctor's orders as well as your dad's."

In the van again, Elaine shut the door. "You sure are tough on your only child."

Dad turned the key. "Darn right." He nudged her knee. "Fasten your seatbelt."

"I am, I am," Elaine said, clicking the belt.

"Much better. Besides, if you think I'm tough on you, wait until Joe finds out."

"Why does he have to know?"

"Wouldn't you want him to tell you if he had an accident and got hurt?"

Elaine considered the question. Normally she'd agree, but she wasn't the clingy—oh, I'm just a pitiful woman, wait on me—type, so she'd rather Joe didn't know. She faced Dad. "If he wasn't hurt bad, I wouldn't mind not knowing."

The dashboard's lights illuminated his frown. "That doesn't sound like someone who understands how important honesty is in a marriage, honey." He left the hospital parking lot. "Know what I mean?"

Elaine didn't answer. He was right—it was rare when he wasn't—Mom too. Like all couples, they had their squabbles, but they usually settled their differences by suppertime. That was the kind of marriage she wanted. In fact, she wouldn't settle for anything less. "I'll call him but not tonight, it's too late. Thanks for rescuing me."

"You looked pretty comfortable when I got there. Were you really napping?"

"I dozed off. When I heard you drive up, I thought I'd mess with you."

"How'd you know it was me?"

"Who else would've yelled my name like you did?"

Dad shook his head. "Maybe I should haul that Harley to the junkyard and sell it for scrap."

Chapter 7

The next morning, Elaine crawled out of bed and stretched. Every muscle in her body ached, and the skin around her wrist puffed out, giving her hand and lower arm the appearance of having no bones. Her ankle, tight and sore, caused her to favor it as she donned her robe and limped toward the living room and the phone. She wouldn't do the kids any good, in pain and half-hobbling around. The soreness should ease with breakfast and a couple of ibuprofen, and since she'd fallen into bed right after coming home last night, a hot shower might help too.

She called the school and went to the kitchen, where Mom was washing dishes. Elaine sank into a chair, and Mom glanced over her shoulder. "Your dad left early to help someone without any water. Can I fix you something? There's leftover bacon, coffee too. It'll only take a minute for eggs. Over easy or scrambled?"

"Scrambled is fine. Did he say anything about the Harley?"

"He said it steers to the left so bad, he could hardly drive it home."

Elaine pushed up from the table with her left hand and eased over to the coffee maker. "It didn't feel like the deer hit me that hard. Maybe hitting the ditch did it."

"He said it scared the deer as much as it did him."

Elaine poured coffee. "What do you mean?"

"That deer left a stinky calling card down the side of your bike. I heard that sometimes happens when a car hits one. I'm surprised it didn't poop on your jeans."

"Yuck." Elaine sipped coffee. "The handlebars must've gotten knocked out of alignment or bent. You're glad to hear that, aren't you? I can't ride it until it's fixed." She returned to the table, wincing at her sore ankle.

"Joe will be glad to hear it too," Mom said. "Your dad said you were going to call him today." She brought a plate to the table. "Do you have time before school?"

"Isn't it obvious I called in since I'm walking around like Uncle Thomas when he was still walking? Can I borrow your phone to text Joe to call me between classes? I'll tell him then."

"That's right, yours got broken in the crash. Mine's on my dresser, I'll grab it for you. Oh, your dad parked the Harley in the shed in front of the tractor. Maybe I'll run it over with it."

"Don't you dare. Then Dad will get you for wrecking the tractor."

Mom returned with the phone. Elaine crunched bacon and swallowed. "Did Dad tell you about the doctor asking about my arm being broken when it never was? That was weird."

"No, he didn't." Mom poured coffee and sat across from her. "That *is* strange. What made the doctor think that?"

"He said the X-ray showed a place in the bone called a 'callus.' According to him, that's calcified bone from where it heals. I never heard of it."

"You never broke a bone either." Mom sipped coffee. "I'm going into town later. I can drop your phone off to have it checked."

"That'd be great. I'll shower and text Joe after I eat." Picking up a fork, Elaine winced and dropped it as a sharp pain shot through her wrist. "Ouch!" She flexed her fingers. "I sure hope that shower helps me feel better."

* * *

As Joe left his soil microbiology class, relieved the final exam was over, his smart phone vibrated. The text from Elaine said to call the land line at her parents' house when he had time. With thirty minutes before his next class, he went outside and took a seat at an out-of-the-way bench beneath a row of maple trees lining the sidewalk between this and the next building.

He read the text again. Why was she at home instead of school, and why did she want him to call the land line instead of her smart phone? Only one way to find out.

"Hey, babe. You can imagine the questions running through my mind when I got your text. What's up?"

"As long as we've been together," Elaina said, a hint of exasperation in her voice, "you know what I can imagine. Your forehead wrinkled and you asked yourself why I wasn't at school since I had you call here."

"And why I had to call the land line too." Joe touched his forehead. She was right about it being wrinkled.

"Well," she said, the exasperation even worse, "I sprained my ankle and my wrist and took off from school."

"What the heck were you doing to sprain both?" Joe asked. "Did you sprain your phone too?"

"I didn't want to tell you. Dad said I should."

"Your dad knows happy couples don't keep secrets from each other. Why didn't you want to tell me whatever it is that happened?"

"Because I got hurt when I crashed my Harley."

"And all you got was a sprained ankle and wrist? What's the bike look like?"

"Your tone says you don't believe me." Elaine exhaled a hard breath into the phone, which Joe recognized as her huff of impatience whenever they had an argument.

"C'mon," he said. "If you wrecked the bike, why aren't you hurt any worse?"

"Do you wish I was hurt worse?"

"I'm sorry, babe, you know not that's not what I want. Why didn't you call me when it happened?"

"Because I wasn't hurt any worse, meaning you might have sped here and wrecked too."

"That's true." Joe almost asked her if she'd been speeding on the Harley like on Saturday, on the way to the river, but it wasn't important since she was okay. "What happened?"

"You know what they say about most accidents happening near home? I was almost home last night after painting at the house in town, and a herd of deer ambushed me. I saw them when I rounded that last curve before our drive. I probably wasn't going much more than twenty miles an hour, and one ran into the front wheel. It was just a brown blur and then wham, I went in the ditch."

"That's the stretch that has all that thick grass, right? Thank God for soft miracles, huh?"

Elaine laughed and Joe smiled, extremely glad to hear her laugh and extremely glad she'd made it through the crash with only a couple of sprains. He couldn't imagine being without her for any reason, and he didn't care to try.

"That's for sure," Elaine said, done laughing. "My phone's the worst victim. Mom's dropping it off in town. I'll pick it up tomorrow if they can fix it."

"You're working tomorrow?"

"I think so. After one of Mom's breakfasts and a couple of ibuprofens and a hot shower, I feel a lot better."

"Glad to hear it." Joe glanced at his watch. "I need to run, babe. My next class calls."

"Call me later tonight and I'll tell you about my painting."

"Will do, bye."

Joe slid the phone into his pocket and hurried across campus to his next class, plant genetics, where the exam was scheduled for Friday. In the room, Professor Propst already stood, talking beside a projection screen. Joe took a seat near the back while the professor lowered a laser pointer from a strand of plant DNA on the screen. Joe glanced at his watch. Sure, he'd just gotten here, and sure, DNA interested him, but this subject wouldn't help him much in the field.

The professor turned the pointer off and faced the class. "I'm sure many of you doubt the necessity of this information unless you're in the lab. Still, DNA research is a fascinating field, even more so with humans. Did you know identical twins share the same genetic code? Also, there have been instances where a person could not be prosecuted for a crime because their DNA matched a twin."

Joe raised his hand.

"Yes, sir, Mr. Matthan?"

"I was wondering how long DNA that can identify a person lasts?"

"Quite long. Samples have been recovered from bone that are hundreds of thousands of years old."

"What about hair samples, or blood?"

"Hair follicles, you mean. The shaft itself contains no DNA. As far as the follicle and blood, if kept cool and dry, the DNA can easily last a hundred years or more. Does that answer your questions?"

"Sure, professor, thanks." Professor Propst faced the screen, pressed a remote, and a different picture appeared. He turned on the laser pointer and aimed it at a cell of some kind. "Here we have the cell from a corn leaf. In it ..."

Joe leaned back in his seat. If his dreams meant he really was the reincarnation of his 1944 self who died in the Ardennes Forest, could he prove it by finding a DNA sample from himself back then? He bit his lower lip. Not likely. His 1944 self was buried in the Ardennes American Cemetery in Belgium. Even if he managed to visit, what could he tell the officials that would allow him to gain access to his body—if it was his body—to get a sample? The obvious answer was nothing. Still, when a problem presented itself, he enjoyed solving it, unless this problem had no solution.

Class and lunch over, he trotted to the library. He'd never taken the time to research the reincarnation aspect of his theory—how he was his own great-grandson—and it was time. His laptop had decent speed, but between all his class notes and pictures of him and Elaine, not much memory. He really needed to pick up a few memory sticks and download the pictures for safekeeping.

The librarian led Joe to several desktop PCs. He sat in front of one of the latest models, afforded by the college due to a recent donation from a business tycoon who, when he'd made the donation, had said, "Neither opinion nor emotion is the key to education. That, ladies and gentlemen, lies with knowledge."

Joe certainly agreed. Maybe he could find a bit of knowledge to help him on his quest to find the truth of his theory. Or, if it were the case, to discount it. Regardless, he intended to get to the truth of the matter before he mentioned it to Elaine.

In the search bar, he typed "interesting cases of reincarnation." From the resulting list, he clicked "ten compelling cases of reincarnation." A website popped up, along with the first names of the ten people. Scrolling through the list, the cursor trembled at one of the captions, mirroring his trembling right hand.

I Am My Own Great-Granddaughter

Joe took his hand from the mouse and lowered it to his lap. This was exactly what he was looking for, so why the hesitation? Was it because his theory was fun to think about, and now, that he'd actually found a corroborating story, it wasn't fun to think about any more? He scrolled back to the top.

The first story was about a woman, who, when she was a young girl, claimed to know a couple who lived out in the country, south of an unnamed town in Kansas. In fact, the girl claimed to have been neighbors of the people, but the only knowledge she had of the area was from hearing her adoptive parents, who lived in the same town, talk about its rural name. That's when she'd made her claims—eventually making them so often that her parents took her to the area and drove around until she pointed at a house and told them that's where she lived when she was a little girl. They stopped to ask the people next door who lived in the house where the girl claimed to have lived her previous life, and they were told no one now, because the family—a mother and father and their son and daughter— had died in a car accident. The girl's parents asked when this had happened, and the neighbor's answer floored them—the accident had happened on the night the girl was born.

Joe paused from the article. Wild stuff. Hard to believe stuff. Even with the addition of the young girl's testimony and her corresponding death and birth dates. Joe ran his fingers through his hair. Maybe he really *did* need a mental evaluation.

He scrolled to another story of a man who claimed to be his own great-grandson. This story was similar, in that the man told people where he used to live, but it included the names of his neighbors. The information was verified when he visited them, including the names of something that wouldn't have been public knowledge: the names of his family pets from the eighteen-year span in which he'd claimed to live there, before joining the Navy in the late 1950's. The interesting side note to this story was how, up until he'd happened upon a set of World War II dog tags that bore his name at a thrift store, he'd only had the dream occasionally, like Joe was having. Upon finding the dog tags, his flashbacks and dreams had occurred more often, with more scenes from his previous life. That's when he'd questioned his relatives about his great-grandpa. He'd been killed in the Pacific in World War II, and the Marines had returned his personal effects to his family, along with the dog tags that had languished in the thrift shop until the man had bought them.

Joe closed out the website. Too bad he didn't have Great-grandpa's dog tags. He assumed they were buried at the Ardennes American Cemetery with the ashes of Great-grandma Elaine. Grandpa said he and Ruth buried several personal items in the mahogany chest where the ashes were kept. He'd have to call Grandpa and—

Grandpa? If Joe's theory proved correct—that he was his own great-grandson—that would make Grandpa his—

Son?

Also, if his theory proved correct, that would make Elaine his—

Great-grandma?

Yep, straightjacket time.

Or was it?

None of that mattered. The fact that he and Elaine were meant to be together mattered, and if they'd returned to the future to be together in the present because they couldn't be together in the past, that was all the proof he needed, though he'd like to have more.

If the dog tags were buried in Belgium, he couldn't afford a trip to ask about them, which he'd like to do before he and Elaine were married.

Time to figure out a way to get to Belgium.

But how?

Chapter 8

After supper, Elaine grabbed her latest paperback, her repaired phone in case Joe called, and went out onto the back deck. In the garden spot to the right, Mom and Dad planted tomato seedlings. Elaine wanted to help but didn't want to reinjure her wrist. Instead, she needed to get back to school in the morning, since the kids—even elementary age kids—could severely try a substitute teacher's patience.

Book partially open, her cell rang with Joe's tone: a tractor's rumbling engine.

"Hey, Mr. Soon-to-be-graduate. I was just about to take a minute for myself."

"Yeah? Wanna make it one of *those* phone calls?"

"Excuse me, Mr. Pervert, I meant reading. I rarely have time to do that for enjoyment and not school. As far as what you mean by *those* phone calls, we don't do *those* phone calls."

"Wanna give it a try? How about—"

"Do you want to hear about my painting or not?"

"Okay, okay. Tell me what you've done to what I hope will soon be our new home."

"I started priming one of the walls in that horrid purple living room. The stuff Mr. Hansen at the hardware store recommended did a great job."

"It's a good thing you started before you hurt your wrist. How is it?"

"It's better. Let me tell you about my weird X-ray. After the bike crash, Dad took me to the ER because he was worried about my wrist."

"What was so weird about it?"

"The doctor showed me a place on the bone above my wrist and asked when I'd broken my arm. I've never broken my arm. Weird, right?"

"What did the place he show you look like? I thought a bone healed and that was that."

"It was sort of like a white mark. He said it was called a callus."

"I've heard of that." Joe paused like he sometimes did before making a joke. "That's those places on your feet that dent concrete when you walk on a sidewalk barefooted."

"When you come home," Elaine said, "I'll dent your—"

"Just kidding. You've got the sexiest feet in Alma ... maybe in Nebraska ... maybe even in the—"

"Mr. Matthan?"

"Yes, the soon-to-be Mrs. Matthan?"

"Shut up." Elaine laughed, and loved doing so. Her and Joe's joking was one of the qualities she adored most about their relationship. To her, laughter was like an aphrodisiac, and she'd often asked herself if they would make love on their honeymoon or laugh at each other half the night. Then she'd scold herself, because she looked forward to that night for more important reasons than laughter.

"Okay," Joe said, "I'm shutting up."

"Are the job recruiters still coming tomorrow?" Elaine asked.

"I saw the list today. I wonder what the income range is?"

"Me too. We'll need a good one to afford a big family."

Joe didn't say anything, but Elaine could almost see his brows furrowing, or either his right brow rising, which she considered quite sexy. "Well, Mr. Matthan?"

"Exactly how big a family is big?"

"You know us 'old souls,' at least half a dozen."

"Yeah, right. I might be an 'old soul,' but I'm not a dumb one. How about three?"

"As quiet as you were, I thought you might have taken me seriously. Three's fine."

"Maybe you'll have triplets and get it over with in one pop."

"Even if I have one at a time, I'll have you, you big kid, to deal with." She checked her watch. "I'm gonna read and get some sleep so I can face my little angels tomorrow."

"Me too. Gotta be ready for the recruiters. I love you, babe."

"I love you too."

Elaine left the phone on the table but didn't open the paperback. In the garden, Dad knelt beside a mound of dark earth that stretched in a row of about fifty feet, digging a hole with his hands. To his right, he'd planted ten tomato plants, and Mom was watering them with a garden hose.

Over the western horizon, the sun hung over the distant trees, a yellow ball in the middle of its transformation to orange. Within fifteen minutes it'd be red, and when it disappeared behind the trees, it would darken to the color of embers glowing in her and Joe's previous fire at the river.

Ever since she and her parents had moved here, she sat here as often as possible to watch the sun set. More often than not, birdsong accompanied the dimming twilight, as well as the warm breeze that blew from across the fields, bringing the natural aromas of both plant and animal. In early spring, like now, the air also held the slight hint of the cooler night to come.

Elaine stood and stretched. Her aches from the accident had lessened, but her back was stiff, and she winced when she attempted to place her full weight on her ankle.

Dad rose and stretched also. Mom watered the last tomato plant he'd set into the soil. Elaine waved. "I'm turning in early to read, goodnight."

***

Classes done for the following day, Joe entered the gym with a folder of his class records. At four-thirty he was late. The recruiters would be here until five, but he didn't think there'd be this many people. Hands in his pockets and the folder beneath his arm, he shuffled to the end of a long line of fellow job seekers.

Every few minutes he glanced at his watch, and twenty minutes later took a seat at a table. A young woman with corn-silk blonde hair half way down her back, and gorgeous sky-blue eyes, offered her hand. "Good afternoon. I'm Jillian Bauer, with Organiks."

Joe took Jillian's warm hand. She squeezed his and smiled an amazing smile that—he shouldn't go there—possibly rivaled Elaine's. No, there was no "possibly" to it. This woman holding his hand was absolutely stunning. Jillian … a pretty name too. Wait a minute, did she say her last name was Bauer, like Kurt's last name? Joe released her hand. "If you don't mind me asking, with your last name and blonde hair, are any of your ancestors German?"

Jillian picked up a pen. "I'll tell you my secrets if you tell me yours."

A tingle ran up Joe's back. Was she flirting? Maybe not but maybe so, since she might have thought he was flirting by asking her such a personal question.

"No secrets here, I'm an open book," he said. "I'll start with my name—it's Joe Matthan."

Jillian's blonde eyebrows arched. "What an interesting last name. Jewish, isn't it? That would make us mortal enemies back in World War II."

"My step-great-grandpa would disagree. His last name was Bauer. He fought with—was forced to fight with, I should say—the Nazi's. He was no enemy of the US, but he had every reason to be."

"Why's that?"

"Because he was captured and brought here as a POW to work on the farms around Alma. That's where I'm from, Alma, Nebraska."

"I've been through there, lovely country."

Jillian's voice was a mix of sultry and sexy, but a little on the low side for Joe's taste.

Her lips quirked with a slight grin. "A previous boyfriend and I used to skinny dip in the Republican River in the next county over, where I'm from."

Joe swallowed. Imagining her naked, standing on the bank of the river before diving in, was hard to ignore. If she wasn't trying to flirt with him, she was doing a poor job of it. He glanced behind him. "Maybe we should talk about your job opening. I'm sure the people behind me would like to see you before five."

Jillian slid a pad in front of her. "That's very considerate of you, Joe." She clicked the pen. "Consideration for others is extremely sexy. As far as our job openings, is there anything in particular you're interested in, such as research or field work, or perhaps some of both?"

Joe swallowed again. *Extremely sexy?* If that wasn't flirting, what—

Jillian tapped his hand with the pen. "Come on now, work with me here." She waved her hand in front of his eyes, and the sweet aroma of her perfume wafted in the air.

Joe cleared his throat. Time to get his mind back on why he was here. "Definitely field work. Research is interesting too, especially with organics. I understand it's a growing field" — he grinned at his pun— "so to speak."

"Nice smile, Joe. Nice pun too, I might use it some time. You're in luck with our openings. We're considering opening an office within an hour's drive of Alma. Are you planning on living there after you graduate? That would be convenient."

"My family lives there." *His* family lives there? Why hadn't he said his fiancé works there?

Jillian gave him a card from a nearby stack. "I like being considerate too. Take my card and I'll help everyone waiting behind you. Also, do you know of a decent place around here for dinner? Perhaps a cozy, out-of-the-way restaurant with a great wine list? We could talk more about my last name and your last name and what I've got planned for you." She smiled that same stunning smile. "I mean, of course, what Organiks might have planned for you." She leaned over the table and pointed toward his lap. "What do you have there, that looks promising."

A tingle of adrenaline shot through Joe. "I—" He looked down. Sheesh, she was pointing at the folder he'd forgotten and not at— He placed the folder on the table. "Uh … yeah. You might want to take a look at that."

"I certainly would, I'm *extremely* curious about what I'd find." She opened the folder while Joe shifted in his seat, glad she was looking at his resume and not at his warming cheeks that had to be turning red.

She read, tapping the pen on the table … turned a page … turned another page … and raised those gorgeous blue eyes to Joe again. "Your GPA is above average. Do you—" On the table, a phone vibrated. She glanced at the screen. "Let me take this, it's from my boss." She raised the phone to her ear. "Hi, Terry. Yes, that's good news, I've got a candidate right here who might fit perfectly. Yes, his GPA and majors are exactly what we're looking for. No, he's local to Alma, so no relocation. I'll meet with him later to discuss the job and more of his background and get back with you then."

She ended the call. "Interesting conversation, don't you think?"

"It sounds like the 'considering' phase of building that office near Alma is done."

"You're quite the lucky man to get in on this project." Jillian sat back in the chair and ran her fingers through her hair. "How about that restaurant?"

Earlier, since it seemed she had more on her mind than the job when she mentioned the restaurant, Joe was going to decline. Now, with the possibility of a job, including an office near home presenting itself, he'd be crazy to decline.

"There's a place like you described near the south end of the campus. What time?"

"Around seven's fine. How about I meet you there?"

"Sounds good. It only takes a few minutes to walk there from my apartment." Joe clenched his jaw. He shouldn't have told her that. She might think it was an invitation to stop by after dinner. There was no way that could happen. Elaine would kill him if she found out he had another woman in his apartment, and he wouldn't blame her one bit. He'd feel the same if the roles were reversed.

He stood with the folder, and Jillian held out her hand. "If you don't mind, I'll read the rest of your records and return them when we meet. What's the name of the restaurant?"

"The Lamplighter. If you take the main road that circles the campus, you can't miss it."

Jillian responded with her stunning smile. "See you then."

Chapter 9

On the way to his apartment, Joe recalled the name of the company Jillian represented. Organiks was an up-and-coming force in the agricultural world, specializing in large scale organic agriculture. The company was based in Belgium, but its market was expanding, even locating to the small town of Alma, of all places. Whatever. When an opportunity like this presented itself, only an idiot would ignore it.

What about Jillian? Would she try to take advantage of his wanting a job by expecting some kind of sexual reciprocation? He had no reason to think such a thing, but the tension—*sexual* tension—between them had been thick enough to make him fear what might happen tonight if he gave her any idea that he was interested in her. Still, admitting his engagement to Elaine would've put that issue to bed, so why hadn't he said so already? Did Jillian's stunning smile, gorgeous blue eyes, and corn-silk blonde hair down her back make him forget he was engaged?

He shook his head while unlocking his apartment door. Unsettling thoughts for sure, ones to have sorted out before that wall of sexual tension formed a door he might walk through.

Showered, shaved, and dressed in a well-worn pair of jeans and a button-up white shirt, Joe took a seat on the sofa.

Somewhat surprised he hadn't heard from Elaine, he checked his phone and frowned. When did he turn it off? He couldn't remember, which wasn't like him at all. After logging in, a series of texts from Elaine surprised him again.

Hi, sweetie, I love you.

Hi again. Letting you know I'm feeling good enough to paint more tonight.

Hi again, sweetie. Good luck with any recruiters you met today. Do whatever it takes to get a job!

Good luck with the recruiter? Do whatever it takes to get a job? Yeah, right.

Joe sent Elaine a text saying he loved her, he hoped the painting went well, and he'd call her later to tell her about the recruiter. With that promise on his list of to-dos, maybe he'd have the presence of mind to not *do* anything with Jillian he'd regret—or that Elaine would never forgive.

He checked his watch. Six-thirty. How many people at the gym got to see Jillian? He hated holding anyone up, but— He rubbed his forehead. Was his brain turning to mush? Jillian and the other recruiters would be there tomorrow, so everybody seeking a job would have the same chance. He leaned back on the sofa and closed his eyes.

The possibility of a job could speed up his and Elaine's marriage plans. He'd graduate in three weeks. In addition, they had a place to call home, so there was no reason to wait.

Or was there?

He'd had no new dreams concerning his past—his past that he believed could be his past—but he wanted to tell Elaine about it. Since she'd mentioned her déjà vu feelings while they were at Ruth's house, he wanted to know if they were related to what he'd been experiencing. After all, if what he believed was true—that he could be the reincarnation of his 1944 self—she might be the reincarnation of herself from back then also. As far as the similarities in love stories between his Great-grandpa, Joe Matthan, and Elaine's great-aunt Elaine, the coincidences were almost undeniable.

He opened his eyes to check his watch. Time to walk to the restaurant.

When he arrived at the parking lot, a car horn beeped. In a sleeveless red dress with what Elaine called spaghetti straps, Jillian got out of a car. The dress fell mid-thigh of her long, tanned legs, and she wore matching high heels. Not only was she breathtaking, she was also as stunning as any model on any cover of any of the fashion magazines Elaine occasionally read. Joe didn't know if he should go inside or run. Elaine ... Elaine ... got to keep his mind on Elaine.

Jillian strolled over. "I feel overdressed. Is casual okay here?"

Her sultry voice knocked Joe for a loop. "Seeing as we might be future co-workers, would it be sexual harassment to tell you how great you look?"

"Not at all, since we're not co-workers yet."

Joe wanted to smack his own forehead for telling her she looked great. What the heck was wrong with him? He loved Elaine. They were engaged. She was the love of his life. They were going to get married just as soon as—

Jillian linked her arm with his. "Let's go, I'm starved."

On their way to the door, Joe caught the scent of her perfume, with its subtle, musky sweetness. If he had to guess, the high-heels she wore were three-inches at least, because she almost reached his six-foot height. She glanced at him and smiled, and he caught a whiff of her shampoo, intoxicatingly similar to the honeysuckle blossoms at home. At the steps, her blonde hair shined in the light that shone from the two lamps on either side of the door, illuminating the fine strands.

A greeter met them inside. "Two? Table or booth?"

"A booth," Jillian said. "Is that round one in the back corner taken?"

"Nice choice," the greeter said, with the hint of a smile. "The most romantic booth in the entire restaurant, not to mention the coziest." She took two menus from a nearby rack. "Follow me."

Joe slid into the booth and Jillian slid in beside him, bumping his hips with hers. "Slip over a little more so I can set my bag beside me."

Joe waited until the greeter left. "Aren't you demanding? What happened to please?"

"Is that the magic word?" Jillian licked her lips. "Will you do most anything I ask if I say please?"

Joe rubbed his lower lip and immediately regretted it. Elaine said it turned her on when he did that.

"Ah, you're considering it," Jillian said. "Or have you been considering it since we met?"

"Well, there's no telling what I might do since a job might be on the line." Joe lowered his finger from his lip. Where did idiotic line come from?

"Your merit at college will get you that job, not your merit elsewhere."

Joe wasn't about to ask where "elsewhere" might be, but the bedroom was a good guess. He slid a menu to Jillian. "Take a look and see what you want." He inwardly cringed. Yet another idiotic line.

Jillian ignored the menu. "I know what I want." She touched Joe's arm. "You're something else, you know that?"

Joe closed the menu. "How so?"

"Here I am, sending you all these signals, and you've got your mind on food. You're really the shy farm boy, aren't you?

Don't you know how absolutely gorgeous you are? I could eat you up."

Pinching the bridge of his nose, Joe chuckled. "My shyness shows that bad, huh?"

"To me it does." Jillian opened the menu. "Didn't I say I was starved? Maybe they have a good—"

"Welcome to the Lamplighter," a waitress said. "Would you like a drink to start, or are you ready to order?"

"A rare steak would be great," Jillian said. "Have the chef cook it just long enough to silence the moo. Add a baked potato and a salad with house dressing, I'll be good to go."

"Make that two," Joe said. "But take a bit more of the moo out of mine—medium rare, please. I think the lady would like a glass of wine to go with that also."

Jillian eyed him. "Aren't you the attentive one?" She faced the waitress. "Not a glass, a bottle. Your best Cabernet Sauvignon, please."

"I'll get your order in and be right back with the wine. Would you like an appetizer?"

"My appetite is quite well without." Jillian cut a sideways glance at Joe. "You?"

"I'm, uh … I'm good."

The waitress hurried away.

"My goodness, farm boy, you're right about saying please. See how well she responded? Would you *respond* as well if I said please?"

"If you keep up with all that sexual innuendo," Joe said, despite his nagging conscience, "you'll have this shy farm boy blushing. Tell me more about your company. Organiks is headquartered in Belgium, right?"

"In Liège. Are you familiar with the Ardennes American Cemetery? It's a short drive from there."

Joe opened his eyes a bit wider than normal. Only yesterday he'd been thinking about the very same cemetery and how his—or his great-grandpa's—dog tags were buried there.

"That's quite a coincidence," he said. "My great-grandpa's buried there. I've always wanted to visit his grave. My grandpa did back in 2001, I think it was."

"Interesting," Jillian said. "This afternoon you mentioned having a German step-great-grandfather with the last name of Bauer, like mine. I take it he liked Nebraska even though he was brought here as a POW and used as farm labor."

"Not too many people know about that," Joe said, glad the sexual innuendo had left the conversation.

"I wrote my college thesis on that interesting bit of American history," Jillian said. "Please don't think I'm prying, but did your great-grandmother marry the same two men, or did one great-grandmother marry one and the other marry Kurt?"

"She married my namesake first. After he was killed, she married Kurt a few years later."

Jillian sighed. "How romantic, to overcome the stigma of being an enemy soldier to eventually woo and marry your great-grandmother. Kurt must have been a special man. For all your great-grandmother knew, he could've been the soldier who killed your great-grandfather. Now wouldn't *that* have been a coincidence?"

"I'm not sure about—" Joe paused. "Here comes the wine."

The waitress opened the bottle, filled their glasses, and Jillian asked for a glass of ice-water. When the waitress brought it, Jillian took what resembled a compact of birth control pills from her purse, popped one into her mouth, and washed it down with the water. Joe sipped wine and glanced at Jillian, who waggled her finger at him. "Don't look at me like that, my doctor prescribed them for migraines. I imagine with all my *innuendo*, as you called it a minute ago, and these" —she shook the pills at him and returned them to the purse— "you think I'm quite the floozy."

Joe laughed. "'Floozy?' I might have said something else, like ..."

"Careful, farm boy."

"I better shut up."

"Very intelligent of you."

"Which is why I bring this up—what you said about skinny dipping with a previous boyfriend, that might be considered 'floozy' behavior too, you know."

"Mmm, mmm, mmm," Jillian said, shaking her head. "For you to believe I'm not a floozy, or loose, or whatever else you might call it, I'll have to tell you my deepest, darkest secret."

"That's up to you," Joe said, then sipping wine.

"I'm a virgin."

Joe strangled on the wine and coughed while Jillian eyed him. "Does that mean you don't believe me?"

Joe wiped his lips. "It means that was the last thing I expected you to say. You really know how to surprise a guy, or make him choke half to death."

"It's true. I happen to think I'm special enough to wait for the right man to come along." She placed her hand on his. "Don't you think I'm special?"

Joe didn't answer right away. If she were telling the truth— and she could be—it was an amazing admission. How would she feel about his own dark secret? There was only one way to find out. "I knew you were special when I saw you. Since you've been acting like I'm special too, there might be a similar reason why."

"You're a virgin too?"

"Amazing, huh?"

"In this day and time, darn right."

Joe raised his wine glass. "A toast to 'special' people everywhere."

She clinked her glass to his. "I completely agree."

They both sipped wine, set the glasses on the table, and Joe faced her. "As far as your name, Bauer, do you have German relatives?"

"Remember what I said during our interview about how we'd have been enemies during World War II? I also have family in Norway, several generations back." Jillian paused for wine. "What about Matthan? Have you researched your ancestors further back than your great-grandfather?"

"I have enough trouble keeping those straight. You know, with having a German step-great-grandpa too."

Their supper arrived. The steaks sizzled on the hot platters, sending up the delicious aroma of seared beef. The baked potatoes ran with butter and sour cream. Joe asked about the job and how long it might be before the office near Alma was built, and Jillian said by the end of the summer.

Joe swallowed the last bite of steak and washed it down with his second glass of wine. "Wow, that was great."

The waitress had already left the bill on the corner of the table. He checked the total, took his wallet from his back pocket, and Jillian popped his hand. "No, sir. That's going on my business account."

"If you don't mind, I'd rather pay for mine."

"Want any more?" she asked, touching the wine bottle. He said no and she filled her glass. "I think I'm a closet wino. That's four glasses, isn't it?"

"Not sure, I had two."

"Instead of paying for your meal, you can do me the flavor" —she giggled— *"favor* of driving me back to my hotel. I'm feeling a bit woozy, and I'd hate to get a ticket." She giggled again. "Then I'd be woozy floozy."

Joe held in a laugh. "I thought you weren't a floozy."

"I'm not—certainly I'm not. I just like how it rhymes. Will you drive me? I'll say please … pretty please … whatever might—"

"Okay, okay, you said the magic word."

The waitress returned with Jillian's credit card, and Joe walked her to the car, placing his arm around her slender waist when she got wobbly on those sexy high heels. He opened the door and waited while she climbed in. Since she made no move to put her seat belt on, he leaned over her to pull it across her lap, and she sniffed. "Oh my, farm boy smell."

He stood. "What? *Eau de* cow pile?"

"Not at all, sweetheart. Did I tell you that after I get to know someone I like—I mean *really* like—I call them sweetheart? It's a short list. You should be pleased you're on it."

Joe closed the door. She was definitely in no shape to drive. He climbed in and buckled his seat belt. Jillian sat back with her eyes closed. He hoped she could make it to her room without any help. Her hotel room was off limits—*bigtime* off limits.

At the hotel parking lot, Jillian faced Joe. "I left your resume in my room, and I've got a box of them in the back seat. You can carry them in for me." She poked at the seat belt latch. "You can undo this thing for me too." She grinned at him and batted her eyelashes. "Oh, darn, I didn't say the mashic word. Please? Purty, purty please, with kisses all over your sexy farm boy lips?"

Joe took the offered keys and went to the passenger door, chuckling the whole time. She was a mess—a *drunk* mess. Either that or she was faking to get him into her hotel room, along with leaving his resume there. Regardless, he should be able to control himself long enough to get in and out after grabbing his resume.

He opened the door, leaned over to unbuckle the seat belt buckle, and Jillian sniffed again. "There it is, that farm boy smell. I think I'm in love."

Joe pressed the button. "I think you're drunk off your—rear end." He stood and shook his head. He'd almost said, *I think you're drunk off your sexy behind.* Had he checked her out? Fool. Sure, he'd checked her out, which was another thing on the long list of things he shouldn't be doing. He held out his hand. "Ready to go, floozy?"

Giggling, Jillian swung her feet to the pavement. "Woozy floozy. Yep, lesh go."

Joe helped her up and walked her to her room. Apparently, the walk and the cooler air had cleared her head—maybe. She held out her hand at the door. "Keys, farm boy. If you didn't lock my car, you can go back for that box in the back seat. Do I have to say please?"

Back with the huge box, Joe knocked on the door. It opened, so he went in and closed the door behind him. A sliver of light shone beneath a door at the far end of the room. Bathroom, probably. He placed the box on a table and started toward the sofa but sat in the chair instead. Better not take any chances with Miss Woozy Floozy.

The door opened. Jillian came out, kicked off her high heels, and fell on the bed. "I was about to pop." She raised up on her elbow. "Don't you need to go?"

Joe stood. "Good idea." In the bathroom, after flushing, he eyed himself in the mirror. He needed to get his resume and get the heck out of here—like *now.*

Leaving the bathroom, he noted how the huge box sat in the chair he'd just left—the one chair in the room—and Jillian sat on the sofa. She patted the cushion. "Come here, sweetheart. I've got a headache from that wine and need a strong shoulder to lean on."

Joe swallowed. What choice did he have? He had no idea where the resume was and— What an idiot he was. Just ask. "I would, but I've got an early exam and need to get to bed."

"And?"

"If you could get my resume?"

She glanced at her watch. "It's just eight 'o clock. Please, sweetheart?"

Joe swallowed again. To be in this young woman's room— this *stunning* young woman's room—was the last place he wanted to be. No, that was a lie, because not only was he attracted to her, he was *extremely* attracted to her. Still, being here was as wrong as anything he'd ever done. Still again, he needed the job so he and Elaine could get married. That's right, Elaine … just think about Elaine.

He shuffled to the sofa and sat. "Tell me about Liège."

Jillian slid close. She wrapped her arms around his and snuggled into his shoulder. "No talk. My poor head hurts."

Joe closed his eyes. The list of things he shouldn't be doing just got longer.

Jillian rose from the sofa and stretched. "Maybe it's a tension headache. My neck and shoulders are sore from sitting in the gym all day. If I let the girls out, that might help."

Girls? Was she talking about—

Jillian tried to reach the dress's zipper, but every time her fingertips neared it, she groaned. She held her hand out to Joe. "Come on up here and give a lady a hand. Oh, yeah, please."

Joe started to rub his lip but managed to stop. If he did this one thing—another thing on the growing list of what not to do—that'd be it. He stood. She turned around, gathered her hair, and raised it from her neck. "Go ahead and zip it all the way down. Then, when I go to bed, I can slip the dress right off." Blue eyes glanced at him over her shoulder. "Okay?"

He touched the zipper with a trembling fingertip, bit his lip and pulled the zipper, revealing a back as tanned as her legs and the clasp of a bra. He dropped to the sofa, beads of sweat breaking out on his forehead.

Blue eyes over her shoulder again. "Oh, sweetheart?"

Joe wiped his forehead. "I'm still here."

"Since I can't unzip my dress, I can't undo my bra. Please?"

Joe stood again. Another thing on that freaking list. He waited, attempting to build his nerve as his breaths came in quick, tiny bursts.

Jillian giggled. "That's quite the tickling little train you've got back there with all your huffing and puffing. I think I like it. Go ahead, sweetheart, don't be nervous. If you've never been with a woman, you need the practice. Slip your index finger between the clasp and my skin. Then pull the clasp out a bit and give it a slight push with your thumb. That's all there is to it."

Joe did as she said. Beneath his fingers, her skin, smooth and warm, felt amazing. Sheesh. One more thing on that list. He started to push the clasp but stopped. Adrenaline burned through him, the kind that made him want to do anything *but* run. Jillian's skin glowed in the lamplight, completely unblemished. The muscles beneath her right shoulder blade flexed as she raised her hair, which brushed his face and nose. Honeysuckles ... sweet, inviting honeysuckles. His mouth watered. What would it be like to kiss her neck, to taste her skin, to—

He pushed the clasp and it opened. The bra fell, dangling behind her, and he dropped to the sofa once more. He couldn't take much more of this. Maybe he could find the resume and—

"Thanks," Jillian said. Facing him, she slid the dress's spaghetti straps off her tanned shoulders. Then she pulled one arm through the shoulder strap of the bra and did the same with the other, pulled the lacey, pink cups free and tossed the bra to the bed. Beside Joe again, she patted his knee. "That feels so much better, sweetheart. The girls are happy—definitely happy. Aren't you glad you don't have to wear one of those things?"

Joe opened his mouth but nothing came out. He laughed, hard and long, and Jillian sat up to eye him until he stopped laughing. "What'd you do?" she asked. "Did you imagine yourself wearing my bra?"

"Maybe it was nervous energy being released."

She snuggled close again, fingering the top button of his shirt. "I love your farm boy laugh. If you do it again, I might take your shirt off and put my bra on you. Do you have the pecs for it?" She rubbed his chest. "Mmm, I think so." She sat up on her knees and looked him in the eye. "Okay, it's like this—I'm special and you're special. Meaning we've never had sex. Meaning we're both healthy with no STDs. *And*, as luck would have it, I'm on the pill, so ..."

Joe started to get up, but she wrapped her arms around his neck and kissed him, as fine a kiss as he'd ever experienced.

And she didn't stop.

She opened her mouth and touched her tongue to his, and he slipped his arms around her. He'd never wanted a woman more—almost as much as—

Elaine!

He pushed Jillian away and jumped to his feet, breathing like a full-blown locomotive and not some little train, like she had said earlier.

"Jillian, believe me, I want—you can't imagine—maybe you can, but ..."

She ran her fingers through her hair. One thin spaghetti strap had slipped off one tanned shoulder. She pulled it back into place. "I understand, you're nervous." She stood. "But I'm still calling you sweetheart, sweetheart." She went to a desk, took a folder from the drawer, and returned to hand it to him. "Remember when I said you'd earn the job by your merit?"

"I remember."

"I used the hotel fax machine to send a copy of your resume to Terry. Did I tell you he's my boss? That's right, you were at the gym when he called. Anyway, he's impressed and wants me to offer you the job." She went to the desk again and wrote on a pad by the phone, returned to Joe and gave him the paper. "That's your starting salary if you accept. Of course, there'll be other benefits ... insurance, 401k, vacation."

Stunned at the amount, Joe dropped to the sofa. He and Elaine could get married. They could build their dream home at the river. They could have those three kids. They could afford all their needs and some wants too, especially with her teaching salary added in.

Jillian sat beside him and ran her fingertips through the hair above his ear. "Sweetheart, if you don't leave soon, you might not leave. I don't want you to do anything you'll regret." She kissed his cheek. "That's the last thing I want." She rose from the sofa. "Can I get your cell number before you go? I'll call with more information if you accept. Do you think you will?"

"I'd be a fool not to." Joe could hardly believe his luck. He looked up at Jillian. "What about training? What about getting to know Terry? Will he be my boss too? What about—"

Jillian offered him her hand. "Up, farm boy, before I sit in your lap again."

Like a thoroughbred horse, question after question galloped through Joe's brain. He wanted to know the answers now so he could make plans with Elaine. "Wait a minute, Jillian, what about—"

"And I'm not wearing panties."

Chapter 10

Joe jumped from the sofa. After he and Jillian exchanged phone numbers, he left for his apartment. During the walk, his heart nearly beat out of his chest, not only from the job offer but from nearly losing his virginity to someone he genuinely didn't want to lose it to. That privilege belonged to no one but Elaine. Since that was the case, he needed to be honest with Jillian about being engaged—and soon. The last thing he wanted was to hurt her, and if she was thinking about a serious relationship, that would happen.

* * *

Rolling over in bed to check his phone the next morning, Joe found a text from Jillian waiting for him.

Good morning, sweetheart. Could you sleep? It was hard, wasn't it? Could I see you around four? The recruiting will be done today at three, and I'll be beading home shortly after. J.

Joe scratched his head. He shouldn't think this, but if it weren't for Elaine, he'd date Jillian in a heartbeat.

In the bathroom, he rubbed sleep from his eyes while staring at his reflection in the mirror. What a fool, thinking about dating Jillian. He shaved and brushed his teeth, threw on a pair of jeans and a T shirt, and sat on his bed.

Phone in hand, he texted Jillian. He didn't want to tempt fate by meeting her in her hotel room, so he suggested an early dinner at the restaurant to discuss the job. The phone vibrated with her text.

Sounds good. No wine this time. See you at four. J.

No wine and no calling him sweetheart in the text; Joe didn't know whether to be disappointed or not. She was leaving too. What did he expect, that she'd stay around and flirt with him the next three weeks until he graduated? Dumb … *more* than dumb. Why was he thinking about Jillian when he was going to marry Elaine?

Since today's first exam wasn't until eleven, Joe ate a quick bowl of cereal, slipped on his running shoes, and headed out for a jog around campus. Maybe the fresh air would clear his frazzled brain of the honeysuckle aroma of Jillian's hair, not to mention her long legs, tanned back, and tantalizing kiss. He locked the door and smacked his forehead with his palm. If he kept thinking about her amazing attributes, including her suggestion to sleep together, their meeting later might get him into more trouble than he could handle.

He hit the sidewalk with a steady pace. Within five minutes he regretted not changing into shorts. His T shirt stuck to his sweaty chest, and perspiration ran down his back.

Marrying Elaine.

From the first time he saw her in the door of Mrs. Hansen's English class, no other girl stood a chance of getting his attention. There'd been times when other girls flirted with him in college, but none tempted him like Jillian did. Was it because she was different than most girls, or that he'd never had a girlfriend other than Elaine? His mother once suggested he and Elaine see other people, if for no other reason than to make sure they really wanted to be together. Joe had given the suggestion a single night's consideration—and no more. He hadn't shared the idea with Elaine either. They already knew they were meant to be together without any kind of test.

Tests.

Jillian had tested him last night. Had he passed? Barely. What would Elaine say? Failed, flunked, high dive in the shallows of the river? Splat, face first in the mud?

No doubt about it, and she'd be right.

Because whenever they had a disagreement, they tried to look at it from each other's point of view, and it usually kept a mild annoyance from turning into a serious argument. If she ever found out about last night though, no amount of shared perspective would help.

He checked his watch. Instead of making another round, he returned to the apartment, showered, donned clean jeans and a shirt, and checked his phone. No messages, so his date with Jillian was still on. He raised his hand to smack his forehead again but lowered it. Not a date, a meeting, likely about the job. If he didn't stop thinking dumb things, he'd slap his forehead black and blue.

The remainder of the day crawled along. Two 'o clock class over, he hurried to his apartment to wash his face and under his arms, including two more swipes of deodorant. He rubbed his chin and decided against a shave. Since he'd been in class, his phone was off. Powered up, it received a text from Elaine, sent an hour ago.

Hey, sweetie. Painted again last night and it looks great. Sorry I didn't call or text. Busy! Hope you had good luck with the job hunt. I love you! Elaine.

Joe grinned. She hadn't called him "sweetie" in ages. Maybe their engagement was giving her romantic thoughts. Or either she was practicing for when she'd say, *Sweetie, can you take out the trash? Sweetie, can you mow the lawn? Sweetie, let the toilet seat down so I don't get a wet behind in the middle of the night.*

Joe grinned again. He wouldn't mind her requests. He'd love every minute of being with her, no matter how many requests she made.

He snapped his fingers. The job! He shoved his hand in his jeans for the note Jillian had given him concerning his salary, but remembered it was in the jeans he'd jogged in, now in the hamper in the bathroom. His memory, or lack thereof, sucked. Maybe it was the combined excitement of being engaged, taking final exams, having a beautiful woman proposition him, and getting his dream job, all within the span of a few days. With the crumpled note fished from the smelly jeans and spread out on the small table where he ate, he took a picture of it with his phone and added a text message: *How's this for good luck with the job hunt?*

He started to press send, but the phone vibrated in his hand with a text from Jillian.

We still on? My line's empty and I can meet you at 3:30, okay?

Joe frowned. He kind of missed her calling him sweetheart. Hey, he had a great woman waiting for him at home, one who loved him and called him sweetie. That meant he could do without Jillian's *sweetheart* as long as he had Elaine's *sweetie* to look forward to.

He replied to Jillian that he'd meet her at 3:30, grabbed his keys and wallet, and ran to his pickup.

She hopped out when he pulled up beside her car. She wore the same business suit she'd worn at the gym yesterday, but with a different blouse, and she'd tied her thick, blonde hair in a ponytail. After a long day she still looked great, blue eyes smiling.

Joe climbed from his pickup. "Look at you, a hard day at work and you look as fresh as a honeysuckle bloom."

Jillian's eyebrows rose to an arch as she grinned a cute, one-sided grin, almost as gorgeous as her smile. "That's a first. What happened to fresh as a daisy?"

Joe wasn't about to tell her how he loved the fragrance of her shampoo, exactly like honeysuckle blooms. She might take it as a sign of his being interested in her. "Is anything wrong with being original?"

"Not a thing, farm boy. Let's grab a bite. I've got a long drive and I don't want to stop anywhere for dinner."

Beside her, Joe strolled to the restaurant. This time she didn't slip her arm into his. He tucked that observation away, contributing it to being early afternoon instead of night. "Do you still live one county over from Harlan County?"

"I sure do. I live and work in Arapahoe."

Joe opened the restaurant door. "That's not far from Alma. Is Organiks planning a facility in every county in Nebraska?"

"They keep those decisions to themselves. Have you been to Arapahoe?"

"I've never been much of anywhere. Right where we stand is as far north and east as I've ever been."

"All of this great big world we live in and you've been no farther east or north than Omaha, Nebraska? We need to fix that."

"Does having my passport count?" A couple of months ago, he and Elaine had considered a trip to Cancun, sort of a graduation present for them both since she didn't do anything like that when she graduated last year. Their parents even offered to help pay for it. Either that or give them the money for a future wedding present. They took the money instead, leaving him stuck with an unused passport.

A greeter took two menus from the rack. "Good afternoon, booth or table?"

"Table," Jillian said.

"This way, please." The greeter led Joe and Jillian to a corner table, where he sat across from her.

"You're making me wonder about you," he said. "No more sweetheart and no more booths and no more wine."

"That's one of the reasons I wanted to see you before I left."

"Which reason is this? Because I'd like to know why the huge change."

Jillian placed her hand on Joe's, which lay on the table. "Where'd your nervousness go? Would you rather we forget dinner and return to my hotel room to pick up where we left off last night?" Joe eased his hand away, and Jillian giggled. "I didn't think so, shy farm boy." She sat back in the chair. "I want to apologize about last night. I was out of line—no, I was *way* out of line. I pressured you to the point of being unfair. This morning, when I re-read that text where I called you sweetheart, it even embarrassed me. Anyone reading that would think we were lovers."

"I thought it was hilarious."

"I wasn't trying to be hilarious. What part was funny?"

"The part after you asked If I'd gotten any sleep, where you said, 'It was hard, wasn't it?'"

Jillian's cheeks reddened. "You thought I meant …?" Her eyes lowered, as if she were looking through the table to Joe's lap. "Well, well, well, and I thought *I* was naughty last night."

Joe's face warmed.

"Aw, the farm boy is blushing. Do you see why I apologized?"

"I need to apologize too."

"I have no idea why, other than *not* taking me in your arms and carrying me to bed." She slid forward in the chair and leaned close. "I really am a virgin. Do you realize how much I think of you to let you be the first man to make love to me?"

About to apologize for not telling Jillian about Elaine, Joe hesitated. He needed to tell her—tell her this instant—because if she were having such strong feelings for him after just meeting him, she needed to know. "Jillian, I— Well, as far as why I should apologize, I'm engaged. I hope you don't hate me for being dishonest."

"I wondered if you had someone special and that was why you weren't responding to my shameless advances like most men would." She placed her warm palm to his cheek. "Your tone tells me you're sad. Don't be, okay? I should have read your shyness for what it was—a girlfriend. She tapped the tip of his nose with a fingertip, smiled, and sat back in the chair. "Since you mentioned me not saying it, I'll say it one last time. "Sweetheart, I don't hate you. Between the pressure of final exams and the pressure of applying for the job, not to mention the pressure I placed on you in my hotel room, that was a lot for any man to handle. If you were mine, I'd be proud, okay?"

Joe could hardly believe how understanding she was, but there she was, teasing, grinning, and understanding exactly how he felt. "Thanks for being so understanding. What was the other reason you wanted to see me? You mentioned it when we came in."

"It was about seeing the world and— Our waitress is on the way. Let's wait until we order."

The waitress took Jillian's request of grilled salmon, a side salad, and water with lemon, and Joe's of the same, but with sweet tea. "All right, what's this about seeing the world?"

"What do you think of seeing Belgium? Organiks sometimes sends new hires to their headquarters for orientation. New hires the recruiter recommends."

"That's a lot of money to spend on someone they don't know much about."

"That's why they only consider recruiter recommendations. Didn't you mention how your great-grandfather was buried in the Ardennes American Cemetery? Wouldn't you like an all-expenses paid trip to facilitate visiting his grave?"

Joe couldn't believe his luck. A great job with a great salary and now a trip to see his—or his great-grandfathers'—grave.

"I sure would like to see it. Now that we've cleared the air concerning our—I guess I'd call them romantic entanglements—oh, and my engagement—what do I have to do to convince you, dear recruiter, to recommend me for a trip like that?"

"Not a thing." The waitress brought their drinks, left, and Jillian patted Joe's hand. "I just hope it doesn't bother you or your girl."

"Why would a trip to Belgium bother us?"

"Because I'd come with you."

"That won't be a problem. After all, we've worked out our— I'll call them entanglements again. As far as Elaine, she won't hear about any of that from me."

"Sounds good to me, farm boy." Jillian raised her glass. "Here's to a smooth tractor ride from here on out. That's what farmers say instead of sailing, did you know that?" Joe raised his glass. She clinked hers against it, drank, and returned it to the table. "Have you and Elaine decided on a date? Lovely name. What's she like, a blue-eyed blonde like me?"

"Completely opposite—a sun-streaked brunette with dark brown eyes. Like you she's definitely fun to be with. As far as a date, not yet. We found a good deal on a small house in town to rent. She went ahead and signed the lease and is doing some painting. This job should help move things along."

Jillian took her phone from her purse. "Can I get the address? I'd like to send you both a wedding present."

"That's sweet, but you don't have to do that."

"It's sweet because *I'm* sweet. Haven't you figured that out yet? Besides, I don't do things because I have to, I do them because I want to." Her finger hovered over the phone. "Address, farm boy—now."

Joe gave her the address, and the waitress returned with their meals. Between bites of salmon and salad, washed down with sips of tea and water, he and Jillian discussed what his new job entailed—field research with organically produced crops, including testing and documentation—and a monthly meeting in Arapahoe with equivalent co-workers from other counties. Jillian surprised him by saying the orientation trip would be this coming week. Surprise or not, he could make the trip. At college, the week after final exams was one where students, for the most part, weren't doing a lot, so the trip wouldn't interfere with his schedule, either at school or at home. He and Jillian also discussed their smart phones, and Jillian confirmed his model, like hers, would work in Europe. He was glad to hear it. With a new job, a trip where he could visit the Ardennes American Cemetery, and a plan to marry the love of his life, things were looking up.

Joe insisted on thanking Jillian for her help by paying for both meals, and they stepped outside to her car. Dinner traffic was increasing. A car pulled in, slowed by Joe's pickup, and stopped beside Joe and Jillian. The window slid down to reveal one of Joe's soil microbiology classmates. Joe had shown him a picture of Elaine but couldn't recall the guy's name. Good thing, because the guy had talked about women as if he'd conquered half the college campus. The guy stuck his head out the window. "Whatdaya say, Matthan? Does Elaine know you're stepping out on her? Better not let her find out." He laughed, pulled into a space on the other side of the lot, and strolled into the restaurant, occasionally glancing back over his shoulder at Joe and Jillian, still grinning.

"What a jerk," Jillian said. "Some people never grow up."

"Yeah," Joe said. "He needs a good swift kick."

"And I know where." Jillian opened the car door. "I'll call with our travel itinerary. I guess I don't have to tell you how important this trip is. You could move up the ladder quickly if things go well, along with how well you perform the work."

"I like the sound of that. How long have you been with Organiks?"

"Two years. Terry's set to retire in a year or so. I hope to have a shot at his job, which is regional manager."

"Would you move from Arapahoe?" Joe was glad they'd worked out their entanglements, but he'd miss seeing her. He rubbed his lower lip. He shouldn't be having thoughts like that.

Jillian took a step toward him. "Aw, you look sad. Would you miss me if I moved? Answer carefully, sweetheart, because—" She shook her head. "Well, I blew that didn't I? I said I wouldn't call you that anymore." She turned away for a second, then faced Joe again. "I'm going to do something else I shouldn't." She palmed his cheek. "This is the last time, I promise."

At Jillian's "sweetheart," Joe's heart had skipped a beat, and when she touched his cheek with her smooth, warm palm, it skipped two. He had an idea what she meant, but he asked anyway. "The last time you do what?"

She eased forward, touched her nose to his, and slid it along one side and down the other. Her breath, sweet from the peach cobbler they'd shared for dessert, warmed his lips.

"You do things to me inside that no man should be able to do. If you and Elaine don't work out ..." She stepped back and shook her head. Her chest rose and fell as she breathed with the same quick, shuddering breaths Joe had breathed when he'd unzipped her dress.

Her throat muscles worked with a swallow, and she lowered her head. "I apologize. I was going to ask for a kiss, but that wouldn't be respecting you or Elaine."

Joe couldn't speak. He wanted to kiss her, wanted it as badly as she did. What the hell was wrong with him? The only woman in the world he should want to kiss was Elaine.

"Jillian?" She raised her head, tears glistening in her eyes. Joe wanted to take her in his arms and tell her not to cry, but he shoved that want, that need, away. He slipped his hand into hers. "Now I get to tell you not to be sad. You are— Shoot, I don't have words to describe you. If I could come up with the words, they'd be good words. That's how you do things to me inside too. You're right, us kissing is wrong on so many levels, it surpasses wrong. I love Elaine and want to marry her more than anything."

Jillian squeezed his hand, allowed her fingers to slip from his, and her hand fell to her side. "I'm happy for both of you. I realize we just met, but I trust you. I know you wouldn't say you loved her if you weren't sure. I better go." She took her keys from her purse and climbed in the car. Joe grabbed the door before she could shut it and knelt beside her.

"Hold on, farm girl. I need to see that knockout smile before you leave." He grinned. "Pur-r-r-rty please?"

Jillian smiled. "You're terrible, you know that?"

"I hear the same thing all the time from Elaine."

"I'm sure. Okay, since I just smiled for you, I need to run."

Joe stood and closed the door. She backed out of the parking space, waved, and drove away.

In his pickup, Joe sat back in the seat. He never thought he'd meet someone who made him feel anything remotely similar to what he felt for Elaine.

Similar.

That was the difference between what he felt for Jillian and what he felt for Elaine. The two feelings were nothing alike. One was mostly lust while the other was a gift, a gift or love that would last a lifetime and more, along with a gift of hope from their pasts to the present—him as his great-grandfather, her as his great-grandmother—with them in love all over again. Imagine how that gift could make their relationship even more spectacular if he could prove it by visiting his own grave in Belgium.

Chapter 11

Done with his last exam on Friday, Joe jogged back to his apartment to pack and climbed into to his pickup. Since he hadn't sent Elaine the text with the picture of the Organiks salary offer, he planned to tell her in person. She'd be thrilled to start making wedding plans.

He spent much of his four-hour drive from Omaha to Alma imagining Elaine's reaction to his job, but he spent part of it thinking about Jillian. She'd be back in her office by now, planning their trip to Belgium. In no way did he consider himself well-traveled as he'd admitted to her, and his curiosity about the trip grew with each mile.

What he might find at the Ardennes American Cemetery intrigued him more than the trip itself. What could be buried with his great-grandma's ashes in the grave? All Grandpa had told him was "personal" items, and since he dropped his head and grew quiet at that moment—an obviously emotional moment—Joe didn't pry. Along with the dog tags, if they were there too, those items—since they were placed with Elaine's ashes—might be something extremely personal to her. If that were true, like with the man whose memories were triggered when he received what he believed to be his dog tags, the items might trigger Elaine's past memories of their time together. If so, and if the dog tags helped Joe recall more of his memories from their time together so long ago, that'd be all the proof he needed to verify his beliefs.

As Joe passed the sign marking Alma's town limits, his phone vibrated. Instead of checking the phone, he flipped the signal, pulled into a service station, and glared at the Closed sign. He'd bought a twenty-four-ounce bottle of water at his last stop. If he didn't get to a bathroom soon, he might not need one.

He sat up straight in the pickup seat, winced as he squeezed his legs together, and checked the phone. Jillian had texted him, saying to meet her at Kearney Regional Airport on Monday morning at eight, where they'd start their fifteen hour-plus journey to Belgium. She also added to remember the passport he never used and signed off with a smiley emoticon. Joe texted that he'd be there, and on time too.

The pressure in his bladder worsened, and he squeezed his legs together harder. Should he make a run for the rear of the service station? Instead, he dialed Elaine's cell. "Hey, babe. Are you in town painting?"

"Hey, sweetie, I sure am. Are you on the way?"

"Almost there now. I thought you might be painting and wanted to see you."

"Come on by. I'll see if you're as good with scraping window trim as you are with kisses."

"Which you'll get as soon as I step in the door. See you in a few." He slipped the phone in his pocket. He'd use the bathroom first and give her all the kisses she could handle after.

Elaine was waiting on the porch when he parked behind her car. He jumped out and ran up the steps. "Can the kisses wait? I need the bathroom—like now."

She followed him inside. "What about the recruitment, did you get an offer?"

Joe wrinkled his nose at the aroma of fresh paint. He took his phone from his pocket and tossed it to her. "I'm about to bust, darlin'. Look for a text with a picture of my salary offer." He stopped at the bathroom door. "You won't believe your eyes." Done in the bathroom, he returned to the living room.

Elaine sat on the sofa with his phone on the coffee table. She swiped something from the corner of one eye while her lower lip trembled. "You're right" —her throat muscles contracted with a hard swallow— "I don't believe my eyes. I never would've thought …"

Was she crying? Joe started toward her—and stopped. Jillian's text—the one she'd sent calling him sweetheart—he'd forgotten to delete it. That was the only thing on his phone that would make Elaine cry. "Elaine, it's not what you—"

"Not a word," she said, raising her hand. She picked up the phone. "Guess what I just read? I'll read it back in case you don't remember, but I doubt you'd ever forget something like this. 'Good morning, sweetheart. Could you sleep? It was hard, wasn't it? Could I see you around four? The recruiting will be done today at three, and I'll be heading home shortly after. J.'" She dropped the phone and it clattered to the table. "I assume you were gonna say 'it's not what I think.' How in the hell could it not be what I think?"

Joe had seen Elaine angry before, but this was entirely different. Her eyes blazed at him, narrowed like a cat's eyes before fighting with another cat. Her voice, low and steady, had quivered with each word. Angry didn't describe what he was seeing, and he didn't know what to expect.

"Babe, I—"

"Don't call me that."

"Babe, please, I—"

"Didn't you hear me?" She snatched the phone from the coffee table and threw it at him. It flew by his head and hit the wall behind him, clattering to the wood floor like it had on the table. "Because if you can't hear me, you might as well leave and take that damn phone with you. Then you and this—this *J*—whoever she is, can live happily ever after."

Joe wanted to run to Elaine and take her in his arms. He wanted to beg her forgiveness and promise to never do again what she thought he'd done. Instead, he needed to diffuse the situation and let Elaine calm down, because her anger was making her assume too much from the text without knowing anything. He went to the chair at the wall opposite the sofa and sat. "I understand why you think the worst about that text. Believe it or not I can explain, so when you can talk instead of throw things ..."

Using the palm of her hand, Elaine pushed more tears away as if she were trying to rub the skin from her cheeks. Eventually she stopped, sniffled, and crossed her hands in her lap. The red of her cheeks matched her eyes glaring at him. "I don't know how you can explain 'good morning, sweetheart. It was hard, wasn't it?' Really? 'It was hard, wasn't it?' I'm not—" She snatched the engagement ring from her finger and dropped it on the table. "I'm not even sure I want you to explain. I feel so ... betrayed is the best word I can come up with."

Joe allowed himself a slight sigh. At least she was talking and not throwing things. "I understand how you feel, okay?

If it were the other way around—you know, if I found a text like that on your phone—wouldn't you hope I'd give you a chance to explain, especially if the message could be *honestly* explained?"

"I would, but I'm having a hard time believing anything you say—or *might* say." She wiped another tear. "Go ahead, I'm listening."

Tempted to sigh once more, Joe held it in. She was going to listen, a much better position from which to straighten this mess out. "I need my phone. There's supposed to be a picture on it of a piece of paper with my salary for the job offer I've accepted. That's what I wanted you to see while I was in the bathroom. It'll make more sense when you read it."

Joe retrieved his phone and returned to the chair, but the phone refused to power up. Great. Now he couldn't prove what he'd just said. "My phone's broken. I'll start from the beginning."

He told Elaine about meeting Jillian in the gym. At the part where he told Jillian about his parents living in Alma, Elaine held up her hand. "Stop right there. Why didn't you tell her your fiancé worked here too? That would have stopped her flirting—what she said about you telling each other your secrets and that remark about swimming naked—right away."

Joe leaned back in the chair. He'd done a good job of being honest so far. No reason to stop now. "I didn't tell her about you because I was willing to let her think I was single as long as I was still trying to get that job. I want to earn a living like you. I want to get married like you do too. We've waited—"

"Forget getting married for now." Elaine pointed at the ring. "This gets nowhere near my finger until I trust you again."

"Don't you think a woman might do the same thing? Then, when she gets the job, she lets the recruiter know she's not available? That's what I did … what I did for us."

"I *might* can see that. What happened next?"

"After she looked at my—"

"'She?' Go on, say her name."

Joe wanted to shake his head but didn't. Patience would win Elaine back, not signs of frustration. "After Jillian looked at my class records, she said she was impressed. Next thing I know, she wanted me to have dinner with her."

Elaine crossed her arms. "What does this Jillian person look like?"

Joe couldn't help shaking his head this time.

Elaine smirked. "Uh-huh, my exact opposite, right? A tall, blue-eyed blonde with legs up to her neck and a killer body. You men are so predictable. That includes predatory women like *your* Jillian too."

"She's not *my* Jillian, okay? It's hard enough to explain with commentary like— Oh yeah, her boss called in the middle of the interview. She told him we were gonna talk about the job later. See how you're making me forget stuff? Can I please finish?"

"You're doing so well, go right ahead."

"So, as I hope you see, I needed to see her later." Joe waited for another comment.

"Don't stop now. I don't want to make you forget anything important. I'm dying to find out how she started calling you sweetheart."

"That happened at dinner" —Joe scratched his head— "I think. Anyway, she mentioned how—when she gets to know someone—she might call them sweetheart. Remember the cashier at the grocery? She does the same thing."

"Go on, I'm listening."

"She drank too much wine at the restaurant and asked me to drive her to her hotel. Oh, she forgot to bring my resume so she could give it to me at dinner too. She told me she'd do that when she mentioned having dinner."

Elaine sat back on the sofa, took in a huge breath, and let it out slowly. "I said predator earlier. I should have said Black Widow. You know she left your resume in her room on purpose, don't you? She might've even drunk all that wine on purpose."

"I'll admit that crossed my mind." Joe paused to get his thoughts—thoughts he'd done a poor job of remembering so far—in order. He intended to be honest, but he wanted to avoid revealing the kiss. "We sat on the sofa. After a few minutes I asked about my folder. I told her it was getting late, and—"

"I know exactly what Miss Widow said. Oh, it's not too late, sweetheart. Please, oh pur-r-r-ty please, stay a while longer. Or did she kiss you right then?"

Joe's mouth fell open, and Elaine closed her eyes. "I knew it." She opened her eyes. "How long a kiss? Were tongues involved? How about the bed?" Her eyes narrowed: the cat ready to fight again. "Answer me, Joe Matthan."

"The kiss only lasted a split second, that's—"

"Details. Tongue. Something else you forgot."

Heat building in his cheeks, Joe jumped out of the chair. "That only lasted a split second too before I got the heck up off of that sofa. Satisfied?"

Elaine twisted her lips to one side. "You swear you didn't sleep with her?"

"When I jumped up, she gave me my resume and told me I had the job. That's when she wrote my salary on that slip of paper I took a picture of. After that I was gone."

"That's it?" Elaine's voice, more normal now, not the low tone she used earlier, gave Joe an inkling of hope. He dropped to the chair.

"There's more."

"Oh, I bet there's mo—"

"More that's a lot better, so hush and listen. See? You already forgot the text that got you so mad. As far as her asking if I could sleep, she could've meant I was excited about the job. As far as the 'hard' comment, that could've been the same thing too. In fact, when I asked her about it the next day—you read where she wanted to see me—she said that's what she meant."

Elaine took the ring from the table and held it out. "This is getting closer to my finger. What did she want the next day?"

"That's when I found out she's not the person I thought she was. Maybe it *was* the wine that caused her to come onto me like she did." Joe risked a grin. "Would you blame her, even without the wine? Don't you remember the chest licking you gave me at the river when I gave you the ring? Come on now, time to be honest."

Elaine covered her eyes, peeked from between her fingers, and grinned too. "I'm not going there. What did she say?"

Joe left the chair to join Elaine on the sofa. "She apologized for coming on to me. That's when I told her about you. She even said she liked your name and that she wanted to send us a wedding gift. Wasn't that nice of her? I'm sure she'd love to meet you sometime."

"I'll decide about 'nice' when I'm sure she won't make any more passes at you. As far as meeting her, no time soon."

Joe took the ring from her. "Do you mind?" He slipped the ring on her finger and kissed her knuckles. "Much better. May it never leave that sexy finger again."

Elaine stood and turned around. "Don't you think a paint-splattered blouse becomes me? I didn't see any need in wearing a clean one."

"Not sure, turn back around." During her turn, Joe popped her behind. "Yep, looking good, babe."

Elaine's eyes lit up with her familiar expression of playfulness, with a slight crinkling at their corners. She smiled—barely a hint—and unbuttoned the first two buttons of her blouse. "I hope your blonde-haired, blue-eyed recruiter hasn't been on your mind. If so, maybe I can do something about that." With two more buttons undone, and with the white lace of her bra showing, she tousled his hair. "Think so?"

A band of tension drifted across Joe's shoulders—not an unwelcome feeling. Jillian had nothing on Elaine, absolutely nothing. The wedding couldn't come fast enough. "I know so, babe. You're killing me."

Joe's eyes opened wide as Elaine finished the last buttons and let the shirt fall to the floor. "I like killing you. Are you ready to be embalmed yet?" She placed one knee on the sofa, then the other, and settled onto his lap. "Hmm, I think not."

Joe swallowed. "Either we fly to Vegas and get married right now or you get up. Otherwise, we'll have nothing to look forward to on our honeymoon."

Elaine wiggled in his lap. "I think I have a *feeling* what I'm looking forward to." She stood, put the shirt on and buttoned it, and sat beside Joe. "Tell me about your job. Do you think you'll like it, other than the money? Oh, how much money? Since I broke your phone and can't see the note, sorry about that."

"No problem. Like I was saying about looking at our disagreement in reverse, I would've been as mad, but I might not have thrown anything."

Elaine punched his arm. "Are you saying you *might* have thrown something?"

"Let's hope not. I'll see what the cellular place can do with it tomorrow. I'll need it next week while I'm out of town."

"Where are you going? As long as you've got a couple of weeks of school left, you'll be there, not here."

Since she'd gotten over her anger, Joe hoped she'd be okay with the trip. After all, he'd accepted the job for both of them.

"I'll tell you about my salary first. It's in the lower six figures and—"

"Oh, please, you're not worth that."

"I haven't told you the name of the company yet. It's called Organiks. They're big into organic farming and they're adding a facility in our county. Since I live here, that helped me get the offer. That and my grades."

"I've heard of them. I like how they're into organic farming. Aren't they based in Europe?"

"Belgium, not far from the Ardennes American Cemetery where my great-grandparents are buried. I don't need to be at school next week and Organiks wants me to fly to Belgium for orientation. I was really impressed when Jillian told me that. It must mean they—"

"Whoa." Elaine's brows rose to form a serious row of wrinkles across her forehead. "You're flying to Belgium next week?"

"Yep." Joe laced his fingers behind his head and leaned back on the sofa. "Your sweetie's gonna be a globetrotter, at least to one small part of it."

"Is anyone going with you? It better not be Jillian."

Joe unlaced his fingers and leaned forward to look her in the eye. "I thought you were over all that?"

"That doesn't mean I trust her. Tell her you can't go, or ask if someone else can go with you."

"You don't have to trust her. If you believe what I said about the text and the rest, that means you trust *me*."

"She's attracted to you. For all I know she'll reserve adjoining hotel rooms with the lock on her side of the door." Elaine shook her head. "Nope. Maybe you should turn down the offer and be done with Organiks—and Miss blue-eyed blondie while you're at it."

Joe stood. She was being ridiculous. "I want a job now—*this* job. If you trust me like you say you do, I'm not turning it down."

Elaine stood too, eye's narrowed like earlier. She snatched the ring from her finger and shoved it toward Joe. Her chest rose and fell, and a tear slipped down one reddening cheek. "Take it. Better yet, take it with you to Belgium. While you're with Jillian you can decide what the hell is important—that job or me."

Joe didn't take the ring. She dropped it on the floor and whirled and ran to the bedroom, to slam the door and click the lock. He squatted to the floor, fell back on his rear, and stared at the ring. The diamond reflected the overhead light. He never thought looking at this ring would make him sad, but there it was. It belonged to Elaine, belonged on her finger. What had he done that was so wrong? She'd understood at first, so how did all this mess happen? No, not a mess, a *damned* mess, and he didn't know how to fix it.

Pocketing the ring, he went to the bedroom. Elaine sobbed behind the door, with huge gasps in between. Her crying frightened him, and a tear slipped down his own cheek. What frightened him more was the genuine possibility of losing her. No, they were meant to be together. From the past to the present they were meant to be together, and this job, Jillian, or no one else would make him doubt that.

He tapped the door. "I'm taking this job so we can build our home at the river and our children can have great lives. I hope you'll think about that while I'm gone."

Elaine stopped crying. "Go, leave, get out of here!"

At the front door, Joe locked it from the inside, closed it, and stepped out onto the porch, to half-walk half-stumble to his pickup. He leaned his back against the cold metal fender and searched the sky. Clouds gathered, sweeping across the sliver of moon, hiding the stars like Elaine's heart was hidden from him. His chest ached. More tears came, hot down his cheeks. He climbed into the pickup. Beneath the window at the side of the house, the glow of the light from the bedroom where Elaine was crying illuminated the shrubbery.

He'd planned on trimming the overgrown hedge tomorrow.

Planned on dinner with Elaine.

Planned on a visit to the river and lying on the quilt with her in his arms.

But those plans—like the stars and the moon and the love of his life hidden behind clouds and sadness—were gone.

Chapter 12

Elaine stopped crying. She sat on the side of the lumpy mattress to wipe her burning eyes with a tissue from a box on the nightstand. Her throat hurt from sobs deeper than any she'd ever experienced. At the door, she listened. Had Joe left, or was he waiting for her to come out? She hadn't heard his pickup crank. Holding her breath, she pressed her ear to the door.

Nothing.

Good. She couldn't face him now—if ever.

She unlocked the door and peeked down the hall. Was the front door locked? He would've done that if he'd left. The deadbolt position showed it was locked. She went to the living room window. Her car sat alone in the driveway.

He didn't have a problem leaving when she told him to, so why couldn't he turn down that job when she told him to?

She dropped to the sofa and ran her fingers through her hair, snagged a tangle and winced. Pain? Why no pain in her heart? It was as if she were ice-cold inside, more dead than alive, almost like one of the calves born too early this spring.

Dad found it in a clump of frost-bitten grass beside the fence near the barn. Its mother mooed while she stood over it. The calf belonged to neighbors, and Dad did the neighborly thing.

Although the calf barely breathed in short ragged bursts of white fog from its blue nostrils, he took it inside and wrapped it in a blanket. Mom heated milk in the microwave, and Dad sat on the floor with the shivering calf's head in his lap so Elaine could drizzle milk into its mouth with a large spoon. Within minutes the calf's nose, starting at the base and working toward its nostrils, changed from blue to pink. Within an hour, after the rising sun warmed the morning air, Dad returned the calf to its mother, who promptly gave it a bath with her coarse tongue.

Elaine sat back on the sofa and wrapped her arms around herself. If Joe had listened and refused the job, he'd be here now, his arms around her, warming her, bringing her to life after the previous long week without him.

Was she wrong to tell him to not take the job? Elaine plucked her lower lip. If she trusted him like she'd told him a short while ago, the answer was yes. But did she trust him, *really* trust him? She believed she did. Ever since receiving their driver's licenses, one or the other would invariably find their way to the other's house on Saturday morning, unless their parents had plans. If the weather allowed, they'd make their way to the river, to fish or hike along the bank, or to simply lie under the shade of the oak and talk.

With both knees pulled to her chest, she hugged them. She and Joe had always been able to talk, working out small disagreements before they blew up into large ones. This was a first—one of them walking out on the other—and she hated it because she'd been the one to do so first, especially since she trusted him.

Jillian, on the other hand, couldn't be trusted. No matter if she apologized, no matter if she was as 'nice' as Joe had said, the mental image of another woman—likely a stunningly beautiful woman locked in a passionate kiss with Joe—made Elaine cringe.

No, regardless of what Joe said, Jillian couldn't be trusted. Elaine dropped her feet to the floor and slammed her hand on the sofa. Dust rose from the old cushion. Maybe, just maybe, when Joe returned from the trip, she'd talk to him, if for no other reason than to grill him on what, if anything, had happened. Until then she had no intention of calling him or taking his calls, and, if at all possible, she'd attempt to banish him from her thoughts entirely.

A ratty, old cuckoo clock from the thrift store hung on the living room wall Elaine had first painted. 8:45. She didn't know it was that late, but she had no idea how long she had cried either. The clerk said the clock likely dated from the early 1940's, causing Elaine to smile. She loved that era, full of history, full of nostalgic stories of war heroes and heroines, full of women who worked in the factories while the men fought in Europe, in the Pacific, and in north Africa.

She rose from the sofa and stretched. Her parents, early risers that they were, should be in bed by the time she got home, which suited Elaine. They knew Joe would be coming home and would ask about him, and the pain of their argument, as fresh as a scraped knee when she'd crashed her bicycle into the barn at age eight, needed to be wrapped with the bandage of silence, or she'd burst into tears again.

With the paint and cleaning supplies gathered in a corner, and the back door locked, Elaine switched the car's ignition on. The automatic headlights illuminated the house. Since the issue with Joe had occurred, maybe she'd be better off here than with her parents.

She put the car in reverse, backed out of the driveway, and headed out of Alma.

* * *

Joe drove to the hardware store to park. Since he and Elaine had met, whether he was a kid with his parents or after he got his license, this place drew him like steel to a magnet. He couldn't explain it, but every time he entered, with the brass bell ringing overhead, an eerie comfort washed over him.

He reclined the seat and opened the window halfway. The earlier clouds had drizzled a shower, wetting the blacktop to shine in the streetlights, and the aroma of wet asphalt entered the window. He started to turn the radio on but didn't. If any of his and Elaine's favorite songs played, he'd likely break down into a sobbing mess.

He took the engagement ring from his pocket and held it to the window. The facets reflected a nearby streetlight. A thread of hope remained. She hadn't said she wouldn't marry him, only that she wanted him to take the ring on the trip so he could decide whether the job was more important than her. More than likely she expected him to change his mind about taking the job over the weekend.

He returned the ring to his pocket. Not gonna happen. This job was as much for her as it was for him. So was the trip, since he'd be able to visit his—or his great-grandpa's—grave.

Seat raised and window closed, he left Alma.

At home, the lights were still on in the living room window. Great. Mom and Dad would ask about Elaine and he'd have to tell them what happened. He should've stayed in town until past their usual bedtime. Nope, they'd question him in the morning, so he couldn't avoid it. Might as well get it over with.

He gathered his luggage and went inside. When the front door thudded shut, Dad looked up. "College boy made it home. Come on in and tell us about your week. I'll turn the TV off."

"Let me carry this stuff to my room first." Joe did so. In the living room, he took the chair opposite Dad's recliner and yawned. "I'm beat after that long drive. Can I tell you about it over breakfast?"

Mom folded a newspaper. "Did you get a job offer? You can sleep late in the morning, unless you and Elaine have plans."

At least Joe could tell the truth about that. "No plans."

"And?"

"I accepted an offer with Organiks. They're building a facility in the county."

Dad raised the recliner. "You don't sound too excited. European, right? They lowball you on the salary?"

"It's enough, along with what Elaine makes, to save a nice down payment for the house we've always wanted to build overlooking the river."

Mom dropped the paper on the coffee table. "Then why aren't you any happier about the job than what you sound like? You must be really tired if—"

"I know," Dad said, "you want to tell Elaine tomorrow and surprise her, right?"

Mom nudged Dad's knee. "Don't interrupt me, I—"

"I saw her," Joe said. "She's surprised."

Mom huffed. "You men won't let a lady get a word in edgewise."

"C'mon, Anne, if we didn't take over the conversation once in a while, you'd never get a chance to take a breath."

Mom crossed her arms. "Maybe I should cook a less appetizing dinner so you get a chance to take a breath while you scarf it all down, Joseph Albert Matthan the third. What do you think of that?"

Mom only called Dad his full name when he gave her a hard time. She usually called him Al, which lessened the name confusion since she could've called him Joe also.

She stood. "You can tell me about your job in the morning." She faced Dad. "Staying up?"

"I'm curious about farm boy's fancy job."

Joe cringed at Jillian's pet name she'd stuck him with.

Mom left, and Dad returned to Joe. "Why the long face? This job sounds like a great opportunity."

Joe moved to the sofa. If the conversation turned to what had happened with Elaine, he didn't want Mom to hear. "I didn't know I had a 'long face.' Why do you say that?"

"I'll let you in on a secret," Dad said, keeping his voice low. "I always know when something's bothering you."

"If you have such a special insight into me, why's it a secret?"

"Us guys have to stick together. If your mom and Elaine knew all our secrets—like the facial expressions we make when something's up—we'd never get a minute's peace, would we?"

Joe nodded. "Boy, did I need that."

"I figured as much. You and Elaine have a fight?"

"I thought you wanted to know about the job?"

"Elaine's more important, right?"

That was the last thing Joe needed to hear. "I'll tell you about the job first."

"You already did. It's with a rising company that does research in large-scale organic farming. It's opening a facility in the county and they're offering you a sizable salary. Now tell me what's going on with you and Elaine. With all that great news, I'd think everything would be fine."

Joe tightened his lips.

"Uh-huh, there it is."

"There *what* is?"

"Your secret. I'm surprised Elaine hasn't mentioned it. When you frown like that, one side of your mouth goes up and the other side goes down."

"That's good to know. I'll try to keep it under control when I'm around her. Hey, it sounds like you know more about Organiks than you were letting on. How did you know they were into large scale organic farming?"

"Your old dad isn't as dumb as he looks. When I left research agriculture to farm, I knew I'd better keep up with all the latest and greatest, right?"

"Makes sense."

"It sure does." Dad paused. "Is there any chance your problem with Elaine concerns another woman? I'm sure your college is filled with them. Don't tell me one has turned your head."

"Well ..."

"Doggone, Son, that looks says it all. If it happened at college, how did Elaine find out?" Dad's normally tension-free forehead wrinkled. "I'm not trying to pry. I'll tell your mom just enough when I go to bed to keep her from harassing you in the morning. You know how she can be."

"That's not a bad idea. I'd like to keep this thing between Elaine and me to myself as much as possible."

Dad stood. "I think there's some leftover pot roast from last night's dinner in the fridge. Since the kitchen's on the other side of the house from mine and your mom's bedroom, we won't keep her up."

In the kitchen, Dad took a large bowl from the refrigerator. They both filled smaller bowls, microwaved them until the delicious aroma or beef, onions, potatoes, and carrots wafted about the kitchen, and sat at the table with a glass of milk each.

Dad downed a forkful of beef and onion, followed it with milk, and wiped his mouth with a napkin plucked from the holder. "Your mom sure knows what to do with a pot roast." He dropped the napkin by the bowl. "Go ahead. I'll be glad to share any advice concerning women that I might" —he grinned— "or might *not* have picked up over the years."

Joe swallowed milk, licking his milk moustache. "It's something I never meant to happen. Elaine—"

"I hope you didn't tell her that. That's one of the oldest excuses in the book."

"Let me tell how it started. I'll get to how Elaine reacted after."

Joe explained how he met Jillian and how she flirted with him, how they had dinner together and how she kissed him. At the part where Jillian apologized the next day, Dad nodded. "Seems like a decent gal after all." He rubbed his lower lip the same way Joe did. "Tell me something."

"What?"

"Where'd you get all that willpower from? From the way you describe her—blonde and blue eyed and long legs— what kept you from staying on the sofa and kissing her back?"

Joe shoved Dad's shoulder. "And I thought you knew me and my secrets so well. You tell me."

"Yeah, dumb question. The same thing—or person, rather—that would've stopped me in that situation. The love of my life, your mom, and Elaine for you."

"When Elaine popped into my head, I got the heck up from that sofa. I'll be honest, I was tempted. Thank goodness I overcame it."

Joe followed up with how Elaine took the text from Jillian, how she threw the phone, and how she eventually calmed down after he explained everything, including the news about the job.

In the middle of a swallow of milk, Dad set the glass down. "What's the problem then?"

"I'm flying to Belgium Monday, to Organiks' main headquarters for orientation."

"What's wrong with that either? You need to see the world, or at least some of it. Is it anywhere near the Ardennes American Cemetery? You could visit your great-grandpa's grave if it is."

"It's only twelve miles away, so Jillian said. She also said if I do well with the work, I could move up in position. I feel like I need to take advantage of this opportunity. I can visit the cemetery too, which is something I've always wanted to do."

"Are you saying Elaine doesn't want you to go?"

"She doesn't want me to go because Jillian is going."

Wrinkles created a veritable ladder on Dad's forehead. "Son, you've got yourself quite a mess. You're still going, right?"

"I'm doing it for me but I'm doing it for Elaine too. This is a great chance."

"I guess Elaine's afraid Jillian won't keep her hands to herself during— How long is this trip anyway?"

"A week."

"Are you staying in the same hotel?"

Joe didn't answer right away. When Elaine made that same remark, he hadn't taken it seriously, but it made sense.

"Since Organiks is paying for it, their visitors probably stay in the same hotel."

Dad took their bowls and glasses to the sink, refilled the glasses, and returned with a bowl from the fridge and two forks. "We can split the last of this fine peach cobbler your mom made a couple of days ago. That'll put a smile on your lips."

Ever since Jillian had almost kissed Joe in the restaurant parking lot on the night she left the college campus—her breath warm and sweet with the aroma of the peach cobbler they'd shared after dinner—he'd been attempting to rid his memory of that moment. Would he have to give up one of his favorite deserts to do that?

"No thanks, Dad." He sipped milk. "After this I'm going to bed."

Chapter 13

Sunlight streamed through Elaine's window and fell across her pillow. She touched her cheek. Why couldn't the argument with Joe never have happened? Why couldn't their evening have been filled with the warmth of his kisses on her cheeks, lips, and neck rather than fighting? A tingle of desire ran through her, replaced by tears.

Done with crying, she sat on the side of the bed. Sunlight beamed through the window and shone on her naked ring finger. Another tear slipped down her cheek. Maybe she shouldn't have forced the ultimatum on Joe, especially when she'd added the significant gesture of making him take the ring with him on the trip.

She slowly stood on her ankle that had stiffened overnight. It would loosen as she moved around. She worked her fingers and shoulders, sore from painting and cleaning. Those aches would work their way out also, but she wanted to move enough of her clothes and bathroom items into her new home today to stay. That meant the soreness would return each morning until she finished her work.

First things first, which meant a visit to a furniture store for a new bed. She'd sleep in town tonight if the store delivered a replacement for that musty mattress, and a new sofa to replace that dusty beast in the living room wouldn't hurt. Maybe all that would take her mind off her problems for a while. She sniffed the air. Along with a slice or three of that bacon Mom had sizzling in a pan.

Clothes on and hair brushed, she headed to the kitchen. Would her parents ask about Joe? He didn't always visit on weekends, and during the week she'd said nothing about him coming home. Maybe they wouldn't ask and she could get the move to town underway without their worried looks on her mind every hour.

Elaine poured a cup of coffee. Mom took bacon from a pan, placed the sizzling strips on a plate lined with paper towels, and gave it to Elaine. "Take the bacon to the table. Your dad wants his eggs over easy, you?"

"That's fine." Elaine took a seat across from Dad, who was reading the local paper. "Anything interesting, Dad, or just the same-old-same-old?"

"Pretty much the same old thing." He folded the paper and set it on the table. "You working on the house today?"

"After I run by the furniture store for a bed. If they can deliver today, I might sleep there tonight and start moving the rest of my stuff." Elaine sipped coffee. "I need a sofa too. The one already there is so dusty, it might stir up my allergies."

"Do you need a vacuum cleaner?" Mom asked, placing three plates on the table. "I've got an old one that still does a decent job." She sat between Elaine and Dad.

"Then why'd you get a new one last month?" Dad asked, peppering his eggs.

Mom buttered a slice of toast and slid the container to Elaine. "As you can see, you might want to rethink getting married."

To keep the conversation from leading to Joe, Elaine said nothing.

Dad slid the pepper shaker to the middle of the table. "Don't listen to my old battleax. I can't think of anything Joe would do to make you reconsider marrying him."

Mom popped his hand. "I can think of reason to divorce you, calling me 'battleax.' You've worked under many a kitchen sink over the years. How many women have seen your underwear?"

"Why, dear, didn't you know I don't wear underwear on the job? If I did, I'd be depriving women all over the county the pleasure of seeing my butt crack. You don't want me to lose half my business, do you?"

Elaine stood with her plate and coffee. "I'll finish my breakfast on the deck before I lose my appetite."

Outside, she took a seat and sipped coffee. Morning had dawned gray, mirroring her mood despite her parents' joking. At least she'd managed to use their carrying on as an excuse to slip away before one of them asked about Joe. She'd have to tell them, but not now. Like immediately after the motorcycle crash, the pain lingered: raw and tender to the touch.

Breakfast done, she took the dish and cup to the sink, where Mom was washing dishes. "Your dad left on a call. Someone on the other side of town has no water. He said he might stop by your place after."

Elaine turned to leave.

"Elaine?"

Elaine dreaded the question that had to be coming. She turned around.

"Why are you in such a hurry to move?" Mom asked.

No question about Joe, thank goodness, and this was a question she was prepared to answer. "Weren't you ready to get out on your own when you were my age?"

Mom dried her hands. "That doesn't mean I won't miss you. Your dad and I might forget to tell you, but we're extremely proud of you. Now that you're ready to get married, it makes us even more proud, especially since you're marrying someone as wonderful as Joe."

Elaine swallowed. Joe didn't seem exactly wonderful at the moment. "I'll be back for a few things if I manage to get a bed. See you later."

During the drive to Alma, Elaine relived her and Joe's argument, questioning herself endlessly about how she'd handled it. If the proverbial shoe had been on the other foot, and some guy had stuck his tongue down her throat in his hotel room, Mr. Joe Matthan would've had a fit. What was he thinking, going to that hotel room? He admitted this Jillian woman had been flirting with him, so he had to have known her saying she'd drank too much to drive was a ploy to seduce him, including how she left his resume in her hotel room. As far as his not telling that blonde bimbo about his engagement, no job worth having was worth lying for.

Then again, Elaine had told Joe she believed him. If that were true, why keep putting herself through the agony of reliving it, including the torture of imagining him kissing another woman?

At the furniture store in Alma, she lucked up on a bedding sale and purchased a king-sized mattress set at half price. The clerk told her both the bed and the new sofa she'd bought would be delivered by three o'clock.

Next, she stopped at a department store for bedding and a new pillow. For a moment she considered a second pillow for Joe but declined. He could buy his own pillow, but only if she was satisfied with his story of how the trip with Ms. Blue-eyed She-devil went.

At the house, in preparation for the new sofa, Elaine cleared the empty paint cans and other supplies from the living room. In the bedroom, she unplugged the lamp and slid it and the nightstand out of the way. No need in giving the furniture people the opportunity to break anything.

Her stomach growled. The old cuckoo clock on the wall read 12:30, but the refrigerator held nothing she wanted, mostly water for while she painted. Maybe she'd drive to the closest fast-food place and bring back a burger in case the furniture people arrived early. Purse and keys in hand, she opened the door—and stopped.

Dad, with one hand up to knock, raised two paper bags with his other hand. "Hey there, workin' girl. How about some lunch?"

Elaine welcomed the aroma of burgers and fries, but if Dad stayed very long—and he would since he carried two bags— he'd likely bring up the subject of Joe. She forced a smile and held the door open while he stepped inside. "I guess you were reading my mind—or my growling stomach."

"My own, more than likely. Did your mom tell you about the job I had this morning? Anyway, I finished early and thought you might be so busy you'd forget to eat."

Elaine took him to the kitchen. They sat at the table to unpack the food and drinks. Dad glanced around. "You've cleaned up. Are you happy with everything?"

Elaine unwrapped a burger. "There's a deck and a nice backyard. You saw that the other day."

"How about a grill?" Dad took a bite of his hamburger and frowned. "Then Joe can cook a decent burger and not have to buy stuff like this." He opened a pack of ketchup, removed the bun, and squeezed it on the wilted lettuce.

"We'll have to look at those, I guess." Elaine took a bite of her own burger, more like a tasteless mass of bread, bland meat, and mushy tomato. The icy soda washed it down crisp and cold. Since Dad had mentioned Joe, how long before—

He set his drink on the table. "I think I saw Joe's pickup at his parents' place when I went to that job. You didn't mention him last night. If he came in late Friday like he usually does, didn't you see him yesterday?"

Eating fries, Elaine held her finger up. Dad nodded and continued eating.

What should she tell him, or how much *could* she tell him and not flat-out lie? She never cared for lying, especially to her parents. Whose side would Dad take if she told him? Would he sympathize with Joe by saying the kiss was innocent and the job was a great opportunity? Probably. Maybe she could twist the truth enough to steer the conversation elsewhere.

Elaine swallowed soda. "He stopped by for a minute on his way home. He would've gone straight there but he needed to use the bathroom. I'll probably see him soon."

"'See him soon?'" Dad asked, surprise in his voice. "You don't sound very excited. You didn't even mention the news this morning."

Elaine took another bite of hamburger. Was he talking about Joe's new job? How could he know that already?

"Tell you what, workin' girl, you eat and I'll talk. Maybe you were a bit too overwhelmed with fixing this place up to mention it. Heck, you're probably wondering how I know. Al told me at the hardware store this morning while I was picking up supplies for that job. Joe's job offer sounds like a great opportunity. You two will be married and building that dream home overlooking the river before you know it."

The last of the burger went down like a rock—a large rock that stuck in Elaine's throat. Forgetting the soda and her fear that Dad would take Joe's side of their argument, her eyes filled with tears. She dropped her head, her shoulders shook, and she waited for the question that had to be coming.

"Elaine, honey, what's wrong?"

She plucked a napkin; they all fell from the wooden holder. After soaking that napkin, she took another, stealing a glance at Dad. He sat patiently, arms folded. She needed to talk it out, so why not Dad? He *should* understand, even though he might take Joe's side.

She wiped her eyes one last time, threw the soaked napkins in the trash, and returned to the chair. Dad picked up the spilled napkins, folded them, and returned them to the holder. "Those didn't look like happy tears to me, honey. If you'd rather talk to your mom ..."

The disappointment in his downturned eyes crushed Elaine. He must think she'd rather confide in mom more than him. She slid the chair over and hugged him. He usually forwent shaving Saturday morning, and his whiskers scratched her cheek. She finished the hug, plucked what she hoped would be the last napkin, and wiped her eyes again. "I'm just as much a daddy's girl as a momma's girl. Don't ever think I wouldn't talk to you about something personal if I need to, okay?"

He fingered moisture from the corner of one of his own eyes and gave her a weak smile. "You read me pretty good, baby girl." He laughed. "Where'd that come from? I haven't called you that since ... well, since you were a baby girl. Don't tell me Joe did something to upset you? I think an awful lot of that boy for him to do something like that."

To settle her nerves, Elaine took a swallow of the soda, now cool, not cold. She set the cup on the table. "Joe told me about the job last night when he got in from school. You're right, it does sound like a great opportunity, but ..."

"I can't imagine a downside to a job like that."

"It's not so much the job as it is the person who recruited him, or the *woman* who recruited him, I should say. It's her flirting with him. It's how she got him back to her hotel room. It's how she kissed him. To top it all off, it's the text she sent him the next day say, 'Good morning, sweetheart.' It makes me want to smack her."

Dad's eyes widened. "Whoa, honey, don't work yourself up, your cheeks are getting red. Did this woman know Joe was engaged? If so, I could see why you'd be mad at her. Joe shares part of the responsibility though, because— Wait a minute, since the kiss happened in her hotel room, how far did it go?"

"He said he left right after."

"Did he tell her he was engaged? I'd think he would've told her as soon as she started flirting with him."

"I would have thought so too." Elaine stuffed a cold fry in her mouth.

Dad shoved his food away. "He didn't tell her? Are you sure he didn't sleep with her? If he'd lie about being engaged, who knows what else he lied about." Face reddening, Dad stood. "I'll get it out of him, honey, don't you worry about—"

"Dad!" Elaine jumped from the chair. "This is my business and I'll handle it." She sat. "Sit down, you haven't heard everything. I believe him and I'll tell you why, okay?"

Dad sat, his face a shade less red.

"First," Elaine said, "thanks for taking up for me. Before I told you—you know, when I was crying—I wasn't sure how you'd take it."

"You're my daughter. That should tell you how I'd take it."

"Did you forget what you said a minute ago? About how you think an awful lot of him?"

"That's true, but—"

"There's no need for 'buts.' Maybe I'm making it sound worse than it is. I'd better fill you in. I feel better, so we can eat too. I *am* hungry."

Eating a cold fry here and there, Elaine told him the rest of the story, including how Joe was afraid he might lose the job if he didn't act friendly toward Jillian.

Dad finished the last of his burger. "I'm glad you stopped me from rushing over and talking to Joe, because this Jillian person would've been next. Maybe she's okay, since she apologized."

Elaine smirked. "That remains to be seen."

About to drink soda, Dad lowered the cup. "Don't tell me he'll be working with her."

"Organik's main offices are in Belgium. Joe's flying there for a week on Monday with—"

"Oh, no. With Jillian?"

"You got it." Elaine held up her hand and wiggled her ring finger. "I've already given him a going away present. I told him to keep it while he was gone to remind him of what was important—me."

Dad swallowed soda. "That means you're not breaking the engagement. Unless ..."

"If he messes up ... if I get the slightest hint ... the wedding's off."

"Can't say I'd blame you, honey. I wonder what your mom will think of this?"

"Please don't tell her," Elaine said, her voice plaintive. "As far as she knows, Joe will be back at school."

"What if she sees Anne in town. You know they'll talk about it."

"I haven't thought of that." Elaine sipped the now-warm soda. "Can you tell her just enough so she won't ask me about it? Tell her not to mention it to the Matthans either, that there's no need because I didn't break the engagement and things will work out."

"I can do that. I think Joe will be the gentleman he's always been while he's in Belgium." Dad wadded his empty burger wrapper and stuck it in one of the bags. "It'll work out."

Choking down the remainder of her meal, Elaine considered what might happen when Joe returned from the trip. If he knew what was good for him, he'd *better* be a gentleman with this blonde, blue-eyed Jillian person. If not, what? Could she stand to lose him? She'd never considered the possibility, could never bear to think of him not being there for her and her for him. Tears stung her eyes again. She took a deep breath, threw the trash away, and returned to the table. "It'll be okay, Dad. If not, after you and Mom kill him, I'll kill him too."

Chapter 14

Joe opened his suitcase to pack. He'd spent a restless Saturday and Sunday hiking the fields around home, wondering what would happen between him and Elaine when he returned from Belgium. Jillian had called him on his new smartphone—his old one was beyond repair—and had given him the itinerary for their trip. She also said their flight had been changed, so he needed to be at Kearney Regional at six a.m. instead of eight.

Mom hadn't questioned him concerning the argument, so he owed Dad bigtime. Still, Joe did catch her eyeing him wistfully a time or two, a slight frown on her usually cheerful face. A souvenir from the trip would definitely be in order—for both of them.

He took clothes from drawers and hangers, folded and fit them into the suitcase, and stopped when he came to an old pair of pajamas he hadn't worn in ages. A Christmas present from Mom—she didn't know he slept nude—the PJ's red plaid screamed "yuck." What if Elaine was right about Jillian booking adjoining rooms with the lock on her side of the door? What if she conveniently forgot how she respected his engagement and slipped into the room during the night in some kind of flimsy, see-through nighty? Joe added the PJs to the suitcase. At least he could jump out of bed without her seeing him naked.

Suitcase nearly full—he'd pack his bathroom items in the morning—he sat on the bed. The last time he'd seen Jillian, when they'd said goodbye at the restaurant, sparks had flown, especially when she'd almost kissed him. But since he and Elaine had argued—fought, more like it—the thoughts of kissing her, or doing anything else, had vanished like a haystack in a tornado. Was Jillian beautiful? No doubt about it? Was she a blast to be with? No doubt about that either. Did they share common interests? Doubt number three blown away like the grenade that had killed his great-grandpa—or him—if his reincarnation theory, or whatever it was, held true. How about if he were single, what then? No doubts there either, but he wasn't single and didn't want to be. All he wanted—all he'd ever wanted since meeting Elaine—was Elaine.

He started to rise from the bed, and a cold chill enveloped him. He swayed on weak knees and collapsed, the mattress squeaking with his weight.

The chill faded, and he knew what had caused it. How did he know his great-grandpa had died from a grenade blast? Had Grandpa told him? Not that he remembered. Had anyone else? No. Could it be a latent memory attempting to surface from the haze of his likely past? Possible. Or could it be an unlikely past? Why? Because all he had so far to make him believe the strange version of his possible previous life was the dream of Elaine wearing 1940's era clothing with a yellow ribbon in her hair while kissing him, including the dream of them making love beneath the oak at the river after being married. Those two dreams, along with his learning the guitar incredibly fast, were difficult to ignore. Still, doubt occasionally nipped at his belief, as it likely nipped at

Elaine's belief in him. Maybe his belief could be further verified—or discounted—in a cemetery in Belgium.

Joe's empty stomach gnawed at his backbone. Mom and Dad were eating supper out, and he didn't care to join them. Despite her silence on the subject of his and Elaine's argument, the last place he wanted the topic to arise was in a public place, so he declined when they had asked him to go. He opened the fridge. Nothing caught his eye or his appetite, so he climbed into his pickup for the drive to Alma.

Wheat covered Dad's fields in a lush, green blanket that swayed in the day's dying breeze. The pickup neared a field left fallow, and a murder of crows flung themselves upward, their wingbeats painting the gray sky with slashing, black brush strokes.

Joe lowered his window and took in the aroma of rain, though no rain fell. Over the treetops about a half a mile away, lightning slashed a crooked Z earthward. He counted … one … two … three … *boom!* Shortly after his birthday, he, Mom, and Dad had sat out on the front porch swing to watch a thunderstorm roll in from the west. Dad had told him how, after seeing lightning, every five seconds until it thundered meant the storm was a mile away. The storm now hanging over those distant trees, with black clouds scudding about in the distance, wasn't far away at all.

Nearing town, he pulled into a fast-food place and purchased a bar-b-cue sandwich with extra sauce and coleslaw, an order of fries, and an iced tea with lemon. He likely wouldn't get those tastes in Belgium. He took a left to drive along main street and parked in front of the closed hardware store.

Sunday night in Alma was quiet. The walk-in movie theatre had closed years ago, and a For Sale sign leaned against the window from the inside, propped on the sill. A car rolled by with a smiling young man at the wheel, maybe on his way to see his girl. A minute later another car rolled by. An older man tapped his fingers on the steering wheel while mouthing the words to some song playing on the car's radio. Maybe he was headed home to see his wife and kids. Joe lowered his window to better hear the song.

Lightning flashed in the rear-view mirror. Thunder rolled in waves, echoing amongst the red-brick buildings until it faded into the night. Fireflies danced around one of the maple trees lining the street, their lights flickering on, off … on, off.

A sudden wave of sadness hit Joe. He cranked the pickup, ready to speed to Ruth's old house and try to make Elaine understand why she had nothing to worry about concerning Jillian. He turned the key, killing the engine. She probably wasn't ready to see him. Her demanding he take the ring proved that well enough.

He faced the hardware store. The firefly flickers reflected in the glass door. What was it about this place? Why did it attract him like it did, exactly like Elaine attracted him to her?

Lightning flashed again. Thunder rumbled several seconds later. Huge raindrops splattered on the windshield. The main body of the storm had skirted Alma to the north, but one section of clouds, enough of one for it to rain, was moving over town. Joe raised the window, but not before several warm drops hit his arm. He finished his meal while the errant shower turned into a downpour, falling on the roof of the pickup as if it pounded hundreds of tiny metallic drums. The aroma of rain slipped inside the pickup's vents, giving the gray moment an even grayer smell.

The lightning gradually lessened to an occasional flash in the east, followed by the low rumble of distant thunder, but the downpour continued. Joe wanted to at least see if Elaine was at her new house. He bit his lower lip. Yes, at the moment it was *her* new house, and he had no claim to it—or her—except the claim she had on his heart. Not wanting to drive by and risk her seeing his pickup, he took the keys from the ignition and left. The walk would take about ten minutes, and he'd be soaked within seconds. Not important. He had to be near her before he left in the morning.

Joe didn't hurry. Hands stuffed in his pockets, head down, he walked with a medium-paced stroll, but not a stroll he enjoyed. The rain soon soaked him. By the time he arrived at Elaine's street, the shower had lightened to a half-drizzle, except the drops were cold, almost like liquid ice streaming down his forehead, cheeks, and back. Shivering, and with his teeth chattering, he stopped at the end of Elaine's driveway. Her car sat near the house. A light shone in the living room window. He waited between two large bushes by the street.

Elaine walked into the living room from the direction of the hall and looked out the window. Joe slipped deeper into the bushes, and a cascade of cold water fell from the leaves, running into his eyes and down his back. He winced as one of the limbs scratched his arm.

A leafy branch blocked his view, so he pulled it aside. What looked like a new floor lamp with a beige shade illuminated a different color sofa, blue instead of brown. Maybe Elaine went shopping to get her mind off of him. She probably bought a new bed too.

She left the window and sat on the sofa. Her thick brunette hair, streaked with sun, shined under the light. What he wouldn't give to be snug and warm in her arms, without kissing or caressing or saying a single word, just holding her close.

She ran her fingers through her hair, causing the memory of the aroma of her sweet floral-scented shampoo to burst upon Joe, like the day he rode behind her on the Harley. With his hands around her waist and her back tight to his chest, he hadn't wanted the ride to end. If they'd been on a long stretch of highway instead of the curvy country road leading to the river, he might have teased her by rubbing her legs. She might have leaned into him or giggled—Joe would have loved either. Her spontaneity, as well as all her other attributes of honesty, love of children—as with being a teacher—and a kind and caring nature that tended toward the basics in life rather than the superficial, drew him to her as intensely as the past he believed they shared. In fact, regardless of his dreams of their possible pasts together, he loved her exactly the same.

Would she ever love him the same since he admitted to kissing Jillian?

He left the bushes and sat on the ground, leaning against the base of a tree. The rain slowed to a steady, bone-chilling drizzle, even colder than before, while the thunder and lightning faded away to darkness and silence. The overcast broke apart to reveal a sliver of moon, similar to a ghostly white sliver of fingernail hanging in the sky, along with a scattering of stars. He pushed the button on his watch to illuminate the digital numbers. Nine o'clock, not too late. He'd stay until Elaine either went to bed or until ten. It'd take him an hour in the morning to shower, shave, get dressed, and finish packing, and he could grab something from the fridge for the hour's drive to Kearney Regional airport.

Elaine remained on the sofa, possibly watching TV. Maybe she bought one of those too. Joe yawned and checked the time: 9:50. Another fifteen minutes or so wouldn't hurt. He yawned again and closed his eyes. They stung slightly, maybe from the water that had doused him as he hid in the bushes. He'd rest them for a minute and check on Elaine again.

* * *

Joe snapped his eyes open. His new phone vibrated in his pocket. Lucky the rain hadn't ruined it. He checked the screen. "Hey, Dad, what's up?"

"What's up is your mom and me are wondering why you aren't home in bed. You've got a long day tomorrow."

Joe checked the time on the phone. He hadn't noticed it when he checked the caller ID. "I lost track of time."

"Glad to hear it and glad you're all right. You didn't leave a note. I started to call earlier but thought you might've been trying to make up with Elaine."

"I'll be home soon."

"We're already in bed. Usually are by twelve, you know. Talk to you in the morning."

Joe ended the call and rose from the base of the tree to stretch in an attempt to loosen his stiff back. Elaine's living room window was dark. He ran down the street beneath the moon and the stars stitched into the black quilt of sky, still aching to run to her door instead. No, he wouldn't be welcome.

His tennis shoes splashed through puddles. The cool night air chilled his sinuses.

Would she welcome him when he came back from Belgium? He didn't know, but he sure hoped so.

Chapter 15

Beep-beep-beep-beep-beep-bee—
Joe rolled over to jab the alarm clock button and groaned. Four in the morning. He hadn't gotten into bed until one and had tossed and turned all night—all three hours of it—waking to glare at the clock each thirty minutes or so.

Several stumbling steps later, he peered at his reflection in the bathroom mirror. Whatever had made his eyes sting from the bush had left them red, either from that or from the lack of sleep. Regardless, the effect was the same: eyes that look liked he had pulled an all-nighter, drunk and stumbling home in the dark. He shaved and showered, toweled dry enough to dress, and hurried to the kitchen, where he welcomed the aroma of coffee. Thank goodness farmers rose early.

Mom flipped sausage patties in a pan. " Do you have time for breakfast? I can make scrambled eggs for a couple of sausage and egg biscuits for the road."

"I think I've got time to eat here. I'll fill one of our travel mugs for extra coffee for the drive."

A tractor rumbled outside. He went to a window overlooking the backyard, including a half-mile wide field where Dad drove a huge, green tractor with the headlights on. The engine growled as it reverberated across the open land. Diesel smoke poured from the exhaust while slices of earth rolled up the plow's blades, falling to the side in dark, overturned sections. Joe could almost imagine the smell of life within the loamy soil.

Mom joined him at the window. "He sure loves farming."

"If we had chickens, he'd wake them up," Joe said, trying to lighten his mood. "Maybe we should call him rooster."

"Son?"

Recognizing her pleading "mom" tone, Joe faced her.

"I know you don't want me to bring it up," she said. "I'm your mom, so …" She held out her hand. A gold chain with fine links dangled from her fingers. "I thought you might want to put Elaine's engagement ring on this and wear it around your neck. You know, as a reminder of—"

"What? Keeping my hands to myself while I'm with Jillian?" Joe glared at the chain. "I guess you're taking Elaine's side in this mess."

She left the chain on the table and returned to the stove to stir the eggs. "It's not like you to assume. It sounds like this mess—a perfect description—is bothering you more than you're willing to admit." She faced him, cheeks flushed, and pointed the spatula his way. "Don't you know I'd take *both* sides?" She returned to the eggs. "Assumptions. I'd have to *assume* you and your dad are the first three letters in that word if I *assumed* anything, since you both think I'd worry you to death about the job and that trip."

At the table, Joe took the ring from his pocket, slipped it over the chain, and placed the chain around his neck. "What do you think? As a fashion statement, I mean?"

She came over to raise the chain and release it, so it slid inside his collar. "Next to your heart is a better statement." She patted his chest. "I've often marveled at how you and Elaine seem made for each other. I understand why you need to make the trip, with the job and all. You two will work it out." She returned to the stove

"I'm sorry I snapped at you," Joe said, feeling guilty. "You're right, I should know better. As far as Dad knowing better, you'll have to take that up with him."

Mom turned and grinned. "Maybe a sprinkle or three of cayenne pepper on his sausage and egg biscuit would make him see the error of his ways."

"Add a little Ex-lax," Joe said, glad humor was entering the conversation. "He'll get the message then, and it'll last a lot longer."

"That might be too much of a message, especially while he's bouncing on that tractor." Mom made two egg and sausage biscuits, wrapped them in wax paper, and put them on the table. "These should keep you full until you have that airline lunch. Better fill that travel mug too."

"Didn't you hear me when I said I'd eat here?"

She pointed at the wall clock. "I don't think so."

At the cabinet, Joe grabbed a mug and filled it. Where had the time gone? Dumb question. It had disappeared while he was learning another life-lesson from Mom.

Bathroom items packed, suitcase in the pickup, coffee mug in the console and biscuits in the passenger seat, Joe roared down the road.

At the intersection of US-136 and US-183, where he needed to take a left, he was tempted to take a right into Alma and swing by Elaine's. He smacked his forehead. Not only would she slam the door in his face, she might not even open it. He took the correct turn and drove north toward Holdrege, the halfway point of the journey.

He marveled at the scenery, mostly farmland watered with rotating irrigation systems. Difficult to see from the ground, the huge circles showed green in satellite images on the internet.

A few miles passed before he opened the first biscuit, took a bite, and washed it down with coffee. Good thing Mom had made his breakfast. If not, he might nod off while driving the dead-straight highway.

At Holdrege, after stopping at a fast-food place for a quick run inside to relieve his aching bladder of the coffee, he took US-34 east. In spite of his yawning, he managed to keep his tired eyes open, and soon he was taking a left on state-road 44, to head north again.

The circular fields accompanied him during the entire drive, except for the random traditional square field like Dad preferred. Farm houses with tractors, plows, and assorted machinery were a common site also, as well as the lush green of corn—the most important crop in Nebraska for cattle feed. He also passed wheat, soybeans, and quite a few lesser-known crops, such as sugar beets and potatoes.

In the large town of Kearney, his phone vibrated. It was Jillian. "Uh-huh, you're checking up on me," he said. "I'll be there in a few minutes."

"I'm not checking up on you," Jillian said, her tone serious. "Are you in a bad mood? I expected a better greeting for your future co-worker with whom you're about to spend an entire week. Try again, something like, 'Mornin', farm girl, are you ready for our week together in romantic Liège?"

Enjoying Jillian's tone, which had changed from serious to perky, Joe considered his own perky comeback. "'Whom'? You're mighty formal for a farm girl, farm girl."

"I have my formal side at times."

He yawned. "Look, I'm almost there, so—"

"What's with the yawning? Didn't you get enough sleep last night?"

"Not as much as I needed. Talk to you soon."

Joe ended the call, shaking his head and dreading the questions she'd likely pepper him with during the flight. How in the world would he keep her sidetracked? He snapped his fingers. By going to sleep.

Leaning against her car, dressed in faded jeans and a button-up white blouse, blonde hair in a ponytail, Jillian waved to Joe as he parked beside her car. He met her at the front of his pickup, suitcase in hand. "Mornin', farm girl."

"Back atcha, farm boy." Her exquisitely plucked eyebrows rose. "You forget to comb your hair as well as go to bed? I know, Elaine gave you a late night going away party. Nice and cozy too, I bet."

"Can we save the questions for later? Like next year maybe?"

"Sure, Mr. Grouchy. Let's catch our plane."

A small airport, Kearney Regional didn't require Homeland Security's stringent search procedures that the international airports would. Joe was glad. By the time he boarded the Organiks private jet, he could hardly stand.

He dropped into the seat, buckled his seatbelt, and closed his eyes.

Since he and Jillian were the only passengers—there'd been no other recruits from his district—she'd taken the seat across the aisle. She poked his arm. "For someone who's never flown, you seem to be taking it for granted. Did you bring any airsickness medicine?"

Joe popped his eyes open. "Does that happen much?"

"I brought some in case."

Joe closed his eyes again until the plane took off, giving him the sensation that it had left his stomach on the ground. He burped and tasted sausage grease. "Can I have one of those pills?"

Jillian took a bottle from her purse and shook two pills into his hand. "You'll get used to it, unless we have severe turbulence. People have hit the roof and gotten concussions and broken bones."

"I thought the pilot warned passengers to put on their seatbelts when that happened?"

"They don't always know it's coming. Talk about surprises."

Joe took the pills. "Any water on this tin can?"

"Don't make fun of this plane," Jillian said, her tone serious like earlier. "You'd hate for it to let you down. I'll get you a bottle from up front when we can get up. This 'tin can' has water, wine, snacks." She patted his hand. "A couple of the seats in back even open into beds."

"I might take you up on that—the sleeping part, that is." Joe reclined his seat and closed his eyes again. "Just place the cold bottle to my cheek when you get it."

"Sheesh, were not on the plane five minutes and you're already treating me like we were married. Can you at least say please?"

Joe opened one eye. "Please."

The jet's twin-engine-whine lulled him in and out of sleep. Cold touched his neck and he jumped, but only until the seat belt restrained him. He took the bottle from Jillian. "Thanks."

She returned to her seat with her own water. "The list of things you owe me for grows, farm boy." The plastic bottle crinkled when she twisted the top.

Joe did the same, popped the pills, and washed them down with the ice-cold water. "Man, that's good. I almost feel human again." He unbuckled his seat belt.

Jillian swallowed water. "Why are you so worn out? I've seen ground hogs crawl from their holes that look better than you."

"Phooey." Joe tousled his hair. "I'm blond, they're brown."

"Right, a blond ground hog. Why do I have the feeling your lack of sleep has nothing to do with a late-night celebration with Elaine and everything to do with her not wanting you to go?"

Joe said nothing. How did women seem to have a six-sense that told them when something was wrong with any man they knew?

"Are you zoning out on me?" Jillian waved her hand in front of his face. "You realize we'll be together hours and hours and hours before we land in Belgium. You might as well tell me what's going on and get it over with."

Joe considered ignoring her, but, like she said, he might as well get it over with. "Aside from being a recruiter with Organiks, do you read minds too? Yes, Elaine and I didn't have what you'd call an amiable parting. Satisfied?"

"Too bad. I've spent the last few nights dreaming you two would break up so I could have you."

Joe faced the window.

"Hey, farm boy, I'm kidding, okay?"

With the weight of his fight with Elaine, as well as his lack of sleep bearing down on him, Joe said nothing. Another job, like Elaine had told him, might be a good idea.

Jillian sat beside him. "Is it as serious as your sad face says it is?" She grabbed his arm. "Don't tell me you didn't delete the text I sent calling you sweetheart and she saw it?"

"That's exactly what happened."

"Didn't you tell her how I sometimes call a person that after I know them for a while?"

"Would you believe that story?"

"That's all she knows, right? You didn't say anything about helping me with my bra or the kiss?"

Joe turned to face her. "What kind of questions would you ask me if you were her?"

"Well, I'd—"

"Don't even try. You'd grill me until I blabbed almost everything."

"Don't interrupt," Jillian said. "I was going to agree. You said 'almost everything.' Does that mean you didn't tell her everything?"

"She didn't ask about undressing, so I didn't tell her the bra story. She did ask if we slept together. I could answer that honestly, thank goodness."

"Well, that's something." Jillian paused. "Does she know her way around a shotgun?"

"I'm probably making it sound worse than it was," Joe said, hoping it was true. "She didn't break the engagement, so that's a plus."

"Then why, as you said, was your parting not amiable?"

"It was pretty doggone amiable for a while. I eventually made her understand nothing had happened. She said she believed me too, until she found out about this trip."

"Because I'm going with you, not the trip. That means she might trust you but she doesn't trust me. Do I have all that figured out too?"

Joe sighed. "That about covers it."

"Your Elaine sounds like a tough lady. When do I get to meet her? I could run by when we get back and explain—"

"Don't even think about it. If she kills *me*, fine. I can't have your death on my conscious too."

Jillian poked his side. "How would you know? You'd be dead too. Besides, we could go together. Doesn't that sound romantic?"

Despite the tension between them, Joe couldn't help grinning. "It wouldn't be boring." He nudged her knee with his. "It should work out, as long as you didn't book adjoining rooms so you can sneak into my bed in the middle of the night."

Jillian nudged him back. "The lock's on my side too." She laughed. "You won't get any more sleep in Belgium than you did your last night in Alma. You'll be wide awake worrying if I'm going to attack you."

"Not when you promised to respect mine and Elaine's engagement after our last dinner. Maybe she's right, and I can't trust you."

Jillian moved back to her seat. "I might joke around, but that doesn't mean you can't trust me." She faced the window, the back of her neck turning red. "Believe it or not, I'm a good person."

The part of her cheek Joe could see was turning red too. "I didn't say you weren't, but—"

"Don't say another word until we get to the next airport. I'll be forced to speak to your smug, Mr. Perfect-self then."

"Look, I—"

"Not—another—word."

Joe settled back into the seat and drank water, capped the bottle and closed his eyes. The commute to the next airport, where they'd board a full-sized plane, would be fairly short, but it also would be long, quiet, and tedious while he tried to figure out why he couldn't seem to please the opposite sex no matter how hard he tried.

He touched his shirt, where Elaine's engagement ring hung from the gold chain.

At least he could still count on Mom.

Chapter 16

A jolt startled Joe awake. He sat up from his slouch and looked out the window. The jet had touched down and was slowing on the runway. He couldn't remember buckling his seat belt, but there it was, snug around his waist. If Jillian, who was reading a paperback across the aisle, had buckled it while he slept, maybe she wasn't mad at him anymore. The plane taxied toward the off-load area, but she never looked his way. Yeah, she was still mad.

The plane stopped. She clicked her seat belt loose, took a carry-on from the overhead compartment, and zipped the paperback into a side pocket. "We've got a long way to go and I'm trying to get over being mad at you. Let's clear the air, do you trust me or not?"

"I do, I really do," Joe said, using his most plaintive tone "Can't we forget all that stuff? I'm down enough about Elaine. I don't want to feel down about you too."

"Good." She started down the aisle with the carry-on. He grabbed her arm to say he was glad, but before he could, she turned around, eyed his hand, and then him. "Getting physical, are we?"

Joe let go of her arm. "Look, I like joking around like anyone else, but not right now."

"Since you're making demands, is anything else on your mind, farm boy? Maybe you want the lock on your side of the door at the hotel so you can sneak in and catch me naked. All you have to do is ask. I guarantee you'll like what you—"

"See?" Joe made a growling sound in his throat. He hadn't meant to complete her sentence. "I meant *see* how it is with your joking? I'm not making demands, I'm politely asking."

Jillian pouted and fought a grin at the same time. "Aw, poor baby doesn't care for my sexual innuendo. You didn't protest when you helped me with the girls." She tapped her chin with a perfectly manicured fingertip, red polish glistening. "It seems I recall your hot breath on my back too, care to explain that?"

Joe took his suitcase from the overhead compartment. "All I want is to get on a plane full of people so I can get some privacy."

At the TSA search line, when the metal detector beeped, he had to show the agent the necklace with Elaine's ring. Lucky for him, Jillian was occupied with her own search, so she didn't see it. If she had, her questions would start again.

After receiving his suitcase—minus toothpaste and deodorant—he sat on the other side of the TSA line to tie his shoes that were checked for metal. Jillian sat beside him, slipped on her flats, and waited while he finished. "Too bad, farm boy."

Joe stood. "What are you talking about? That whole experience was bad."

She stood also. "Too bad I couldn't have been the person checking you out while they were doing the scan. I understand they're quite revealing."

"You act like none of this bothers you."

"It's better than getting blown up by a terrorist." She picked up her carry-on. "Let's go."

Joe followed. All manner of individuals, some strolling, some hurrying, some in mad dashes, moved around as if eddies within currents at the river. He caught up to Jillian as she rounded a corner. "I hope I don't have to travel a lot with this job—at least not flying. I'm not crazy about having my personal items pawed, or having my doggone toothpaste and deodorant confiscated."

"Oh, hush. I'll help you find some when we get to Belgium. I'll show you the approved travel items if you have to fly again. It's no big deal."

Her ponytail bounced against her back, and Joe puffed as he tried to keep up with her long-legged pace. "Didn't it bother you to have your personal items searched? What if it were some pervert who liked fondling your panties?"

She cut her eyes his way. "Fondle my panties and tell me if you like it. Then I'll know whether to be bothered or not."

Shaking his head, Joe followed her to the boarding gate.

On the plane, Jillian stashed her carry-on. "Our row has three seats. Maybe it's just us."

"Good," Joe said, trying to keep frustration from his voice. "With all your teasing, we might need some space."

"Like one seat apart will stop me." She pointed. "Do you want the window?"

Joe stashed his suitcase and closed the compartment. "Nope. That way I can escape to the restroom if you worry me too much." They sat, and Joe leaned the seat back slightly. "Not bad." He stretched his legs and wiggled his feet. "Plenty of legroom too."

Jillian sat. "This is what they call 'Premium Class.' I'm hoping Organiks will start flying its people Business Class, but we can forget First Class."

"Why's that?"

"Only celebrities and the wealthy can afford it. Businesses have to watch costs, so ..."

"Have you ever flown Business Class?"

"A time or two. The seats are wider and will recline farther. The meals are better too."

"I'm all for that." Joe rubbed his stomach. "Mom made a couple of biscuits for the drive and I could use a bite."

"I could use a bite too." Jillian tilted her head and pulled her ponytail away from her neck. "Right here."

"Good grief, woman, you're too much. Still, thanks for forgiving me when I intimated I couldn't trust you."

Jillian's eyebrows raised. "My, what a word, 'intimated.' It's so close to intimate, isn't it?"

"Elaine's a teacher, did I tell you that? I pick up the occasional interesting word from her."

"That's a fine one. I don't hear it very often. What grade does she teach?"

"Third at Alma Elementary. She loves teaching, even though the kids are a handful sometimes."

"How many kids do you two want?"

"Maybe two or three."

The jet engines muffled whir transformed into a whine and then a roar, and the announcement came for the passengers to buckle their seatbelts. Joe clicked his and so did Jillian. The jet rolled down the runway, picking up speed. He covered a burp, tasting the hint of sausage grease like earlier. "Can I have some more motion sickness pills? I want to have them when they bring us something to drink."

***

Jillian looked up from her paperback. Joe lightly snored. The plane had re-fueled in New York and now soared over the Atlantic with the familiar monotone rush of air and engine.

Shortly after takeoff, passengers had received lunch and beverages, and Joe had taken two motion sickness pills with his water and roast beef, saying the airline cooks could learn a thing or three from his mom when it came to cooking. He'd been asleep over two hours, possibly because of his and Elaine's argument. It must've been severe for him to lose so much sleep over the weekend.

Jillian wished she hadn't worded the text like she had. She didn't care to be the cause of their troubles. His blond hair, curling at his ears, fluttered with the air coming from a nearby vent. She'd known him less than a week, but he seemed like the clean-cut type, likely getting a haircut before it grew that long. How would it feel to run her fingers through those curls—soft, silky, and entirely too sexy with his cute self? No, not so much cute as a mix between boyish and handsome, with a bit of his farm-boy innocence thrown in for good measure.

She'd wanted him that night in her hotel room—*seriously* wanted him. He probably hadn't believed she was a virgin, or how she took the pill for hormonal migraines, but she didn't mind. The truth was the truth, and if he hadn't been engaged, and if he'd wanted to have a relationship with her, he would've discovered the truth about all that eventually.

Outside the restaurant, when she'd almost kissed him despite knowing about his engagement, her feelings had been serious as well. What was it about this farm-boy who had gotten to her so completely, making her flirt with him like she never had with any man? And the fantasies! Her cheeks warmed, as well as other parts of her body, when another fantastic moment entered her thoughts—of him looking into her eyes right before kissing her mouth and neck, and then moving lower and lower and lower until—

Jillian squirmed in the seat. She needed to stop all that. He was engaged and engaged he'd be, since he obviously loved his girl so much. Still, Ms. Elaine better take him back soon, or all bets were off.

She returned to the paperback, and Joe groaned. She marked her place with a finger and waited. His eyes fluttered open, and he sat up to look past her toward the window. "Nothing but blue down there," he said. "*Way* down there. How high are we?"

"About 35,000 feet, give or take."

"How many times have you been to the Organiks headquarters?"

Jillian dog-eared the paperback and slid it between her thigh and the seat. "This is my tenth trip."

"That makes you a regular globetrotter by my standards."

"Joe?" She placed her hand on his arm.

His eyes focused on hers. "What's up with those wrinkles across your forehead?"

She touched her forehead. "You're not supposed to tell a woman she has wrinkles. I want to apologize—again."

"For what?"

"For what you said about my joking. I should stop since I know about you and Elaine. I'm sorry about my text too. I wish it hadn't been so— Well, I was definitely flirting when I called you sweetheart, although I do that after I know someone a while." Joe's eyes wondered over the passengers sitting nearby. Was he afraid they might hear? What an innocent soul he was— an endearing and sweet innocent soul. She placed a finger on his chin and turned his face toward her. "Hey, farm boy, I'm over here."

"I'm not used to having a personal conversation around so many strangers."

"You said it'd be more private."

"I should've deleted your text before I went home. I got sidetracked and forgot about it."

"What sidetracked you?"

"Well …"

"*Well*, what?"

"Okay, I'll be honest. I forgot about it because you had me so frazzled. You're entirely too good at that."

"Are you saying that's one of my more endearing qualities?"

Joe laughed. The passenger sitting ahead of him glanced rearward, raised an eyebrow, and turned back around.

"Endearing's as good a word as any," he said.

Jillian loved his laugh: in the middle of the male tonal spectrum, not too loud, not too soft, blue eyes grinning. If it weren't for Elaine, this coming week would be as interesting as it got. "Enough laughing, farm-boy, especially after you said I joked around too much."

"Whatever you say, farm-girl. How many days are we expected to be at Organiks? Do we get any time to sightsee? You know I want to visit the cemetery where I'm—I mean where my great-grandpa is buried."

Jillian hesitated. Joe had clearly began saying the cemetery where *he* was buried, not his great-grandpa. It could have been a slip, but it was difficult to ignore the certainty in his voice. She'd let it lie unless she had reason not to. "They expect the recruiters to take first timers out and about. Belgium is beautiful as well as romantic." Why'd she say that? She needed to get those comments under control.

"Maybe I could talk Elaine into coming over for a visit." Joe snapped his fingers. "Or—and this is a brilliant idea if I do say so myself—a honeymoon."

Jillian wanted to say, *sure, if she takes you back*. She nodded instead. "It depends on when you get married. If you care about the nicest time of the year, July and August are considered the peak tourist season."

"Now I know when we *wouldn't* want to visit. I imagine June and October—when the crowds are less—would suit us fine." He glanced at his watch. "What time will it be when we land?"

"It's a seven-hour difference. The first flight took about an hour. Adding the search and seizure at the airport, the second flight of about three hours, the refueling, the—"

"Sheesh," Joe said. "It's gonna to take us nearly fourteen hours to get there. We left Kearney Regional around seven. That means we'll get there around nine at night our time, which means it'll be about four in the morning."

"Don't worry, we don't have to show up at Organiks until about one. They'll feed all the newbies a fine lunch and take you on a tour of the facilities."

Joe reclined his seat. "I'll grab another nap. I've never experienced jet lag, but I bet it's hard to get over. Aren't you sleepy? We got up early."

Jillian took the paperback from between her thigh and the seat. "Not really. I'll wake you around six for dinner. You need to be able to sleep when we get to the hotel too."

Jillian opened the paperback. What kind of week would she and Mr. Farm Boy have together, and what else might he tell her about his and Elaine's argument? More importantly, would Elaine call and break their engagement? If so, those adjoining rooms might come in handy for something other than business. talk.

Chapter 17

At the Brussels airport, Joe endured another security search and left the bustling terminal with Jillian to meet the company car. The drive to Liège, where Organiks' main headquarters and the hotel was located, would take about an hour. Jillian mentioned how Liège had an airport, but since the drive was so short, it made no financial sense to pay for another flight.

During the drive, as the moon played hide and seek with the clouds and the stars, Joe constantly yawned, exhausted from his lack of sleep as well as the grueling flight. At the hotel, he followed Jillian inside. She requested the reserved rooms, signed the register, and they shuffled behind a porter rolling their luggage on a chrome cart. Joe promised himself to get a better look at the hotel in the daylight, when he didn't feel like a fuzzy-eyed and fuzzy-tongued beaver gnawing on a log at dawn.

Teeth brushed, faced wiped with a washcloth soaked in cold water, he collapsed into bed, nude as usual. Pulling the air-conditioned sheets over him, he said a silent prayer for his and Elaine's family, turned the bedside lamp off, and almost turned it back on to set the alarm clock. He closed his eyes. Jillian had said she'd wake him.

What was Elaine doing? It was four-thirty, eleven-thirty back home. She'd be in school, attempting to get her classes ready for third-grade graduation. In the dark, Joe kissed his palm and blew the kiss in the air. "Goodnight, darlin', I love you. I hope you still love me too."

***

Knock, knock, knock.

Joe opened his eyes. In thin, yellow lines across the bed, daylight attempted to shine its way through the closed curtains.

Knock, knock, knock. "Joe, are you up?"

Blinking and rubbing his eyes, Joe sat on the side of the bed. "You don't have to beat the door down."

"Does Elaine know you're not a morning person?"

On the way to the bathroom, Joe answered by slamming the door.

In the bedroom again, he studied the door that joined their rooms. Inset into the polished wooden frame, a full-length mirror reflected his naked self. He tapped on the door. "Do you have a mirror on your side too? This thing's huge."

"I have one, but it's not a regular mirror?"

"How so?"

"It's a two-way electronic mirror. There's a switch that lets you turn off that feature. I turned my side off before I went to bed."

Joe shot his hands over his crotch. "I never heard of an electronic mirror."

"Then why are you covering up?" Jillian giggled. "Looking good there, farm boy."

Joe jumped away from the mirror and jerked his previous day's jeans on. He ran his finger around the edge of the mirror, couldn't find any switch, and knocked. "Are you dressed? I need you to show me this doggone switch."

Jillian opened the door. "Come on in." Joe went inside and faced the mirror, which reflected his frowning face. Jillian shoved his arm. "Do you believe everything anyone tells you?"

"But you said you saw me covering up?"

"What else would you have done? Get dressed, I'm hungry."

Joe closed the door behind him. Regardless of her teasing him, it *was* funny. There was no telling what might happen before the end of the week. He knocked on the door again. "Do I have time for a shower? I need to wake up."

"You *do* look like a half-asleep raccoon shaken out of its tree. Don't be long, they have a great brunch here."

"Not raccoon, I hope." In the bathroom, a massive granite shower of gray, green, and red-flecked stone greeted him, including several pulsing shower heads. Too bad he didn't have time to stay and soak.

A quick shampoo and a body scrub cleared his mind, along with a shave. He dressed in clean jeans, loafers, and a golf shirt, although he didn't golf. Jillian, wearing jeans, a button-up blouse, and open-toed sandals, signaled that casual was fine as far as Joe was concerned. He knocked on the door. "Ready when you are."

The door opened. "It took long enough, let's go."

Joe patted his back pocket. "Let me get my wallet."

"This is all on Organiks' tab, but I wouldn't go ordering any Bloody Marys."

Joe followed her into the hall, where she stopped to close the door. "It locks automatically. Make sure you have your key card when you go out." She left for the elevator, and he had to rush to keep up with her long-legged stride along the plush, blue carpet.

"What's the big hurry?" he asked.

They were lucky enough to have an empty elevator waiting. Inside, Jillian pressed the lobby button. "I'm looking forward to a spinach omelet. The coffee's great too."

The reality of Joe's empty stomach doubled with the elevator's speedy decent. The doors slid apart to reveal the opulent lobby. Brilliant white tiles lined the floor, likely marble. Tucked in inconspicuous corners, thickly upholstered sofas and chairs, in either red or black, welcomed guests for reading or relaxing.

Jillian nudged his arm. "Nice, isn't it? Would you believe it's a renovated factory? Wait until you see the lounge. The ceiling is all white brick arches."

"I don't care what it looks like as long as the rooms are clean and the food is good. I guess I was too tired to notice everything last night."

Jillian led Joe through a door and into a room that opened up into what could have been a miniature cathedral. Like she'd said, white brick arches curved to the ceiling and down, coming together to end in columns set into the same white marble floor. Joe brushed his fingers along the white brick. "Wow, if the food is as impressive as the atmosphere, it'll be great."

"Take a whiff of the coffee, isn't it wonderful?"

Joe sniffed. "I hadn't even noticed, and I love great coffee." He glanced around. "Do we seat ourselves or …?"

Wearing black slacks, a white shirt with a gray vest, and a black bow tie, a dark-haired young man emerged from a door to their left and gathered two menus from a stand. "I am so sorry for you to wait. Cleaning from the morning rush, you know. Table for two for brunch?" Sorry was soory, wait had plenty of w in it, and rush was more like rosh.

"Please," Jillian said, "and goede morgen."

The waiter smiled. "En goede morgen naar jou, mis. Spreek je nederlands?"

Jillian shook her head. "Oh no. All I can manage is goede morgen, goede avond, and en ik hou van je"

The young man smiled at Joe. "I see, follow me, please." He led them to a table by a window overlooking two streets. Beyond the streets a river rolled by, and tall trees, fully clothed with foliage, lined the opposite bank. Several red-brick buildings ranging from ten to twenty stories stood like shadowed soldiers beyond the trees. The young man placed the menus on the table. "If you have noticed, we have a fresh coffee, just brewed. We also have several fresh juices. What may I get you?"

"Coffee, definitely." Joe opened the menu. "Orange juice would be great too."

"Very good, sir. For the lady?"

"I'll have the same." She opened the menu and read for a second. "I know what I'd like, but my companion might need a minute or two."

"I will be back shortly with your beverages."

Joe faced Jillian. "You mentioned having a spinach omelet. Would you believe I've never had an omelet?"

"We'll have to remedy that, but you might like to add bacon and tomato. I'm trying to stay slim, so I'll just have spinach and tomato."

"You've got slim down to a science, you look amaz—" Joe closed the menu. "I'm sorry. I asked you to stop the suggestive jokes and I do the same thing."

"I'll take your 'amazing' comment as a compliment, although you didn't finish it. How about that?"

"Thanks. So, you speak a little Dutch. What did you tell the waiter when he kind of grinned at me?"

"Goede morgen is good morning. Goede avond is good evening."

"What about that last one? En ik hou …?"

"En means 'and.'"

"What about the rest? That's when he grinned at me."

Jillian looked away. "Well …"

"Why the big hesitation?"

She looked back. "In Dutch, ik hou van je means I love you."

"Oh. He must have thought we're together."

"Obviously, farm boy. I'll teach you and you can tell Elaine when you get home."

Joe didn't reply, and Jillian looked away again. Could she be in love with him after meeting just a week ago? No way. Sexually attracted, sure—more than sure after the hotel room incident where she'd kissed him and tried to get him to make love to her, but the way she was acting now suggested otherwise. If she did love him, or thought she did, would he be better off knowing or not knowing? She'd already agreed to no more sexually explicit jokes, including how she would she'd teach him to say "I love you" in Dutch so he could tell Elaine. Since he didn't care to bring up the subject of her feelings for him, he'd rather not know.

He pointed out the window. "What's the name of that river? It reminds me of the one back home."

Jillian took a tissue from her purse and wiped the corner of one eye.

Was she crying? If she was, it was a good thing he'd decided not to ask her about her feelings for him.

She balled up the tissue and dropped it into the purse. "It's called the Meuse. When I look out over the city, it's hard to believe World War II ever reared its ugly head here. Not long after I started traveling here for Organiks, I did a little research into Belgium's history. It attempted to stay neutral in the beginning of the war, but lost the claim when the Germans invaded in May of 1940. The government surrendered after only eighteen days of fighting."

"That's interesting. I like history, especially World War II hist—" The waiter brought their coffee and orange juice, took their orders, and left.

Jillian sipped coffee. "What were you going to say about World War II history?"

"My dad sometimes watches those World War II documentaries, maybe because of his grandpa who's my great-grandpa. It's unbelievable what the world had to deal with in those six years."

Jillian said nothing.

"Okay, enough of that dreary talk," Joe said. "Teach me to say I love you in Dutch."

She faced him, grinning, which Joe was glad to see. "Okay, farm boy, repeat after me. Ik, as in 'ick, that's nasty.' Hou, as in 'how are you?' The next one's tricky. It's spelled v-a-n, but it's pronounced like 'fine,' with hardly any of the 'f' sound. That last part is j-e. It sounds like 'yeah,' but without saying the e and h. Ick-how-fine-ye. Simple."

"Ick-how-fine-yeah. How's that?"

"You're putting too much emphasis on the 'f' and drawing out the 'yeah.' Let's try this." She slid her chair close and took his hands in hers. Soft and smooth and warm, these were the same fingers that had held his face while she kissed him in the hotel that night. She eased her face close to his, but not so close he couldn't see her lips, lightly shaded with pink lipstick. "One more time. Ick-how-fine-ye."

"Ick-how-fine-yeah."

"Much better, but you're still drawing out the 'yeah.' Jillian flicked her tongue across her lips. "I'll say it exactly like it should be, in Dutch. Ik hou van je … ik hou van je." She slid forward a bit more, and a tingle ran up Joe's back.

"Jillian?"

"Hmm?"

"I love Elaine more than I can say, but I can't take much more of your lips within inches of mine, or that honey-suckle shampoo you use."

Instead of pulling away like Joe expected, she eased forward.

Boys are weak. That's just the way you are.

Joe looked around. "Who said that?"

"Who said what?" Jillian's breath warmed Joe's cheek.

"I could swear I heard a voice."

"Did this voice say to kiss me?" She placed a fingertip to his chin, turned his face toward her, and someone nearby cleared his throat.

"Very sorry to disturb you, but your omelets would be best eaten hot." The waiter left their plates, and Joe picked up his fork. That kiss had been entirely too close. How in the world would he get through a whole week with Jillian when he'd almost kissed her on their first morning here?

Boys are weak. That's just the way you are. The voice had sounded exactly like Elaine's when she teased him. Could it be one of his 1943 memories returning to stop him from kissing Jillian? No one had ever told him that line about boys being weak, so how could it pop into his head like it had?

Jillian had already started on her omelet, likely thinking he'd made the voice up to get out of kissing her. Joe forked omelet and swallowed. "Thanks for telling me about this, it's great."

"You mentioned visiting the Ardennes American Cemetery. We can go whenever you want. Our schedule at Organiks isn't written in stone."

"Sure. I can't wait to see my great-grandpa's grave."

Chapter 18

Elaine filled her cloth brief case with her standard Tuesday quizzes and left school to stop by the hardware store for more cleaning supplies. She hadn't scrubbed the floors and wouldn't feel at home until everything felt smooth under her bare feet.

Then again, the status of her and Joe's engagement kept her from feeling completely at home. The house was meant to be his home too, and the problem had been nagging her with spurts of late-night questions, old movie tears, and longing to hold him close again.

With her cleaning supplies bagged, she sat on the bench by the wood stove. Did she really hear that music from the radio in the back, or could it have been something else—something like déjà vu but in sound form? She waited for five minutes and heard nothing except the comings and goings of customers and Mr. Hansen's friendly banter.

On the way home she stopped by the grocery for dinner items. As she loaded the fridge, her cell phone played Elvis's *I Did It My Way*. She closed the fridge and took the phone from her purse on the table. "Hi, Elvis, what's up?"

Mom laughed. "You're always teasing me about my ringtone."

"It *is* a little out of date."

"Says the old-fashioned country girl. How're you getting along in your new place?"

"I'm fine."

"Have you heard from Joe lately? I hate how you two had a squabble."

"He's probably learning all about his new job." Elaine smirked. He *better* be, instead of learning about that floozy Jillian.

"I'm sure he has his hands full with all kinds of things."

"That's an understatement, Elvis."

"It sounds like your still upset with him."

"I'll get over it. I've got some things to do, okay?"

"Okay, honey, talk to you later."

Elaine returned the phone to her purse and filled a new tea kettle and set it on the stove. She glared at her reflection in the polished stainless steel and then at her naked ring finger. Sure, she'd get over her and Joe's so-called squabble, but when?

The clock on the stove read 4:35. When all else failed, maybe cooking supper would help.

The broiled chicken, tossed salad, and iced tea went down tastelessly. What had Joe been eating and drinking? Caviar followed by filet mignon followed by chocolate mousse, all washed down with red wine? And for a late-night dessert, chocolate covered strawberries with a champagne chaser in bed, Jillian at his side wearing a skimpy negligee, her blonde hair across his shoulder while she nestled in the curve of his arm?

Elaine dropped the dishes in the sink and the glass shattered. Lucky the strainer was in. She'd leave the broken glass until tomorrow. Lucky it broke in the sink or she might've thrown it through the window. Then she'd have a window replacement to pay for since she hadn't learned that skill.

In the living room, she collapsed onto the sofa and flipped through TV channels, passing and returning to an old black and white scene where a tall, dark man and a gorgeous, blonde woman were locked in a passionate embrace, kissing as if it were their last moments on earth. Elaine stuck her tongue out at the pair. If the man were blond, she might've gotten a glass to throw at the TV. She pulled her tongue back in and bit her lower lip. If she stayed mad and threw glasses for real, she'd soon be out of glasses.

Flexing her right bicep, she studied it, and then her left. Not bad from her lifetime of helping Dad around the house with various projects. Well defined—she poked one—and firm too. If she ever laid eyes on Jillian, could she take her? She shook her head. Ridiculous, of course she could. No, considering violence to solve her problems was ridiculous, but the idea was fun to think about.

TV off, she stepped out onto the front porch and into the cool of the evening. The moon hadn't risen yet, and the sky sparkled with stars. A dog barked down the street, and the aroma of someone's dinner—a dinner they'd likely tasted, fried chicken maybe—drifted on the breeze from the opposite direction. Mom made the best fried chicken she'd ever tasted, though Joe had said the same thing about his mom's, as he should. How hard would that recipe be, and would Joe love her chicken as much as his mom's? Would he help her in the kitchen? Would he make a great dad? Would he make love to her and tell her he loved her until they both grew too old to worry about love making?

She trusted him—liked to think she knew him inside and out—so the answer was yes. As far as Jillian, even though Joe should be trusted to control himself, how much temptation could he stand?

Boys are weak. That's just the way you are. Boys are weak, that's just the way you are. Boys are weak, that's just the way—

Feeling the electric jolt of adrenalin, Elaine whirled around. "Who said that?"

No one answered, except the dog barking down the street again.

She sank to the steps. Even her stupid subconscious was telling her how Joe would sleep with Jillian. She covered her face while hot, angry tears wet her hands. Her sobs faded to hiccups. When the hiccups ended, she looked at the stars, twinkling as if they were filled with life, energy, and hope.

I have to believe you'll come back to me, I have to believe you'll come back to me, I have to believe you'll come back to me.

This time, as unbelievable as it was, the words were coming from her own thoughts, as if she'd said them in another lifetime.

* * *

Joe snapped upright in bed, chest heaving.

Still in the hotel in Liège. Still with Jillian next door.

He dropped to the pillow to catch his breath. A new dream from his past with Elaine had woken him, and he wanted to remember as much of it as he could in case it slipped away. He closed his eyes.

She wore a yellow dress and a yellow ribbon around her ponytail, exactly like the yellow ribbon she'd worn in church when they sang. Holding a huge daffodil, she ran away from him through lush, tall grass, laughing. Her ponytail streamed behind her, and he managed to pull the ribbon. She dashed away from him even faster, laughing while her sun-streaked hair billowed behind her.

The dream flickered through his mind like an old theatre film through a projector, and he fought to catch hold of another scene. Elaine stopped, and he gave her the ribbon. Instead of keeping it, she shoved her hand—and the ribbon—into his pants pocket. Her warm hand so close to certain areas of his physique startled him, yet teased him also. Then she raised on tiptoe and kissed him—a long and luscious toe-tingling kiss that he never wanted to end—until she pulled away, cheeks reddening.

Joe opened his eyes. What a dream—one he wanted to relive over and over and—

Another scene exploded in his mind, with a sexual urgency he had never experienced since ... never?

He stood behind Elaine and lifted her hair to kiss her neck. He must've taken the daffodil, because he raised it to trace a teasing line along the wet trail he'd left on her neck with his kisses. Pulling the collar of the dress lower, he kissed from her neck to the curve of her shoulder. Trembling with his touch, she pressed against him, which increased his sexual urgency to where she must've known how aroused he was. She whirled away, cheeks even redder, chest heaving like his did when he woke up.

The pure sexual need of that moment—almost like when a bull mounted a cow, bellowing and slobbering—tempted him past reason.

Jillian's bare back when he'd unfastened her bra. Jillian's kiss on the sofa in her hotel room. Jillian's long, tanned legs that had to be smooth and silky and—

Boys are weak. That's just the way you are.

Joe sat up and looked around. Could that be Elaine's 1943 voice warning him of what might happen if he kept thinking about Jillian?

Boys are weak. That's just the way you are.

Although Elaine's words were clear in his mind, his dream of making love to her, along with Jillian's tempting him with their almost kiss at breakfast, made him afraid of what might happen before he got back home.

He rubbed his wrinkled forehead. He hated to consider it, but would he make love to Jillian regardless of loving Elaine? Were people like animals in heat, allowing lust to completely override all reason?

Joe fell back on the pillow. He couldn't believe it—people were better than that. At least he considered himself to be. Liar. How many times had he thought about Jillian since he'd met her? How many times had he imagined her exquisite body beneath him, over him, her hair hanging in his face while her blue eyes bore into his?

A promise is an important thing. It means you're trusting another person to honor their word. If we make a promise like that, we'd better respect and keep it.

Realizing he'd been asleep again, Joe snapped his eyes open. This new dream had to be another remembrance of his and Elaine's past, like with his dream of making love to her at the river after being married.

He slapped his forehead. What an idiot he was. He needed to put the whole dream together so he could make sense of it.

And there it was, all right before him.

She'd told him how *boys are weak, that's just the way you are,* and had kissed him as an example of what she'd meant. Then she'd allowed him to do the same to her, which was when he'd kissed her neck and shoulders. All their kissing and touching and learning exactly what forces of human nature—and sexuality—they had to face had caused them to simply promise not to go too far until they were married.

And they had kept that promise, even now, in the present.

The next time Jillian's beauty and intelligence and absolutely delicious aroma of honeysuckles tempted him, would he take her like the animal that existed within him?

What did he want? Clearly, to keep his promise.

For his and Elaine's sakes, he hoped he would.

Chapter 19

*B*eep-beep-beep-beep-bee—
Joe smacked the alarm clock and checked the time with blurry eyes. Eight a.m. He rolled to the middle of the king-sized bed and stared at the blindingly white ceiling.

A glance at his watch confirmed his hazy belief that it was Wednesday, and he was glad. Tuesday, because of an unscheduled seminar at Organiks concerning the future of using farm animal manure in large-scale organic farming, which meant he and Jillian had to grab a quick morning bite in their rooms, he had avoided another intimate breakfast with her. The seminar was interesting, but his eyes had opened and closed, opened and closed, and Jillian had to nudge him several times until he grew more tired of that than he did of simply being tired.

Monday, after what he called the "near-miss-kiss-brunch" with her, his day at Organiks had consisted of a meeting with college recruits from all over the world, as well as shaking the hands of the CEO. A tour of the facility, with its endless white halls, laboratories with uncounted numbers of white coated technicians, and warehouse-sized greenhouses filled with experimentally-grown organic crops from all over the world, filled the remainder of his day, while Jillian attended a recruiting seminar.

Yawning, he faced the window. The worst thing about their busy schedule was how it had delayed their visit to the Ardennes American Cemetery.

After a quick trip to the bathroom—he really needed to start wearing those pajamas he'd brought instead of sleeping naked—he opened the blinds. Rain drizzled down from the gray overcast. He touched the space between his eyes, where a deep furrow formed a valley in his brow. If his life didn't get back on track soon, he'd resemble Elaine's great-uncle Thomas.

Joe took his pajama bottoms from the dresser drawer, slipped them on, and sat at the foot of the bed to stare into the mirror on the adjoining door. The gold chain his mother had given him, with Elaine's engagement ring dangling from it, hung around his neck, but with a knot in the links. He slipped the chain over his head, worked out the knot, and slipped the chain back on.

Knock, knock, knock. "I heard your alarm, farm boy. Are you ready to rise and shine?"

"I guess we're not going to the cemetery today."

"I saw the rain. Don't worry, we'll make out."

The V reformed in Joe's brow. What a choice of words. Maybe he should strip his pajamas off and tell Jillian they should go ahead and sleep together and get it over with.

"Still there, Mr. Matthan? Let's go shopping after breakfast. We'll pick up one of those huge golf umbrellas and walk the streets until we're tired and damp and ready for a warm shower when we get back."

Joe fell back on the bed. She'd said "shower," not "showers," as in they'd shower together. Why did every other word she spoke, whispered, or murmured seem to carry the never ending sexually explicit connotation? Without warning, his imagination conjured up a scene of him and Jillian in the huge granite shower in his hotel bathroom. Steam rose around their naked, entwined bodies, slippery from the hot water and soap they'd lathered each other with. He managed to banish the thought but only for a moment, evidenced by a certain part of him that kept thinking on its own. Maybe a shower—a *cold* shower—would help.

He knocked on the door. "I'm gonna shower. Go ahead and eat if you want."

"Do you need someone to scrub your back?"

Joe closed his eyes. Just. Too. Much. "I got it."

"Okay." Jillian's voice was light and airy and entirely too perky. "I can wait. I'm still working on the paperback I was reading on the flight over. Knock when you're ready."

In the cold shower, as that certain part of him finally relaxed, Joe set the water a bit warmer. "'Knock when you're ready,'" he mumbled. When was he *never* ready around Jillian?

Done bathing, Joe emerged from the steamy bathroom to dress and face the day—and Jillian.

He hoped.

* * *

After a sexually uneventful breakfast of apple-spice oatmeal, fruit, coffee, and orange juice, Joe and Jillian, with newspapers over their heads, left to search for the huge umbrella she'd mentioned. To keep from tempting fate, he planned to buy two. If not, he would have to walk practically arm-in-arm all day with her, or get wet in the rain.

They hurried along the sidewalk, splashing through the occasional puddle while passing the rare person venturing out into such a wet, cool day. The papers over their heads soon sagged and fell apart. Jillian pulled him under an overhang, where they huddled out of the rain. "I feel like a drowned beaver," she said, fingering soaked hair from her eyes.

Joe wiped rain from his face. "Well, you're— No way would a beaver drown." He'd almost said, *well, you're the sexiest drowned beaver I've ever laid eyes on.*

Jillian missed the slip. "Tis true, fair sir. Wouldst thou have thy lady be a drowned rat instead?"

"What the—? Where'd that come from?"

"I love Jane Austen's books. She wrote during the Regency period in England, when everyone talked like that. You should read one sometimes. I especially like those that criticize women's roles during that period, or I should say the roles men placed women *in* during that period."

"I know what you mean. I caught the tail-end of one of the books made into a movie once with Mom." Joe eyed the rain that seemed to have no intention of slowing. "I hope we find an umbrella soon."

"Only one way to find out." Jillian took off down the sidewalk, shoes splattering water around her ankles whenever she hit a puddle. Joe ran after her, his soaked hair falling into his eyes. He caught up as she dashed under another overhang. She checked the door and went inside.

Lined with shelves on each side, the store, a miniature version of the old hardware store back home, warmed Joe immediately. In the rear, an elderly woman stood by an old wood stove similar to the hardware's, rubbing her hands together. "Welcome, welcome," she said, waving them in. "Come in out of such a dreary day and dry yourselves, young lovers."

"I like her already," Jillian said.

"Maybe she has some umbrellas," Joe said.

At the stove, he rubbed his hands over the hot metallic surface like the woman did. Jillian offered her hand. "Goede morgen. My" —she glanced at joe— "lover and I are searching for a large umbrella for our walk. Would you have one or two?"

With gray hair in a bun, piercing gray eyes, and an old-style yellow dress, the wrinkled woman smiled a knowing smile. "What do two such as you need with an umbrella when you have arms for holding each other close? Why, I would imagine you have all the warmth you need between you, in which to dry rain, water, or even tears of sadness. Do you not agree?"

Jillian raised an eyebrow at Joe, who shrugged. She faced the women. "Why would you say that?"

The woman winked. "I have a knack for knowing. My name is Elaina … Elaina Matthan. I am at your service."

Joe wobbled on unsteady legs. What were the chances of this woman having almost the same name as Elaine's name if they were married? He eased into a nearby wooden chair, which creaked and groaned with his weight.

Jillian remained standing. "How would you know that about us?"

"I am a fortune teller. If you will allow it, I would like to tell your future. I'll leave the young sir to his rest, for his ashen pallor tells me he needs it."

"Two umbrellas are all we need." Jillian took her wallet from her purse and offered a credit card. "I'll pay double."

The woman hobbled to a nearby wooden table covered with so many layers of patina that it's black surface resembled coal. She pulled out a matching chair and sat, lifted a black cloth from over a large crystal ball, and motioned toward the chair opposite her. "Sit, sit, it will only take a moment."

Jillian faced Joe. "Are you okay? I'm sure that name got to you. For a second I thought you were going to pass out."

"What a coincidence, huh? Go ahead. Maybe she has a freaking umbrella and we can get the heck out of here."

Jillian went to the table and sat. "Now what?"

"Your hand, please."

Jillian placed her hand in the woman's, who spoke so quietly Joe couldn't hear her. Move closer or not? Not. He would stay in this rickety chair as long as it would hold him.

Several whispers later, the woman covered the crystal ball and stood to reach behind a counter to produce a large umbrella. She hobbled to Joe. "For you, young sir. Please keep your lady dry and warm, for I fear your arms will not."

"How much do I owe you?" Joe asked, standing to take his wallet from his pocket.

"That," she said, tapping the umbrella with a swollen-knuckled hand, "is my own and a gift. I have another at home, only a short walk from here."

"I can't take your umbrella, ma'am. You'll get wet."

She faced the store front. "It will clear by the time I close and rain again soon after I arrive home." She returned to the stove, rubbing her hands together exactly as she had when he and Jillian had arrived.

Jillian grabbed Joe's hand. "Get me out of here."

Outside, as Jillian started down the sidewalk toward the hotel, Joe opened the umbrella, caught up to her, and grabbed her arm to stop her determined rush. "What the heck happened in there? What did that old woman—"

"Take me back to my room." Tears filled Jillian's eyes. "I might tell you and I might not. That's all I can say right now."

Except for the increasing patter of rain and the occasional car passing by, its tires nearly splashing them, silence filled the small space beneath the umbrella. Every few steps Jillian either sniffled or fingered tears from her eyes. Joe couldn't imagine what the old woman had said to upset her so much.

In the hotel again, he entered his room, and Jillian opened the adjoining door. "Do you mind? I feel too much like I'm alone otherwise, and I don't—" She swallowed. "I don't want to feel like that."

"Sure, no problem."

"I'll undress in the bathroom. A shower would feel …" She entered his room. Her hair, still wet and dripping from the rain, hung in her eyes. The thin shirt clung to her body, revealing the lace of her bra. She fingered Joe's own wet hair from his eyes, sending a sizzle of adrenalin along his shoulders. She wavered between a smile and no smile as her fingertips traced a warm and tingling line from his forehead to his mouth. Pausing there, she cupped his cheek in her palm while sliding her thumb slowly over his lips. Her startling blue eyes bore into his.

Joe could barely breath. Was this how he'd break his promise to Elaine? Was this the day he'd lose her forever? Was his sleeping with Jillian inevitable, really and truly inevitable as he'd thought earlier?

A soft smile slowly formed on Jillian's lips. "No worries, lover, I'm not going to attack you." She took her hand from his cheek. "But I could eat you up."

"You better run for that shower and lock the door," Joe said. "I've had about all of us I can take, if you know what I mean." He took a step away. "What did that old woman say when she told your so-called future? You said you'd tell me."

"I said I *might* tell you. I'm going for that shower and you might as well do the same. I don't want to be cooped up in these rooms with your stinky self."

In the bathroom, when Jillian shut the door, it bounced halfway open without latching. Joe went to the adjoining doorway. How far did his temptations have to go? Was this a test of his character before he could marry Elaine? It better not be, because he'd failed in every category, so what would another test or two or three or a dozen matter? He headed to his own bathroom and slammed the door behind him, making sure it latched.

* * *

Freshly showered, shampooed, and shaved, Joe left the bathroom. The adjoining door and Jillian's bathroom door remained opened. The water ran, so she was still in the shower. Was she singing? He listened but couldn't make out any words, only her soft and extremely feminine voice he'd fantasized about while in his own shower. How would it sound to have her whispering in his ear, telling him things that'd make a grizzled old farmer blush?

He stomped into his room's entranceway and snatched a bottle of water from the college-dorm sized fridge. What the heck was wrong with him? Minister Mattaniah would tell him he was going to hell as sure as he stood there, with things going on beneath his robe that never should—unless it was with Elaine after they were married.

He returned to his bed and sat. Jillian's shower and singing stopped. Joe, staring at his feet with the water bottle hanging between his knees, slowly rolled his eyes to the left, toward the half-open bathroom door. He caught a glimpse of her curved behind and jerked his eyes back to his feet. A hair dryer whirred. He rolled his eyes toward the door again. There she was, totally nude while drying her hair at the sink. Jerking his eyes to his feet once more, he dropped the bottle. When it banged on the hardwood floor, he expected Jillian to stick her head out of the bathroom, give him a knowing grin, and *maybe* close the door.

No such luck.

Close the adjoining door or not? That might upset her, since that old woman had said whatever she'd said, and he didn't want that.

Still, sitting here with a naked woman—a *gorgeous* naked woman—only a glance away was absolutely unbearable. Then why was he bearing it? Why didn't he go over by the window, anywhere, somewhere, instead of sitting where he could check her out?

The hair dryer stopped its whir. Joe cut his eyes toward the bathroom door. Bent over with her rear facing him, Jillian was brushing her hair. If he had false teeth like Uncle Thomas, they would've fallen out of his gaping mouth. He was going to hell, going to hell, going to hell, going to— Without looking, she mercifully closed the bathroom door. Joe sucked in so much air it stretched his ribs and whistled in his nose.

He got up to put his horrid red-plaid pajamas on, donned the robe too, and returned to the bed.

Jillian left the bathroom. She wore one of the hotel's thick, white robes, and her freshly shampooed and dried hair flowed about her shoulders like liquid gold. With a wave and smile, apparently over her dreary mood, she came to the door. "Hey, lover. I saw a bag or two of microwave popcorn in the cabinet by my fridge earlier. How about popping one while I find us an old movie on TV? We can cuddle up on the couch as snug as two bugs in the proverbial rug."

She disappeared to the left. Joe opened his mouth, but all he could manage was a thin squeak. He found the popcorn and popped it while she surfed channels. Her robe slid open to reveal a long leg, smooth and tanned. Red polish shined on her toenails. She even had sexy doggone feet, delicate with sensual arches. The microwave dinged—no burning, thank goodness.

Joe opened the bag to the aroma of melted butter. Whoa, a beer would— Nope, no alcohol. He was headed for hell as it was.

On the sofa, Jillian pulled her feet under her and patted the cushion beside her. "I saved you a seat, lover. For our viewing pleasure, I found a classic—*Casablanca.*"

Joe took the offered seat. Why fight it now? They munched popcorn while enjoying the tragic romance of Rick Blaine and Lisa Lund, played by two greats in the acting industry: Humphrey Bogart and Ingrid Bergman.

Jillian stood and stretched luxuriously, the robe rising up to her thighs. Joe covered his eyes but peeked anyway. Going to hell, going to hell, going to— He jumped from the sofa. "Want a water? I do."

"Water's boring. Call room service for champagne and chocolate covered strawberries."

"What about Organiks seeing that on your credit card bill?"

"I have my own card, lover. No worries."

"Can you call? I don't ... I don't ..."

"You sound like a broken record, lover. You don't want the hotel to know you're in my room, do you?" Jillian glided to the phone.

"Damn right."

"That's the spirit, lover. Pop us another bag. We'll eat that while we're waiting for dessert." Phone in hand, she called room service while Joe stared.

At the microwave, Joe waited on the popcorn. Jillian seemed different, as if she were attempting to overcome her earlier sadness at whatever the old woman had told her. It made sense. People often overcompensated when overwhelmed with one emotion, or so his psychology professor had said. As far as her calling him "lover," she must have gotten that from the old woman too. He needed to find out what that eerie, so-called fortune teller had told Jillian before her dangerous mood ended with them in bed. The microwave dinged, and he removed the steaming popcorn bag. He'd put himself at enough risk already, barely hanging onto the edge of control. What would happen next? He ran his fingers through his hair while returning to the sofa. Who the heck knew?

Joining him on the sofa, Jillian tugged at the leg of his pajamas. Red plaid PJs? How in the world did I miss these? I'm like a bull when it comes to red."

Afraid to ask exactly what she meant, Joe stuffed a handful of hot, buttery popcorn in his mouth. Jillian did the same, and they returned to the movie.

A knock came at the door, and Jillian hopped up. "About time." With the server tipped and the tray of huge chocolate covered strawberries on the table before them, she handed Joe the champagne. "Please do the honors, lover. I saw an opener and glasses in the cabinet over the fridge."

Joe returned with filled glasses, handed her one, and sat beside her.

"Mmm," Jillian said, sucking chocolate from her finger. She swiped the same finger through the chocolate on the strawberry again and pointed it at Joe. "I bet it tastes better on my finger." In the middle of munching one of the super-sweet berries, Joe held up a palm, and Jillian frowned. "I don't have all day." She wiped the chocolate across his cheek and giggled.

Joe swallowed the mouthful of berry and chocolate. "You sure are a big kid sometimes."

Jillian pouted. "Aw, lover, don't be mad, I'll take care of it." She grabbed his face and licked the chocolate from his cheek. "Mmm, so good." Grinning, she started to pull away but stopped—to lift the chain from around his neck. The grin, including the amused twinkle in her eyes, faded. "Is this Elaine's engagement ring. You didn't tell me she gave it back."

Joe took the ring and dropped it back inside the robe. "She told me to take it on the trip so I'd remember what was important."

"Was it your idea to wear it around your neck?"

"Mom gave me the idea. The chain too."

Jillian sat back on the sofa. "And because of me you're having a hard time remembering what's important, right?"

"I'm not totally innocent either and you know it. Look, you never told me what that old woman said. Since it seemed to make you sad, I'd like to know. Did it have anything to do with us, like when we were leaving and she said my arms wouldn't be able to keep you warm? She was saying everything *but* that when we went in her store."

"I—" Jillian lowered her head and raised it again. Moisture gleamed in her eyes. "I'll tell you but ... but can you hold me while I do?" Joe raised his right arm so she could slide close, and she stood from the sofa. "Be right back."

He waited while she rummaged through a dresser drawer, eventually taking out a pair of pink sweatpants and a matching top. I'm going to get out of this robe and slip these on. Can you close your eyes, or do I have to run to the bathroom?"

"I'll close my eyes, but why change?"

She nudged his leg with her foot. "Like I said when we met, you tell me your secrets and I'll tell you mine. You put those pajamas on to discourage anything happening between us, or I should say, anything happening sexually between us, right?"

"Well ..."

"Don't tell me," Jillian said, humor in her eyes. "Like me in the hotel that night, you're not wearing panties."

Joe threw a sofa pillow at her. "You have no sense. Give me that pillow so I can cover my eyes while you change."

Jillian handed him the pillow. "Good idea, Mr. Matthan, you're not to be trusted."

"*I'm* not to be trusted? What about—"

"Hush and do as I say, or I'll never get around to telling you what that woman said."

"Okay, okay. All covered, as you can see."

"There." Something soft fell on Joe's head. "That's my robe, for a little extra protection."

Joe waited, inhaling her clean scent from the warm robe. What in the world was she about to tell him concerning that old woman? "Are you ready yet? Your robe's hot."

She pulled the robe off him and then the pillow. "You were the perfect gentleman." Joe rubbed his lower lip. Not according to all those fantasies he'd been having about her he wasn't. Jillian sat beside him, snuggling close while pulling his arm around her. "I want to ask you something first." She faced him, apparently so she could see his reaction. "Do you believe in past lives?"

For a split-second, Joe's throat clamped shut. This was the last thing he expected to hear from her. "Well, like what exactly?"

"Some might call it reincarnation, I suppose. Do you believe in it?"

"Does this have anything to do with what that woman told you?" He refused to call her Elaina Matthan. The resemblance to Elaine's name—if they got married—gave him a chill.

Jillian turned away. Her shoulders beneath Joe's arm shuddered, and she covered her face. Not knowing what was making her cry, Joe lacked the most basic of comforting words. He started to put his other arm around her, but she uncovered her face, wet with tears. "I was … I was afraid of this. I cry terribly. I sob and shake and shudder. Once I get going, it'll feel like you're holding an earthquake. That's why I need you to hold me better than you are now. It won't be quite as bad, or last as long if you do. Only my mom and my dad know that about me. When I was twelve, my grandpa died. We were really close. He took me fishing and let me ride the tractor with him. Anyway, when I saw him at the funeral home the first time … well, it was all my mom and dad could do to comfort me. If they hadn't been there, I guess I would have cried until I passed out."

Jillian stood. "Can I sit in your lap facing you? I want to be as close to you as I can, with your arms around me tight. Please?"

The story about her grandpa touched Joe's heart. He opened his arms and she eased into his lap, pressing close to his chest. Though the pink sweat pants and matching top blurred the definition of her fit body, they didn't blur it entirely. He shoved those sensations from his mind. She was going to cry, probably a lot. It was time to think of her as a person who needed comforting instead of an attractive woman.

She lay her head on his shoulder. It was all he could do to ignore her honeysuckle-scented shampoo. "Whenever you're ready," he said softly.

"I asked about past lives because that old woman said we were star-crossed lovers who lived in Belgium in the 1800's. I was a serving maid to a woman who hated her husband, and I was in love with him. I never told you—or him, rather. He—you—loved me too, but you couldn't leave your wife because it would have been such a scandal. That old woman only said one more thing." Jillian squeezed Joe so tight he didn't know if he could breathe, and her shoulder's shook with a single sob. "Joe, she said we were passing each other in time in different lives, and we'd only have one chance at happiness."

"C'mon on now," Joe said. "You don't believe that nonsense, do you?"

"Maybe not that part. It was the last thing she said." Jillian squeezed him again and her entire body tightened.

Joe stroked her back. "Shh, I got you. If it's that upsetting, I don't need to know."

Jillian pulled away and looked him in the eyes with such sadness that he was afraid of exactly how much she'd cry when she started. "Joe, that woman said this life—right here and right now—was when we'd finally make love. Only once though. After that we'd never meet again." She collapsed against him, attempting to speak between the sobs and the shaking of her entire body. "Joe, please, I can't … I can't be the reason you and Elaine break up. You love her, I know you do. Please don't let it happen." She sobbed again, holding onto him as if she were viewing her dead grandpa once more.

She shuddered exactly as she'd described—like holding an earthquake—and Joe simply held her as tight as he could without hurting her. Eventually her crying slowed, but she pressed herself against him tighter than ever. Another minute passed. She pulled away to kiss his cheek and look him in the eyes. "You are the sweetest man I've ever known. If I weren't sensible—" She laughed, light and teasing like the Jillian of happy times. "I was going to say if I weren't sensible, I'd be inclined to believe that old woman's story. I imagine you know I'm half in love with you as it is." She kissed his cheek again. "Don't worry, my reasonable half will keep hoping I can find someone else as sweet as you one day."

"You will," Joe said. "I don't doubt that one bit. As much as I hate how that woman upset you, I'm glad we cleared the air.

Well, our *sexual* air. The way things were going, we would have ended up sleeping together before the end of this trip. My willpower was about shot."

Jillian eased herself up from his lap. "Mine too." She took the rest of the strawberries and champagne to the fridge and threw away the half-eaten bag of popcorn. "Do you want any supper? We can go out or eat downstairs. We can have the rest of the strawberries and champagne for dessert." She went to the window. "Oh, the TV listing by the phone says *Casablanca* is coming on again around eight, so we can catch that too, but without any drama of our own." She opened the blinds. "Would you look at that."

Joe left the sofa and joined her at the window. "Good grief."

"'Good grief' is right, Charlie Brown." Jillian glanced at her watch. "It's almost five, which means that old woman was right about having a dry walk home after closing. Do you think she was right about us making love too?"

"You better smile when you say that, Lucy." Joe bumped her shoulder with his. "That'd be like pulling the football out from under both of us."

Chapter 20

Done with her week at school, Elaine drove to her parents' house for dinner. Like the weekend, the past five days had been filled with long nights and occasional tears, plus questioning whether she should call Joe or not.

When she reached the top of the porch steps, Dad opened the door. "Hi, honey, how's my girl?"

Elaine followed him inside. "I'm okay." She sniffed the air. "Is Mom making pot roast?"

Dad patted his stomach. "Since I've managed to lose a few pounds with your mom's help, she's cutting me some slack and pan-searing an incredibly marbled porterhouse steak."

"Only one? What will Mom and I eat?" Elaine elbowed Dad's ribs.

"I hear you. She said it was big enough for all of us. We're having sautéed mushrooms, tossed salad, and a cantaloupe she bought at the Farmer's Market too."

"That sounds great. I'll see if she needs a hand."

Wearing an apron and standing by the stove with a large fork in her hand, Mom faced Elaine. "I thought I heard you drive up." She eased the steak over with the fork; the huge cut of beef sizzled and hissed when its unseared side hit the hot cast-iron pan.

The delicious aroma rising from the pan made Elaine's mouth water. "Can I help with the salads?"

"I tried to get your dad to do it. He said it's bad enough eating salads all the time without having to make them too."

At the sink, Elaine washed her hands. "Joe's already turned renegade on me, Dad. You better behave, or Mom and me will move into my house and you'll have to cook and clean for yourself."

Dad sat at the table with the local newspaper. "Have you talked to him this week?"

"I thought about calling him but didn't." Elaine dried her hands with a paper towel. "He didn't call. I wouldn't have answered if he had. He needs to take our engagement seriously enough to respect my feelings. After all, he's spending an entire week in the same hotel with a gorgeous woman."

Mom turned the steak again. "When your dad told me about all that, his face turned red. You might not like what I'm going to say, but I'm going to take Joe's side in this mess."

"Why's that? You know how men are when a pretty woman walks by, they about break their necks looking. Dad probably does the same thing."

Dad lowered the paper. "Hey now, I'm the one who took your side, remember?"

"Confession time," Elaine said. "Do you or don't you look at women when they walk by?"

Mom cleared her throat. "Listen to you, putting your own father on the spot. I can only imagine how you treated Joe over a simple kiss. After all, he stopped it right away, didn't he?"

"He should have told her he was engaged. That would have stopped any kissing."

"You're being mighty judgmental, young lady. If your dad glances at an attractive woman occasionally, it doesn't mean anything. We're human, so we fail. I've checked out a nice piece of beefsteak now and then myself." She winked. "I don't mean in the supermarket either. That doesn't mean I'd cheat on you dad."

Elaine shook her head. "My own mother, a floozy. I'd never have believed it."

Dad chuckled. "You've never heard her in the bedroom, when we're—"

"Jimmy Johnson!" Mom pointed the fork at him. "Not another word, she's traumatized enough as it is." She faced Elaine. "Honey, Joe loves you. He won't sleep with that woman. I say that because I've trusted him ever since I met him. There's something about him … a presence that seems wise beyond his years. I know you trust him too, or you would've broken off the engagement."

"'A presence that seems wise beyond his years?' That big kid?"

"You both act like big kids when you're together—that's a good thing. If you're that happy now, your marriage will always be fresh and new, like on your honeymoon."

Dad winked. "Listen to her, honey, she knows what she's talking about." He rose from the table to step over and slip his arm around Mom's shoulders. "I remember our honeymoon, Nor, don't you? I hope our bride-to-be doesn't throw Joe's back out like you did mine when—"

"Dad, please!"

Dad returned to the table and patted the chair next to him. "Come on over, this conversation hasn't ended yet. Your mom won't mind making the salads."

Elaine did as he asked. "Are you taking her side now?"

"Hear that tone, Nor? Reminds me of the time— Heck, there were lots more times than one. Anyway, honey, your mom made me see how, in the grand scheme of things, like with life and love, and like the love you and Joe have, this is a bump in the garden of life. You two will get over it and grow and flourish, like in the garden too, okay?"

Mom placed a foil covered plate on the table. "I'll let this rest while I make the salads." She sat beside Elaine. "After I say this. Elaine?"

Elaine didn't face her, or answer her.

"And here I was, thinking you'd lost that stubborn streak a long time ago. Look at me when I'm talking to you, this is important."

Elaine's eyes moistened. They were treating her like a child. Why couldn't they understand how Joe had betrayed her? He'd made absolutely no attempt to listen when she'd asked him not to go to Belgium with Jillian. She raised her head, and tears ran down her cheeks. "I don't want to lose him, Mom, but ..." Mom slipped her arms around her, and Elaine cried like when she'd been a young girl who'd lost her first pet: a Beagle pup that had run into the pasture and died when a bull trampled it.

Dad rubbed her back while Mom stroked her hair. "Of course you don't want to lose him, but" —she placed her hands on Elaine's cheeks and lifted her face— "that's up to you more than it is him. You only have two choices—love him or not. If you choose the latter ..."

"I know, Mom, I know." Elaine sat up and plucked a napkin from the holder. "He might be as hurt as I am now. If he is, he might run straight into Jillian's arms."

"I hadn't thought of that," Dad said. "I know how much it would've hurt me if your mom broke our engagement way back when. That would've been an awful lot of hurt to bear by myself." He grinned. "Yep, I'd have run straight into Myrtle Swanson's arms for sure."

"Oh, please, Jimmy, have you seen her lately? She's thin as a rail, probably can't cook a lick."

"Good thing we stayed together then." Dad gave Elaine another napkin. "Come on, honey, you're not gonna let that happen, are you?"

Elaine threw the balled-up napkins on the table. "And miss the chance to break Joe's back on our honeymoon?"

"'Throw out' his back, not break. Your mom rubbed out the kinks and had me back in the tractor seat the next night."

"You worked during your honeymoon, and at night?"

Mom left for the refrigerator. "That's farm-speak. It's what we say instead of 'back in the saddle,' like cowboys do."

"Cowgirls too," Dad said.

"Did you have horses back then?" Elaine said. "I don't get it."

"How much did I spend on your education?" Dad said. "Think about—"

"I got it, I got it." Elaine shook her head again. "With all this 'back-throwing-out,' as well as 'tractor riding'—whatever you want to call it—how did I end up as an only child?"

"Because," Mom said, bringing over the salads, "I'd have killed your poor dad if we'd wanted more than you."

* * *

After supper, Elaine helped Mom with the dishes while Dad, out on the deck, alternated between adding ice and rock salt and turning the crank on the ancient ice cream freezer. Homemade strawberry ice cream, what a treat.

Elaine rinsed a glass. "Why doesn't he buy an electric freezer? That old thing reminds me of a wooden barrel like the one in the corner at the hardware store, but a lot smaller. Is it sanitary?"

Mom gave her a sideways glance. "Do you think I'd put my ice cream mix in that thing if it wasn't safe? Besides, the inside is stainless steel."

"An electric one would be a lot easier."

"You don't get it, do you?"

Elaine huffed. "I guess I don't get much of anything, Mom. What am I missing?"

"Your cheeks are getting red. They always do that when—"

"Fine, don't tell me." Elaine took a dish from Mom, who strode to the table and sat.

"You need to cool off, young lady. I realize you've got a lot going on, but I won't be on the receiving end of your attitude."

Shame stung Elaine. She rarely snapped at anyone like that, especially not her parents. The issue with Joe was causing it, of course, causing too much of her sadness, anger, and confusion about how to handle it. She sat beside Mom. "I'm sorry. Will you tell me what I don't get about that ratty old ice cream freezer?"

"Your first taste of ice cream came from that freezer. That's the most important reason we keep using it. Also, I like how he gets a bit of exercise when he cranks it, and I think he does too. Whenever we use it—which isn't as often as when you were little—I'll catch him poking his bicep later."

"I understand that about me, that's sweet. Anything else?"

"I realize we're well into the twentieth century. We have smart phones, tablets, laptops, the internet. Electric cars will probably be the next rage, followed by personal single-engine aircraft. Anyway, your dad, since he works with his hands like farmers, thinks of himself as a man of the earth. Like with farmers, his job can be hard one day and easy the next. You know how it is with farmers, there's nothing easy about that life."

Mom went to the door, and Elaine followed. Dad glanced at them and smiled. Elaine returned the smile and waved. "He looks happy."

"Because, like the working men and women of this world, he's doing something for us."

"Is that it?"

"Think about it ... good men and women—potentially great husbands and wives, fathers and mothers—are happiest when they're doing something for those they love. Isn't that why Joe took that job and went to Belgium with Jillian?"

Elaine held back a smirk. "I wish you wouldn't say her name."

"Since Joe might see her on the job from time to time, you might as well get used to it if you marry him." Mom took her by the arms. "You are, aren't you? Why don't you give him a call?"

Elaine pulled away. "I can't. Every time I think about him, all I see is his lips touching some other woman's lips. If I *ever* meet her ..."

Mom returned to the sink. "You'll do nothing. Your dad and I didn't raise you to believe in violence, if that's what you mean. Besides, you can't get married while you're in jail for assault."

"You wouldn't bail me out?"

"How would you learn your lesson? Don't you teach the kids at school how they have to be responsible for their actions?"

Elaine said nothing. If anyone should call anyone, Joe should call her. After all, he's the one who left. Then again, like she'd already decided, she wouldn't answer him anyway.

Chapter 21

Done in the bathroom, Joe opened the blinds. The morning sun lit the street outside. What a great day to visit the Ardennes American Cemetery.

The visit should go even better because the sexual tension between he and Jillian had faded. Bathroom doors remained closed when in use, pajamas and sweat pants and tops replaced hotel robes, and no one smiled suggestively, touched inappropriately, or called anyone anything other than their given name. From time to time, Joe was tempted to tease Jillian by calling her 'lover,' but he didn't because it might upset her like it had when she'd been afraid they were destined to make love, like the old woman had predicted.

He tapped the adjoining door they now kept closed when one or the other might be undressed. "Are you up yet, Jillian? I'd like to have breakfast and get going." She didn't answer, so he tapped harder. "Rise and shine, farm girl."

A muffled groan came from the other room.

"I'll take that as meaning you shouldn't have had those four glasses of wine with dinner last night." He tapped the door again. "Are you okay in there?" She groaned again. He tried the door, found it unlocked, and stuck his head inside. "Jillian?"

"Over here." Her weak voice came from the direction of her bed. "I'm not feeling well."

Joe went to the bed. "What's wrong?"

"My stomach. I think it was those mussels I tried. You tried a couple, what did they do to you?"

"That's what that was? I burped a lot. They were worse the second time."

"You should"—Jillian burped— "taste them when you throw them up."

Joe pulled over a chair from the desk and sat. "Can I do anything?"

She attempted a weak smile. "You could have held my hair while I barfed my guts up." She puckered. "How 'bout a kiss instead?"

"Always the joker, even when you're sick."

"You bring it out in me. I managed a few swallows of water, but there's no way I can go with you."

"Maybe you'll feel better after lunch."

Jillian's cheeks bulged as she burped. "You really know the right thing to say, don't you? Go ahead, I'll be fine. Besides, between the rain since Wednesday and our schedule at Organiks, this is the best chance you've had to visit the cemetery all week. You don't want to come all this way and not see it, do you?"

Joe couldn't stand the thought of not visiting the cemetery, especially since he'd taken this trip against Elaine's wishes for both the job and to visit the cemetery. The mystery of discovering what might be buried in his great-grandpa's—or his—grave made his decision for him.

"Is it hard to find?"

"There's a bus that goes five times a day. It'll take you right there."

"You're the best, you know that?"

"No, farm boy, Elaine's the best. Still, if you ever find yourself available ..."

Joe stood from the chair. "Feel better, okay? You want to be in decent shape for the trip home tomorrow."

"What I want is to feel better for dinner. That steak you had last night looked great."

"It was. I'm glad I only tried two of those mussels of yours. I would've wasted a good meal otherwise." Joe went to the adjoining door. "I think I saw a pamphlet about that bus you mentioned in the lobby downstairs. I'll grab one on the way to breakfast, see you later."

In the lobby, Joe stopped at a rack of tourist brochures and located the bus schedule to the cemetery. His excitement concerning what possible discoveries might await drew him along like Christmas morning drew him down the stairs at four a.m. when he was a kid.

After a breakfast of scrambled eggs, light and crusty homemade rolls, and savory local sausages, a five-minute walk through the cool morning air, fresh and clean with the aroma of the Meuse River rolling by, brought him to the bus stop. Since this was the first ride to the cemetery for the day, the bus only carried an elderly couple and a much younger couple. The older couple spoke English—clearly American—while the younger couple spoke French.

The route paralleled the slightly off-color Meuse as it wound through Liège for the first few minutes of the ride. Then the road crossed a railroad yard that must've had a dozen tracks, many with freight cars as well as empty flatbed cars staged in the distance. Entering the countryside, the bus took a long, wide curve, and the centrifugal force pulled Joe to one side.

The remainder of the trip consisted of a tree-lined road with scattered homes and shops, a large complex of hotels, and a section of the Université de Liège. Joe took the pamphlet from his pocket to check the travel time but put it back when the air brakes hissed as the bus slowed and turned right. A low, white stone wall stretched about fifty feet on either side of two opened black-metal gates that looked to be about ten feet tall, and the bus passed through.

The driver parked. Joe and his fellow passengers exited. Ahead, at the end of a wide concrete walkway, the white surface of a huge building gleamed in the sunlight, and Joe, awestruck, swallowed. He'd researched this hallowed ground on the internet—the final resting place of exactly 5,329 Americans who gave their all, not only for their country but for the world. Still, he hadn't been prepared for the full effect of actually being in the presence of the final remains of those brave souls.

The size and scale of the huge building hadn't been apparent on the internet either. Sculpted into the limestone façade, an eagle of at least thirty feet tall spread its wings. Alongside it to the right, two similarly sculpted figures stood—both female and about twenty feet tall. Between the eagle and the women, another woman knelt, holding a sword beside her. Opposite them, on the left side, two rows of sculpted stars lined the lower section of the building: one row of six with another row of seven beneath them.

Joe continued toward the building. A few feet away, the elderly couple walked. "I sure am glad I made it back," the man said. "I've been wanting to see this place for so long now, I didn't think I'd ever make it."

The woman patted the man's arm she was holding. "I'm glad too."

They silently approached the building, which sat in the center of a platform of what Joe assumed was limestone also, with seven steps on all sides. He wanted to walk around the entire structure and take a look at the tablets engraved with the names of the missing, but he'd do that later. According to the information on the website, there was supposed to be a staff member inside answering visitor questions. He opened one of the double doors, held it while everyone stepped in, and left the warm morning sun for the cool of the huge stone building.

Equally awe-inspiring, the walls, covered with marble and brass inlay depicting battle maps of the entire European World War II campaign, reached almost as high as the outside. At the far end of the room above a white marble altar, a guilt metal angel hung from the wall.

While the elderly couple spoke with what appeared to be an Army chaplain, almost as old as the couple themselves, Joe studied the maps and the angel. They thanked him for his help and left, and Joe approached the man. "I realize it might be a stretch, but my grandpa visited here back around 2001. He and his step-father's wife buried my great-grandma's ashes in the same grave as my great-grandpa."

"Would you like me to escort you to the grave?" the chaplain asked. "All I need is the name."

"I'll look first. I was wondering if there were any records of what might've been in the chest with my great-grandma's remains. Grandpa mentioned something about it but never said exactly what."

"Couldn't you have asked him, or— I'm sorry, has he passed away, and that's why …?"

"I got sidetracked with a few things and completely forgot about it," Joe admitted. "One of those things was the surprise of coming here due to work. I recently asked my girl to marry me too, so …"

"I'm sorry," the chaplain said. "We don't keep records of what family members might've placed with—" A flash of what Joe assumed was recognition crossed the chaplain's face, and Joe held his breath. "Could I have your name?" the chaplain asked.

Joe offered his hand. "I'm Joe Matthan." The chaplain took Joe's hand, and a spark of energy similar to static electricity passed between then.

He released his hand. "I'm Chaplain Mulhaney. I imagine you'd like to know why I wanted to know your name. Is Joe short for Joseph?"

"It is. Does that help you remember anything?"

"Your last name certainly did. If it had been different, I likely wouldn't have recalled a thing. After all, that was about twenty years ago. Matthan … you and your grandfather and great-grandfather have a rare last name. There's only one Matthan buried here. I recall that day because I attended your great-grandmother's service."

Joe's insides shook with nervous energy, including that strange spark he'd experienced a moment ago. Was he about to have all of his questions concerning his past answered? "I'm glad to hear it, sir. As far as what was in the chest …?"

"The lady and I spoke about it. I believe her name was Ruth. Since that was twenty years ago, I suppose she's no longer with us."

"You're right," Joe said. "Ruth died of heart problems a year later."

"I'm sorry to hear it." The Chaplain smiled. "Ruth was a very memorable lady. She told me to call her Ruth instead of Mrs. Bauer. She said she and the lady whose remains were being laid to rest had been best friends. The ceremony was extremely hard on her and your grandfather. The tears flowed freely that day, I can tell you. During those ceremonies we have a service member from the same military branch as the fallen attend. A young Private with the Army was with us, and even he cried. I've never known that to happen—before or since—and I've attended more than my share of those services."

"That's interesting about the Private," Joe said. "My grandpa never told me about that. What did Ruth tell you about the chest, or rather, what she placed within it?"

"I saw everything," the chaplain said. "She placed a letter in the chest and said it was written from Mrs. Bauer to Private Matthan. That'd be the lady whose ashes were in the chest, not Ruth."

"Could my great-grandpa's dog tags have been in the envelope?"

"Ruth told me your grandfather wanted them as a keepsake."

Disappointment filled Joe. "I sure wish I hadn't forgotten to ask him. Was there anything else you know of, anything other than the letter?"

The chaplain rubbed his brow. "Seems there was something else. My memory isn't what it used to be. Whatever it was, it was extremely personal to both Private Matthan and your great-grandmother. Since she wanted to be buried with him, I can only imagine—" He snapped his fingers. "I recall one thing. Ruth mentioned placing a few pictures with the letter, pictures that your great-grandfather had with him when he was killed."

"I guess they were pictures of my great-grandma."

The Chaplain's brow furrowed, and he rubbed it again. "No, now that I think of it, I believe they were pictures of both of them. Yes, that's right. Ruth said one of them was taken at a river and one was when they got married. The last one was at the train station, when he was about to leave for boot camp." He paused. "Oh, and she was giving him a yellow ribbon."

The chaplain hesitated; his face changed from his glad-he-remembered smile to a sad frown.

"What is it?" Joe asked.

"Ruth said this last thing was very upsetting. You see, until she called here, no one involved with arranging the ceremony considered searching for Private Matthan's personal belongings, like the pictures or the dog tags, but after that ..."

"Where were those things kept?" Joe hardly believed something so important could be forgotten.

"They're usually sent home with the deceased. Since your great-grandfather's family chose to have him interred here, it's possible that issue was overlooked."

"Where were they kept?" Joe took a breath. He couldn't stay here all day, and he wanted to see the grave and look over the grounds and the outside of the building.

The chaplain stepped closer. "Can I tell you something in the strictest of confidence?"

"As long as it helps me find out what's in that chest."

"Since I'm retired Army, it's not like I'll get in a jam. I'd still appreciate you not telling anyone."

"Don't worry, I won't."

"The Army managed to lose some of those personal items during the interim between the burials and when this site was officially dedicated in 1960. They're now stored in a classified location and brought here when a similar request is made, such as the one made by Ruth."

"I'll forget all that right now," Joe said, glad he was about to learn a vital clue about his death in 1944. "What's that item?"

"The same yellow ribbon your great-grandmother gave Private Matthan in that picture at the train station."

"How could that be as upsetting as Ruth said?"

"Because it was stained with your great-grandfather's blood."

Joe took a step back from the chaplain. "I didn't know anything about that ribbon. Since my grandpa—who's my great-grandpa's son—saw the ribbon, I understand why it'd upset him too. He has the dog tags. Is there anything else?"

"That's it. I'm glad to meet you. I'm always glad to meet any descendants of those who served our country and are at rest here. This is a very special place."

Joe glanced around the building's interior. "I'd better go see if I can find that grave."

From a nearby table, the chaplain took a brochure from a holder and opened it. "Here's a map. The cemetery is in the shape of a Greek cross. It's a bit over ninety acres, so you might need the map. If I remember correctly, the grave is over by what's known as the Youth Statue, just to the right of it in one of the last two or three rows."

Joe accepted the brochure. "I appreciate all your help. Thanks for your service also. I'm sure you're a comfort to the visiting families." He started toward the rear exit but stopped.

"What is it?" the chaplain asked.

"I told you about getting engaged. If I can work it out, I might come back for my honeymoon."

"I'd be glad to meet your young lady. I imagine she's very special."

"She sure is. Let me see if I can find that grave."

Outside, the enormity of the ninety-plus acre cemetery caused Joe to appreciate the chaplain giving him the brochure. Over five thousand white crosses in row upon row, shaped in the Greek cross like the chaplain had said, gleamed in the mid-morning sun. At the far end, a flagpole towered, flying the red, white, and blue United States flag. What an awe-inspiring sight.

Joe made his way down the steps and continued along the center walkway that ran the length of the headstones.

The day couldn't be more beautiful. The sun shined bright in a cloudless blue sky, and a slight breeze stirred the aroma of freshly mown grass.

At the center of the cemetery, where he needed to turn right, he paused to look around. The young French couple had stopped at a grave near the center of the section to the left. The man knelt by a cross while the women held a camera. The elderly American couple were doing the same thing, but near the location where Joe was headed.

He walked toward the Youth Statue the chaplain mentioned. Instead of turning to the right and searching for his—or his great-grandpa's—grave, he continued to within an arm's length of the statue. Made of bronze and holding a sword and a wreath, the figure was of a young man who symbolized American youth. Joe slowly shook his head. If his body from the past lie in the grave here, he'd been killed at eighteen, in the prime of his young life as symbolized by the statue before him. War … what a waste of so many good people all over the world … people with dreams of life with families and loved ones. Why did some so-called leaders choose war over peace, death over life, and tragedy instead of hope?

He returned to the last rows of crosses, turned between the final row and the next, and continued until he found the name.

Joseph S. Matthan

PFC, 106th Infantry Div., Nebraska

Dec. 17, 1944

Sucking in a huge, wheezing breath, Joe almost fell to his

knees. The grave was really here, exactly as Grandpa and Ruth had described. He reached out a trembling hand and drew it back. That tingle he'd experienced when he shook hands with the Chaplain … what might happen if he touched this gleaming white cross? Anything? Nothing? Would his past fall upon him with the weight of his previous life as well as his present life?

He reached again but hesitated. If he were really his great-grandpa re-born, how would knowing that affect him? More importantly, how might it affect him and Elaine? If it were true and he could prove it, either here or later when he managed to hold the dog tags like the man in the story on the internet, would he regret that knowledge, or would it bring him and Elaine closer like he hoped it would?

Joe couldn't be sure of any of that without knowing his past first. After that, and after he talked it over with Elaine and convinced her to search for the same answers, possibly through some of the same physical connections he'd experienced, he'd find out then.

He reached toward to cross again, with fingers as steady and unwavering as his will to finally know the truth about himself. Would he receive the same slight shock he'd received from the chaplain's handshake? He touched the stone with one fingertip and felt nothing but warmth from the sun. He placed his hand on the top of the cross and closed his eyes to wait, and waited … and waited … and waited.

Nothing … absolutely nothing.

Hadn't there been a small rug beside the table when he and the chaplain had shaken hands? Joe rubbed his wrinkled forehead. That was probably where the static spark had originated. What an idiot he was, thinking he'd have some kind of revelation by simply touching this stone cross. What he needed was to get his hands on that letter and the ribbon stained with his own blood—if it *were* his own blood. Could he sneak in here in the middle of the night with a shovel and— No, that was just another idiotic idea that would land him in jail.

What could he—

The dog tags! What if he could bring them back and ask to have them buried with Elaine's ashes and bring Elaine with him? When she read the letter, saw the pictures, and held the ribbon, which was bound to hold memory after memory, including the pain of his death, couldn't all that emotion filling those objects make her remember their past lives together?

Joe knelt by the cross and traced the engraved letters with his fingertips exactly as Grandpa had said he'd done. "I'm not sure who you are down there … if you're me and if I'm you … but I'll find out." He touched his fingers to his lips and placed them to the stone. "I'll find out the truth about you too, Elaine. I can't imagine what you went through when you found out I wasn't coming home. If I can make up for it by coming home to you again, I plan on doing exactly that." Joe stood. "But first you've got to let me come back to you in *this* life."

At the memorial, the elderly couple had climbed the steps to the raised podium surrounding the main building, and they were reading one of the twelve slabs of dark gray granite with the engraved names of the missing in action. Joe climbed the steps, neared one of the slabs of granite, and the old man—his wife had called him Elmer during the bus ride—came over. "Hey there, young fella, you look a lot like that statue." He pointed a gnarled finger. "The one the brochure says is called Youth."

"I don't know about that, sir, but thanks. It's a shame so many young men and women service members had to die in a war that should have never happened."

"Civilians too. If you don't mind me saying so, you looked

pretty intense out there when you were kneeling by that cross. A family member of yours?"

"My great-grandpa. I read in the brochure that eleven sets of brothers are buried side by side here."

"Yep." Elmer glanced in the copy of his own brochure. "792 of those crosses mark the graves of men who couldn't be identified either. Imagine the family back home never knowing for sure what happened to a loved one."

"I agree. Nice talking to you, but I want to get a look at these inscriptions."

Elmer took a chain from his pocket." Got something I'd like to show you before you go." A set of dog tags hung from the chain, glinting in the sun. "These are my brother's." He gave Joe a slight smile. "Much as I miss him, I'm glad I'm not beside him, if you know what I mean. He was ten years older than me. Did the folks here give yours" —Elmer shook his head— "I mean your great-grandad's dog tags to his family back then?"

"My grandpa has them. I'll read a few of these names and get back to town."

Joe read several more of the names on the granite slabs and caught the bus back to Liège. On the way, he made a mental list of everything he had to pack for the trip home in the morning.

Off the bus, he stopped at a store for a gift for Mom and Dad, and Elaine too. Inside the shop specializing in glassware, he studied the fragile items. Whatever he bought, he'd have to make sure they were wrapped well for the flight home. He chose a beer glass for Dad and a candle holder for Mom, but rubbed his forehead while searching for something for Elaine. The entire store seemed devoid of an item she might like—until Joe walked by the front window. The sun glittered on a small, white vase with raised daffodils on its lower, larger surface that narrowed at the neck and flared again at the opening. This would be perfect. It could hold the daffodils she loved so well, and more than enough grew at the river. Purchases paid for and wrapped and bagged, he headed to the hotel.

Elaine hadn't called, not even a text, but he hadn't expected her to since she'd been so mad. How might her week be going? Would she be working on the house, buying more furniture, and maybe, just maybe, thinking about him?

Who knew, but he'd find out soon.

Chapter 22

Done scrubbing the floors, Elaine threw out the dirty water and sat at the kitchen table with a glass of iced tea. On the table, her phone played Mom's Elvis song.

"Hi, Mom."

"Hi yourself. Did our ice cream last night ever cool you off?"

"If you called to remind me about our argument, I'd rather not go over it again."

"Maybe I should bring more ice cream when I pick you up to visit Uncle Thomas. I'm sure he'd love a visit."

Elaine wanted to keep busy working on the house—both to get the work done and to keep her mind off of Joe—but seeing Uncle Thomas might get her mind off Joe too.

"What time?"

"Look out your front door."

"You're already here?"

"Isn't that what 'look out your front door' means?"

"It's unlocked. I need to change clothes."

Wearing clean jeans and a blouse, Elaine left the bedroom to find Mom standing in the hall. "Have you heard anything from Joe? I was wondering because—"

"No, Mom. Since he went on that trip regardless of my wishes, it's obvious he thinks I'm in the wrong and I should call him."

"If you had that snippy attitude with him during your argument, I don't blame him for getting away from you for a week. You should know marriages are about compromise."

"That explains it—we're not married."

"You're not likely to get married either if you keep this up. Let's go."

Outside of town, Mom glanced at Elaine. "Do you think that daughter of mine who still loves Joe" —she poked Elaine's side— "who's still in there somewhere, might go to his graduation? It's in a week, you know. He supported you by going to yours."

Elaine faced the window. Joe's graduation had completely slipped her mind. They had made so many plans, and now, who knew what might happen.

"I'm not sure."

"He'll be devastated if you don't."

"Like I was when he went to Belgium? With that … that …"

"Don't you dare call that young woman a bad name. You don't know a thing about her, and she's someone's daughter too. Joe admitted to not telling her about your engagement, so it's not all her fault."

"She better keep her hands to herself. If I find out different, I'll—"

"You'll behave. Remember what your dad said about not bailing you out?"

Elaine said nothing. A night in jail might be worth it.

"Look at me, Elaine. A woman who's willing to fight for her man sounds like a woman who's still in love with her man. If you two don't talk before his graduation, it might be a good time to make up."

Mom turned into the rest home and parked near the wing where Uncle Thomas lived. "I'll leave you alone for now. Let's go have a nice visit with your great-uncle."

Elaine followed Mom through the double doors and into the facility. The medicinal aroma reminded her of a hospital or a doctor's office.

She enjoyed visiting Uncle Thomas on his good days, but walking through these white halls, usually scattered with elderly men and women sitting in wheel chairs in various states of sleep or wakefulness, saddened her if she allowed it.

And it was hard not to allow it.

An old woman stood by a window; her chin almost rested on her chest. Gray eyes followed Elaine. Wisps of white hair barely covered her scalp. Wrinkles etched the corners of her eyes as if she'd squinted her entire life. Did she think Elaine might be a daughter come to visit, or a best friend, or an elementary school playmate?

Rounding a corner, Elaine nearly stepped on the sock feet of an old man pulling himself along the hall in a slow-motion shuffle in a wheelchair. He smiled with pink gums. "My, my, you're a pretty young gal." His voice squeaked as if it were the barn door at home that needed oiling. "Could you roll me to where the finches are?"

Mom stopped. "Why not? Their cage is on the way."

"I'm sure glad they brought them here for us to watch," the man said as Elaine pushed the wheelchair down the hall. "Most are yellow but some are red and blue. They remind me of the candy my folks used to put in my stocking at Christmas."

Elaine said nothing. Maybe her mood would lighten when she saw Uncle Thomas, as long as he didn't confuse her with his sister, who was Joe's great-grandma. Even when lucid he constantly remarked on how alike his sister and Elaine were, from their hair to their eyes, even to their carefree personality. Unfortunately, her cares were anything but free because of Joe.

She and Joe were distantly related, but she'd never attempted to figure out exactly *how* they were related, and since neither her nor Joe's parents had made an issue of it, Joe included, she hadn't considered it important either. Maybe Mom had figured it out.

"Mom, do you have any idea how Joe and I are related? He's my great-aunt Elaine's great-grandson, and she's Thomas's sister. That's means we're what, third cousins?"

"It does. Once, when all of us were at the river having a cookout, your dad and I talked with Al and Anne about it. You and Joe were down by the river."

"Why were you talking about it?"

"Just curious. Why, are you looking for a reason to not marry him? If so, that's not good enough. Third cousins are too far apart to worry about."

Not caring to continue discussing her and Joe's relationship any further, Elaine said nothing.

Mom nudged her hip with hers. "I'll take this gentleman to see the birds while you go visit Thomas. I want to talk to his doctor too, if he's here today."

Elaine stepped aside, Mom took her place, and the old man looked up at them. "I sure feel special. Got all kinds of pretty ladies willin' to push me around." He chuckled. "I mean that in a good way, ya know."

At Thomas's room, Elaine knocked and went in. She found him sitting in a recliner in the corner while a TV hanging from the wall at the end of his bed blared. He pulled his attention away from the TV. "Well look here, my great-niece has come to see me. Have a seat, Lainey. I'll turn that noise-box off. Nothin' worth a hoot on anyway."

Elaine hugged him. His sweatshirt held the same medicinal aroma of everything here, and his whiskered cheek scratched hers as she pulled away. She took a chair across from him. "How've you been, Uncle Thomas?"

"Oh, I'm hangin' in there. At my age—" He frowned. "Doggone, just how old am I this year? Heck fire, what year is it anyway?" He waved the questions away. "Never mind, as long as I can breathe and have my family visit me, I'm good to go."

"Have you been out of your room today?"

"Had breakfast and puttered around. How's that beau of yours? You make him an honest man yet?"

Elaine held in a smirk. That remained to be seen, but she'd darn well see when he returned from Belgium. Then again, would she be ready to see him? Not likely.

Thomas cleared his throat. "Mighty deep in thought there, Lainey. Whatcha got on your mind? I could always tell when something was bothering you, ya know. When Joe died in that damned war— 'scuse my language—I wondered if you'd ever recover. Thank goodness that German fella Kurt showed up. I know how much you loved Joe, but Kurt was as good a husband to you and a daddy to Joseph as a man could be."

Elaine never knew how to answer the questions that came when Thomas slipped into the past. She usually played along, since not doing so might upset him.

"That was a tough time for Joseph and me. We're doing fine now." She glanced at her watch. The attendants normally offered snacks around one. She looked up. Thomas had nodded off.

The story of Joe's great-grandma, Elaine, who married Kurt after Joe was killed in the war, was well known in both families, including how Elaine herself was named after her. As amazing as her marrying a German who'd fought against the United States in the war had been, it was even more amazing that the 1944 Joe and Elaine had only been married one day before he had to catch a train in Holdrege, back to what had been Fort Leavenworth in Kansas, where he'd trained before heading to Europe. If not for their single honeymoon night, the current Joe, including his dad and his grandpa, would've never existed.

Elaine's eyes filled with tears. She couldn't imagine Joe never existing. She swiped the tears away. Since that was the case, why couldn't she get over their argument and all the reasons behind it?

Thomas moaned and raised his head from his chest. "Hey there, Lainey. I must have been snoozing and didn't see you sneak in. Have I seen you since you and Joe sang at church? I sure enjoyed that." He paused to glance out the window. "You've heard me talk about my sister. You know you're named after her, right? A few years after Joe died, she started singing in church. Boy did she have a set of pipes. You sound exactly like her." He covered a cough. "Can you run 'round the corner and fetch me a bottle of water? I'm as parched as a dried-out wheat field."

Elaine did as he asked, glancing down the aisle for Mom. With her nowhere in sight, she returned to Thomas's room to open the bottle. He took several swallows and placed the bottle on a nearby table. "Mmm, that hit the spot. Tell me now, since you and Joe are getting hitched, have you two set a date?"

Elaine tried not to frown. No matter where she was or who she was with, there was no escaping the topic of her and Joe. "We haven't talked about it yet. He still has to graduate too."

"Didn't I hear you tell the minister you wanted to rent his house, the one he bought when Ruth passed on?"

"How'd you hear that? I thought you were asleep."

Thomas grinned. "Oh, I have my good days and bad days. That was a good day. When I'm having a good day, I can remember more than on those bad days."

Elaine patted his leg. "I'm glad you have good days."

"Me too, Lainey, me too. It's gonna be a good day when you and Joe get married. I can feel it in my creaking old joints." Thomas clapped his hands. "I know, let's have the weddin' at the river. That'd be a fine place to honor my sister's and Joe's memory. It'd almost be like they were there instead of over in Belgium in that cemetery."

Elaine didn't answer. Before her and Joe's argument, she'd considered having the wedding at the river. Now, with everything up in the air, who knew where, when, or even *if* there might be a wedding.

"There you go again," Thomas said, "off in la-la land. I ever tell you how much you and Joe remind me of my sister and Joe from back in 1943? Sure, I was only a sixteen-year-old kid with fishin' on my mind, but I knew love when I saw it. I never had any idea a boy and a girl could fit together so perfect. I think I heard Dad say it was like all the holidays was wrapped up in one when you two—I mean those two—was together." Thomas paused for a swallow of water. "You and Joe are just like that, ya know?"

"I … yes, that's how we are. Well, for the most part." Elaine stood. "Mom's here, I'll see if I can find her. I'll be right back."

Thomas picked up the TV remote. "Tell her to bring me a candy bar. My sweet tooth's actin' up."

Instead of looking for Mom, Elaine hurried down a side hall that led to an outdoor gazebo. Taking a seat, she didn't know whether to cry or smile. Thomas's words had brightened her day but had saddened her also. Of course she believed she and Joe were meant to be together, exactly like their 1940's counterparts were meant to be together. She'd never believed otherwise since meeting him. Their overnight romance—as much of a romance as two twelve-year-olds could have—had seemed as natural as breathing. From that moment on they'd texted, video chatted on their laptops, and had their parents drop one or the other off at one or the other's home on Saturday morning. Usually she'd go to Joe's house, where they'd almost always end up at the river.

Although she'd joked with him about their first kiss the last time they were there, she'd instigated it. Naturally, he didn't mind one bit.

Elaine peeked out from under the gazebo's circular roof. When had they discussed not making love until they were married? Try as she might, the answer avoided her like an egg under an old hen pecking a hand. They must've talked about it. If not, how did they always manage to stop when their kissing and touching and groping got to the point of no return? It was almost like they'd made a pact to not go too far no matter what. Whatever. She had enough to worry about now with Joe coming home.

When was that exactly? The week had passed with such a tornado of emotions, it was hard to keep the days and nights straight. No, he would come back Monday because he left last Monday, and the trip was supposed to last a week.

Elaine left the gazebo. At least she would expect him if he showed up on her door step. The last thing she needed was another surprise, and since he'd been away with Jillian all week, any surprises concerning her were *not* welcome.

Chapter 23

In his hotel room after returning from the cemetery, Joe found the adjoining door open and Jillian on her sofa, eating what smelled like chicken soup. In the middle of a spoonful, she swallowed. "They've got the best chicken noodle soup here you'll ever taste if you're hungry."

"It sure smells good." Joe left the brochure on the nightstand by his bed and joined her on the sofa. "You must be feeling better."

"With any luck I'll be able to handle that steak later."

"No wine, okay? I mean for both of us too. We don't want that strange woman's prediction about us making love coming true on our last night together."

Jillian nudged his knee with hers. "Like it'd be so terrible."

Joe returned the nudge. "You sure run hot and cold. Where's the weeping Jillian who vowed to never allow that to happen because she didn't want to be responsible for breaking Elaine and me up?"

"I'm just messing with you" —Jillian gave him a peck on the cheek— "lover."

"You're still too much, but too much of a *good* thing. I'm gonna miss you."

She placed the soup on the table in front of the sofa. "I know what you mean. Do you have any idea how things might go with Elaine when you get home?"

"She still hasn't called or texted, and I'm not. I think she should be the one to break the ice on our frigid engagement. I'm just trying to get a job so we can get married and earn the money for our dream home we planned to build at the river."

"I don't think you mentioned that. It sounds exactly like what I'm looking for." She tapped the tip of his nose. "Don't forget what I said about my being interested if it doesn't work out between you two. Then we can make that old woman's prediction come true."

Joe stood. "I've got some packing to do, Ms. 'Prediction.' I don't want to wait until the last minute."

"I did mine while you were gone. How'd the cemetery visit go?"

"I'll tell you later during dinner. I want to grab a shower for our early start. I'd like to be well-rested and not have a repeat of my flight over here."

Jillian rose from the sofa and ran her fingers through her hair. "I won the shower race too. I love the smell of my honeysuckle shampoo, don't you?"

"You gotta be kidding, right?"

"How so?"

"After our week together, I'll probably smell it the rest of my life."

* * *

Joe swallowed a bite of *carbonade flamande*, a sort of Belgian beef stew. "That's everything I saw at the cemetery."

"What did you think of the Youth Statue?" Jillian sipped water. "I thought he was quite handsome. You know, like a certain farm boy I know."

"That's funny. There was an elderly American couple there. I spoke with the man while his wife read some of those tablets with the names of the missing."

"What's funny about that?"

"He said I reminded him of the statue too. I bet his reason isn't the same as yours."

"Uh-huh. You'll find out *exactly* my reason if Elaine doesn't take you back."

Instead of answering, Joe allowed silence to resume while they ate. As much as he'd enjoyed the trip, especially since it meant he'd soon be starting work at a vocation he loved, he missed home—and Elaine. How could they get past the extremely large bump in their relationship road? He was sure they could, but with her engagement ring on the chain around his neck a constant reminder of their unexpectedly violent argument, he had no idea how that might happen.

"You're mighty deep in thought there, farm boy. Do you think Elaine will attend your graduation?"

"I guess it depends on what happens between now and then."

"Do you want her to come?"

"As long as we get things worked out." Joe sipped water.

"Then I'd better not ..."

Strangling on the water, Joe coughed. "Attend my graduation? I don't think that's a good idea."

"I told you I'm fond of you and I meant it. I'm sure your parents will be there. If she's not coming, someone should be there to give you a sincere hug."

"Mom and Dad will hug me."

Jillian narrowed her impossibly blue eyes. "That's not what I meant and you know it." She placed her hand on his, and its warmth, as well as the warmth of her eyes gazing into his, made him swallow. "Sweet farm boy, I joke a lot, but I also meant what I said. If things don't work out between you and Elaine, I'd love to date you and see what happens."

Joe pulled his hand away. "Jillian, I—"

"Oh, hush. I know you're in love with her, or we'd have spent the entire week in one bed instead of two. I won't bring up the possibility of you and Elaine not working through your troubles again." Jillian glanced out the window toward the Meuse and faced him again. "But I won't stand by as silent as those graves at the cemetery while she makes you miserable either."

"You care that much? Seriously, that is?"

"I told you I'm a good person. Do you doubt it?"

"Not at all. If things don't work out between Elaine and me—I don't see the possibility though—I'll let you know about the graduation."

"Do you think it'll be settled by then?"

"I darn well hope so, but I don't know what kind of nudge she—or we—will need to make that happen."

* * *

Finished with dinner, Joe packed everything except a change of clothes and his bathroom items and knocked on the adjoining door. "You decent in there?"

Jillian opened the door. "Always, lover. What a shame, huh?"

"You need to behave."

"No way, farm boy. We don't have much time left together, and I need to tease you as much as I can before we get back home."

"Then it's a good thing we're going home tomorrow." Joe sat on the sofa. "Thanks for the info on the timeline for the construction of Organiks facility near Alma. That and the definitions on my upcoming job duties will help me get ready a lot faster."

"What do you think of the construction of the Alma facility being delayed and us being co-workers until it's ready?"

"I can deal as long as you stop your teasing."

"No worries, lover. Will the drive to Arapahoe be a problem?"

"The problem is what Elaine will think of us working together."

"No worries again. Once you get your training, most of your work will be studying the effects of Organiks' various experimental all-organic fertilizers on its designated crop type. Since that takes place in the field, we won't see as much of each other as you think."

"If Elaine and me get our problems worked out, she'll be glad to hear that." Joe yawned. "I better get some sleep."

"Me too. We've got a long day tomorrow, and you might have some excitement when you and Elaine see each other again."

Joe stood from the sofa. "No freaking joke. It probably won't be *good* excitement either."

***

Jillian rinsed her toothbrush and left it out for after breakfast in the morning. Joe closed a dresser drawer with a muffled thud, which she heard through the adjoining door she'd shut when he left her room. She'd enjoyed the week—especially her time spent with her sweet farm boy-new hire—but her feelings about returning to life at home were mixed. On one hand, she wished Joe all the happiness he deserved, and if that happiness was with Elaine, so be it. On the other hand, Miss Huffy Pants better get her act together. If not, a certain farm girl from

Arapaho wouldn't stand by and watch him pine over Elaine to the point of throwing his life and job away.

Jillian crawled into bed and pulled the air-conditioned sheet and coverlet over her naked body. How would it feel to have Joe's warmth next to her? No goosebumps from the cold sheet, no doubt. She shook her head and turned out the lamp on the nightstand. That likely would never happen. Closing her eyes, she snuggled into the equally cool pillow, intent on a decent night's sleep.

* * *

Jillian blinked her eyes open and rolled over. The green LEDs on the nightstand clock read two a.m. Her aching bladder informed her she'd drank entirely too much of the restaurants' delicious mineral water with lemon. She climbed out of bed, flipped the room's overhead light on, and hurried to the bathroom.

Instead of returning to bed after, she went to the adjoining door. Was Joe on his phone? Who could he—

Crash!

She opened the door and peeked inside. In the light from her room, Joe was rolling side-to-side in the bed with his arms flailing about. The crash must've been when he knocked the lamp off the stand.

"No … can't … can't. Need to get back. Don't want …" He rolled over again and slammed is hand on the nightstand. "No! No! Got … got to get back!"

How could he stay asleep through all that? Afraid he'd hurt himself, Jillian ran to her bed, jerked the sheet off, and wrapped it around her. He continued rolling about, growing even more violent. She didn't know what to do, but she couldn't let him hurt himself. She stepped closer to hold his arms, but stopped at a scene that broke her heart.

Joe's eyes were clamped shut in an anguished grimace, and tears flowed down his cheeks while he continued to roll back and forth as if he were in a fight for his life.

Jillian hesitated. What could she do?

"No! Can't! Can't!"

Since his rolling and screaming didn't wake him, which meant she couldn't wake him, there was only one thing she could do.

In case he was naked, she pulled back the coverlet, left the sheet over him, and climbed into bed to wrap her arms around him. "Hush, Joe, it's okay, I've got you."

He mumbled a few more words, twitched a few more times, and quieted when she kissed his cheek. What could've given him such a bizarre nightmare? The only reason she could think of was how much he wanted to get back to Elaine, since he'd yelled how he needed to "get back."

His breathing slowed to an even, consistent ebb and flow, the rhythm of sleep, and Jillian held him tighter. "Don't worry, sweet farm boy. I'll make sure you get back to your Elaine."

Chapter 24

Within the haze of wakefulness and sleep, Joe felt an unaccustomed warmth beside him, as well as a gentle, comforting pressure on his chest. If he didn't know any better, Elaine was holding him while they lay on the quilt at the river. What a great dream. He pulled the covers to his chin, allowing the warmth to settle him into sleep and into his dream. Elaine snuggled into his shoulder, and he pulled her closer.

From the sweet aroma of her hair to the softness of her cheek next to his, the dream couldn't be any more real than if it *were* real. "Elaine, I miss you."

"Aw, go on, farm boy, you know you've had all of me you can stand."

Joe snapped upright. Lying beside him with a sheet wrapped around her, Jillian smiled. "Good morning, lover."

"Jillian, what— What are you doing in—"

"Calm down, that old woman's prediction didn't come true."

Joe raised the coverlet. He'd gone to bed naked. At least the sheet kept them separated, and the sheet she was wrapped in covered everything but her feet.

"That's right, lover, I had enough sense to take precautions." Jillian left the bed with the sheet around her and sat in the chair by the desk. "Questions? I'm sure you have plenty."

"Can you get me the robe hanging on the inside of the bathroom door? I need to … you know."

"Uh, huh, that's what woke me too." Jillian retrieved the robe, dragging the sheet along while her tanned legs shown from beneath it. Joe's eyes widened. What exactly had they done last night? If she were lying and they had slept together, how could he not remember?

Jillian gave him the robe and returned to the chair to close her eyes. "Go ahead" —he stood— "but I won't promise not to peek." Joe jerked the robe around himself and she laughed. "Look at you, scared to death I saw you in your naked glory."

"Doggone it, you should know."

"I'm not looking, sweetheart." Jillian traced a cross over her heart. "Farm girl swear."

Joe stopped at the bathroom door. "Okay, so-called farm girl, I'm covered up and going in the bathroom."

She opened her eyes, which crinkled with her familiar mischief. "Go on now, so I can tell you about last night." The crinkles left her eyes. "You scared me half to death, you know. No, you *don't* know. Go ahead. I'll slip on something more appropriate for the conversation we need to have."

"What the heck do you mean by that? You said we didn't— you know."

"We didn't, so watch your tone." Jillian stood to tuck the sheet under her arms and around her breasts. "Scoot before you wet your robe." She whirled and left through the door, closing it behind her on the sheet. "Oops! It's a good thing you're on that side of the door!"

Joe locked the bathroom door behind him. With a woman like Jillian in the room next to him, he couldn't take any chances.

At the toilet he winced. Any longer and he might've wet himself exactly like Jillian had said. He finished and tied the robe, wet a washcloth with cold water and wiped his face and eyes. What had happened last— In the mirror, his reflection's eyes opened wide. A nightmare about him dying? He closed his eyes and concentrated. An explosion bloomed in his mind. Brightness swallowed him while searing bits of impossibly hot *somethings* pierced him from head to toe. Then falling … falling … to land in— Joe opened his eyes. Snow?

A knock came at the bathroom door. "I'm decent."

Joe ran his trembling fingers through his hair. What had he seen? He had to know more, whatever it was, but what would it take to remem—

The dog tags.

"Be there in a minute."

Tell Jillian? Not in a million years. What had she heard during the nightmare? Apparently, she was about to tell him.

Joe reached for the doorknob. A chill ran over his entire body.

I have to believe you'll come back to me, I have to believe you'll come back to me, I have to believe you'll come back to me.

His fingers trembled again. It was as if Elaine had spoken those words, like when she'd said, *Boys are just weak. That's the way you are.*

At the sink once more, he ran cold water on the washcloth and pressed it to his face, neck, and eyes. "What the hell is going on with me?"

He wiped his face again and opened the door. Jillian had returned to the chair. Instead of the sheet, she wore pink sweat pants and a top, possibly the same outfit she'd worn when she cried while sitting in his lap.

"Okay, farm boy. I grabbed the sheet and ran in here when I heard and saw you were having a night— Well, I wouldn't call it a nightmare." She pointed. "I looked in because you knocked the lamp off the nightstand."

Joe sat on the bed. "I did that and didn't wake up?"

"Does your hand hurt? You slapped the heck out of the nightstand too."

Joe flexed his fingers. His joints ached like the time he'd smacked a stubborn cow's rump when she wouldn't go all the way into a trailer. "That must have been some nightmare."

"It was, to the point I thought you'd hurt yourself. I had to do something, so ..."

"It worked?"

"You calmed down almost as soon as I wrapped my arms around you." Jillian giggled.

"What the heck's so funny?"

"If Elaine asks you if we slept together, you'll *have* to lie now."

"Not funny. Besides, she won't be talking about sleeping." Joe checked the time on the clock on the nightstand. At least he hadn't knocked that off. "How long were you gonna let me sleep? We barely have enough time to get out of here."

"While you were in the bathroom, I called the airport and managed to get a later flight. I set everything up with Organiks too. Our jet to Kearney Regional will modify its schedule to match."

"You're just a regular tornado of organization, aren't you?"

"I do have an ulterior motive—we can order breakfast here and eat while you tell me about your nightmare. Do you have them that often?"

"Order breakfast first. I need to wake up."

"Okay, okay, I'll leave you alone for now. How about a traditional farm boy—and girl—start for our day? Does eggs over easy, bacon, and hash brown potatoes sound good?"

"Plenty of coffee too."

Jillian stood and winked. "You're reading my mind, sweetheart. I believe that old woman was right about us being soul mates."

"Excuse me, doggone it. She said star-crossed, not soul mates. Watch that 'sweetheart' business while you're at it. Since we'll be working together until the Alma facility is built, our co-workers might get the wrong idea about us if you keep that up."

"True. I rarely like someone enough to call them sweetheart anyway. See how special you are to me?"

Joe grabbed a pillow and threw it at her. "Breakfast! Now!"

* * *

As Joe took a slice of bacon from the plate on the coffee table in Jillian's room, she elbowed his ribs. "I'll miss being here with you. Are you ready to tell me about that nightmare?"

"I don't like cold bacon and eggs, and forget cold coffee."

"I'll tell you what you said. Maybe that'll jog your memory if it needs it. Does it need it?"

"Everything's still fuzzy, except waking up to you snuggling me in nothing but a durn sheet."

Jillian's full lips, now with her familiar light shade of pink lipstick, slowly formed her entirely too-attractive smile. "Glad to hear it. That memory will probably haunt you the rest of your days with Elaine. Maybe you'll even fantasize about me when you and she are—"

Okay, okay, enough of that." Joe crunched the bacon and followed it with coffee. "Go ahead, what the heck did I say?"

"You were extremely dramatic, yelling 'no, no,' and saying something about getting back." Jillian paused. "No, that's not right. You said 'got to get back.' Does any of that help? I imagine you were dreaming about Elaine."

"I guess." Joe declined to offer the parts he'd remembered, about the explosion and falling in the snow. If he told Jillian all that, she might take him to the nearest mental health facility for evaluation. It'd be best to simply allow her to believe the nightmare had been solely about Elaine.

"I guess this whole thing with the engagement has me more worked up than I thought."

"Obviously." Jillian sipped coffee. "Have you given any thought to if she'll come to your graduation?"

"I said I'd let you know. Didn't I say I'd let you know? I know I said—"

"Okay, grumpy. Let's finish eating and get back to Brussels so we can catch our flight." She glanced at her watch. "It's nine here and three in the afternoon at home. Our plane leaves at twelve, so between the flight and the refueling—"

"Don't forget having to practically undress for those security searches. Maybe we should walk through naked to make it faster."

"Now who's teasing?" Jillian asked with a grin. "As much as I'd love to see your buff self completely in the nude, that would be the quickest way to get yourself arrested. Now, as I was saying before you gave me such an intriguing mental picture, since it usually takes fifteen hours to get from Liège to Kearney Regional, that means we'll get home at about—"

"As much as you make this trip, I'd think you'd automatically know when you'd get home."

"Then *you* figure it out, smart aleck." Jillian sighed. "One week together and we're snapping at each other as if we were married for twenty years. Are you sure you don't want to re-think getting married altogether?"

"Would you please just tell me what time it'll be when we get home?"

"I know why we're grumpy, sweetheart. Our sexual frustration is taking over. Can I sit in your lap again?"

"You said you did that because you were upset. So what—"

"Hush. You'd just be that much more frustrated. We should get back around nine tonight, Nebraska time."

"You mean it'll be like three a.m. our time now, right? I hope we can sleep on the plane."

"Me too." Jillian sipped coffee. "I don't think we could stand another night together, meaning we'd have to rent a hotel room to get some rest before driving home."

"We'd have separate rooms."

Jillian kissed Joe's cheek. "And miss out on all the fun? No way, farm boy."

***

Jillian stepped off the Organiks private jet at the Kearney Regional airport. At the bottom of the stairs, she took a deep breath. "Mmm, mm, I can smell that sweet Nebraska air regardless of those jet fumes. No matter how often I make that trip, it's always good to get home."

Beside her, Joe stretched. "I'm glad we got enough rest to drive home. I'm ready for my own bed though."

"You won't see Elaine when you get back?"

"Remember what I said about her being the one to fix this mess? I still feel that way."

"No calls or texts?"

The pilot came to the doorway of the jet. "You two might want to head wherever you're going before I takeoff."

"Good idea." Jillian picked up her carry-on.

Back at their vehicles, after they put their luggage away, she faced Joe. "So, no calls or texts?"

"Not a one. We'll work it out. I'm just not sure how."

Jillian stepped closer. "Joe, I'm sure you know I hope the best for you, but ..." She turned away. He probably thought she'd been joking when she'd told him what she was about to say again. She hadn't—anything but—and he needed to know. Tears stung her eyes, and Joe touched her shoulder.

"Are you okay, farm girl? It's not like you to turn away from me." He eased her around. "Jillian, what—?"

"Aren't I a mess?" She dug a tissue from her purse and wiped her eyes. Thank goodness he waited without saying anything. Eyes reasonably dry, the threat of more tears gone, she glanced around. A single street light illuminated the airport parking lot, empty except for her car and Joe's pickup. She took another step closer and fingered a button on his shirt. "I doubt we'll ever be alone like this again." She surprised herself with a weak laugh. "That's a good thing. The sexual tension between us during this trip has been unbearable, for me anyway." She raised her head to find Joe smiling. "Look at you with your farm boy grin. How will I get by without it?"

"There's lots more farm boys out there willing to make you smile."

"None like you. Do you mind holding me one more time?" Joe pulled her into his arms and rubbed a slow circle between her shoulder blades. She snuggled into him, breathing in his clean, fresh scent from his shower this morning. "I'm not trying to say you and Elaine won't work things out, but do you remember what I said to do if they don't?"

He raised a hand to her head, stroked her hair. "You thought I thought you were joking, didn't you? I knew you weren't."

Jillian pulled away. She had to see those blue eyes up close once more. "That's good to know. So if ...?

"I'll remember."

She gave him a slight smile to keep tucked away near his heart, though not deep inside like she wanted it to be. Tears threatened again, but she swallowed, choking them back. "Could I get a goodbye kiss?" She lowered her head. "I'm sorry. I shouldn't …"

Joe placed his fingers beneath her chin to lift it. When their eyes met, the familiar boyish charm left his face completely, and he transformed into a sad farm boy, with no smile whatsoever. "I won't lie. That sexual attraction about drove me crazy too. That kiss at college, in your hotel room … if it hadn't been for Elaine …" He grinned. "I think you know what would have happened. Not just because of sexual attraction either."

Jillian raised her palm to his smooth-shaven cheek. "I guess that's something. Besides, if we kissed, and if Elaine asks you if we kissed, you'd have to lie. I don't want you to have to lie about us, I want us to part with fond memories." She pulled his face toward her and kissed his cheek. "Oops, I better wipe that lipstick off." She gave him another tissue from her purse.

"Thanks." He scrubbed his cheek, checked the tissue, and scrubbed his cheek again. "I'd never hear the end of it from Mom and Dad if I went home like that." He returned the tissue. "You better take that with you."

She dropped the tissue in her purse. "Maybe I should stop by Elaine's and show it to her. You *did* give me your address, remember?"

"You better be joking, farm girl."

"You know I am."

"Good. I hate to ask, but are we gonna be all right when we work together?"

"Not at all. I'm going to sexually harass you every chance I get." She poked his stomach. "Yes, sweetheart, we'll be okay working together."

He returned the poke. "Just making sure."

"No problem. We better get on home. We have more than an hour to get there as it is."

In the car, Jillian waved to Joe as she drove by. He returned the wave but didn't follow in his pickup. "I see you, farm boy, turning on that phone you left off during the entire trip back home. Miss Elaine better get her big-girl panties on soon. If not, *this* farm girl might have something to say about it."

Yawning as she passed through Holdrege, Jillian pulled over for a soda from a machine. She took a swallow of the fizzy, lemon-lime flavored drink and set it in the car's console. Why not check the address Joe had given her for his and Elaine's house she was currently renting? She found the address, dropped the phone in her purse, and took it back out. Joe had told her his parent's names, so maybe she could find *their* address. She snapped her fingers when it popped up, dropped the phone in her purse, and pulled back out onto the road.

Instead of continuing west on highway 34 toward Arapahoe, she took highway 183 south to Alma, where she checked into a hotel, got ready for bed, and set the alarm for eight a.m.

Whatever morning brought—a fight, a fuss, or making up, *or* Joe turning to her for love—something had to give between him and Elaine.

Jillian turned the lamp off.

"And I'm just the doggone farm girl to do it."

Chapter 25

No lights shone in the windows when Joe pulled into his parents' driveway. He yawned and checked his phone once more, but he didn't know why. Obviously, Elaine thought he should apologize. "Not gonna happen, Elaine. I can be just as doggone stubborn as you can."

On the front porch, he set his suitcase down to unlock the door. Halfway to his room, the floor of the old house creaked. He stopped, not wanting to wake Mom or Dad, and continued.

In his room, all he wanted was to fall into bed, but he didn't care to neglect his teeth. His back ached while bending over the sink, brushing and flossing. The long hours of sitting during the flight had done him no good whatsoever, so maybe a good night's sleep would. He spat into the sink and glared into the mirror. Maybe, maybe not. He'd have to hit the road again Monday for the drive back to college. At least he had all day Sunday to recuperate. Of course, he'd have all day to answer any questions about the trip from Mom and Dad.

Done in the bathroom, Joe stripped off his clothes and fell into bed to pull the familiar cool, crisp, and clean sheets over his naked body. "I agree with you, Dorothy. I feel like I've been inside a tornado. That means there's no place like home."

* * *

Elaine smacked the alarm and glared at the clock. Watching old movies until twelve, including emptying half a leftover bottle of wine, was *not* the way to a good night's sleep. Her mouth could've been a storage container for cotton balls, while her crusty eyes could've been in a commercial for eye drops.

She forced herself up to the bedside, yawning and blinking in an attempt to feel human again instead of the somewhat depressed wino she might've become. No, she hadn't gotten drunk, and that bottle had lasted all week. At least she wasn't too far gone yet.

She touched her lips. Had two fuzzy caterpillars taken their place last night? She burped rancid grape flavor. No more wine. She rose from the bed, weak-kneed, and shuffled to the bathroom. "Good grief, girl, you've got to pull yourself together." She burped again. "And the first thing that'll make that happen" —she burped once more, tasting bile— "is to throw up."

Elaine heaved until she feared her stomach would flop into the toilet, but she brought nothing up but sticky strings of vile tasting grape flavor. She brushed her teeth and returned to bed with a cold, wet washcloth on her forehead.

What day was it? Saturday? No, one of the reasons she'd drank all that wine was that it was Saturday night and she wouldn't have to go to work. Sunday. That's right, it was Sunday. What she needed was to get her sorry rear end up and shower and go to church. She burped once more, but no nasty bile rose in her throat. Take it slow, have a few crackers and ginger ale. Maybe by this afternoon she could stomach some—

Sunday? Was Joe back? No, since his trip lasted a week, he should be back Monday. His graduation was this coming Saturday. Go or not go? She should go, that was certain. He might not forgive her if she didn't. Forgiveness. Concerning their current mess, who should do the forgiving? If she were honest with herself, and she darn well better be, both should. How would that happen if no one made the first move?

She turned the now warm washcloth over and returned it to her forehead cool-side down. Since she'd made the huge deal about him going to Europe, and yes, acting like a drama queen by attempting to force him into not going, then crying when things didn't go her way, it was possible she should apologize first. Thank goodness her week of self-pity—with a healthy dose of self-examination due to her parents' advice—had sunk into her stubborn self.

* * *

Lying in bed awake, Jillian rolled over and turned the alarm off. Either her nervousness at her plan had kept her awake, or she'd gotten enough sleep on the flight back from Belgium to be well-rested. Regardless, she got up to dress and double-check both Elaine's and Joe's parents' addresses. With what she planned, she couldn't be too careful. She checked out of the hotel and drove around to find a place for a quick breakfast. Instead, she settled for a pack of nabs and a water at a service station vending machine. Now, in the quiet little town of Alma, Nebraska, it was time to start World War III.

Jillian followed the GPS on her phone to Joe's house. She parked behind his pickup and jogged to the porch to knock on the door. Footsteps thudded on what must've been a wood floor inside, coming closer. A man who resembled an older version of Joe, a bit heavier and with thinning hair, opened the door. "Good morning, young lady. Can I help you with something?"

Jillian offered her hand. "Mr. Matthan, I'd know you anywhere. You're just as handsome as Joe."

Smiling hugely, he took her hand. "With an introduction like that, you can call me Al." He released her hand. "I bet you're

Jillian." He stepped aside. "Come on in, Joe's finishing breakfast. Is he expecting you?"

"I'm sure the look on his face when he sees me will answer that question."

A woman who must have been Joe's mom came down the hall. "Al, who're you talking—"

Al held a finger to his lips and waved her closer. "This is Jillian, Anne. Joe's not expecting her" —he smiled at Jillian— "I don't think. This should be interesting."

"I hope you know what you're doing, Albert Matthan."

"What are you two talking about?" Joe said, his voice coming from a room down the hall."

Al grinned. "He's all yours, young lady."

"No, sir," Jillian said. "He's all Elaine's, and I'm here to make sure that happens."

Jillian went down the hall toward a kitchen, Al and Anne behind her. Joe jumped up, hitting the table and knocking over a cup of coffee. "Jillian? What the heck are you— I thought you'd be home by now?"

"Yep, that's the reaction I expected," Al said. "Anne, pour this young lady a cup of coffee while I wipe up Joe's mess. Then he can—"

"I'm good, Dad. Would someone please tell me what's going on?"

Jillian faced Al. "Thanks for the offer. I have more important things on my mind." She grabbed Joe's hand. "Come on, farm boy, we've got somewhere you need to be."

Joe pulled his hand free. "I'm not going anywhere until you tell me why you're here."

Anne took Al's hand. "Let's go outside while they talk."

"And leave before all the fun? I don't think—"

Anne jerked Al away. He let her lead him toward the back door. "Nice to meet you, Jillian. Joe will do a fine job for Organiks, I guarantee it."

Joe faced Jillian. "Doggone it, what the heck—"

"Hush, Joe Matthan, doggone you doggone it." She shook her head. "Now you've got me saying it. One question—do you love Elaine?"

"You know the answer to that."

"Fine. One more for the record didn't hurt, did it?"

"No, but—"

"Hush, that was rhetorical." She took him by the hand. "Come on. We're going to see your bride-to-be and I'm not taking no for an answer."

Joe jerked his hand away. "I'm not going anywhere. I told you she needs to apologize."

"You can go with me or I'll go alone and tell her all about me sitting in your lap and you ogling me while I was naked in the bathroom."

Joe's eyes bulged. "You—you knew?"

"I hope you enjoyed it. It'll never happen again."

"Jillian, I—"

"Are you going or not?"

"Would you really tell her all that?"

"Darn right."

"I guess I don't have a choice."

"Darn right again, farm boy."

Joe opened the back door. His parents were sitting at a patio table on a deck. "I'll be back" —he glared at Jillian— "but I don't know when."

Grinning, his dad gave a thumbs-up. "Keep him straight, Jillian, and Elaine too. Those two hardheads need a good dose of reality and you're just the gal to give it to them."

"Good luck with Elaine," Anne said, winking at Joe. Joe let go of the door. As it closed, Anne added, "Nice to meet you, Jillian!"

Outside, Jillian led Joe to his pickup. "You better drive yourself in case you stay. In fact, if I do my job as well as I think I will, you *might* stay all night."

"I can't. I've got to head back to college early."

"That's right. Oh well, first things first."

At his pickup, Joe faced her. "You're not gonna tell her anything that might break us up, are you?"

"You idiot, do you have chicken poo in your ears? I'll back out and follow, let's go."

She opened the car door, and Joe stuck his head out the pickup window. "We don't have chickens!"

"Who the heck cares, I was making a point!"

Jillian followed Joe back to town. Why didn't she just go on home last night and let Joe and Elaine's relationship blow up? Then she could pick up the pieces, comforting him, loving him, and making him as happy as Elaine ever could. No, she couldn't do that, because it was obvious he and Elaine belonged together, and if they broke up, he'd end up blaming his love-sick recruiter for the entire mess.

Yes, she was doing the right thing, and yes, like Joe had said, she'd find another farm boy to make her smile.

They entered Alma and continued down main street. A few turns later, Joe pulled into a driveway. Jillian parked behind him, took a deep breath, and climbed out to meet him at the front of his pickup. So far there was no sign that Elaine knew they were here, but a car parked ahead of Joe's pickup meant she was home.

Joe faced her. "I hope you know what the heck you're doing."

"She doesn't own a shotgun, does she?"

"Not unless she bought one while I was gone."

"Pepper spray?"

"Not that I know of."

"You go first. If she answers the door with that stuff, I need room to run."

They eased up the steps, stopped when they creaked, and continued. At the door, Joe tapped it, and Jillian eyed him. "She'll never hear that, scaredy cat." She shoved him aside, raised her knuckles, and the wooden door opened to a wide-eyed Elaine Johnson, the love of farm boy's life. Jillian lowered her knuckles. "Oh, wow. Joe said you were stunning, but not exactly *how* stunning."

From behind the screen door, Elaine cut her eyes at Jillian and then at Joe. "Have you lost your mind bringing her here? Or is your little head doing all your thinking instead of the one on your shoulders?"

Jillian snorted laughter. "It's the chicken poo in his ears. He's not thinking straight."

Joe tugged on the screen door. "Elaine, I—"

"It's latched. Why should I let you in?"

"Because he loves you," Jillian said.

"Then why are *you* here?"

"I'll tell you if you let us in."

Elaine cut her eyes from Joe to Jillian again and again, lips tightening with each withering glare. She unlatched the door. "This better be worth my time. I've got pepper spray in my purse if it isn't."

On the way in, Jillian nudged Joe's side with her elbow. "I thought you said she didn't have pepper spray?"

"I didn't say that, I—"

Elaine let go of the screen door, which slammed behind them. "I bought the pepper spray in case this jackass tried to force his way in." She pointed. "Living room. That way. Sit."

In the living room, Jillian shoved Joe toward Elaine. "No sitting. You two kiss and make up, doggone—" She covered her eyes, uncovered them, and faced Elaine. "See what I've had to put up with all week from farm boy here? Please kiss him. You know you're both dying to."

Elaine crossed her arms. "What if I don't want to?"

Jillian grabbed Joe and whirled him around. "I can show you how." She took Joe's face in her hands, pursed her lips for the coming kiss, and pulled him toward her.

Elaine stuck her hand between their faces. "Don't you dare."

Jillian stepped away. "He's all yours—always was, always is, always will be. Give him a good one while you're at it. I'll be watching to make sure it isn't just for my benefit so—"

"Watch all you want, maybe you'll learn something." Elaine wrapped her arms around Joe. "Do you swear nothing happened in Belgium?"

"Not even a kiss. I'm sorry about— Are you sorry too? I think we both need to realize that before—"

Elaine raised on tiptoe, placed her palms to his cheeks, and pulled him to her for a kiss. And another. And another.

"Sheesh, you two," Jillian said. "Come up for air."

Elaine dropped to her heels, cheeks reddening. "I sure missed that." She grinned. "I see why she tempted you, sweetie, she's hot. Maybe I should give *her* a kiss."

Jillian whirled and headed for the door. "My work is done. See you at graduation, farm boy. You too, farm girl. Have fun!" She hurried out the screen door, which slammed behind her, and climbed into her car. In the living room window, Joe and Elaine were at it again, kissing passionately, hands roaming where hands ought to roam when two people loved each other as much as they did.

Jillian grinned. She might've missed her calling. Maybe she should've been a pre-marriage counselor. She cranked the car. But she would have to draw the line at kissing her clients.

Chapter 26

The warmth of Elaine's soft lips brought the same surge of sexual need to Joe as in his dreams of her. He ended the kiss and pulled away enough to look her in the eye. "Darlin', if we don't stop now ..."

"I need you, Joe. Don't you know how much I need you?"

"What we *need* is to talk about something."

"Run to the drugstore. I'll be in bed waiting."

"Good grief, woman. What about *waiting* until we're married?"

"If you don't want to talk about birth control, what *do* you want to talk about?"

Joe led her to the sofa. "Let's sit, okay?"

On the sofa, he removed the chain and the ring and put the chain back on to give to Mom later. "I kept your ring with me like you said. Can I put it back where it belongs?"

"Good idea, sweetie. My finger felt naked without it." Elaine offered her hand, and he slipped the ring on her finger.

Joe had no idea he was going to discuss this subject now, but it was as good a time as any. "Darlin', every time we almost—well, you know—go too far with our kissing, we manage to stop. Have we ever made a pact or a promise about having sex before we get married?"

"I didn't want to stop just now."

"That's probably because of all the mess with Jillian and being apart for a week while worrying about it. Intense emotions almost always make people do things they regret later."

"I'm sure we talked about it. Wasn't it at the river after our first kiss, or sometime later?"

"It seems I recall you saying 'boys are weak, that's just the way you are.' Did you ever tell me that?"

All the color drained out of Elaine's face. "I don't—" She fell back against the sofa. "I didn't tell you that. While you were gone, I was out on the front porch, thinking about you. All of a sudden those exact words popped into my head. They sounded like my voice too, and they made me think you were weak to the point of sleeping with Jillian while you were in Belgium. I sat on the steps and cried as hard as I ever have. Joe, how could we both hear me saying that but not remember when I said it? It doesn't make any sense."

"I have a theory about it, but I'm afraid you might haul me to the nearest doctor for a mental evaluation if I tell you." Joe patted Elaine's hand. "Then again, you probably thought I'd lost my mind by coming here with Jillian."

"You got that right."

"Believe me, it wasn't planned. She showed up at my parents' house this morning and practically drug me here. I had absolutely no idea what she had in mind until it happened."

"She's really a take-control kind of woman. I was joking about liking her—and kissing her, of course—but I can see where she could grow on a person."

"That's Jillian alright. We shouldn't get sidetracked. I've wanted to tell you my theory about me—maybe about us—for a while now."

Elaine sat forward on the sofa. "What do you mean 'about us?'"

"Because if what I think is true, it involves you too."

"I admit I was scared about us hearing those same words. Now I'm intrigued, spill it."

"Some of it involves our supposed conversation about waiting until we were married to make love, when you said that about boys being weak."

"Do you remember when I said that?"

"I don't remember it, I dreamed it."

"That's a strange way to remember something. When did we have this talk? I can't remember, other than what I guess I said."

"I'm not sure how you're going to take this, but we had that conversation in 1943, and I dreamed about it while I was in Belgium."

"Yeah, right," Elaine said, rolling her eyes. "Did you and Jillian stop for a drink on the way here?"

"I'm trying to be serious. Something else happened while I was in Belgium. You know one of the reasons I wanted to go there was to visit the Ardennes American Cemetery, right?"

"I assume you went."

"I even spoke with the chaplain who was there when your— I mean your great-aunt Elaine's ashes were buried. You know, when Ruth and Grandpa flew over at Elaine's request."

Elaine tilted her head to one side. "Why did you start to say Aunt Elaine's ashes were *my* ashes?"

"Grandpa told me how Ruth had placed some of Elaine's personal effects with her ashes before they were buried. He didn't say what and I needed to know, to help verify my theory."

"Are you saying the chaplain knew what Ruth placed with the ashes?"

Joe paused. He'd tell her what was in the chest but not include the bloody yellow ribbon. If he piled that on top of what he was about to tell her, there was no telling how she'd react.

"According to the chaplain, Ruth placed a letter written by Elaine to Great-grandpa with the ashes. She included a few old photographs of her and Great-grandpa before and after they were married too."

"That's interesting … romantic even. What does it have to do with us?"

"Before I tell you, promise you won't think I need to get to the nearest mental health facility."

"Come on, now. It's not like you think I'm a reincarnation of my great-aunt and you're a reincarnation of your great-grandpa, reborn so we could be together again because he was killed in the war."

Joe took his phone from his pocket and gave it to her.

"Why do I need this?"

"So you can call 911, because that's exactly what I believe."

Elaine dropped the phone in his lap. "This is no time to be joking, Joe Matthan, no time at all."

"I'd like to have the chance to tell you the rest before you make any knee-jerk judgments."

"Go ahead." She sat back on the sofa and crossed her arms. "I'll listen, even though I don't want to."

"After I spoke with the chaplain, I walked out to Great-grandpa's gave. I'll call it his grave for the time being instead of mine. I guess I expected something to happen like with the dreams. When I touched that white cross with my name on it, it was a humbling experience, but that's all."

"What did you expect, Joe?" Elaine's nostrils flared as she spoke. "Rockets and fireworks announcing to the world how you were its one and only reincarnation of a World War II soldier?"

"Don't be like that, you said you'd listen." Joe's neck ached from looking at her sideways. He turned on the sofa so he could face her. "I'm not the only World War II soldier who thinks that. I'll get to that in a minute. No, nothing happened then, but it did later. Back at the hotel that night, I had the worst nightmare of my life. I knocked the lamp off the table and hurt my hand and didn't even wake up. I sure remembered the next morning. It was like I was in the center of an explosion, or maybe a grenade. It was like all these hot bits of metal were going through me while this brilliant light flashed around me. I remembered something else that morning, and it was the last thing. Like when I heard your voice telling me 'boys are weak, that's just the way you are,' it was the same, but—"

Elaine eyes widened.

"What's wrong?"

"That day I told you about, when I heard my voice saying 'boys are weak, that's just the way you are', I heard something else." She swallowed. "In my own voice too."

"I bet I know what it was. 'I have to believe you'll come back to me.'"

Elaine nodded. "'I have to believe you'll come back to me.'" Eyes blinking, she slowly shook her head. "What does it mean, Joe? Are we both going insane?"

"No one's insane, okay? All we are is in love. We always have been from when we met back in 1943 until now."

"It's so hard to believe."

"All you have to believe in is us." He palmed her cheek. "Don't you believe in us? I do."

"I do—you know I do. What did you mean when you said that about another soldier thinking he was reincarnated too?"

"It's sort of a long story. Let me call my folks and tell them we're fine. Then we can scramble some eggs and make coffee and toast and I'll tell you about it. Jillian interrupted my breakfast."

"Don't you need to get back to college?"

"No worries, darlin'. We're what's important now."

* * *

Joe emptied his coffee cup. "Does all that make sense?"

"That story about the man's memories returning when he found his World War II dog tags is interesting."

"I lucked up on my professor talking about how DNA can be used to identify long dead relatives. I might not have thought about it otherwise."

"You still haven't told me how that information relates to us."

Joe stood. "We might as well be comfortable on the sofa while I tell you." He followed Elaine to the living room and sat beside her. "Other than the things we remember you saying, did anything else strange happen?"

"I hate to mention it. You'll think I need a trip to have my head examined too." Elaine paused for a deep breath. "Remember when I had that déjà vu feeling the first day we stopped by to check out the house?"

"I was wondering if some of your past might be returning to you then. Did something else happen?"

"I thought it was interesting at first, but for the longest time I thought I could hear music when I visited the old hardware store with Dad. The other day, when I picked up the painting supplies, I heard it again. Have you ever heard it?"

"You asked Mr. Hansen, didn't you? Now you know about the radio in back."

"I felt like an idiot, trying to figure out if I were hearing some sort of ghost music."

"You're no idiot, darlin'. That would make two of us if you were."

"I'm inclined to believe that after hearing our tall tales. What did you hear?"

"It's not what I heard, it's what I dreamt."

"I'm glad it was a dream and not another self-destructive nightmare. Is it a good one?"

Joe gave Elaine a kiss that lasted longer than he intended. How could he have ever thought Jillian could take her place? He ended the kiss. "Does that give you any idea how good it was?"

"It does, sweetie. Want to try again?"

"What I *want* is to tell you about the absolute best dream I've ever had in my entire life."

"No! You dreamed we …?"

"You got it, and it was great."

"Yeah? I've got to hear this."

"We were at the river. I was dressed in World War II fatigues and you were wearing a floofy yellow dress that looked like it was from the 40's. You wore a yellow ribbon in your ponytail too."

"A floofy dress? I don't wear floofy dresses."

"You would back then. Anyway, other than our making love on what I think was our honeymoon night, I sang to you. Near the end you joined in to sing those lines you sang at church the last time we were there. That's how I knew you'd sing so well before I ever heard you in our present time."

Elaine unbuttoned the top button on Joe's shirt. "I'm not worried about my singing. What else did I do well?"

"I'll save that for our future honeymoon night. I don't need you to have a heads-up on me."

"You'll have a heads up on me, Mr. Matthan, and that's not fair. Aside from that, even if we think we might be from the past, your theories are just theories and your dreams are just dreams."

"If I can, I want to prove my theories before we get married."

"What about our conversation you dreamed where we agreed to not make love? The one you said took place in 1943?"

"It was … uh … would you believe it was as sensual as our honeymoon?"

"How's that?"

"Kind of like forbidden desire, I guess. We pretty much teased each other with kisses and touching to make the point of if we went too far, it would be trouble. You know what happened with us after Jillian left. That's the first time you ever asked me to run to the doggone drug store."

"Well, I guess I'm just a weak girl like you're a weak boy. How will you prove your theories about us?"

"Don't you want to know why?"

"I figured you were just curious about it."

"Don't you want to know if it's true? It might bring us closer together. Heck, we might even remember more of our past lives. Wouldn't *that* be interesting?"

"As long as we keep it to ourselves."

"That's a given." Joe took his phone from his pocket.

"Who in the world are you calling in the middle of our conversation?"

Joe held up a finger, dialed Grandpa's number, and Elaine sat back on the sofa.

"Joe, is that you? This thing tells me it's your number."

"Hi, Grandpa, how've you been? Are you still beating old man Willis next door at cards? What was that game Grandma liked so well, Rummy?"

"That's it, God rest her soul. That sweet woman whipped me so many times at Rummy I lost count. I was tempted to ask her to play strip Rummy when we were younger, but she wasn't going for that business, ya know."

Tempted to laugh, Joe waited until the urge left. "Grandpa, I need to ask you about Great-grandpa's dog tags. Do you still have them?"

"I do, I do. Been thinking about passing them on to you. Of all of us Matthan men, you were the one most like Dad, so I was told by Mom all that time ago. How's that gal of yours, Elaine? Thanks for the pictures you sent at Christmas. Mmm, boy she's pretty. She looks just like Mom did when she was a young woman. I got some pictures around here somewhere of her when she and Joe were dating back then. I haven't seen 'em in a while though."

"I think she's pretty too, Grandpa." Joe winked at Elaine. "If you're thinking about sending me the dog tags, I'd appreciate it. You have my address, right?"

"Still got it on the envelope you sent the pictures in. I'll get it to you first thing in the morning. Look, I've got to run, my laxative's kicking in. Send all my love to everyone, and give me a holler when you get those dog tags. Bye."

Joe returned the phone to his pocket, and Elaine leaned forward from the sofa. "What do you need those dog tags for?"

"I need them so we can go to Belgium and have them buried in the chest with the rest of the things Ruth placed there. Before that we'll take a look at that letter and those pictures and see if you remember anything."

"When do you plan on doing that, not to mention affording it?"

"Did Alma Elementary close for the summer yet? I forget when that is."

"Friday's the last day."

"I graduate Saturday, so we can leave Sunday. Do you still have your passport from when we thought we were going to Cancun?"

"You never said how you'd afford going to Belgium."

"We'll just stay long enough to visit the cemetery and fly right back after."

Elaine smacked his hand. "Money. How? Where?"

Joe grinned. "I'll pay them off when I start work with Organiks."

"You'll pay *what* off?"

"Credit cards. It's the American way."

Chapter 27

Joe unbuckled the airliner seatbelt. "What a crazy weekend."

Elaine unbuckled her seat belt too. "I'm not sure about Jillian, not after her comment at the restaurant after you graduated."

"What comment was that?"

"You were talking to your dad and didn't hear it. She said she hoped the restaurant had the same peach cobbler you two shared for dessert. That sounded too darned cozy, Mr. Matthan."

"You let that go without saying anything?"

"I told her she seemed to like returning to the scene of her crime too much, especially since she wrangled you back to her hotel room for a kiss."

"You won't ever forget that, will you?"

"Would you if it were the other way around?"

"Okay, I get it."

Turbulence shook the plane, and Joe grabbed Elaine's arm. "Doggone, I never had to deal with feeling like the plane was about to drop out from under me on either flight, both coming over or going back home."

In the seat by the window, Elaine glanced out. "This reminds me of when we rode the roller coaster at the state fair last fall." She faced Joe. "Did Jillian let you hold her arm like this?"

"I just told you we didn't have turbulence on either flight, okay?"

"Okay, sweetie, grab all you want." She patted Joe's hand. "I'm glad our folks didn't give us a hard time about coming over. I guess that means they bought our story of how this trip is a graduation present to yourself. Did your mom or dad say anything about our sleeping arrangements?"

"Not a word, probably because they didn't know I could only afford one room."

"And for two nights only. Still, they're gonna be interesting, don't you think?"

"Don't forget our promise neither one of us can remember making."

"It's you we have to worry about. Boys are weak. That's just the way you are, remember?"

"Yeah, right, like you were good when you were kissing my chest at the river after I gave you the engagement ring. Do I have to remind you how good you were when Jillian left too? Let me see if I can get it right. 'Oh, Joe, I *ne-e-e-e-e-d* you.'"

"Like you didn't enjoy it. Regardless, I'm glad you weren't weak while you two spent an entire week together."

"That makes both of us."

"I'm glad your grandpa mailed the dog tags in time for the trip. Why haven't you taken them out of the box?"

"Remember what I said about that man who started having his past life memories return when he held his dog tags? I'm not touching them until you have that letter and those pictures in your hands. I'm positive that's when you'll remember our past lives."

"What if I don't? I know we both heard those words I supposedly said, but what if they're a coincidence, like the music I heard all those years in the hardware store being from a radio?"

Joe said nothing. If both of them hearing those same phrases didn't give her pause, he had no idea what would. Then again, all that might change when she held the letter and old photographs of him and her together.

Elaine nudged his elbow with hers. "I see that wrinkled forehead. You don't like me doubting you."

"Regardless of my wrinkles, you're gonna believe what you believe until you believe otherwise."

"We'll see." Elaine took a paperback from her purse and opened it, putting an end to the conversation.

Joe didn't like how she scoffed at the coincidences they shared. How often did two people hear the exact same thing in their heads? Still, like they'd always done when arguing—though that hadn't worked with the original argument about Jillian—he tried to look at the situation from Elaine's point of view.

He'd dreamed those initial dreams of her wearing the 1940's dress and kissing him, plus the dream of their honeymoon at the river, a long time ago. He couldn't even recall when, and they'd become a part of him now, like a pair of broken-in work boots so comfortable he hardly knew he was wearing them. For her, his attempt to fit her into his theory must be the opposite, like being forced to wear new shoes that chaffed and blistered until all the wearer wanted was to jerk them off and run barefooted.

"Darlin', I know my theory is hard to believe. You didn't have to come on this trip and I appreciate it."

"You must've been sitting there trying to put those big feet of yours into my shoes," Elaine said, closing the paperback. "I was doing the same."

"And?"

"And I'm curious about what might happen at the cemetery. I didn't mention it, but it's strange how Uncle Thomas confuses me with his sister, who, according to you, could be me."

"I agree about Uncle Thomas. I've always liked him, and now I know why—his theory matches mine."

"I didn't say that, but …"

"I see that wrinkled nose of yours. You're holding something back. What happened while I was gone?"

Elaine rubbed her nose. "Mom and I visited him and—" She took a tissue from her purse and dabbed her eyes.

"That must've been some visit if it makes you cry."

Done with the tissue, Elaine dropped it in her purse. "I asked how he was doing, things like that. Right out of the blue he asked if he'd ever told me how much you and I reminded him of his sister, Elaine, and Joe from back in 1943. Then he said even though he was only a sixteen-year-old kid with fishing on his mind, he knew love when he saw it. He also said how he never had any idea a boy and a girl could fit together so perfectly, and how he'd heard his dad say it was like all the holidays were wrapped up in one when we—I mean they—were together. He said we were just like that."

Elaine's voice cracked with her last words. Joe said nothing, afraid she might cry again.

She balled the tissue in her hand. "Hearing that made me happy and sad at the same time. I had to go outside and sit in the gazebo until I could get myself together. I'm sorry for doubting you. I agree there are entirely too many coincidences concerning our past and our present to ignore."

Joe could hardly believe what she'd said. "So that means …?"

Elaine gave him a slight smile, nodding at the same time. "That means I believe you, and I want to find out exactly what our past means concerning our present."

"I think we will." Joe slipped his hand into hers. "Like Uncle Thomas said, and like we've known ever since we met on the first day of sixth grade, our past is gonna show us exactly how much we're meant to be together."

* * *

At the hotel, Joe paid the cabby, had him pop the trunk, and took his and Elaine's carry-ons to the hotel door. He set them on the sidewalk and tapped his watch. "We've been gone from home over ten hours. It's almost 11 p.m. here."

Elaine rubbed her behind. "My sore butt could've told you that."

"Mine too. Let me set my watch so I can keep the time straight." He lifted the carry-ons. "Come on inside and get a look at this hotel. I got the room here since I was familiar with it."

Inside, Elaine glanced around. "This place is fabulous. No wonder you could only afford one room for two nights on your credit card." Joe caught her comparing her watch to what looked like a hand-carved wooden clock on the wall over the clerk's desk. She set her watch and faced Joe. "We even gained six hours to relive again. It's too bad we can't do that in real life."

"And go through everything our 1943 selves did again?" Joe asked. "No thanks, I'll stick to having you remember all that and enjoying this life instead."

"Good point." Elaine went down the hall and peeked into the restaurant area. "Wow, I love the arches." She returned to the clerk's desk and rang the bell. "Let's check in so we can enjoy our fancy room for as much time as possible."

A clerk came from a door behind the desk. "May I be of assistance?"

Joe took his wallet from his pocket. "A reservation for Matthan, please."

The clerk studied a laptop monitor. "Joseph Matthan and company for two nights, correct?"

"That's us."

"If I may have your credit card for the balance, you can register and see if your room is satisfactory."

Done with everything, Joe gave Elaine the key card and took their carry-ons to the elevator. At the door, it took her two swipes for it to open. "Maybe that's a sign we shouldn't stay in the same room, sweetie."

Joe took the carry-ons inside. "We've been good all these years, we can be good until we get married."

Elaine peeked into the bathroom, looked out the window that overlooked the road in front of the hotel with the blue-gray waters of Meuse beyond it, and sat on the bed to pat the mattress. "This bed looks like a full. I thought it would've been at least a queen or a king. It'll be a tight squeeze."

"Can you handle it?" Joe sat beside her.

"That depends on what you brought to sleep in? Since we both sleep naked, naked is out."

"Got it covered, darlin'." He sat his carry-on on the luggage rack in the corner and took his red-plaid pajamas out. "How about this?"

"What if red affects me like it does a bull?"

Joe couldn't believe Elaine had just said the same thing Jillian had said about his pajamas. "We'll handle whatever 'bullish' feelings you might have. What did you bring?"

She took her carry-on to a chair, faced away from him and unzipped it. "Knowing us like I do, I brought this." Facing him, she held the slim straps of a black lace negligee up to her shoulders. "Will this make you snort, Mr. Bull?"

"Doggone, darlin', you might as well sleep naked if you wear that."

Elaine dropped the negligee on the bed and slipped her arms around his waist. "If you'd like." She stood on tiptoe and kissed his nose. "I packed that just to see the look on your face, and it was worth it. I brought some PJs I used to wear—very conservative PJs, okay?"

"Good. Otherwise your opinion that 'boys are weak, that's just the way you are' would be proven beyond a shadow of a doubt." Joe took his shaving kit with a toothbrush and other items from his carry-on. "We need to get an early start to the cemetery. Do you want the bathroom first?"

"If you don't mind." Carry-on in hand, Elaine stopped at the bathroom door to blow him a kiss. "Make sure you wait up for me, lover." She closed the door, and Joe shook his head. Talk about déjà vu.

Chapter 28

Behind the curtains, the morning light glowed a dingy yellow. Joe turned the alarm off before it could wake Elaine. She rolled over to face him, eyes still closed. With her hair curling about her tanned cheeks in silken swirls, she pursed her lips, pulled the sheet up to her chin, and sighed. He leaned close to sniff the floral aroma of her shampoo—the same aroma that had swirled about his face while she drove them to the river on the Harley, on the day he asked her to marry him. How could he have told Jillian he'd consider dating her if things didn't work out between him and Elaine? If any way possible, Elaine would remember her past life at the cemetery, and they'd be married as soon as they could make the arrangements.

Since it was almost eight, the time they'd agreed to start their day, Joe kissed Elaine's forehead. "Rise and shine, darlin'."

Elaine's lips slowly formed a slight smile, and her brown eyes blinked open. "Mmm, I could get used to waking up like this." She placed her hand over her mouth. "Do I have morning breath? Yours is fine."

"There's only one way to find out." Joe took her hand from her mouth and kissed her. He ended the kiss, but she pulled him down to kiss her again.

"I *really* could get used to that. We better get up before we don't, if you know what I mean."

"I *definitely* know what you mean." At the window, Joe opened the curtains. "We've got a nice day." He faced Elaine, who wore a thin, blue nighty with spaghetti straps over her shoulders—and no bra. She raised her arms to stretch at the foot of the bed, and the nighty rose up to reveal pink panties. He faced the window again. "Doggone, those PJs are driving me crazy."

"Poor baby." Her footfalls thumped on the carpet, heading in the direction of the bathroom. "As much as I'd love to try breakfast in that gorgeous restaurant downstairs, order room service while I get ready. Bacon, scrambled eggs, orange juice, and coffee for me. That'll get us to the cemetery sooner."

Still facing the window, Joe gave her a thumbs-up. "Will do, darlin', will do."

* * *

Joe took a seat on the bus to the cemetery, and Elaine sat beside him. "You didn't forget the dog tags, did you?"

He patted his pants pocket. "Right here."

"And Chaplin Mulhaney has everything ready for the service?"

"He's the same chaplain who officiated when Ruth and Grandpa were here."

"Is that a yes or a no?"

"You heard me talking to him on the phone."

"I just don't want anything unexpected to happen." Elaine peered out the window past Joe. "I had no idea we'd pass through the Université de Liège." She poked his side. "How do you like my attempt at Dutch?"

"Can you use that accent on our honeymoon night? It's kind of sexy."

"Only if you learn some phrases in French."

Joe raised an eyebrow. "Uh-huh, been reading one of your romance novels again, haven't you? How about this? French fry."

"We'll stick to English."

"It doesn't matter since you'll be moaning. That language is universal."

Elaine poked him again, harder. "What would you know about it? Did Jillian give you a sample?"

Joe attempted to hold in a grin. "Well …"

"*Well*, my behind. I see your eyes crinkling."

"I can't get a thing by you, can I?"

"Never have, never will. Can I see the cemetery brochure again?"

"No need." Joe pointed. "We're here."

The bus passed through the black iron gates and entered the parking area. The huge, white limestone building loomed ahead, its eagle and three female figures gleaming in the sun. Elaine lowered her head to look through the bus's windshield. "I see what you mean about this place being special."

The bus parked, and Joe climbed out ahead of Elaine. "See that building with ivy on the red-brick walls? That's the visitor center. We're supposed to meet Chaplain Mulhaney there."

Elaine slipped her hand into his. "Are you nervous?"

"Some, but nothing happened the last time until I had that nightmare. I think your memories might return when you read the letter."

"I won't read that letter, or open it."

"Then how do you expect—"

"It's too private, Joe. I'll hold it. I'll even place it inside my blouse next to my heart. Besides, if anything could make me remember, I think the yellow ribbon Ruth placed in the chest with everything else would. Didn't the chaplain say Ruth mentioned how Elaine had given it to Joe before he went to Fort Leavenworth?"

Joe could hardly believe what Elaine had just said. He grabbed her shoulders and looked her in the eye. "Elaine, I didn't tell you about the ribbon when we talked about the letter and pictures."

"You must have. I remember it perfectly."

"I swear, I didn't mention it. Maybe being here is helping your memory come back."

"We'll see." Elaine took a few steps toward the visitor's building and stopped to rub her arms. "I just had one of those weird déjà vu feelings." She faced Joe. "Why do I have the feeling you aren't telling me everything about the ribbon?"

"Why do you think that?"

"That doesn't matter and you know it. If it's going to upset me, I'd rather know."

"I should've told you when I told you about the letter and the old pictures. Remember what I said about my nightmare, that it was like I was in an explosion of some kind, like a grenade? Great-grandpa or me, if what I believe is true— must've had the ribbon with him when he was killed."

Elaine's chin trembled. "You mean …?"

Joe nodded slowly. "I'm afraid so."

"I'll look at that letter and pictures." Elaine whirled away from Joe. "You can forget that bloody ribbon."

"I won't make you look, okay? I was hoping you'd read the letter since it's from you to me—I mean from your great-aunt to my great-grandpa. Can't we go in and start slow?"

"As long as you don't make me look at that ribbon."

Joe opened the visitor center door and followed Elaine inside. At a desk to the right, Chaplain Mulhaney stood. "Hello there, young Mr. Matthan. I take it this is your new bride?"

"No, sir, not yet." Joe faced Elaine. "I told the chaplain we might come to Belgium for our honeymoon."

"No, sir," Elaine said. "We're not married yet."

"It's a wonder. When this young man of yours was telling me all about you, it was obvious he was smitten." The chaplain gestured to a table near the room's center. "I had the chest brought here for privacy. Emotions can run strong when families visit the cemetery. As you see, we have several boxes of tissues around."

Joe took a seat in one of two beige arm chairs that sat on a blue-patterned rug. Elaine sat across from him in the other chair. The chest, resembling mahogany, sat on the table between them. Below the latch, which shined as if it were brass, an engraved plate similar to the latch also shined. Joe read the engraving. "Elaine M. Bauer."

The chaplain went to the door. "There's no rush. Dial zero on the phone on the desk when you're ready." He started to leave but turned around. "You might wonder how the chest is in such good shape. Ruth and your grandfather wrapped it in a heavy plastic bag. She did the same with the letter before she put it inside."

The chaplain left, and Joe rubbed his stomach. "Doggone, my insides are practically shaking."

Elaine set her purse on the floor beside her. "Mine too. How do you want to do this?"

"Do you want to open it? After all, it might be your ashes inside."

She glared at him. "You can pick the worst times to crack a sick joke."

Joe pointed at his mouth. "I wasn't smiling, so I wasn't joking." He took a deep breath. "Okay, let's see what we find." The lid creaked when he opened it. A clear plastic bag bulged up and out of the box. He took the bag out and set it on the table, peeked inside the chest and closed the lid. "There's nothing else inside but a black cloth bag with a withered daffodil on top that looks like it might turn to dust if I touch it. I guess the bag is for the ashes."

Elaine slid forward in the chair and unfolded the plastic bag. "I see an envelope but I don't see the pictures. No ribbon either, thank goodness."

"The envelope is kind of bulging." Joe slid forward in his chair also. "Everything's probably inside." He opened the bag, took the envelope out and offered it to Elaine. "Do you want to hold it to see if anything comes back?"

"I guess." She took the envelope and turned it over. "It has your name on it."

"I saw that. It looks a lot like your handwriting."

"I don't write J and M with all those curlicues."

"The rest is close, right?"

Elaine didn't answer.

"Do you remember anything?" Joe asked, hoping she did.

"I really hadn't planned on putting it in my shirt like I said." Elaine unbuttoned the top button of her blouse. She slipped the envelope inside her blouse, and its square corners pressed out against the thin material of her blouse over her heart. She placed her hand there. "I'm sorry. I don't remember anything at all, Joe."

"Can't you leave it there at least a minute?"

"What did you think was going to happen?"

"I don't know, I just—"

"You act like I'm supposed to fall out in the floor in convulsions and swear my undying love to you because I miraculously remembered every minute we ever spent together in the 1940's."

"Are you thinking about us back then, like maybe at the river, since the Joe and Elaine of the past spent so much of their time there too?"

"I wasn't thinking about anything, but that makes sense. You realize you're buying me a nice dinner at the hotel restaurant tonight, regardless of your credit card bill."

Joe stuck his tongue out at her. "Maybe I can wash dishes to pay the bill. Try closing your eyes."

Elaine did as he asked. Her chest rose and fell three times. Eyes still closed, she raised a fingertip to wipe a single tear from her cheek.

Joe said nothing. If she were remembering anything, he didn't want to break the possible spell of her recollection that could be happening before his very eyes. Heart thudding in his temples, he continued to wait. He wanted them to be in love as much as possible—in the present, after they were married, and in the future—and this might be their last chance to reclaim the love they shared in the past, which would make all that come true.

She opened her eyes, took the envelope from her blouse, and returned it to Joe.

"You were crying. What did you remember?"

Elaine took a tissue from a nearby box and wiped her eyes. "The same as before, nothing. I was crying because this overwhelming sadness came over me. It was probably because while I was thinking of them—us, whatever—at the river, all I could think about was her wearing that ribbon and how he probably loved seeing her hair up like you did mine that day we sang in church."

"I know what you mean. Imagine how it'd be for us now if I had to go off to war. Regardless of what war or when, I don't know how families deal with it." Joe pulled the flap on the envelope open. "You better turn around. You said you couldn't handle seeing the bloody ribbon."

"I'll look at my lap. Let me know when you're through with everything and I'll hold out my hand for the pictures." Elaine lowered her head.

Joe took the pictures from the envelope, followed by the letter and the ribbon. He half expected his fingertips to tingle like the day he shook hands with the chaplain. Nothing happened, but he didn't have the dog tags out either. He tucked the ribbon between his leg and the chair's armrest so Elaine couldn't accidentally see it and studied the pictures.

In the first, Great-grandpa and Elaine's great-aunt stood on the bank of the river, with the huge oak to their right. She wore a dress similar to the one he'd dreamed about, with her hair tied in a ponytail with a yellow ribbon. Smiling, they must have set the camera up to automatically take the picture. The second was of them standing beside a passenger train car. Her arms were around his neck, his were around her waist, and a yellow hair ribbon—what must've been the yellow ribbon beside Joe's leg—dangled from his fingers. The third was taken in what looked like an office. Joe, in a full-dress Army uniform from the time period, and Elaine, wearing what appeared to be the same dress in the first picture, but with her hair down, faced each other, smiling hugely.

The hint of tears stung Joe's eyes. He and Elaine resembled Great-grandpa and her great-aunt in every way possible, from his blond hair and six-foot height to her sun-streaked brunette hair and head that rose to his chin. So much love, all lost in an instant when what Joe believed to have been a grenade had exploded.

He fingered moisture from his eyes. "The ribbon's hidden where you can't see it." Elaine raised her head, and he gave her the pictures. "When you finish, tell me when and where you think they were taken. I have my ideas, but I'd like to know if they match yours without me telling you."

"I heard you sniffle. Did the pictures upset you?"

"They look exactly like us. Like when you held the letter next to your heart, it upset me to think about how that grenade—if that's what it was—ended all their love in an instant. Go ahead. They're great pictures, regardless of being yellowed. Don't forget to tell me when and where you think they were taken. Oh, and look at them in the order I have them. That's a hint."

"I'm going to take a peek at all of them first. That way I can have some kind of clue as to what you're talking about." Elaine lay the pictures side-by-side on the table. "I see what you mean, it's amazing."

"About us looking like them, or the order I put them in?"

"About us looking *remarkably* like them. I'll comment as I go instead of waiting." Elaine slid the first picture aside. "I agree with your order. This one, where they're standing by the river, must have been taken before the other two. I see the 'floofy' dress you mentioned, but Joe's wearing jeans." She placed a fingertip on the second picture. "This one is so sad. It looks like he was about to get on the train to leave for basic training, and she'd just given him the yellow hair ribbon that was in the chest." She picked up the last picture. "This one's happy and sad at the same time. Since he's in uniform and she's in a dress, and since it was taken in some kind of office, I assume they'd just gotten married." She slid all the pictures back to Joe. "They *are* great. Does my opinion of when and where they were taken agree with yours?"

"It does. Do you remember anything?"

"I'm afraid not. I hope I don't wake up screaming with a nightmare tonight."

"You might remember anytime. I didn't have the dream of our honeymoon at the river until after we met. Still, like I've said before, I don't remember exactly when." Joe returned the pictures to the envelope and removed the letter. "Are you sure you don't want to read this? It might help you remember, especially since it's possible you wrote it."

"You read it first. I may or may not, depending on your reaction."

Joe's eyes stung again when he read the first sentence. He sniffed and fingered tears from his eyes.

Elaine handed him a tissue from a box on the table. "What's wrong?"

"My ... I guess my allergies are acting up. Let me finish, okay?"

"Go ahead."

Joe finished reading. Elaine had to read this, which is why he lied about having allergies. He offered her the letter. "If this doesn't make you remember, I don't know what will. There's also a hint in it about my theory concerning us, so you really need to read it."

Elaine didn't take the letter. "I don't remember you having allergies. I'm not sure I want to."

"No, darlin', I don't have allergies."

"Don't *darlin'* me. First, you're dishonest by not telling Jillian you were engaged. Now you tell me you have allergies."

Joe shook the letter. "You need to read this, doggone it. I can't be more honest than that."

Elaine eyed him, the letter, and then took it. "If this makes me cry ..."

"It might, but I think you'll see it's worth it. Read it out loud."

"Why?"

"Just do it for us, okay?"

Elaine snatched several tissues from the box. "I have a feeling I'll need more of these." With the tissues in one hand and the letter in the other, Elaine focused on the single sheet of paper.

"Dear Joe, I don't know where to start, but I wish I could start over with you again, back at the river after we were married. As I write this, I remember that night as if it had just happened. You and that place were my heaven, and I hope you know that.

Our son looks and acts so much like you. He's serious, of course, like you were before I loosened you up, but he's blessed with a wife who can make him laugh, and that laughter, as silly as it may sound, keeps their marriage fresh. You would have been a wonderful father, and I wish with all my heart that you could have known him, if at least for only a brief moment."

Elaine paused. "She must have written this a lot later in life for your grandpa to be married."

"That what I thought. Go ahead."

"When the news came of how you were killed, it almost killed me too." Elaine wiped her eyes. "I can't imagine her losing him like that, and with no father for her son."

"I agree, what a way to start a family. It gets better."

"I hope so." Elaine raised the letter again. "But our parents helped me through it, and Joseph kept me centered. Thank you so much for him. As a baby—and a little boy—he was my miracle. As a man, he is my pride.

And, Joe, if you know about Kurt, I want you to know I was able to do as you had hoped because of him. Yes, I had a happy and fulfilling life, and if not for Kurt, and you, I'm not sure that would have happened."

Elaine stopped reading. "How could he have known about Kurt? That doesn't make any sense at all."

"Keep reading."

"I've asked Ruth to do something for me, and I know I can count on her. It's not simple, so it will take some doing. You might even see her there, or you might not. What's important is it's something I really want."

Elaine stopped again. "I assume what she asked Ruth to do was to fly over here and have her ashes buried with your great-grandpa. How in the world could he have been here to see that?"

"I'm not sure, but I have an idea. Keep reading. I'll tell you about it when you're done."

"One more thing. I still have one of my favorite yellow hair ribbons tucked away. It's the one I wore when we went to the river the night after we were married. I take it with me when I go there. I sit on the old quilt and hold the ribbon to my face and daydream of you reaching up to pull it so my hair would fall around my shoulders. I've enclosed it in this letter, and I've asked Ruth to take it from the envelope. If it's possible, I want you to see it one last time.

Hey, I can hope, can't I?

Now I must go. I am so sorry in so many ways about so many things, but I'm never sorry I met you.

With all my love, Elaine.

P.S.

Remember the morning we woke after our honeymoon, when you called me darlin'? That was the only time you ever called me that and I miss it so. Maybe one day, with all the hope I've carried in my heart all these years, I'll hear you call me that again. Love, E."

Elaine stared at Joe. "What does all that mean, or the part about him seeing the ribbon one last time?'"

Joe took the letter. "It sounds like Elaine might've asked Ruth to read this letter out loud at some specific time. Apparently, she believed—how, I don't know—Great-grandpa might be there to hear it, and see the ribbon too."

Elaine wiped her eyes. "That part about her going to the river—when she'd sit on a quilt and hold the ribbon to her face, thinking about him—that's one of the saddest things I think I've ever heard. It sounds like she hoped they might have another chance to be together despite his death."

"It sounds familiar, doesn't it? You don't remember anything yet?"

"No. Are you going to take the dog tags out and see if they help you remember anything?"

Joe took a small, white box from his pants pocket. "That's all I *can* do. Are you gonna turn away while I get out the ribbon? I'll hold everything at once and see if that helps."

"Go ahead."

"Are you sure?"

"Go ahead. I should be able to handle it."

Joe took the ribbon from between his leg and the chair and placed it on the table with the envelope and the pictures. He added the dog tags and picked up everything in both hands. "Here we go." He closed his eyes, counted to sixty, and opened them. "Nothing's happening."

Elaine took the dog tags from him and opened the chain. "Try wearing these."

Joe leaned over to let her slip the chain over his head. He opened his collar to drop the tags next to his heart and closed his eyes to count to sixty again. Nothing. Not a twinge, not a memory, not a whisper from his past with Elaine. Not even the slightest reminder of his death from a grenade.

He opened his eyes and returned the tags to the table. "That didn't work either."

Elaine picked the dog tags up. "After all your dreams and remembering, you didn't get anything at all?"

"I wish I had. If I have a nightmare tonight like that other one, it might freak you out."

"It sounded bad from how you described it. I'd hate to—Wait a minute, you said you knocked the lamp off and hurt your hand but you didn't wake up. It's not hard to knock a lamp off a table, so your hand couldn't have hurt to the point of it still hurting in the morning." Elaine crossed her arms. "I get it now, darn you. Jillian was in the room next to you and came in the adjoining door, like I told you she'd make sure you two had and woke you up."

"You better be glad she did, or I might have sleepwalked. You wouldn't want that, would you, darlin'?"

"That better be all she did, *darlin'*, or I'm gonna kick her butt if I ever see her again."

"I thought we got all that straightened out? Didn't we get all that straightened out? Doggone it, I thought we got all that—"

"It *better* be straight. If she did anything like getting in bed with you, especially since you sleep naked, we'd have a serious problem on our hands."

"I agree. Talk about a *real* nightmare."

Uh-huh, for *both* of you. Call the chaplain. I'm sure he's wondering what's taking so long."

Joe went to a phone on a table in a corner, and Elaine followed. "Maybe I should get you to make reservations at the hotel restaurant."

"For that nice dinner you're forcing me to buy you, huh?"

"You got it, Mr. Matthan. That's the least you can do for putting me through all of these theories of yours."

* * *

Elaine took the last bite of the delicious redcurrant tart she and Joe had shared for dessert. "Wow, this is almost as good as the blackberry cobbler our moms make."

Joe sipped red wine. "I need to see if Mom can make this sausage and mash. It didn't sound like much when the waiter recommended it."

"I agree. Who would've thought sausage and carrots and mashed potatoes would taste so good mixed all up." Elaine sipped wine. "Are you disappointed in how nothing happened during the service at the cemetery?"

"You call both of us crying when I placed Elaine's chest with everything in it in the grave nothing?"

"I'll give you that. I enjoyed you showing me the memorial after. I'll check it out online and tell my students about it."

"Will you tell them about the Youth Statue?"

"I better not. His butt reminded me of yours."

"Get that thought out of your mind, okay? We've got one last night to sleep together, and you need to behave."

Elaine stood. "Thanks for supper, sweetie. I'm going up to shower while you pay. See you in a bit."

In the bathroom, Elaine left the door cracked to tease Joe when he came up.

Sure, she'd cried at the cemetery, but she always got over her sadness quickly when she was around Joe, probably because of how she liked to tease him. Still, with everything he'd told her concerning what he believed to be his past, along with his recently recalled memory concerning how they had agreed to not make love before they got married, his theory that they were the reincarnations of their long-dead relatives intrigued her. But why couldn't she remember anything else, especially after seeing those extremely touching pictures and reading an even more touching letter? When Joe had mentioned his name on the envelope resembling her handwriting, she hadn't thought much of it, but the rest of the letter was the same, even down to how she would have separated each paragraph, each sentence, and written each emotionally charged point.

Done in the shower, she found the door closed and Dutch voices coming from the TV. Joe couldn't stand the possibility of seeing her naked, poor thing.

Her reflection frowned back at her from the mirror while she brushed her teeth. Since she couldn't think of any more options that might help her remember what might be her past with Joe, and since he hadn't mentioned any, it seemed they'd fly home no further along than when they'd arrived in Liège.

She spat into the sink, rinsed the toothbrush, and eyed herself in the mirror.

Unless, like Joe had said, she dreamed about their past tonight. Nope, it wouldn't happen, but something else might.

She cracked the door open. "Can't you find anything except Dutch shows?"

"I'm just flipping until you finish."

Elaine blow-dried her hair, dabbed perfume on her wrists and neck, and opened the bathroom door. Propped on his pillow, Joe wore those horrid red-plaid pajamas that did nothing to attract her.

"Look at you," he said with a smile. "You look as fresh as a daffodil."

"The bathroom's all yours."

"Good, I need to brush some of that sausage out of my teeth."

"What about a shower?"

"I'll do that in the morning. That way my stinky self will keep you from attacking me." Joe left for the bathroom, and Elaine stood by the door to wait.

Water ran in the sink, followed by the sound of him brushing his teeth and rinsing. She skipped to the bed and leaned over. The door opened, and she wiggled her bottom. "Do you still like my PJ's?"

"Good grief, don't tease me like that. Remember what you said about me being a weak boy? Much more of that and I might throw you in bed and have my way with you."

"It might be the other way around. I'm all better from the motorcycle accident. I might rip those yucky pajamas off you and hold you down and have *my* way."

"So I'm not the only one around here who's weak."

Elaine sat on the bed and patted it. "Let's have a test."

"Like what?"

"Come on over and lie down and find out."

Joe did as she asked. "Women like you are why boys are weak. You realize that, don't you?"

Elaine climbed onto the bed on her hands and knees to give him a view inside the spaghetti-strapped top she wore. She sat on top of him. "Test one, lover. Can you handle it?"

"Darlin', please ..."

"You don't have to beg, sweetie." Elaine kissed him—a long, deep kiss that lingered on and on. He ran his hands along her back, pulled her down, and her hips, seemingly on their own, moved back and forth. Her heart pounded in her ears. She rolled off of him before things went entirely too far. "Wow, if that was hint at how our honeymoon night will go, we need to get married soon."

"You're telling me." Joe rubbed his lower lip. "I didn't know you were a biter."

Elaine giggled. "I think it's because I'd never gotten quite that carried away before. You better hope I never catch you in a compromising position, or I might not stop." She kissed him again, but quickly, and pulled away to snuggle into his shoulder. "Better?"

"Perfect." Joe kissed her cheek. "Can I turn the light out, or do you want to read your paperback?"

"I'm ready for sleep." With the room darkened, Elaine returned to his side, loving his warmth, his strength as he held her, and the oh-so-right feel of his body next to hers. "I love you, sweetie."

"I love you too, darlin'. Always have and always will."

***

Elaine jerked upright in the bed and turned the light on. Joe sat beside her, chest heaving, sweat pouring off him. "Joe, did you—"

"Yes." His throat muscles worked. "Night" —they worked again— "mare. I think I woke myself up this time, screaming. I guess that's what woke you too."

She slipped her arms around him. "How much more of this can you take?"

"I have a feeling we're—or I'm—getting near the end."

"How would you know? It seems like we just started, at least it does for me. What was the nightmare about this time?"

"I'll tell you when we get back home. Ever since I read that part in the letter where Elaine said I might know about Kurt, and where she said I might be there, wherever *there* is, something's been nagging at me. You know how, when you're trying to remember a name and it's right on the tip of your tongue but you still can't remember, that's how this is—was.

"Why can't you tell me now?"

"Because I have a feeling I know more about my existence—my past existence—now than I ever have. You've been in my room back home. It used to be Kurt and Elaine's room before it was Kurt and Ruth's room. There's a bookshelf in one corner, and—"

"It has that old copy of *Call of the Wild* from the 1940's in it," Elaine said. "That's one of my favorites."

"I didn't know that. It's my favorite too."

"More coincidences, but I have a feeling that's not what you're talking about."

"It isn't. There's a book there I've never read, but the title's interesting, more now than ever."

"And?"

"After we get home—I don't know what time it'll be—I want to run over and get that book. I'll come back to your place and tell you about it."

"What about after that? I know you said my memories, dreams, whatever, might come back anytime, but I have a feeling we've done all we can to make that happen. Can you think of anything else?"

"I'll tell you after we check out that book. If I'm right, I want to look in an old cedar chest in the attic that might have something inside to help us out. I saw it when I found my guitar."

"You never mentioned that before."

"It didn't seem important at the time. My nightmare and that book just changed all that."

Joe fell back to the pillow. "Now we just need some sleep for the flight home."

Elaine cuddled into his shoulder. "Not to mention that 300 mile-plus drive back to Alma from the airport."

"Ain't that the truth. Kearney regional and that private jet were a lot closer."

"Maybe you should've talked Jillian into letting us use that." Elaine poked Joe's ribs. "Did it have a bed in it?"

"The only bed you need to worry about is this one. Turn that light out. We've got a long day tomorrow."

Chapter 29

Joe opened the pickup door and half-fell, half-climbed out. "Home sweet home, darlin." He took the carry-ons from the back and met Elaine at the front of the pickup, where she was stretching her back.

"To use one of your favorite sayings, 'good grief,' what a drive." After stretching, Elaine straightened. "What time is it? My watch doesn't light up like yours."

"It's a little after eight a.m. in Liège, so it's two a.m. here. I don't know what I was thinking when I said I'd go to my parents' house and get that book. We'll go tomorrow, if you don't have anything planned."

"Nothing but becoming human again. Let's get inside." Elaine took her carry-on and left for the front porch. "As far as going to your parents' house, what about that cedar chest in the attic and how it pertains to your nightmare, and the book too? You said you'd tell me when we got home."

Joe waited while she unlocked the door. "Let's wait until tomorrow. I want my brain to be fully functioning before I explain everything."

He followed her in and took the carry-ons to her bedroom, where she plopped to the bed. "So, Mr. Matthan, are you planning on staying here tonight? The neighbors will have us the talk of Alma if you do. You know how small-town gossip gets around."

"I could pull my pickup around back, behind all those shrubs lining your yard."

"Good idea, lover."

"I'll 'lover' you, lover. We still need to sleep in our pajamas." He patted the bed. "All right, king-sized. A lot more room than that rinky-dink bed at the hotel."

Elaine slipped her blouse over her head, and Joe turned the other way. "I might be used to sleeping with you, but I can't handle seeing you undress. I'll get into my sexy red-plaid pajamas and brush my teeth."

"Don't take all night. I've got to do the same thing, except more."

Carry-on in hand, Joe stopped at the bathroom door. "I know, I know. Like my mom, you've got to take half-an-hour removing your makeup and whatever other mysterious rituals you women perform while you're in the bathroom."

"That's right, and you've already forgotten to move your pickup. Typical man."

Joe set the carry-on down. "Good point."

* * *

At the sound of the alarm clock's shrill beeping, Joe shoved Elaine. "Why did you set the alarm?"

"To get up early enough for you to cook me breakfast, lover." She rolled toward the nightstand, and the shrill beeping ended. "French toast and coffee please."

"Sounds good. Make enough for both of us."

"You think I'm teasing, don't you? I don't tease about breakfast."

"I found that out the last two mornings in our hotel." Joe raised up on elbow to kiss Elaine's nose. "You sure are calling me "lover" a lot."

"You don't like it?"

"If my plan helps you remember your past with me, it'll be a lot more accurate."

"Because I'll remember actually being your wife *and* lover, right?"

"One night's worth until we get married."

"When are you going to tell me about your plan?"

"When we take a look at that book in my shelf at home. Dad will be out working. Mom goes to the Y for yoga on Tuesdays and usually has breakfast with friends. That should give us plenty of time."

"Sounds perfect, lover. You can start my breakfast anytime now."

"When are you gonna do something for me that deserves breakfast? This marriage has got to be a two-way street." Joe rolled over. "How about a backrub?"

Elaine smacked his bottom. "There you go, forgetting something else like you forgot to move your pickup. We're not married yet."

On the way to the bathroom, Joe rubbed his butt. "That stung. Wait until I get a chance to smack your butt. It won't be covered either."

Elaine threw his pillow at him; it hit the door as he closed it. "Too slow, darlin'. Let's grab a quick bite at a fast-food place and eat on the way. I'll have plenty of time to fix you breakfast after we get married."

"Okay, but hurry up. The only thing wrong this house is it has one bathroom."

* * *

Swallowing his last bite of a somewhat unappetizing breakfast sandwich that tasted like burnt grease, Joe parked in his parent's driveway. "Ugh, remind me to not try a fatback biscuit again."

"No problem." Elaine shoved her trash into the fast-food bag. "You're gonna fix me breakfast soon, remember?"

She held the bag open, and Joe dropped the wrapper in. "Do you think so?"

"Even if your plan doesn't help me remember anything, don't you still want to get married soon?"

"You got it, darlin'." He opened the door. "But let's take this plan of mine one step at a time. I'm not giving up on it yet."

In Joe's room, he took the book he'd told Elaine about from the bookcase and gave it to her. "Check out the title."

"*The Ghosts of Longing?* You said you never read it. How do you know if it has anything to do with your—our—pasts?"

Joe sat on the bed. "Have a seat. What I'm about to tell you is different from my theory that we're reincarnations of our previous selves—radically different."

Elaine sat. "*How* radically different?"

"Let's peek in this book. I bet it'll tell us."

"Why, because it has—" Elaine pointed at the title. "Come on now, Joe. You think we're ghosts because it has ghosts in the title?"

"Not now, but I think we became ghosts when we died in our previous lives."

Elaine tilted her head to one side. "You better tell me why you think that before I call 911 and have you committed. That's a *lot* worse than thinking we were reincarnated." She straightened her head. "Wait a minute. You never told me about your nightmare at the hotel. Is it why you think we were ghosts?"

Joe kissed her cheek. "Aren't you smart?"

"Forget that and get to the point."

"It sure was my nightmare. It picked up after the other one with the grenade explosion. Those words we both remembered you saying— 'I've got to believe you'll come back to me'—I heard them as I lay dying in the snow. More is coming back to me, and I remember when you said them, during our honeymoon night at the river."

"I knew you were going to war, so I would've definitely said that." Elaine gave him a slight smile. "Listen to me, it sounds like I'm beginning to believe it as much as you."

"I'm not sure if you will the more I tell you. It's pretty bizarre."

"Let's take a look in this book first. You know how I like to read."

She gave it to Joe. He flipped the pages, magically stopping on one that had popped into his mind for some unknown reason—page forty-four. He read a few lines. "Doggone, darlin', I was right. Read that first paragraph out loud so the whole world can hear it."

She took the book. "Yeah, right. The more you talk, the more 911 is looking like an option. Let's see what's got you so excited."

"'According to some who have reported reincarnation instances, deep hypnosis has revealed that reincarnation was likely not the issue. Instead, multiple examples of other persons revealed that the person had probably existed in spirit form after dying, within the bodies of others while attempting to reunite with a loved one.'"

Joe nudged her knee with his. "Not as dumb as I look, am I?"

"I'm not saying a word. Keep telling me about what happened to you."

"After I died, I was alive again, but in a body. The best way I can explain it is I actually *was* this person, except I had no control over his movements and couldn't hear his thoughts."

"What person are you talk—?"

"Let me finish. It'll go back a lot quicker if you wait until I'm done before you ask questions."

"Okay, okay, go ahead."

"The person was a soldier I was patrolling a section of the Ardennes Forest with. His name was James Daniel, and he was Black." Joe paused. "I see your eyebrows rising. Yeah, I thought about how black and white soldiers were segregated during World War II, but I know from some of the history shows on TV how black artillery units served in the war. It stands to reason that during the Battle of the Bulge, which had some of the bloodiest fighting in Europe, some of those battalions were attacked to the point of the men having to regroup and fight wherever they were needed."

"That makes sense. Anything else?"

"Anyway, James died. I'm not sure how because I blacked out. I guess a ghost can black out from the shock of finding out he's a ghost. The next people I joined, lived in, existed in—whatever you call it—are just flashes in my mind, mostly. The one after James was a boy in a concentration camp. He died in his mother's arms within a few minutes of me being with him. The next thing I knew I was with a British girl who'd been injured, and she died while a doctor was amputating her leg. Then, right away—I mean like that very second— I was with the doctor. The death of the girl upset him so bad, he went to his office and shot himself."

"That's terrible, Joe. I don't know how you didn't go insane dealing with all that."

"What choice did I have?"

Elaine took his hand in hers. "None. What happened after the doctor?"

"I don't know why, but those are even weaker memories than the first. I guess since those were the most traumatic, because they happened during the war, the memories sort of stuck, know what I mean?"

"How long did you live like—" Elaine's mouth slowly fell open. "Oh, my God, Joe, did you live like that until you were— until you were born again?"

"I'm pretty sure I did. I remember the last three people I was with. The first was a boy who lived in Kansas. That would've been around 1999 or so. His name was Sam."

"Why's that name familiar? Could it be because your middle name is Samuel?"

"I have no idea."

"He was just a boy? It wasn't wartime, so what—" Elaine's brow knotted. "Did he and his family die when a train hit their car? That's awfully familiar."

"Maybe you read it when you were a kid in one of those ancient newspapers at the hardware store."

"I'm not sure. It's strange how ..."

"You're remembering things, right? It might not be strange at all."

"What about the other two people you were with before you were born, or is that *re*-born. This is confusing."

"I'll tell you the last. I'm saving the other until ..."

"*Until* when?"

"I have an idea how to make you remember more."

"I guess I don't get to know that either."

"I'd rather we find out with as few hints as possible."

"Fine, what's next?"

Joe stood. "Let's visit the attic."

Chapter 30

In the hall, Joe pulled the string to the spring-loaded door, which squeaked on its way down from the ceiling. He unfolded the steps. "We need a flashlight. Dad keeps a couple in the pantry in the kitchen." He returned to hand Elaine one of the flashlights and unfolded the steps.

At the top, he pulled a second string, and a single lightbulb hanging from a wire somewhat illuminated the musty smelling attic.

Elaine shined a beam of light around. "I'm glad there's a floor, or we might step through the ceiling."

"Uh-huh. I'd have a hard time explaining that to Mom and Dad."

"We're not mentioning any of this to our parents, right?"

Joe turned his flashlight on. "That's a no-brainer, darlin'."

"Good, I'm not into straightjackets."

Joe crept along the creaking wood floor that ran the length of the attic. The planking only covered the center fifteen feet or so of the house. On either side, where the rafters sloped to the overhangs, cobwebs hung near the pink insulation. On the end of the attic facing the sun, slivers of light shined through the eves, falling on several carboard boxes. About half way from the steps to the darker end, he stopped at the cedar chest, lifted the lid, and shined the light inside. "When I found the guitar, I was so excited I forgot about this chest. I'm glad I remembered."

Elaine shined her light into the chest also. "That looks like an old quilt." She moved the light. "There's a couple more, and there's one of those floofy dresses you told me about."

"Look harder. It's not just any floofy dress, it's *the* floofy dress."

Elaine gave Joe the flashlight and lifted the dress. "You're right. It's the dress Elaine wore in the picture that was taken of her and Joe at that office where we think they got married." She held the dress to her nose. "Mmm, I love the smell a cedar chest gives clothes."

"Me too. When we have our home built, I'll drag this one out of the attic for the foot of our bed. You do realize whose it is, don't you?"

"Oh, wow, it must be Elaine's. Since she and Kurt lived here all those years before she died, I bet she kept this at the foot of her bed."

"What do you think of the quilt?" Joe took it from the chest, and Elaine traded him the dress. She turned the quilt over in her hands.

"It's seen better days."

Joe could've grinned or laughed, but he didn't. He wanted to see if Elaine could guess without any hints. "Do you have any idea why?"

"How would I know?"

"Think about the dream I had about our honey—"

"You mean this is the same quilt we made love on in your dream?"

"I recognize the blue and green patches. Since that's the case, I'm sure Joe and Elaine—me and you—took this same quilt to the river every time they—we—went there. No wonder it could use a stitch or two."

"That's amazing. I sure hope I can remember everything you are. What's the rest of your plan?"

Joe dug around in the chest, pulling out more women's clothing, and stopped. "This thing's full of stuff."

"Are you looking for anything in particular?"

"The fatigues I wore on our honeymoon night."

"I doubt the Army would've returned those. Why are you looking for them?"

"I want to recreate our honeymoon at the river. You'll wear that dress and I'll buy some fatigues at the Army Surplus in town, as close to what I wore back then. Then we'll spend the night under the stars by a fire and sleep on this very same quilt. If that doesn't bring back more of my memories, and especially yours, I don't know what will."

"I'm willing, but what if …?"

"I know what you're thinking. We promised we wouldn't make love until we get married."

"What if that's what it takes?"

Joe took out two more quilts. "It's still May. We might need these for the cool nights."

"I have blankets at home we can take."

"I have a reason for wanting these."

"Let me guess—another *secret* reason. Why didn't you answer when I asked if us making love is what it takes to remember?"

"As far as the blankets, my reason won't be a secret for long." Joe closed the chest. "As far as us having to make love for you to remember, it shouldn't take that because of everything I've already remembered. Doesn't that make sense?"

"You never know until you know." Dress in hand, Elaine left for the pull-down steps. "Typical man that you are, I guess you want me to make us something to eat for our experimental night at the river."

"Unless you want a greasy fatback biscuit."

They climbed down the steps and Joe let them up. "What's your plans until we go to the river?"

"We can run by the grocery for the sandwich stuff and whatever you want for lunch. I might watch a little TV or take a walk after."

Joe took the flashlights back to the kitchen. "I'll check out the war surplus place after lunch."

"What about our parents? They were expecting us back today."

"We'll text them our plans. We stayed at the river overnight fishing before, so it isn't anything new. Then we'll be ready to go."

* * *

At the river, Joe took the cooler with the food from his pickup. "I'll come back for the quilts and pillows when I move my pickup down the thickest part of the path that leads to the low ground."

"Your dad sure grows some great sweet corn there." Elaine took the carry-on with the fatigues and her dress from the pickup and joined Joe as they walked to the river. "I think it's a good idea to move your pickup. We want tonight to be as historically accurate as possible if I'm going to remember anything."

Thick grass, green and lush, swished about their legs. A cotton-tail rabbit burst from beside Joe and zigzagged away, its cotton-ball tail marking its erratic path toward the woods.

Joe bumped Elaine's shoulder. "Do you want to run away like that rabbit? Anything might happen tonight."

"I'll be fine if I don't have any of your screaming nightmares." She set the carry-on on the picnic table, and Joe did the same with the cooler.

"I'll put this in the pickup after we eat."

Elaine took off her watch and engagement ring and offered them to Joe. "Lock these in the pickup when you go back for the quilts and pillows. We don't need any reminders of the present."

Joe pointed at his wrist. "Good idea, I forget about my watch." He returned to the pickup, left the watches and ring in the glove compartment, and came back with the quilts and pillows to place them beside the cooler. "I'll take the cooler back and move the pickup after we eat. That way I won't have to walk so far."

Elaine faced the oak. "I don't think we can hide Kurt and Ruth's headstones."

"They're behind the oak. I'll make the fire on this side anyway. I doubt there'll be enough light to see them."

"What about the daffodil greenery that's coming up? Was that in your dream?"

Joe scratched his head. "Can we ignore it?"

"Nope. Run and get your dad's lawnmower."

Joe started toward the pickup, and Elaine grabbed his arm. "I'm kidding, Mr. Perfectionist. Everything around here is green, so it should be fine. Let's spread the quilt and eat."

* * *

Stomach full, Joe took the cooler to the pickup, moved it down the path, and followed the orange glow of the fire back to the oak. The shadows of twilight, romantic and inviting, were settling along the river bottom as the sun lowered into the trees across the wide expanse of water. The fire flickered, its warmth as welcome and romantic as the twilight.

At the oak, he sat beside Elaine on the quilt.

The sun quickly transformed into a red glow that faded into darkness. All around, the sounds of the night serenaded them. An owl cried *who-who-o-o-o* from across the river, and one by one, crickets joined each other in a chorus of chirping. The sky gradually darkened in the west, until the curtain of night darkened the river bottom, except for the circle of light from the fire surrounding the quilt. The final breath of the day whispered through the leaves of the oak, a calm and reassuring rustle.

Joe slipped his arm around Elaine's shoulders. "As much as I love this place, it'd be nothing without you here."

"I feel the same about you, sweetie." Elaine leaned against him, her body firm and warm but soft at the same time. "I know we have a lot of hopes for tonight. If I don't remember, I'll always believe we're meant to be together, okay?"

"I still hope you can remember as much as you can."

"Have you?"

"It seems like every few minutes another memory pops into my head. One in particular was hard to believe, even to the point of making me mad. Then I remembered more and I got over it."

"I don't get to know?"

"I'd rather see what happens tonight, or in the future. Regardless, we'll get married as soon as possible. If you don't remember anything, I'll tell you about it."

Elaine patted Joe's knee. "After the honeymoon, right? We'll be too busy otherwise."

"Got that right, darlin'."

Elaine snuggled closer. "Your memories sound intriguing. As long as we're together, I can wait until after our honeymoon."

Joe stood. "I guess it's time to change clothes."

Elaine stood also. "We didn't think about what to wear while we're sleeping."

"I thought about it but didn't say anything. Do you know why?"

"Because you plan on sleeping naked and turning me into a *weak* girl?"

"We're recreating our honeymoon, so we *have* to sleep naked. I mean *together* naked."

"I don't know about that. Clothes or not, like the last time we were here when I licked your chest, or when we made up on my sofa after Jillian threatened to kiss you, or at the hotel in Liège, when my hips had a mind of their own, I might not be able to handle it."

"It sounds like you're already a weak girl, doesn't it?"

"My weakness has an accomplice and you know it."

Joe opened the carry-on and gave Elaine the dress. "Here you go. You might as well lose your bra and drawers now instead of later."

"Women wear panties, not drawers, you knothead." Elaine took the fatigues and shoved them into his chest. "*You*, Mr. Matthan, can lose *your* drawers. Make sure you put the carry on behind the oak while you're changing too."

"Good idea. We can't have any reminders of the present messing up your memory." Joe started for the oak but stopped. "You realize the Elaine of the past would be a lot shyer than you."

"Meaning?"

"*Sexually* shy. Don't take me into the present with your hip-wiggling self when we're under the quilts naked."

"Don't temp me then."

Joe returned to the picnic table and took the wrapped vase from the carry-on. "This tempted me in Liège. I ran by home for it while I was out for the fatigues."

Elaine dropped cross-legged to the quilt. "I feel like a kid at Christmas. I bet you brought me a present from your first trip to Belgium."

"I see I'll have to double-wrap all your Christmas presents when I put them under the tree." Joe gave Elaine the package. "It's not much, but I'm pretty sure you'll like it."

"Why aren't you completely sure?" She removed the wrapping. "Thank you, sweetie. It'll be perfect for when the daffodils bloom." She returned the vase. "It's modern. You better hide it with everything else."

"One more thing that *isn't* modern." He took a yellow ribbon from the carry-on. "I got this from the chest in the attic while I was at home. I think it's probably the ribbon Elaine took with her to the river."

"How do you know that?"

"Because she would've saved it, wouldn't you?"

"Makes sense." Elaine took the ribbon from Joe. "Thinking about my great-aunt sitting here on this same quilt and missing Joe is one of the saddest things I've ever imagined."

"The time for being sad is over, okay? I've got a few other things I found in the cedar chest. One's in the pickup, I'll save it for tomorrow. I'll show you the other after we change."

"What are you saving until tomorrow?"

"You'll just have to wait and see, darlin'."

"You're being mysterious. I hope it's something I'll like."

"Like I'd show you something you *didn't* like. I'm going behind the oak to change." Joe changed into the fatigues and returned to the picnic table. "Don't you look nice in your floofy yellow dress?"

Elaine turned around. "At least it stops at my knees. That way you get to see my legs from there down."

Joe held the carry-on open. "Stick your clothes in here so I can put everything behind the oak." He took the carry-on behind the oak, took an envelope from it, and left the carry-on there. At the quilt, he offered Elaine the envelope. "I found this in an old purse with Ruth's driver's license in it."

Elaine took the envelope and opened it. "These look like the same pictures in the envelope in the chest in Belgium. They look a lot newer though."

"I remember Grandpa saying Ruth had copies of those pictures. Apparently, she kept the ribbon too. She and Elaine must have been great friends." He took the envelope and pictures. "I'll put these back in the carry-on."

With the pictures safely stored, he returned to the quilt once more to sit, and Elaine squeezed his knee. "You're up and down like a yo-yo."

"Right, like when you'll have me doing chores after we're married. Oh, while I was at home, Mom asked me about work. I told her not to worry about that or us staying here tonight, because I don't have to start work until mid-June."

"When you told me that on the flight back, I was surprised. Still, it gives us more time together before you have to enter the working world."

"Uh-huh, working so we can afford our dream home here." Joe moved behind Elaine and knelt. "Give me the ribbon so I can tie your hair in a ponytail like it was in my dream. We need to be accurate, you know."

Elaine gathered her hair and held it up. "Tie it where I'm holding it. Tie it like you would your shoelaces."

An intense wave of déjà vu hit Joe, making him slightly dizzy. Where had this moment happened in his past? It hadn't happened during the honeymoon dream. A scene blurred into his mind—of Elaine kneeling before him on the quilt, wearing 1940's style jeans and a flannel shirt. Could it be their first date? If so, he might remember the rest tonight.

"What's taking so long, Mr. Weak Boy? Are you fantasizing about kissing my neck and touching it with a daffodil bloom?"

Joe tied the knot and stood to offer Elaine his hand. "Come on up here so we can get my plan going. From here on out, I'll try to recreate our honeymoon like I dreamed it."

Elaine took his hand, rose to her bare feet, and tugged at the olive-drab T-shirt he wore. "Not very sexy, sweetie." She slipped her hands under the shirt, and he jumped at their cold touch.

"Okay, okay, that didn't happen in the dream, but I can still warm you up." He slipped his arms around her. "How's this?"

"Much better." She rested her head on his chest and rocked back and forth. "Too bad you didn't bring your guitar. We could have music to dance by."

"How could I do that and hold you too?" Joe gave her a squeeze and pulled away slightly. The fire's flames had died, leaving the circle around the quilt lit with soft flickers of orange light, which illuminated Elaine's face and reflected within her brown eyes. "I love you, the future Mrs. Matthan. I hope you know how much."

"I …" The hint of tears shone in Elaine's eyes. Joe cupped her cheeks in his palms. "What's wrong?"

"I was thinking how Elaine and Joe held each other right here, probably at this very spot on their honeymoon night. That must have been when she begged him to come back to her, and he couldn't."

Joe held her as tight as he could without hurting her. "She did say that, remember? We talked about it."

"Please don't tell me. I might cry if you do."

Joe pulled away again and kissed her forehead. "Don't cry, darlin', it's all right. You remember, don't you?"

Elaine nodded. "I have to believe you'll come back to me."

"That's right. "I have to believe you'll come back to me. Let's say it together."

"I have to believe you'll come back to me."

"I hope you won't be disappointed." Elaine lay her head on his shoulder again.

"Why would I be disappointed? I'm glad you remembered."

"I'm not sure I remembered. Those words are exactly what I would have said."

Joe caressed her hair, with its sweet floral scent he loved so well. "We have plenty of time. There's a couple more things we need to do. I'm sure you'll like the last one but not the first one."

"You and your surprises. Let's get the first one over with."

"Don't say I didn't warn you. You've got to sing."

"Yeah, right, I sang that night as foreplay. Stop teasing me."

"No foreplay, but that's how I knew you'd sing so well in church when you helped me with *Poor Wayfaring Stranger*. Did you realize you just said 'I' instead of your great-aunt?"

"I might as well start believing in our past as much as you do. Maybe that'll help me remember."

"Do you remember those lines I had you sing?"

"I love that old song. What did we do while we sang?"

Joe swayed side to side. "We danced. Join me on those last two lines like you did in church."

> *I am a poor, wayfaring stranger*
> *While traveling through, this world of woe*
> *Yet there's no sickness, toil nor danger*
> *In that bright world, to which I go*
> *I'm going there, to see my father*
> *I'm going there, no more to roam*
> *I'm only going, over Jordan*
> *I'm only going, over home*
> *I know dark clouds, will gather 'round me*
> *I know my way, is rough and steep*
> *Yet beauteous fields, lie just before me*
> *Where God's redeemed, their vigils sleep*
> *I'm going there, to see my mother*
> *She said she'd meet, me when I come*
> *I'm only going, over Jordan*
> *I'm only going, over home*

Their last words echoed across the river bottom. "Great job, darlin'. Next time we sing in church, you're gonna have to sing the whole song with me."

"Is my voice that good, or are you pulling my leg?"

"'Pulling your leg?' Where'd you hear that old euphemism?"

"Uncle Thomas says it once in a while." Elaine poked Joe's chest. "Where'd you get 'euphemism' from?"

"I'm expanding my vocabulary. After all, I'm marrying a teacher."

"What's the next step in our night's plans, the one you said I'd like?"

"Do I tell you or just do it?"

"You're surprising me every time I turn around. Why stop now?"

"Good choice of words. It involves you turning around."

Elaine whirled about. "Now what?"

Joe took a deep breath. "Can you give me a minute? I've been thinking about this ever since I dreamed it, and I want to take it slow."

"Only if you put your arms around me. Let's stand here and enjoy the night before you do whatever it is you're going to do."

Joe pulled her close and buried his face into her neck, again taking in the sweet aroma of her silky hair. He hardly believed this night was happening, that they were standing here warm and snug in each other's arms exactly as he'd dreamed. Would she have her own dream tonight and remember their past together? Regardless, their lives together—here and now— were the best possible gifts he could ever receive—a gift of hope.

Fresh and crisp, a cool breeze blew, stirring the fire. Sparks burst from the embers, rising with flare and flicker, pinpricks of light dancing upward among the stars until they faded into the black of night. The crickets had long ceased their chirping, but again, the owl called from across the river with its *who-who-o-o-o-o*, while the barest sliver of brilliant moon rose from over the horizon.

Elaine looked back at Joe over her shoulder. "This is as perfect a night as we've ever had together. Thank you for making it happen."

Joe laughed. "Thank you for putting up with all my eccentricities concerning my theory."

Elaine laughed too, soft and low. "My goodness, if you keep learning more big words like 'eccentricities' and 'euphemism,' I might get turned on. Like you said, I *am* a teacher." She turned around and gave him a quick kiss. "I think it's time for that final step."

"You've got to turn around again."

"Okay, Mr. Matthan, but you're making me feel like a merry-go-round."

"Doggone it."

"Don't tell me you forgot something?"

"I probably have some of the steps out of order. It *has* been over seventy-five years since I did this."

Elaine faced him. "What did you forget?"

Joe stepped to the fire. "I like this part. While I put more wood on the fire, you unbutton your dress partway and let it hang off your shoulders to catch my eye. When I look up from the fire and see you, I come over."

"That sounds exactly like something I'd do."

Joe added a few sticks to the fire, stirred the embers, and looked up. Elaine, with her bare shoulders glowing in the firelight, gave him a sideways glance and suggestive smile. He swallowed. She was just as beautiful as in his dream.

He stood and slipped his arms around her. "Can I get a kiss before we get to the final steps? If I kiss you after, it's gonna be tough to stop."

Elaine stood on tiptoe and kissed him. "That's all you get. If I do any more, I might attack you in your sleep."

"What a great way to wake up." Joe gave her a peck on the cheek. "It's time to turn around again."

"Okay, what now?"

"This." Joe pulled the yellow ribbon holding her ponytail until the knot loosened and her hair flowed in soft, silky waves about her bare shoulders. He turned her around and slipped the ribbon into his pants pocket. "I'm sure we want to hold on to that as a keepsake."

Elaine ran her fingers through her hair, stretched and yawned. "Now I know what jet lag is. Do we get to snuggle in the quilts soon? I'm sleepy."

"Remember what you called me the day I proposed?"

"Hot ass, hot ass."

"You're about to get a look at it, or have you forgotten we're supposed to sleep naked?"

Elaine pulled at his belt. "Okay, hot ass, let's get this show on the road."

Joe grabbed her hands. "Whoa, farm girl, you first. Turn around."

"Didn't you say I wouldn't have to do that anymore?" Elaine crossed her arms and turned around.

"You won't regret it." Joe slipped the dress from her shoulders and let it fall to the quilt. He lifted her hair, kissed her neck, and traced a line of kisses along her shoulder. She shivered and pressed into him, moaning softly as goose bumps rose on her skin. Joe stepped away. "I think we better stop. My turn. After that we'd better get to bed." He turned her around, struggling to keep his eyes on hers instead of allowing them to roam over her body, and held his arms up. "Slip my shirt off. You're supposed to help."

She did so. "With the pants too?"

"Loosen them and let them fall. While you're getting under the quilts, I'll put them and the dress on the picnic table."

Elaine loosened his belt. Before she undid the button, Joe lifted her chin. "Ah-ah, no peeking."

"You, Mr. Matthan, are no fun at all."

Keeping her eyes on his, she finished, and his pants fell around his ankles. The chilly night air raised goosebumps on his skin as he took their clothes to the picnic table. He ran the few steps back, his feet wet and cold from the dew on the grass, and joined Elaine beneath the quilts.

She gave him a peck on the cheek and rolled over to face the fire. "Since we have to be good, I'll watch the fire until I go to sleep." Joe snuggled close, and she jerked her bottom away. "Hey! How can I sleep with *that* distracting me?"

"Sheesh, you're hard to please."

"The problem is, I want to be pleased and can't be. Back up. You can keep your arm around me without *everything* being against me, can't you?"

Joe did as she asked. "Better?"

"Thanks, but if we don't get married soon ..."

"I know. Imagine how difficult it is for me since I've dreamed about us making love."

"Let's try to sleep, okay? That's about the only way I can get your warm, naked self off my mind."

"Good night, darlin', I love you."

"I love you too, sweetie. Good night."

Chapter 31

Joe awoke to darkness. Behind him, over the rise leading away from the river, a hint of light shone in the eastern sky.

Elaine still faced away from him, quilts pulled to her chin like when she'd fallen asleep. Apparently she'd had no dreams or nightmares, meaning she wouldn't remember any of their shared past anytime soon.

Wisps of smoke rose from the fire, its embers red and glowing. A stick snapped near the woods to the right. Barely visible, a deer nibbled grass at the edge of the clearing.

Joe pulled the warm quilts around himself and closed his eyes.

* * *

Joe woke to the touch of what had to be Elaine's fingertips. Soft and smooth, they traced warm lines along his forehead, down his nose, and paused to barely touch his lips. His pulse pounded in his ears, and it was all he could do to control his breathing. He didn't want her to know he was awake, because her touching him in such a seductive way—while she thought he was asleep—excited him, and he wanted to see what she'd do next. The quilt rose to allow cool air to nip at his skin, and she rolled over on top of him.

"I know you're awake, sweetie. I could tell by how you were

breathing while I was touching you."

Elaine's lips, soft and luscious, searched his, tasting, tempting. Her body, warm and firm, tensed with passion. As much as Joe wanted to complete their night together by making love, he couldn't break the promise they had made so long ago. He turned his head away, breaking their kiss. "Elaine, please—" She pulled his face around and kissed him again, almost to the point of pain.

Their lovemaking held a passion Joe hadn't expected. Elaine sat up, her skin golden with the rays of the rising sun while continuing her elegant and exquisite rhythm. Joe timed his motion with hers, until she collapsed onto him, their hearts pounding together. Elaine nuzzled his ear. "I hope you're not upset with me."

"Not upset, maybe disappointed. More with me than you."

Elaine raised up. "You shouldn't be."

"But—"

Elaine placed her fingertips to his lips. "You don't understand, Joe." She smiled and kissed his forehead. "I remember."

"Darlin', as much as I want to believe you ..."

"You think I'd fake it? Most of what I remember is our honeymoon night. If I tell you what I said when I woke up back then, won't that prove I'm not faking?"

"As much as I've put you through, I hate to ask you to prove anything. I am curious, though."

"When I woke back then, you were still asleep, and I said, sort of like I was singing, 'Joe-o-o-o ... Joe-o-o-o.'"

Again, Joe's pulse pounded. Had she really remembered? "And then?"

"I said the same thing, but I added 'time to wake up' in the same singing way. You were still asleep, so I touched your face like I did while ago."

"There was one more thing before ..."

"I assume you were going to say 'before we made love.' I said, 'Good morning, my dear husband, I hated to wake you. You looked as peaceful as this place makes me feel."

Joe smiled. "You sure did, and I said, 'Good morning to you, Mrs. Matthan, I hope you slept well.' After that you wanted to make love again. I said we didn't have time, so you pretty much attacked me like you just did."

Elaine rolled over and snuggled into his shoulder. He looked into her eyes. "Are you okay? You know, since it's your first time."

"You couldn't tell? I was more than okay, obviously."

"'Obviously' is right. You pretty much had your way with me."

"You better get used to it, sweetie. As far as my 'being okay,' I have a theory about it. It's about time, don't you think, with you having all of yours?"

"That's for sure. What's your theory?"

"Remember when the deer crashed my Harley and me, and the doctor said my X-ray showed I had broken my arm sometime in my life?"

"Yeah, that was weird."

"Bits and pieces of my past are coming back. I distinctly remember lying on the ground by a red tractor, holding my arm and crying."

"What's that got to do with whether or not making love the first time might hurt you?"

"One thing is how the same tractor is parked beneath a shed at my parents' house. In my memory it's new, not weather-beaten and faded like it is now. Maybe my dad—back then—bought it and I was climbing on it and fell off. And remember what your professor said about how DNA could be used to identify twins? I have a theory about that too. I think our bodies might be twins of our previous selves. If that's true, it means our re-born bodies were the same as when we died, and *that* means I wouldn't be a virgin, not technically. That's why it didn't hurt one bit."

Joe agreed with Elaine's theory, except for one part he regretted.

"Why do you look sad?" she asked.

"Well, I kind of wish we'd waited until we were married."

Elaine tapped his nose. "I can't believe you don't understand yet. There's another reason you should believe me. Since I remember, that means we didn't break our promise. Do you know why?"

Joe smiled so huge it made his cheeks ache. "Well doggone. Because we've been married all this time?"

Elaine rolled on top of him. "Aren't *you* the intelligent farm boy? Now make love to me like you mean it."

Chapter 32

Joe rolled over. Asleep again, Elaine was facing him. Locks of sun-streaked hair fell across her face. Her chest rose and fell evenly, unlike the third time they'd made love again after eating the leftover sandwiches and washing them down with cold water.

Beneath her eyelids, her eyes darted back and forth, and her breathing accelerated. She must be dreaming. She jerked upright. "What?"

"I think you were dreaming, darlin'."

Elaine shook her head, burst into tears, and Joe sat up to hold her. Not a dream but a nightmare. He rubbed her back until she stopped crying. "Are you ready to tell me about it?"

She raised her head from his shoulder and wiped her eyes. "I think I know what memory of ours made you angry. Before I tell you, I have another memory you'd like to know. What do you know about my death?"

"I'd rather you tell me."

"I died from cancer in December of 1997. That day is crystal clear in so many ways. One is because that's when I gave Ruth the letter we read at the cemetery. Another is because that's when I gave her the letter to ask her to take my ashes to be buried with you in Belgium. One more is because when I died, I entered my first person. Any questions so far?"

"No ma'am, not a one." Joe grinned. "But I'm *dying* to know who your first person was."

Elaine tousled his hair. "Listen to you, daring to make a pun about death. No more jokes, okay?"

"Yeah, that was pretty bad. I'll shut up for now."

"Good, because after I tell you this next part, I'll tell you something I think you haven't remembered. When I died, it was like those life-after-death experiences you've heard about, where you're drawn toward a white light. In my case the white light was over a table where a woman was giving birth to a baby, and I was with the woman."

Wincing, Joe shook his head. "Whoa. I'm glad I never had to go through anything like that."

"You couldn't have handled it if you did, *weak boy*. Anyway, it took me a minute to realize what was happening. If it hadn't been for my book—"

"*Your* book? You mean the The Ghosts of Longing was yours? I thought it might've been Ruth's."

"I'm still a bit fuzzy on certain things. I think I bought it because I believed it might give me a clue as to whether your spirit might still exist on earth, and you were trying to get back to me. Didn't you tell me something like that on our honeymoon night?"

As near as I can remember, it was something like 'no matter what happens—even if the worst comes—I'll always be with you.' I think I also said 'as long as hope lives, I think anything's possible.' That could be interpreted as me trying to get back to you, don't you think?"

"I do." Elaine kissed him, a slow, luscious joining of their lips that left him considering if she wanted to make love again. She ended the kiss and tapped his nose. "And you came back to me."

"I sure did. What do you think you've remembered that I haven't?"

"It was about the woman who was giving birth. Her name was Rachel Lewis."

"Sam's mom? You were with her when Sam was born?"

"I said the crash was familiar, remember? She and Adam were great parents, and Hope was a genuine sweetheart. You said you were with Sam when the car pulled in front of the train. If I remember correctly, he was about two when that happened. When did you—for the lack of a better word—*join* with him?"

"About a week after his first birthday. Wait a minute, that means—"

"Exactly right, we were together and didn't even know it. Are you ready to hear about the next person I joined? I only had two. I was re-born to Mom and Dad after—"

"Was it Ruth?"

"How could you know that?" Elaine frowned. "Wait a minute, didn't you say you were with two more people after Sam?"

"That's right. Have you guessed one of them?"

"Was it Kurt?"

"It sure was. Did you remember something in the book that makes you think that?"

"You read more of it when you went back for the ribbon and pictures, didn't you?"

"Yeah, I did."

"You read the theory the author has about the ghosts of people being with someone close to the person they're trying to return too, right?"

"You got it."

"That's amazing, Joe. You joined Kurt and I joined Ruth on the same night the Lewis family died."

"That has to be what happened. I stayed with Kurt until he passed away from cancer."

"I'm glad you aren't jealous about me marrying an ex-German soldier. He was a great dad to Joseph."

"I didn't think much of him at first, but he grew on me. Ruth was an absolute mess. She wouldn't let him get away with anything."

"That's one of the reasons I insisted she marry Kurt when she visited me on the day I died." Elaine laughed. "The day after I joined her, she offered to cook a pot roast and bring it over for their supper. She brought it early and went home to change clothes, but she caught Kurt in his robe when she came back and teased him worse than I ever did. We laughed so hard, I thought she'd wet her pants."

"It was like that for me and Kurt too."

"When Ruth went back home to change clothes, she was worried about what outfit she was going to wear when she went back to Kurt's for dinner. I think that's why I experienced that déjà vu when you and I were standing at the closet."

"She looked great in that turquoise dress." Joe lowered his head for a second. "I hate to bring this up, but since we were with Kurt and Ruth all that time, you were there when he figured out he threw the grenade that killed me."

"I don't blame you for not wanting to bring it up," Elaine said, meaning it. "But, as you say, since we were with Kurt and Ruth at the same time, you were there when she made him understand the war was at fault more than him."

"I'm pretty sure you know it took a while for that to sink in."

"I hated it—you know I did—but Kurt was a good man and a fine person."

"I knew it but I didn't want to admit it. He gave you what I wanted to and couldn't—a happy life. It didn't take me long to forgive him, especially since his guilt gave him a heart attack."

"Did you forgive him then or—"

"Think about it, darlin'," Joe said, interrupting her. "I bet you know when I forgave him."

"Was it during their wedding?" Elaine asked, tilting her head to one side.

"Your memories seem to be coming back as fast as mine did after I had my nightmare on our last night in Liège."

"They are. When Ruth and Kurt kissed, it was like some of our more passionate kisses we've had lately. Who was your last person? Since Kurt died two years after being diagnosed with cancer, you had to be with someone else."

"Remember in your letter, when you said something about the possibility of me being 'there' when Ruth did whatever it was you had asked her to do? Now we know 'there' was the cemetery in Belgium. You were right, I was there, with—"

"I remember, Joe! The soldier who was crying and rubbing his neck—the same one Joseph talked to after the service—you were with him, weren't you?"

"Quite the coincidence, huh? It's strange how, when we were emotional, the people we were with would rub their necks."

"That's true," Elaine said, nodding. "The night Kurt told Ruth about how he thought he killed you, they rubbed their necks until they were red."

Joe kissed Elaine's forehead. "Do you know how glad I am that we've figured all this out? I wanted to tell you for a long time, but—"

"Don't say another word. I'd hate to be fitted for a straightjacket, and that's what I might have thought you needed if you'd told me without the rest of your memories and those phrases we remembered." Elaine gave Joe a quick kiss. "When can we get married? We need to make me an honest woman in the eyes of our modern-day parents."

"Whenever you'd like, darlin'. You want the wedding here, right?"

"Next weekend would be perfect."

"It's a date, but …"

"No, you don't, Mr. Matthan, no excuses. We're getting married next weekend and that's final."

"I was going to say it's a good thing I brought the wedding dress you wore when we got married in Holdrege. That's the other thing I found in the chest in the attic." Joe stood. "Do you want to try it on?"

Elaine pulled him back down. "You better get your naked self back under the quilts."

Joe dropped cross-legged to the quilts and pulled them over his lap. "Yes, ma'am, orders received. We better start planning the wedding, right?"

"I'm sure our parents can help, and Minister Mattaniah will perform the service."

"We need to start saving for our dream home. That'll take a lot of planning and work, not to mention money."

"When do you want to start on kids?" Elaine said, using her usual teasing tone.

"Good grief," Joe said, trying not to frown. "I think we already did."

"The odds are against that. It usually takes more than one time."

"It didn't back in 1944."

"I've always considered Joseph a miracle. If he hadn't been born, who knows how we would've found each other again."

"I've had time to think about all that. I can't—and don't—want to think about it anymore. What matters is we're together again."

Elaine pushed him down, sat on top of him, and leaned over to look him in the eye. "I've got an idea. Let's tempt fate and think about our new house at the same time." She kissed the tip of Joe's nose. "Okay?"

Joe sank his fingers into her silky hair hanging around his face and pulled her down.

"No way, darlin'. If we're gonna do something right, we need to do it one thing at a time."

Chapter 33

Joe placed the first of several burgers on the grill, which sizzled with the delicious aroma of seared beef. Elaine nudged him with her hip. "Lots of people are coming. I can call Mom and ask her to pick up some hot dogs and buns when they drive through town."

"Good idea." Joe finished with the burgers, closed the lid, and wiped his forehead with the back of his hand. "Whew, it's hot out here, or is it because I'm the cook for today?"

Elaine took the empty burger platter from him. "Feel free to cook anytime you please. Did I tell you how much I appreciate you having a dishwasher installed when we designed the kitchen? Oh, the other day, when your mom and I were looking at car seats online, I told her about when you tried—joking or not—to tell me we already had a dishwasher."

"Did you tell her I meant me?"

"You're the dish *dryer*, not the washer." Elaine patted her eight-month-old baby bump. "And don't you dare forget our fifty-fifty rule when it comes to three a.m. feedings and dirty diapers either."

"Gotcha, darlin'." Joe kissed her cheek. "Anything to keep Momma happy."

Elaine pointed toward the river. "Since we managed to not get pregnant down there after all our lovemaking, you've kept this momma quite happy with our practicing for three years."

"Oh, so *that's* why you've been smiling every morning since we got married?"

"Morning, noon, afternoon. Don't forget that time I woke you up at four a.m."

"It wasn't so much you waking me up as it was the *way* you woke me up."

"And you have yet to repay the favor. I like backrubs too, you know."

"Okay, okay, I'll add that to my agenda for tonight." Joe poked his lips out, pretending to pout. "I don't think I like your doctor very much. I looked it up and sex is okay right up to the birth."

"You might not say that if you were the one with the huge tummy. I feel like a duck waddling around."

"Is that what you told her? Why didn't you tell her the truth, that you haven't calmed down in bed yet and you're afraid you might hurt the baby?"

"Look, sweetie, I've warned you about using my bedroom rowdiness against me. That means you get to wash the dishes tonight and dry them too."

Platter in hand, she started toward the back door, and Joe tapped the antique dinner bell mounted to the deck overlooking the river. She'd recently bought it at a yard sale, claiming she'd need it to get his attention when he tuned her out, like all husbands did after a few years of marriage. "Darlin', you forgot, we're using paper plates."

"Well doggone, since you forgot to add them to the shopping list I made when I went to the grocery yesterday—yes, I told you to do that—they completely slipped my mind."

"No problem. I need to get the dirt out from under my nails from planting shrubbery."

"Lucky you, always finding the positive in everything." Elaine opened the door. "I'll call Mom about the hot dogs and the buns. Be right back."

Joe ran to the door and opened it. "See if she can pick up some paper plates too."

"Despite my English teacher ways, Mr. Matthan, *ain't* no way."

Joe returned to the grill and raised the lid to check the burgers. He loved his and Elaine's teasing. It kept them grinning and laughing, holding hands while strolling along the river, and making love with more joy than he'd ever imagined possible.

Gravel crunched in the driveway. He looked around the corner of the house. Jillian was pulling up. She climbed out of her car with a blue gift box wrapped in a pink bow. "Hey there, farm boy-soon-to-be-daddy."

"Hey there yourself, thanks for coming." She climbed the steps. He took the offered gift and set it on a table in the corner of the deck. "I like the color scheme of your box."

"How else would I wrap a baby shower gift when the parents won't let the doctor tell them the sex of the baby? Why are you two being so old fashioned? It's like you're living in the past."

"What can I say, we like surprises."

"Where's Mommy?"

"She's calling her mom to ask her to pick up some hot dogs and buns in case we need them." Joe went to a cooler on another table. "Water and soft-drinks in here. Elaine's bringing out a pitcher of sweet iced tea in a bit." He returned to the grill. "Did I tell you Elaine's great-uncle, Thomas, is coming?"

"I thought he hadn't been feeling well lately?" Jillian took a bottle of water from the cooler. "I hope I'm doing as well when I'm his age. What is that now?"

"His doctor said he might have had a slight stroke. He's ninety-six. Elaine said when she stopped by the nursing home to invite him to the baby shower, he chuckled and said, 'Lookin' forward to it, Lainey. I'll even put my false teeth in for the occasion.'"

"Wow," Jillian said, grinning, "he has a great sense of humor."

The back door squeaked open. Elaine came out and Jillian faced her. "Here's the momma-to-be. Look at you, about to pop."

"You didn't bring Dan? I wanted to tell him it was time he proposed so you can waddle around like a duck when *you* get pregnant."

"No need." Jillian held out her hand, and Elaine's eyes opened wide.

"What a rock. Where is he?"

"You know farmers. He had to get that last field of corn planted before the rain tomorrow, so the forecast said."

"Joe and I know all about that. Tell Dan we said congratulations, okay?"

"Will do." Jillian glanced at Joe and faced Elaine again. "Why don't you want to know the baby's sex? Joe said you wanted it to be a surprise, but I'd rather know so I could buy the right clothes."

"Don't you like surprises?" Elaine asked.

"I guess," Jillian said, doubt in her tone. "But not in this case."

From the kitchen, Elaine's cell phone played Elvis's *I Did It My Way*, and Joe turned from the grill. "Better get that, darlin'.

Make sure to tell her to pick up those paper plates when she stops by the grocery." Through grinning lips, Elaine stuck her tongue out at him and went inside.

Jillian opened the water. "You two sure are happy, farm boy."

"I hope you and Dan will be too. You realize you'll lose your 'special' status on your honeymoon, don't you?"

Jillian slapped his arm. "I'll still be 'special,' aren't you?"

"I'm teasing." Joe raised the grill lid, flipped the burgers, and closed the lid. "Have a seat. Elaine and her mom tend to lose track of time on the phone. They usually end up talking about the baby." He went to the door. Sure enough, Elaine was sitting at the kitchen table, chatting away. He joined Jillian. "I probably shouldn't ask but I am. Do you ever think about that old lady in Liège who called us 'lovers' and said we were destined to make love? Thank goodness she was wrong."

"How do you know she was wrong?"

Joe leaned close to Jillian's ear. "I was there, remember? The closest we ever got was when you sat in my lap, crying."

Jillian snickered. "Why my poor, sweet, innocent farm boy. You never figured out why I kept sitting in your lap after I stopped crying?"

"I didn't think about it."

"I couldn't help myself. I was fantasizing about making love to you." Jillian shrugged. "Think of it this way—like in *Casablanca*, when Humphrey Bogart told Ingrid Bergman, 'we'll always have Paris'—we'll always have Liège."

* * *

The baby shower done, the gifts put away, and the guests on their way home, Joe and Elaine strolled to the river and sat at the picnic table beneath the oak. The wide expanse of blue-gray water rolled by with its ever-present whisper, while a breeze stirred the huge leaves overhead with a soft and gentle rustle.

Elaine slipped her hand into his. "I had another dream last night. It was about the first time you called me 'darlin'."

"That's right," Joe said. "I called you that when we woke up after our 1944 honeymoon. I guess I haven't remembered everything yet either."

"The second time was the day you asked me to marry you."

"I couldn't forget that, could I?"

Elaine nodded toward the two gravestones nestled within the daffodil greenery. A dozen or so huge, yellow blooms remained, shifting with the breeze. "Do you think Kurt and Ruth know we made it back?"

"They're happy about it if they do. That night they talked, when he admitted to killing me, when they both said they'd give up their lives if they could to allow us to have another chance, that told me all I needed to know about the hopes they had for us."

Elaine slid close to rest her head on his shoulder. "When I think of everything we've been through to be together again, from our first date when you took me fishing here to this very moment, I'm amazed. It's like our love bound us together through death itself."

"Don't forget hope. Look at all the coincidences in our past and present lives. Even though Kurt killed me, he managed to come here and work as a POW, meeting you in the process. When I was with him—well, after I got to know him—I couldn't have asked for a better man to be a husband to you and a father to Joseph while I was trying to get back to you. I think our hopes—like with you coming here and wishing we could be together again, and also reading *The Ghosts of Longing* to verify those wishes—had as much to do with us making it back to each other as our love."

"I think about Sam and Hope a lot," Elaine said, looking toward the river. "When they were killed, I hoped they might have another chance at life." She faced Joe again. "Did you?"

"I was the opposite. After living inside other people's bodies for over fifty years, I didn't want them to go through that."

"I hope they find each other, wherever they are."

Elaine gave Joe a smile, pulled him to her for a kiss, and rested her hand on her tummy. "Like with either Joe Jr. or Josie here, whoever he or she might be, hope is the best gift we can have, isn't it?"

"No doubt about it, darlin'." Joe kissed her cheek. "No doubt about it at all."

Joe slipped his arm around her. They both turned to watch the river roll by.

They were like two leaves on the water, where the currents and eddies of life—and hope—had brought them together again.

What a miracle and a blessing—and maybe not a coincidence at all—hope could really be.

Book Club Questions

1. What did you like best about this book?

2. What did you like least about this book?

3. What other books did this one remind you of?

4. Which characters did you like best?

5. Which characters did you like least?

6. If this book were a movie, who would you choose to play the characters?

7. What other books by this author have you read? How did they compare to this book?

8. What feelings did this book evoke in you?

9. If you got the chance to ask the author of this book one question, what would it be?

10. Which character in the book would you most like to meet?

11. What do you think of the book's title? How does it relate to the book's contents? What other title might you choose?

12. What do you think the author's purpose was in writing this book? What ideas was he or she trying to get across?

13. How original and unique was this book?

14. Did this book seem realistic?

15. How well do you think the author built the world in the book?

16. Did the characters seem believable to you? Did they remind you of anyone?

17. What did you already know about this book's subject before you read this book?

18. What new things did you learn?

19. What questions do you still have?

20. Were you happy with the ending?

Readers: please enjoy the first chapter of *The Colors of Eliza Gray*, the first book in the Eliza Gray Series.

Holmes County, Ohio

Of all the times the boy across the table had mocked Eliza, she had never wanted to hurt him.

He was sneaky about it, too. He would stop eating, make sure no one was looking, cover his ears, roll his eyes, and go back to his food, smirking.

But this was different. This was worse.

He had elbowed his fork to the floor, crawled under the table, shoved his hand up her dress to her thigh, and had scrambled back to his chair before she could make sense of what had happened.

She probably could hurt him now, and she didn't even care about the beginning of a beard on his chin.

At the other end of the table, Mama and Papa spoke silent words to the boy's mama and papa. To Eliza's left, Tess and Ethan ate roasted chicken and cabbage soup. Beside the mocking boy, his younger brother drank milk.

Eliza tilted her head to one side, considering the three black bonnets and two wide-brimmed straw hats on pegs by the door. If someone made the mocking boy wear a white kapp, one of the bonnets, a white apron, and a black dress, he might understand how it felt to be her.

She straightened her head. No, that wouldn't work. Not unless he'd lost his hearing as a child. Time to think about something sweet and precious instead of him.

Behind Mama, in one of the boy's old cribs, Ivy pushed her

lips in and out as if she were nursing. Similar to the color of Papa's beard, dark red hair covered her head. Ethan and Tess shared the same hair color, but Mama's hair gleamed in shiny black waves down to her waist when, at bedtime, she removed the white kapp and unpinned her hair. Compared to the women on the magazines at the store in town, Mama was as beautiful as they were. Eliza could've been her sister, except a younger, taller version, with a slender waist, black instead of green eyes, and a sharp nose instead of an upturned one. Mama also had crow's feet, a hint of gray at her temples, and a few wrinkles on her forehead from furrowing her brow. That's what she got for being mean. So much for thinking about something sweet and precious.

Across the table, the boy darted his dark eyes around in preparation for more mocking. Eliza drew her feet back and lowered her head to watch for the fork.

During these meals, when his mocking had begun, back when she was a little girl with curls to her shoulders, she lowered her head to hide like a meek little rabbit in its den of briars, except her den of briars was a kapp sewn from stiff, white cloth. Tears in bed followed. They sometimes followed now, but not as often. Teary nights were never good, when she wished someone would place her in a wooden box and lower her into a hole in the ground.

She counted time in several hesitant breaths. No fork fell, so she raised her head. The boy elbowed his younger brother, who touched one ear and went back to his apple pie.

Being unable to hear meant Eliza had to study people's actions to understand what they meant. In this case, since the boy had only touched one ear, he didn't like mocking her. Eliza managed a smile. Unless he loved apple pie as much as Ethan loved apple pie.

Tess placed a slice before Eliza. Ignoring the mocking boy,

she enjoyed the tart apples and flaky crust, washed down with cold swallows of milk.

Plate and glass empty, she leaned back against the wooden chair's hard slats.

The few words she could remember from long ago, "tree, water, and river," sometimes peeked above the nest of her memories like baby birds stretching their necks for a worm. No matter how hard she tried, no more words revealed themselves, as if the mama bird had pushed them from the nest.

The idea made her teary, but she'd rather do that later in bed.

When she tried saying those words now, people looked at her with widened eyes before turning away, which is why she'd stopped trying to speak as a child. She was grown now, as tall as the adults, and she hated it when they treated her like this. Even worse was when children and older boys and girls treated her like this.

Then there was the boy across the table. One day she'd prove she was no meek little rabbit, and he wouldn't dare touch or mock her again.

Plates cleaned, glasses emptied, the adults exchanged waves on the porch. The boy's mama and papa even included Eliza, giving her a warm feeling in her chest. As they went inside, her family left for the dirt road that led toward home.

The late autumn sun pressed searing rays into the land. On one side of the road, stalks of corn—green at the bottom, dusky brown at the top—filled a huge field. No breeze stirred the slender leaves nor the golden tassels hanging from the plump ears. On the other side of the road, heat waves hovered a shimmering mirage over a pasture, blurring a brown and white milk cow cropping grass in the shade of an oak. The aroma of manure and dark, rich earth filled the air, intensified by the heat.

Eliza lagged behind her family, preferring to walk by herself.

What chores would Mama have for her this afternoon? Pump water from the well and tote it inside? Hoe the withering weeds in the garden? Peel potatoes for—

A hot breeze blew against the nape of her neck, carrying the sour warning that someone was behind her. She turned to peek from beneath the black bonnet.

And there they were, the two boys chasing the meek little rabbit. They carried fishing poles over their shoulders, so maybe they just wanted to see what was biting in the river.

She turned around. No, the oldest boy probably wanted to mock her again instead of fishing—or worse.

Eliza increased her stride to catch her family. Their shoes puffed dust into the air, now dry and still. The sun bore down on their black clothing. Sweat smudged shirts and dresses, darkened underarms and collars.

The oppressive heat surrounded her, concentrated beneath her black bonnet, settled into the hollow between her shoulder blades.

Something lifted her dress. She looked back in time to see the oldest boy jerk his fishing pole away, a grinning smirk twisting his face.

She felt teary again, like the little girl from long ago.

A flash of light caught her eye. To the right, beyond the rolling hills behind her home, the black belly of a cloud bulged and wallowed like a hog covered with mud.

A storm coming.

A cool gust of wind blew the ties of the bonnet around her face. Lightning flashed again, and she turned to see the boys running home, leaving a trail of dust in their wake.

She never expected the boy to touch her leg or raise her dress, but she should have.

Although she resembled Mama, when Papa shopped in town, she compared her reflection in a sunglass display mirror to the women on those magazines, too. Yes, she looked as nice as they did. Young men in the area certainly thought so, because she drew their glances like an apple drew a horse. Regardless, even though the brushes and paste that Papa took home had brightened her teeth, no young man ever approached her with kindness in his eyes.

In the road ahead, another gust of wind swirled dirt and wisps of dried grass. Papa clamped his hand to his hat and walked faster. Beside him, Mama lowered her head over Ivy. Behind Mama, Tess hurried along, black dress swirling about her ankles. Between Tess and Eliza, holding his hat to his head with both hands, Ethan took long, stilted strides. Papa needed to give him a haircut soon. Why would a man or boy want his hair to look like a bowl turned upside-down? The men in the magazines at the store were quite handsome, with thick hair cut either close or curly. How might it be to finger a man's curly hair, especially if it were brown like soil in the garden?

Papa and Mama turned toward the two-story white house, Tess and Ethan close behind. Knees rose and fell. Pants legs and dresses flapped in the wind. Eliza imagined a family of crows in a pasture, all rising and falling and flapping after a grasshopper, whose veined wings fluttered for its life.

From the swirling clouds, lightning flicked a snake's tongue, forked and brilliant, into the trees hiding the river. Papa broke into a trot. The trees swayed and bowed with the wind. Eliza wiped a huge warm raindrop from her cheek. In the dirt road leading to the house, more raindrops fell, evidenced by puffs of dust. The gray aroma of water filled the cooling air.

Everyone piled onto the porch to wipe their shoes on the mat at the door and enter one by one. Papa removed his straw hat to hang on one of the pegs by the door, followed by Ethan. Mama did the same with her black bonnet. Tess climbed the stairs and Eliza followed.

In the dark corner at the far end of their room, she sat on her bed. Shoes, black stockings, bonnet, and apron put away, she sat again to place her hand on the cool window. Huge raindrops struck the glass, sharing tiny kisses with her palm. The grass in the back yard swirled as if caught in the grip of Mama's spoon stirring cake batter. From the swollen clouds, lightning slashed the sky again and again.

Eliza waited. It always came. Always. Like one violent beat of her heart, a huge vibration buffeted her chest, then faded into gentle caresses.

She imagined a gentle man—not some cruel boy who mocked her because she couldn't hear—holding his hand to her heart—a man who enjoyed the outdoors, long walks beneath the trees, and nothing more than the simple pleasure of being together.

Across the room, Tess lit a lamp. Black smoke fluttered sooty fingertips toward the low, plank ceiling. She lowered the wick and replaced the glass chimney, lay her head on the pillow and opened a book from the nightstand.

Eliza took her hand from the window. She needed more paper for her projects. Maybe Papa would visit a store soon, and she could buy some with the few coins that Mama let her keep from making baskets.

First things first: allow the storm to end and gather mud at the river.

If that mocking boy left her alone.

Lightning flashed again, illuminating the rusted well pump at the end of the backyard, beyond the barn and chicken coop to the right, and the woodshed and basketmaking shop to the left.

Eliza reached into her mind for the first page of her memories, when Mama had slapped her as child because she only knew to get water from the river instead of the well. Chin trembling, Eliza had nodded as a single tear rolled down the four streaks of pain burning her cheek. A confused child did not deserve such treatment. If she ever found a way to tell Mama how deep the scars of that day had cut into her heart, she would.

Shaking the memory from her mind, Eliza went to the back porch. The final drops of rain were trailing from the sky in silver sprinkles of light. The trees stood tall as the wind died. She ran through the cool, wet grass toward the barn for an old bucket. Found in the hay loft seasons ago, it made the perfect container for gathering leaves, berries, mud, or any other color a project required.

Along the path to the river, the earthy aroma of mold greeted her as she purposefully shuffled through last fall's wet leaves with her bare feet. In the branches, where green leaves were turning orange, red, and gold, a gray squirrel sat up while nibbling an acorn, furred tail curled over its back. Further on, to the side of the path, a partially eaten ear of corn marked a raccoon's supper, taken from the garden last night. Droplets of green-smelling water fell from the leaves, almost like daytime lightning bugs with crystalline beacons flashing, gathering, and dispersing the sunshine pouring from the clearing sky.

Eliza stopped at the river. The rolling water, tinted green from the leaves overhead, reflected swirls of sunlight sparkling into her eyes.

Around the bend to the left, the end of the boy's rowboat barely stuck out. He was probably at home, disappointed because he wasn't here to mock her.

Eliza left the bucket on the bank and gathered her dress to her knees. The current, slow and steady, kissed bare legs with cool lips. Raising the dress higher, she continued into the water to mid-thigh. Toes wiggling in the mud, eyes closed, she breathed in the spicy aroma of the leaves yet to fall in the woods behind her. The current swirled. She slipped in the mud, almost fell, and stepped back to ankle deep.

Something brushed her calf. Not looking, she swatted the fly away. It lit again and she swatted again. It lit on her thigh between her legs. She looked down to swat it accurately and realized the fly was the tip of the mocking boy's fishing pole, rising to touch where he shouldn't.

She whirled around. He dropped the pole and elbowed his younger brother beside him, then reared back and laughed like a rooster announcing sunrise. The younger brother took a step backward, fear in his widening eyes.

The time for tears was over.

Holding the dress up with one hand, Eliza went to the boy and jerked his hand to her thigh. He squeezed it, slowly licked his lips, and turned to wave his brother away, who ran into the path. The mocking boy faced Eliza again.

His dark eyes denied the shame of his brother's judgement, the desire to take instead of give, the willingness to hurt instead of understand. Swirling within the flecks of green around the black centers, which reflected her face and the river she loved so well, those things revealed something worse than mocking.

Yes, she could hurt him now.

She placed her hands on his shoulders, leaned in as if to kiss him, and drove her knee into his crotch. He grabbed his belly and fell on his side in the mud. She kicked him to his back and clenched her fist. Not his mouth. Why cut her knuckles on his teeth? She drew back her hand, tightened the work-hardened muscles in her shoulder, bicep, and forearm, and with every ounce of strength she could manage, drove her fist into his nose, resulting in a spectacular gush of blood from his nostrils.

She leaned over the boy to wait for his attention. His eyes opened and he jerked away. Blood ran down his chin and neck and into his collar, similar to a male hummingbird hovering near a honeysuckle bloom. Tears squeezed from his eyes, closed again, but that wasn't enough.

Eliza sucked in air until her lungs ached and screamed into his face, demanding that he never bother her again.

She stepped over him as he continued to grimace in pain. He wouldn't dare tell anyone what she'd done. Other boys would mock him like he'd mocked her, so his explanation to his family had better be an interesting one when he finally limped his bleeding self home. Still, now that she'd hurt him, he might hurt her back. Whatever he might plan, she'd be ready.

She grabbed the bucket's wire handle and left for home.

No man nearby would ever care for her, but one somewhere else might. Did he live in town? Far away? Was he sitting by a lake or a river?

Doubt replaced hope, making her teary. Like her, even if he existed, he might know sadness and heartache as well.

Smiling up at the sunshine in the leaves, she wiped her eyes. The only way to find out was to meet him.

About the Author

J. Willis Sanders lives in southern Virginia, with his wife and several stringed musical instruments.

With several novels published and more on the way, he enjoys crafting intriguing characters with equally intriguing conflicts to overcome. He also loves the natural world and, more often than not, his stories include those settings. Most also utilize intense love relationships and layered themes.

His first novel (the first one in this series) is a ghostly World War II era historical that takes place mostly in the midwestern United States, which utilizes some little-known facts about German POW camps there at that time. It's the first of a three-book series, in which characters from the first book continue their lives.

Although he loves history, he has written several contemporary novels as well, and some include interesting paranormal twists, both with and without religious themes.

He also loves the Outer Banks of North Carolina, and has published three novels within different time frames based on the area, what he calls his Outer Banks of North Carolina Series.

Another genre he enjoys is thriller novels, so he has launched a series with a main female character named Reid Stone.

To follow the author's work, please visit any of the following:

https://jwillissanders.wixsite.com/writer

https://www.facebook.com/J-Willis-Sanders-874367072622901

https://www.amazon.com/J-Willis-Sanders/e/B092RZG6MC?ref_=dbs_p_ebk_r00_abau_000000

Readers: to help those considering a purchase, please consider leaving a review on Amazon.com, Goodreads.com, or wherever you purchased this book.
Thank you.

www.ingramcontent.com/pod-product-compliance
Lightning Source LLC
Chambersburg PA
CBHW010537170726
48285CB00008B/2651